OSSIE HOPKINS read English Literature at Durham and then taught English and also rock climbing at a seventies comprehensive. He progressed to management: apprentice to Cheshire's chief education sorcerer. A Masters at Manchester University promoted the career but not the writing.

As deputy director with Birmingham LEA he produced plenty of soundbites for the dailies, Central TV and Pebble Mill but never got round to real writing.

Later he became chief executive at Ribble Valley Council. Strategy papers abounded and leadership's just like teaching: helping people grow. Must get all this written down. Too late! Palace revolution! Ossie leaves the same way he arrived: fired with enthusiasm!

Still, one door closes... And here's a brand new international institute for customer service looking for advocacy in the public sector. Further corridors-of-power to tramp but yet again – more speechifying than writing.

Shown the door...to the open road; and supporting his son's haulage business. Eighteen-hour days afford plenty of material but little opportunity to write it down until long-awaited, enforced leisure produces *Chalk for Cheese* and now *Infinite Riches*.

Also by Ossie Hopkins

Chalk for Cheese

INFINITE RICHES

OSSIE HOPKINS

SilverWood

Published in 2018 by SilverWood Books

SilverWood Books Ltd
14 Small Street, Bristol, BS1 1DE, United Kingdom
www.silverwoodbooks.co.uk

ISBN 978-1-78132-754-8 (paperback)
ISBN 978-1-78132-755-5 (ebook)

British Library Cataloguing in Publication Data
A CIP catalogue record for this book is available
from the British Library

Page design and typesetting by SilverWood Books
Printed on responsibly sourced paper

Prologue

February the fifteenth, 1968

When Stephen promised her a trip to Durham to meet some of his friends, Jill assumed it would be for drinks and a meal.

And when Ed proposed bringing his girlfriend down to the indoor meet that Thursday night, Jay thought nothing of it. Several of the lads brought their *spice* to the Dun Cow. He'd meet them there about 8.30; before that he'd be in the Buffalo Head.

Jill would dress up, but not over. You never knew with Stephen. Sometimes you'd finish up at the Dolce Vita, other times at some dive in Wallsend. Not that she minded; Jill was flexible. Still, if these were new friends she was meeting it would've been nice to know. She'd have asked him but he was working up in Glasgow for the first three days of the week and the only confirmation that they were actually going was a 'phone message passed on by her mam.

'It were that Stephen. He's a canny lad, mind. Yer could do a lot worse, hinny! Said he'd pick yer up boot seven. An divn't be late.'

Still none the wiser, Jill plumped for a modishly short brown skirt and a tight, beige, polo-necked pullover that showed off her figure without making her look a tart. She'd gone to some trouble with her make-up; but no more than if she'd been meeting the lit twins down the Gosforth Park. It would have to do.

Jay didn't worry much about his appearance. His black jeans chose him, secured with the Fascist belt his brother Chris had once coveted, together with a bright orange shirt. As an afterthought, knowing it would irritate Ed; he knotted a black-silk scarf around his neck. Then he stuck his darts in his back pocket and strolled off down the Bailey to the Buff. He bought himself a pint of Fed Special and settled down to a session of shove-halfpenny with Cec, the landlord. After a while a couple of the locals came in to play darts so he chalked the board and then played the winner. He was on form – always handy when his climbing-partner was in the offing – and was still on the board when Ed walked in with his latest bird on his arm.

What a corker! Comprehensively thrown, he tried to pretend he hadn't seen them: not easy in the cramped bar. Shit and derision: she was dazzling! For a second he thought they'd met before but they couldn't have, surely? He'd have remembered. He'd never seen anyone remotely as pretty.

Jill parked her bag on a stool and adjusted her skirt. She took in the room with a lighthouse glance, clocking the boozers propping up the bar as well as the quartet engrossed in their dominoes. She hoped the silk scarf playing darts was not one of Stephen's friends. He looked vaguely familiar but if he was trying to make an impression he was failing miserably.

Jay just couldn't take his eyes off her.

He thought: she's stunning!

She thought: what a prat!

One

A fortnight or so later, Jill woke to a thin, watery sun filtering through the lace curtains of Flat Three, Morpeth Court. It was Saturday but Stephen had already gone to work. She closed her eyes and trawled her hung over memory for any gaffes. Shouldn't be too many. She'd been working split shifts all week and had earned the luxury of the weekend off. Normally she'd be at home, St Peter's Road in Wallsend, where she still lived with her mam and dad, but she'd left early Friday to start at the hospital at eight. Unusually, her mam was still in and, even more unusually, was in a sunny mood. Jill had anticipated a snide response to her, 'I'm just off, Mam. Probably stop over tonight so aa'l see you t'morra.'

'Oh, aye: romantic night oot wi that Stephen? He's aal reet. You have a nice time, pet.'

'Thanks, Mam,' she trilled, reflecting wryly on her mam's reaction. She'd have had a tarter send-off if she'd announced she was stopping over with the *lit twins*. The lit twins were Sue and Joyce, and Jill had known them forever. Joyce Charlton had been her first primary teacher, whilst Sue Lambton was a librarian. They were twins cause the pair had both made an equal, and huge, contribution to Jill's literary upbringing. Joyce would be in her early thirties now, recently promoted to her first headship at an RC infant school in Newcastle; Sue was much younger, maybe twenty-six and was a peripatetic adviser with the city's library service. Jill had been infatuated with her for yonks. It was a shame. Her mam couldn't see how good for her Sue and Joyce were; all she could see were a 'pair o' dykes.'

The ward had been forgettable. Split shifts were such a bind. No time to get home during the afternoon, and the evening compromised by the late finish. Even if you managed to find the girls, it was eight, nine o'clock; most of them were already blotto. And being the only sober one was not Jill's idea of fun. It forced you to choose between hoyin' a few quick ones doon yer neck or getting steadily more morose and sloping surreptitiously off home. For once though she could catch up in her own time and not have to rush to get the last bus.

Sally had said they'd be in the Hotspur 'til nine, so half-past eight found Jill scurrying along Percy Street. There'd be ample time for a bottle or two before she had to head up to Jesmond. She might even get a lift as a couple of the trainee doctors had recently acquired cars and one of them lived in Gosforth. Jill caught his attention by including him in the first round and three bottles of Newcastle Amber later she was rewarded.

'Sure! I'm going after this one. I can easily drop you at the Collingwood. You meeting what's-its-name?'

'Stephen. Yeah, we're having dinner.'

It was where they'd met the week after dancing at the A-Go-Go; it was jam-packed murky. Jill remained the only one of her year who didn't smoke but she didn't object to others doing so, and besides Stephen didn't either. It was one of the things she liked about him: clean breath.

Several Brandy-and-Babychams later they repaired to Falfino's where, once again, Stephen was treated royally. Their corner table was discreet. The previous occasion had been fraught for Jill: she was intimidated by the plushness of the surroundings and worried that Stephen would expect too much. He hadn't; their relationship, though increasingly close, remained chaste. Jill wondered whether it would be after tonight but was relaxed anyway.

There had been an awkward moment when Stephen's flatmate, Alistair had blundered into the living room, but it was only to collect some research papers for the following day. Within minutes a car door was slamming and Alistair had departed for Edinburgh. More drinks had followed and this time Jill had felt no need to plead the sanctuary of the spare bedroom.

It was the first time she'd made love with a man. Stephen was gentle, almost tender, and when he woke her again in the early hours she felt wanted rather than imposed upon. Plus, before he left he brought her a mug of tea!

Stephen was a medical rep for Upjohn and had appointments with pharmacists in Morpeth, Alnwick and Berwick-on-Tweed. He'd be out until mid-afternoon. In no hurry to get up, Jill luxuriated in the downy king-size bed, reflecting on the previous evening and letting her mind wander back over the months since they'd met. Not versed in heterosexual relationships she'd no idea what the norm was. She and her nursing friends had exchanged prejudices, of course, but since Christine was happy to go to bed on a first date and Sally was bi, Jill remained confused. Surely half-a-dozen dates wasn't either loose or tight and last night had felt natural.

Jill liked Stephen and, a tad unexpectedly, had enjoyed the sex. Especially the second time.

She enjoyed his company, too. He was considerate for a man, almost unselfish; plus, he was charming and had a winning sense of humour. Self-deprecating. Jill liked that. Oh…and he were a bit of aal reet! An Olympic-standard fencer, he was due in Mexico that summer. He had a lithe, toned body, which now she'd felt it close up was sensuous in a way she hadn't expected. If he had any major faults they weren't dire. Fancied himself. But didn't all men? Talked too much about himself, of course, and expected her to agree with him. You couldn't blame him for his friends. Alistair, his flat mate, was painfully shy and almost without conversation unless you could feign an interest in archaeology. And as for that bunch down in Durham, they were typical students: brash, immature and self-obsessed. Especially that Jay: what a bullyjock he was with his silk scarf and supercilious smirk.

The evening in the Buffalo Head had started badly when she saw him posing on the darts board. It deteriorated when she realised that this was the friend Stephen had particularly wanted her to meet. He had a stuck-up air and totally ignored them, continuing his game. The bar was lined with locals so, as Stephen pushed his way through for the beers, Jill stood like a spare part, pretending to take in her surroundings with interest. Scarfy-boy was scoring heavily and already on a finish. Jill had played darts quite a bit when her elder brother, Rob, was on leave from various RAF postings. They'd go down the Alma, along from the pedestrian tunnel under the Tyne her dad had worked on as a diver. Just near Brydon's rope works where Rob had once been apprenticed. So Jill knew what *x16* meant on the chalkboard. As Stephen returned with two pint glasses his friend punched the air childishly then turned to greet them.

'Awright, mate. How's it goin? Fancy a game of doubles?'

For a moment Jill thought it was his way of acknowledging her presence. Microscopically mollified she had no qualms about partnering Stephen: she knew he was a decent player. But it turned out the invitation was to play the two lads who'd been on the receiving end 'til now. When Stephen readily agreed she was bemused. Surely he'd twig?

'Yeah, 501? This is Jill Walker, by the way. Jill – Jay Fincher.' And that was it for the next twenty minutes or so. Stephen and Jay won 5-0 and were jubilant. Jill was almost speechless with indignation.

Finally, it was Jay's turn to go to the bar. He didn't ask whether she'd like another, just elbowed his way through the throng and returned, admittedly in double-quick time, with three frothy pints on a tacky metal tray featuring a Federation Brewery logo. Determined not to give him the satisfaction of thinking she was annoyed Jill smiled warmly and took a sip.

'Ooh, Fed Special, didn't know you could get it outside the clubs.'

Jay looked surprised and crowed, 'Can't normally. The Buff's the only pub in Durham that serves it.'

They threaded their way down the narrow corridor into the lounge and found a free table. It was sticky though and they had to park a load of glasses on the hatch. Jill assumed they'd be going for a meal at some stage (she'd noted the Kwai Lam opposite: that was okay, she liked Chinese food) but it gradually became apparent that their destinations after the Buff would be somewhere called the Big Jug and then the Dun Cow. That was where the mountaineering club met. Oh great! Thought Jill resignedly. Maybe she could signal to Stephen that she'd sooner get back to Newcastle although she wasn't banking on it. He didn't seem at his most receptive in Jay's company. The latter hardly spoke to Jill, the talk turning rapidly to climbing.

'Fancy Wales sometime, Ed. The old man took me down to Llanberis recently. The routes in the Pass look fantastic.'

'Okay by me, young Finch.'

And so it went on, Jill's interest piqued only by why Jay who was obviously 'Finch' should call Stephen 'Ed'! She'd a vague recollection he'd told her but would have to ask him, if she ever got the chance. Perhaps it was simply short for his surname – Edrich.

When it was Stephen's shout again Jill and Jay were left, excruciatingly, alone. He seemed completely tongue-tied; but she was determined not to sit in silence. And you *could* even in the midst of a packed lounge.

'So what are you reading?' She was pleased she'd remembered the academic nicety taught her by Joyce, but she hoped to elicit rather more than Jay's terse return.

'English.' Then as an afterthought, 'You?'

It crossed Jill's mind to claim the same. She was confident her 'A' level study of *Lear* and *Midsummer Night's Dream* would suffice for the present conversation but it wasn't in her nature to lie, unless she absolutely had to.

'Oh, nothing. I'm just a nurse at the RVI. Hoping to qualify this autumn.'

'Oh…right.'

For an English scholar he seemed remarkably taciturn as soon as his drinking-cum-climbing crutches were withdrawn and it was a relief when Stephen returned with replenishments. The respite was short-lived.

Someone called *Pard* turned up. He seemed to know Stephen as well as Jay but no one bothered to introduce them and Jay immediately wandered off with his new mate. The last Jill noticed they were playing doms. What an evening!

And what a prat! Snug in Stephen's bed a fortnight on, Jill's opinion stood. The only niggle was why she'd allowed him to intrude on her otherwise pleasurable reverie even for a few drowsy minutes…

Two

Jay sensed the evening had not been an unqualified success.

Thing was, he hadn't been expecting Ed's girlfriend to be anything out of the ordinary. Bit of a boiler, with big boobs. An easy lay. Ed did have a track record, after all. Or so he said. On reflexion, Jay realised he'd only been with Ed in mixed company twice and although both girls fitted the description were they were actually *girlfriends*? Or even come to that, definitely with Ed? They'd been in a gang.

Most of the time they weren't climbing he and Ed were drinking. And talking about climbing. Not girls; except for the occasional boastful fantasy when they were both blitzed. So whatever preconception Jay might've had about an Edrich girl, it certainly wasn't Jill. Boiler? Huh! She was beautiful and entrancing and far too good for Ed; and if he'd had half his wits about him that time in the Buff he'd have tried a lot harder. Cause, from what he could recall of the evening he wasn't at his scintillating best! Unless she was impressed with the darts, of course…he *was* on form that night. But that was all. He'd stuffed up.

For once Jay's course came to his rescue. He had an assignment he simply had to deliver before the end of Epiphany term – three weeks – or he was in deep shit. So instead of whiling away most lunchtimes and evenings in the Buff or the Half Moon, he was prioritising his academic studies. Not the formal bits of course, he couldn't stand group learning. Since the start of his second year they'd been obliged to attend, on average, fifteen lectures a week. Jay had been to six. In eighteen months! His record on seminars was equally dire. Only the tutorials did he assiduously attend, for the sound reason that he'd unaccountably finished up with their associate professor as his tutor. (Jay suspected paternal influence.) Even so, he was forever being threatened with rustication, surviving only because of the quality of his essays. Privately researched and unconventional they might be, but as his tutor grudgingly conceded they were also top notch. And when his track record promised a First they were hardly going to expel him with just four months to Finals, especially when his exam results had been of a consistently high standard too. So he buckled down, spent hours every day in the Stacks researching Jacobean drama and the distinction therein between *horror* and *terror*, and generally ensured that Professor Turner was impressed enough to carry on supporting his wayward protégé.

He didn't have much time to mope about Jill. Indeed, it wasn't until he talked to Jules that he realised he had been. Moping. Julia was the only person in the English school he really got on with. She was twenty-three, engaged to some deadly boring solicitor and like a big sister to Jay; especially since his elder brother, Chris, had been killed a couple of years before. Jay had idolised him. Still did. He'd been a naval officer out in Singapore. Subs. St Cuthbert's Society knew, of course. His moral tutor, Dr Wallace, was supposed to keep a caring eye out for him; which he did that first term. Thereafter only Jules bothered to see how he was doing, and even that solicitude was curtailed by her jealous fiancé.

They'd bumped into each other on Palace Green and gone for tea in the refectory that served the library. Jules was smartly dressed as always: her tight black trousers accentuating her slim figure and the bright green jumper setting off her auburn hair and sparkling silver-grey eyes. Sensing encouragement was required, she hugged him affectionately and smiled warmly before kissing him gently on the forehead.

'You seem a bit down, Jaycy. Why don't you grab a couple of slices of that disgustingly fattening chocolate sponge and come and tell Auntie Jules all about it?'

So Jay shared his recollections of the night in the Buff, concluding dejectedly that he'd blown it. Jules was only partly reassuring, smiling sympathetically but shaking her head sadly, as if at an errant child.

'Well you can be your own worst enemy, you know. I mean the silk scarf and all that. Plus, how was she to know you fancied her if you spent most of the evening ignoring her?' Jay looked positively downcast so Julia continued more optimistically, 'Still, you never know. We girls have much sharper instincts than you lot. It's quite possible she got an inkling of how you felt, in spite of your behaving like a monumental berk.' Jay grinned sheepishly and Jules pressed home her advantage. 'I've told you before: you read too much Hemingway. Most girls don't like that laconic macho attitude; you should try more Fitzgerald!'

This was an old argument. They'd both followed an American Literature option the year before and, just to be contrary, Jay had championed

Hemingway against the mainstream view that Fitzgerald was the finer writer. Jules expected him to rise to it as usual and was concerned when he failed to. Her last, probably forlorn hope was to suggest Jay write to the girl. He might've failed comprehensively to communicate his feelings in person but he could string a phrase or two together, surely! He looked pensive and left her with a rueful smile and a tender hug; but not before paying for tea.

As for machismo, Hemingway was only half the story. Jay Fincher's best friend at Durham was Belasis. Gregory Pardue Belasis, or Pard to his friends. Not that he had many. Pard's dad, Roland, was an ex-boxer and as hard as nails. Roland reckoned their family could trace its roots back to the thirteenth century, when Rowland de Belasis served as a Knight to the Bishop of Durham. He was also a shrewd businessman who could well afford the gifts he lavished on his only son. Pard inherited both his father's sculpted features and physical attributes. Though little taller than Jay ('short-arsed thugs together') he was built like a brick shithouse. He boxed, naturally, which meant he also worked out in the gym a lot. It showed and he knew it. Most of their crowd were afraid of him and Pard did nothing to dissuade them. Only with Jay did he lower his guard.

Pard spent most weekends away from college and it was only after they'd known each other for a year that he confided in Jay that he was married. The society didn't know, and nor did any of their circle. But every Thursday evening Pard would leap into the Triumph1300 that his father had bought as a reward for getting into university (Registration: BJR 740D, noted Jay, whose alter ego Autolycus *collected* car numbers), and screech off up the Bailey cobbles to Cullercoats. He and his wife, Jorja, shared a tiny fisherman's cottage just off the Whitley Bay road. Jay had recently met Jorja. She was petite, brunette and pretty. But he hadn't taken to her, which was tricky as Pard was clearly besotted and expected Jay, as his best pal, to be so too. But Jorja appeared very distant and Jay couldn't tell whether it was him or whether she was just shy. Either way, it didn't matter that much: Jorja wasn't his mate, Pard was.

Mates, but on Pard's terms. And whilst Jay admitted that his friend was tougher and stronger than him he wasn't used to playing second fiddle. So he adopted a similarly macho persona whether Pard was around or not. It got him into a lot of trouble. Or, as Pard put it: *Semper in excretio summus, altum solum veriat!*

This final year they were sharing a room in one of the Georgian terrace houses on the Bailey, overlooking a small quad where the manicured square lawn was currently laid out for croquet. Theoretically it was a college facility but since Room 12 boasted the only balcony with a staircase leading down to the lawn, Pard and Jay had pretty much appropriated it. Their speciality was midnight croquet accompanied by silver teapots, *borrowed* from the refectory and charged with claret. Penalties were liquid. There were dissident murmurs from the *excluditi* but Jay had taken care to get Dr Wallace, now the society's vice-principal, on side. Jay was supervising a doubles match from the balcony when Wally walked in.

'What the devil are those fellows doing, Fincher?'

'Playing croquet, sir.'

'But it's pitch black…surely they can't see?'

'No problem, sir, they're all drunk.'

'Oh right. Fine. Carry on.'

Realizing that the VP had consumed more than the odd snifter himself, Jay seized the opportunity: 'Glass of claret, sir? It's an Haut Brion '64.'

'Thank you, Fincher, don't mind if I do. Have to applaud your taste in music, by the way. The Elgar Cello's long been one of my favourites.'

Jay was chuffed. The concerto was on a 7" Scotch tape superbly reproduced by the TEAC recorder. His father had bequeathed it to him when he'd upgraded recently and Jay was inordinately proud of it. No need to confess that most of his footage was of *Top of the Pops*!

'Recent recording?'

'Yes sir: it's Barbirolli conducting the LSO.'

'With Jacqueline du Pré if I'm not very much mistaken.'

'Spot on, sir.' Jay had noted the satisfaction in his tutor's voice.

Most of the bottle later, Jay played his trump card, 'Don't suppose you'd consider refereeing, Sir?'

'Certainly…what do I do?'

'Just call the penalties, sir, and award the teapots.'

'Teapots, eh? Very good, Finch!'

They were unpopular with most of their neighbours who resented Pard and Jay's exclusive intimacy with Dr Wallace. It exacerbated the duo's tendency to trash anyone who strayed onto their territory. This included the student authorities and they'd already had several run-ins with Robertson, the President of the JCR, and his flunkies.

The day after Jay's heart-to-heart with Jules, Pard had decreed they were gonna try a few. They'd both been working all hours (Pard was reading History with Archaeology as a subsid) and deserved to let their hair down. It was only Wednesday but Term finished in two days or, in Pard's case, tomorrow. They'd start when the Buff opened at eleven and see how many they could down by closing time. Both were big drinkers – despising their fellow students who considered eight pints a skinful – and come three o'clock they were on their twelfth. A break beckoned. The Market Tavern would open again at five.

For some reason neither could subsequently recall, they elected to crash out not in their own second floor room but in an empty spec on the floor above, which turned out to belong to Metcalfe, the JCR Treasurer. Unfortunately, before they could subside quietly Pard needed some air and, hauling up the sash window promptly puked out of it. Most of the mess adorned the wall but some reached the Bailey just as the president and the treasurer were turning into No.9. The latter took immediate umbrage first at narrowly avoiding being drenched and second when he twigged that the malefactors were in his room. His protestations were met with a string of abuse from Pard, which so incensed the worthies that they set off up the three-storey staircase at a gallop. Robertson was a runner, tall and gangly. Taking the stairs three-at-a-time he reached the door to Metcalfe's room whilst the latter was still on the landing below. Pard was ready for him. As the door was flung open and their esteemed president bustled in to lay down the law he was caught by a straight left to the nose which left him bloodied and staggering backwards. Not satisfied he'd finished the job Pard swayed after him and landed an even heavier right hook to the presidential ear, which knocked the already-reeling Robertson down the stairs and straight into the advancing Metcalfe. Caught completely off balance both men tumbled down the full flight to the landing.

To seal their victory – well his really – Pard bawled after them. 'Aye, and yer can fuck off an all, yer lily-livered bastards.'

When he'd sobered up the next morning Jay found Pard had already gone, leaving him to face the music, or in this case, the society principal. On reflexion, Jay was not sure they'd covered themselves in glory. He wondered what Jules would think; or, if she ever found out, Jill.

Three

Jill woke with a start, glanced at her watch and panicked. It was nearly noon. Stephen had promised to be back mid-afternoon. Jill planned a Geordie tea for him, but that meant a shopping trip to the High Street. She didn't know this part of Gosforth well, only how to get to where the lit twins' flat was. She wondered how they were and whether she'd time to call on them.

It would be great to see them and she'd no doubt be very welcome. But maybe she shouldn't just roll up unannounced of a Saturday lunchtime, particularly as it could only be a flying visit. What really gave her pause, though, was Sue. She'd been less than ecstatic when Jill first revealed she was seeing Stephen. She was bound to be curious about why Jill was in Gosforth so it could be embarrassing. She certainly didn't want to upset either of her mentors. She hoped they'd remain a part of each other's lives whatever happened. Did that make her selfish and greedy – wanting both Stephen and Sue? Wouldn't it involve precisely the kind of duplicity she detested? Not so long back her parents' marriage had nearly come to grief when her mam ran off with the manager of the Tunnel Club. They were back together now but Jill still fiercely resented her mam's behaviour. Wouldn't realising her fantasy be just as bad?

She was still agonising when the 'phone rang. It took her a while to locate it, half submerged under a pile of Alistair's research papers, and even then she hesitated. It wasn't her flat. Was she even supposed to be there? What if it was Stephen's mother? Or worse, another girlfriend? On the ninth ring she summoned her resolve and taking a deep breath croaked 'Hello?'

'There's no need to sound so nervous. It's only me.'

'Oh...that's a relief, I thought...well, anyway...'

'Yeah, look I'm really sorry. Summat's come up. I'm gonna have to drive to Edinburgh. Probably won't get back 'til the morning. Whaddya want to do?'

'How do you mean?'

'Well you're welcome to stay over. But if you don't fancy spending the night there alone, I'd quite understand.'

That option hadn't even crossed Jill's mind; she was a bit shocked. Was he taking her for granted, just assuming she'd be there when he was ready to return? She decided to give him the benefit, but didn't disguise the coolness in her voice.

'No it's okay, thanks. I'll get back home.'

'Right ho! Well I'll see you when I see you then,' Stephen concluded cheerfully.

'Yeah, s'pose so.' Jill was unable to keep the disappointment out of her voice, 'Safe journey.' So much for high tea! So much for their romantic weekend and so much for bloody Stephen! Right that does it, she thought dismissively: I'm gonna see the twins.

Still she hesitated. She had a small overnight bag, which she could easily carry over her shoulder, but what impression would that give to whoever opened the door in Moor Crescent? They'd either think she'd come to stay or, worse, was on her way from a stopover. And then she was back to the Sue-Stephen dilemma. No, she needed to leave the bag in the flat and pick it up later. Where did they keep the spare key: kitchen? hall? She located a row of keys hanging from a model sword in the living room and quickly established which one assured her re-entry. Then, before she could change her mind yet again, she set off.

It was almost noon and the late, pale, February sun made the walk down the High Street and along the edge of Dukes Moor Park a pleasure. Her spirits rose: it would be really good to see the twins and she was confident now she could avoid any awkwardness. She paused momentarily outside the town house and then pressed Button Two on the intercom. Her heart was beating outrageously at the prospect of Sue's voice. The crackle ceased and Joyce's delight signalled her to come up.

'Why it's lovely to see you, pet!' The Scots burr in Joyce's refined accent seemed to suit her Gosforth surroundings (her mam would've made some snide remark about the posh side of town) and Jill remembered that Miss Charlton came from Melrose and claimed ancestry back to the Border Reivers.

'You should've said you were coming, mind. Sue's gone into town shopping. She'll be upset to miss you.'

'Sorry, it was just a spur-of-the-moment thing. I won't stay long.'

'Yer fine, chicken. I've to go out at two, but I'm all yours 'til then. Coffee?'

'Hmm, please, though just an ordinary one!' Each smiled at the stipulation. The alternative was *special coffee*, which had done for them both the last night on Lindisfarne a couple of years back. Jill had been invited to spend her eighteenth birthday at Sheldrake Cottage, which the lit twins regularly rented, and the celebrations had almost got out of hand thanks to the rum-laced coffee (or maybe that was the other way round) that had followed a sumptuous birthday dinner. Sue had to put Joyce to bed and by the time she returned to resume their intimate session on the sofa, Jill had fallen asleep too. Joyce presumably didn't know about the sofa but the coffee remained a group joke.

Whilst Joyce made coffee, Jill glanced round the elegant Edwardian living room. Last time she'd visited, the twins had only just moved in and everywhere had been littered with tea chests. Now a three-piece suite adorned a thick-pile beige carpet and the alcove was full of books. Jill made a beeline for them. There was a section of Scottish poets: Gavin Douglas, Robert Henryson, William Dunbar. No prizes for guessing who owned those. Then there was a whole shelf of classy, cream-and-blue volumes entitled *The Oxford History of English Literature*: fifteen of them in all, from *Middle English* to *Writers of the Early Twentieth Century*. Complete set? She'd have to ask Joyce. She pulled out Vol. XV and rifled through the pages until she came to the final chapter, IX, on Lawrence. That was a coincidence. Sue, who was always finding new writers for Jill, had introduced her to DH Lawrence on the Lindisfarne sojourn and Jill had devoured *The Rainbow*, *Sons and Lovers* and, finally, *Lady Chatterley*. Surely the Oxford set was Sue's.

Engrossed, she hadn't heard Joyce pad up. She handed her a steaming china mug and remarked cheerily, 'I see you've found the library. Worked out whose are which?'

'Well the Scots are obviously yours. But I reckon the Oxford set's the librarian's!'

'Well done! And what about the Bard?' Joyce pointed to a lower shelf Jill hadn't yet scanned where there must've been thirty plays at least, all in hardback with pastel-shaded covers. 'They're our prize possession: complete set of *The Arden Shakespeare*.'

'Terrific!' enthused Jill, 'wish I'd been able to read that edition on the course.' Joyce smiled appreciatively; it was only through her pulling strings that Jill had been able to attend the classes at all. A nurse at the RVI as an extra-mural student at Newcastle University? Highly irregular!

'Well, I recall you studied *Lear* and the *Dream* so maybe something different. What about this?' And Joyce pulled out a copy of *As You Like It*.

'Think you'd enjoy it. It's light and funny and altogether wonderful. Plus, it features one of Shakespeare's great heroines, Rosalind. She's witty, pretty and determined. Should suit you to a tee!'

They sat down at opposite ends of the sofa, Rosalind guarding the coffees on the thistle-engraved glass table in front of them. Sue's absence was both a disappointment and a relief. She'd forgotten how kind and thoughtful Joyce was, had always been. To spend an hour or two without complications was a bonus. They had a lot to catch up on. Swapping anecdotes about St Anselm's, Joyce's new school of which she was justly proud, and the orthopaedic ward where Jill had recently found a vocation-within-her-vocation, consumed the next hour-and-a-half.

Joyce was intensely proud of her one-time pupil. She knew her background – the Walkers had it as tough as any other dockyard family – and was gratified that, in spite of missing out on a merited grammar school education, the girl was succeeding by herself. Well, maybe not quite: it would've been immodest to deny her own and Sue's continuing support and influence. The important thing was to help Jill carry on learning...

'Don't suppose you've heard of Lochgelly?'

'No, sorry.'

'It's a mining village near Cowdenbeath in Fife, or the *Kingdom of Fife* as its inhabitants like to dub it. Lochgelly's history is a bit less grandiose: used to be part of what they called *Little Moscow* on account of its Communist leanings.'

'Oh...right' murmured Jill politely.

'Aye, it's where my mother's family come from. She went to Beath Higher Grade School. And so did her friend, Jenny. The idea of the higher grades was that they'd give kids the chance to go on to higher education.'

'So did yer mam?' enquired Jill more keenly, now that they were talking about real people.

'No she didn't. And nor did Jenny. Neither set of parents could afford it. But mum was determined I'd go to college and Jenny got helped by some trust – Carnegie, I think – to go to Edinburgh. And then she did go to university. Read Law and Education. She and mum stayed friends for ages but Jenny moved away and now she lives in London.'

'Er...right,' offered Jill feebly. What on earth would her old teacher come up with next?

'Yeah, know why she lives in London? Cause she has to – she's a government minister! In the Department for Education. She's Jenny Lee!' concluded Joyce triumphantly.

'Sorry, you've lost me. I've never heard of her.'

'Doesn't matter, pet. It's not so much who she is, though that's nice for mum. It's what she's going to do. She's got the PM's backing for a *University of the Air.*'

'What on earth's that?'

'They're calling it that because it's going to conduct its courses by correspondence and – get this – over the radio, and even on TV! But here's the clincher. It's specifically designed to open up degrees to people who never had the chance to go to university.'

Finally, the penny dropped. Joyce meant *her.* 'You mean people like…'

'You and me!' interrupted Joyce passionately. 'You'll soon be a qualified nurse and I'm a head teacher, but neither of us has studied at a university. They say it'll be offering courses quite soon; I'm going to keep an eagle eye on developments, hinny!'

Jill departed soon after, her hand clutching Rosalind's and her head in the clouds…

Four

Jay wasn't hauled before the principal straightaway. Presumably Professor Bleasdale had more pressing matters on his mortarboard with term finishing that Friday. It was only a stay of execution though, surely, as the luminaries of the JCR were bound to press charges. On the evening before he was due to go home a call reached him in the common room. It was Pard.

'Alright squire, how's it goin?'

'Oh, yer know…so so,' Jay was wary. People might be listening.

'Heard owt after our little fracas?'

'Nah. Reckon they'll leave it 'til next term.'

'Probably no bad thing. Maybe it'll all've blown over by then.'

Jay glanced cautiously round the common room. 'Wouldn't bet on it, mate. Rumour is they're after our blood. Especially yours!'

'Hmm…bin thinking 'bout that, mate. S'pose we were to say it was you who'd puked out the window and shouted the obscenities.'

'Hang on, Pard.'

'No, listen. That's the minor offence. The major one's assaulting El Presidente.'

'Well…maybe…if you put it like that.'

'So we share the blame, eh? You fess up to the window job and I say I was just trying to stick up for you.'

Jay could see the logic in Pard's plan but not the justice. He was about to demur when the pips went and a click signalled the end of the conversation. Bollocks, sighed Jay, now what? Oh well, if in doubt, try a few. And off he went to the Buff.

By nine the next morning he was hitchhiking. His tried-and-tested starting point, the lights at Neville's Cross, quickly yielded a Corsair 2000, which took him as far as Scotch Corner. Another good spot: huge round-about. Successive 1100s got him down through Lancashire but the second one was a right cock-up. The driver, a scruffy old codger, had promised to drop him at the East Lancs road where Jay knew there was a sure-fire slipway back onto the M6. But the sod dropped him not at the A580 but the A58, which had no access back onto the motorway. The signpost said Ashton-in-Makerfield; Jay hadn't a clue where that was. The only solution was to scramble back down the cutting to the M6 and walk along the hard shoulder to the A580. It was little more than a mile, two at most: just have to hope the rozzers didn't drive past. It worked, but it cost him nearly an hour and by the time a Cortina 1500 deposited him at the turn for the A41 and he'd trudged the last mile to his parents' place, the journey had taken six hours. Not a disaster, but hardly threatening his sub-four-hour record. Mind, that had included an E-Type!

His mum and dad lived in the cringingly named *Jedka*, a large detached house at the end of a cul-de-sac. It was okay, though not a patch on the mansions they'd enjoyed in Norfolk, before he'd gone up to Durham. His mother had returned to teaching at the local secondary modern whilst his father, a long-standing school inspector, was now something very elevated at the DES, as the education department was currently known. He'd recently been promoted yet again; Jay must quiz him about it as his naturally modest old man was never particularly forthcoming. He was, however, adept at spotting when his younger son needed a shoulder.

Accordingly, that evening found them sharing a pint of Greenhall's and seeking a game of bagatelle at the Black Dog. On their original visit it had been mercifully quiet and the landlord, Charlie, had been on hand to explain the rules and the best shots.

'Always go for that eight-seven break I showed you. Then just try and fill as many pockets as you can. Twice over. That's the way we play: two sticks on the trot. The best players in the League'll finish the season with an average of around seventy to eighty. (Charlie didn't reveal his own average, eighty-two, nor that he'd captained the Dog team to the championship four years out of the last five.) By the end of that first holiday, Jay, with intensive coaching from Charlie, had been averaging sixty-two.

Apart from being entertaining the game could be a money-spinner. (Jay's hero had long been Autolycus, the *Rogue* from The Winter's Tale whom he idolised as 'a snapper-up of unconsidered trifles.' *Trifle = Bagatelle!* Geddit! The irony of his paladin being less of a knight and more of a thief appealed to Jay who was nothing if not opportunistic.) Unfortunately, his Autolyclean skills could not be employed more widely as the game seemed to be restricted to this neck of the woods. Bloody shame: he could've made a fortune in Durham!

For once they couldn't play. There was a match on and even the junior table had been commandeered for practice. So they grabbed an alcove and Jay talked inconsequentially about college life. Downing his fourth pint, he jostled his way to the bar and returned with refills. He took a large swig and a deep breath.

'Actually, there was summat I wanted to mention… I may be in a spot of bother.' And he proceeded to trot out Pard's version of events. Strictly speaking it was lying, which Jay had few scruples about but rarely risked with his dad, mainly cause he always seemed to sus.

His dad listened intently but gave nothing away so Jay was mightily relieved when, after a long pause, he simply announced, 'Leave it with me, son. My round, I think.'

It made sense. There was no tearing hurry. Easter Term didn't start for five weeks and presumably Bleasdale wouldn't summon him in holiday time. It had never occurred to Jay to wonder about the principal's vacation arrangements; he was more concerned about his own. Jay had only spent bits of breaks-from-college there and still knew hardly anyone. Their neighbours were mostly either too young, or too old to have varsity-aged kids. There was Laura, of course, Laura Whittingham, who was in her final year at Nottingham, reading English. Her local boyfriend had survived only one term so she, too, was at a loose end. They got on fine, went out a couple of times for a drink. But neither fancied the other particularly and there was a limit to how long you could spend discussing Augustan poetry. There'd been a bit of a fumble one time they'd walked back from the village after bumping into each other at a twenty-first party that Jay had crashed. They'd lingered on the footbridge over the canal and the kiss had seemed inevitable. But it was hardly a spectacular success and when Jay tried to get his hands up Laura's jumper she removed them with a firm, 'Steady on there, we hardly know each other.' It wasn't unfriendly, might even have meant another time maybe. Jay wasn't sure. But he didn't want to risk further humiliation and the moment passed, leaving just an embarrassing memory.

Most evenings he spent either playing Auction Bridge with his parents or out on the solitary piss round Chester. Several of the pubs had bagatelle tables so he'd sit at the bar calculating both the form of his potential opponents and the characteristics of the table. Did it have a run on it? Was it fast? What about the cushions? What was the favoured opening break? Then when he judged his stars to be in alignment he'd chalk his name on the slate. They always played for money, usually a shilling sometimes half-a-crown, and he was proficient enough by now to win many more games than he lost. It pretty much paid for his beer; his consumption being much more modest than at college, mainly out of deference to his parents.

In late April his dad presented him with a slim, green volume.

'You might want to study this in advance.' It was a climbing guide to Helsby, published by the Liverpool Wayfarers' Club. The Introduction gave a bit of history. There'd been some development before the war but most of the climbs had been put up in the last decade. Unlike the Fell & Rock CC guides to the Lakes there were no details of first ascents. That was frustrating as it used to give Jay a kick when he repeated a route put up by one of his heroes like Joe Brown or Don Whillans, both of whom his father knew well but Jay had yet to meet.

His dad filled in some of the background. 'From what I can gather most of the pre-war activity involved Colin Kirkus; the more recent lines are Hugh Banner's. Probably a bit hard for us, but there are some cracking Severe and VS routes apparently. Anyway, take a look. Thought we'd have a run out there tomorrow. Should be quiet on a Friday.'

They parked the Wolseley by the side of the narrow C-road above Helsby at the bottom of a steep, red-sandy bank. A belt of trees obscured the hill but the sunshine was already filtering through, dappling his dad's pale blue RAF haversack with the crinkled shapes of oak leaves. They struck up steeply through the rhododendrons and, as they emerged so did a striking view of the crag, bathed in warm sunshine. The sandstone looked dry; just as well as there was a marked absence of holds.

'We'll try *Little by Little*, eh. Doesn't look too bad.'

Next thing Jay was up to the mantelshelf about ten feet off the ground. The move was awkward, but he avoided using his knees and was swiftly installed in the corner above. It went easily enough on the left and although the finish was tricky he bridged up until he was high enough to reach an indifferent right handhold over the top.

'Not too bad at all!' he bragged.

'Didn't mean you to solo it!' His dad was still uncoiling the rope and assembling their manky runners. 'You can get off to the left and down that open chimney.'

In a trice Jay joined his father at the bottom. He grinned, proud to have demonstrated his prowess so early in the day.

'Okay, so much for *Little by Little*! Let's have a look at these next three. They're all part of *Oyster Slab* – Severe/Hard Severe. Wanna lead?'

As if there were any doubt! Jay tied on using a bowline and two half hitches, draped a couple of, probably superfluous, runners around his neck and set off. He paused to clean his PAs (recent Christmas present, stood for *Pierre Allain*, the French alpinist who'd developed the soft rubber shoes in the '30s to give a better grip on smooth rock). His dad had said they'd come into their own at Helsby and he wasn't wrong: the route was really thin. Scarcely any proper holds, just small rugosities in the sandstone and the occasional narrow crack. The slab went easily enough in his cherished rubbers, though how his dad would fare in those battered old Vibrams...

Jay belayed and hauled in the surplus rope.

'That's me,' filtered up the thin tones from forty feet below.

'Climb when you're ready.'

'Climbing.'

'Okay.'

Jay leaned as far forward as he could without toppling over in his perch and assessed his dad's progress. Not only did the Vibrams appear up to the task but his father was positively gliding across the wafer-thin slab and within a couple of minutes was pulling himself over the lip and clipping into the belay beside Jay.

'Okay that, son!'

They exchanged satisfied smiles; then rearranged the rope so they could either pull it through from the bottom or use it to top-rope the next route, which was a grade harder. Then they abseiled off in turn. Two more slab routes and they took a break for nuts and raisins, washed down by Guinness as they savoured the sun on the flat summit of the crag.

Suitably refreshed they attacked the rock with renewed vigour, tiptoeing their way up some more face climbs before finishing with the classic of the buttress – *Wood's Climb* – a forty-foot VS which ran up a shallow groove in the main face and was alternately strenuous and delicate. It was a fitting climax to a thoroughly satisfying day; only bettered by his dad's suggestion.

'Fancy a pint? I believe they've a snooker table in the Robin Hood.'

Five

It was a fine May morning and Jill had taken advantage of her split shift to meet Stephen for a swift coffee.

'Jay's coming up later. He's gonna join us at the Brandling.'

'Oh right: that'll be nice for you,' grimaced Jill. Enough uncertainty hung over both her relationship with Stephen and the evening ahead without having to contend with that wazzock. 'You'll be able to talk climbing all evening,' she added, not bothering to contain her sarcasm.

'Thought you liked him,' offered Stephen.

Christ! Men could be so dense! 'He's aal reet, if you like that sort of thing.'

'Whaddya mean?'

'Well…he is a bit of a snob, isn't he?'

'Oh that's just his insecurity. He's quite shy really so he overcompensates.'

'If you say so. Hope he doesn't come wrapped round a silk scarf again!'

This time Stephen had no reply. They were all going on to a party in South Gosforth. Was that really Jay's thing? He'd better behave himself…

Jill had taken more trouble than usual. Her jet-black hair was cut short. She was wearing more make-up than normal: blue eye shadow as well as two days' coating of mascara, and pale-pink lippie. The cream blouse was diaphanous; her black skirt was short and flared. The heels were higher than she was used to. Her basic test was: would Sue approve? If so she was confident she'd turn a few heads, female and male, other than Stephen's, although she wanted his approval too. Impressing Jay wasn't even on the menu. Just inside the porch was a ladies. The full-length mirror confirmed that the skirt almost revealed her stocking tops.

It had the anticipated effect! Not only did she clock several heads turning but the eyes that swept across the lounge bar threatened to burn holes in her bum! Now she really was conscious of how short this damn skirt was. (Just remember later, hinny, if you drop anything let someone else pick it up!) The boys had secured a top table, in a niche on its own but with a good view of the room and close to the bar. As well as Stephen and Jay there was a girl she vaguely recognised: a staff nurse on Pav 3? The Pavilion was miles away from orthopaedics down the longest corridor in the hospital. It housed private patients and some of the staff had a reputation for being stuck-up. Let's hope she's not one of them, prayed Jill: the evening was fraught enough already. She was glad she'd gone to town, though; the other girl was tall, with long blonde hair and was smartly turned out in a scarlet cocktail dress. She had slender, shapely legs and eyed Jill up with cool rivalry. It struck Jill that she might be bi as well… But how come she knew Jay?

Then Stephen introduced them: 'Deborah, this is Jill Walker – Jill, Deborah Burden and Jill realised with a shock that the blonde wasn't with Jay but Stephen. Bummer! It wasn't like she and Stephen were going steady but he'd not mentioned anyone else so she'd just assumed it was a date, with Jay an unwelcome gooseberry. Stephen appeared blissfully unaware of any awkwardness.

Surprisingly, Jay seemed to recognise her embarrassment and greeted Jill warmly, enquiring what she'd like to drink. She glanced quickly at the round table – two pints and a tall glass of chilled white wine. She quite fancied one of those but didn't want to seem conformist.

'That Exhibition you two are on?' And when two nods confirmed: 'Then it's good enough for me. Pint, please.' Jay looked impressed and immediately began the struggle through to the bar. Although they were three-deep at the brass rail he was back with Jill's pint before the atmosphere around the table had become awkward. Hmm, he might be a bit of a berk but he could handle himself in a pub. Deborah's glacial stare augured ill for a convivial evening. What on earth had Stephen let slip?

Jill decided she was being paranoid and, determined to make an effort, asked politely, 'Aren't you Staff on Pav 3, Deborah? What's it like there?' She was conscious it was shop but it was better than climbing. Or silence!

'Yeah. It's okay actually.' She spoke with a barely discernible Northumberland accent (Berwick?) and Jill, not for the first time, was relieved that long-term exposure to the lit twins had considerably softened her own Geordie twang.

'Aren't you on orthopaedics with Sister Watson?' and before Jill could do more than nod, 'Lucky you! She's great, I'll bet.'

That broke the ice. Jill revered Trish Watson, who'd recently suggested she become her staff nurse as soon she qualified. If Deborah liked her, she couldn't be that bad after all. And if she *was* with Stephen, that was hardly her fault. But what the hell was Jill supposed to do with bloody Jay!

An hour and two pints of Ex later, Jill's attitude was mellowing. Whilst the other three were talking she inspected Jay surreptitiously. He wasn't an athlete like Stephen but he was in fair shape: the climbing presumably. Medium height, moved well, especially in search of beer! But he had something sort of helpless about him. Not just his boyish looks. Again, he wasn't in Stephen's league, but he had a pleasant, open face, which lit up when he smiled. Longish, brown hair and striking blue eyes, only partially obscured by the glasses, which gave him a studious, intelligent air. Not much evidence of that so far, though Stephen claimed he was a bright bugger! But there was something else…vulnerability, almost. Anyway, whatever it was, he was clearly trying much harder this time. He'd paid her several reasonably subtle compliments and listened intently through the damn-noisy bar when she'd explained the extra-mural arrangements that had facilitated her A Level Literature course.

'So you did the *Dream* and *Lear*?'

'Yeah, quite a contrast, eh!'

'Which d'you prefer?'

'Depends on my mood. The Mechanicals are a hoot; but in terms of literary merit there's no comparison.'

'What Grade did you get, if you don't mind my asking?'

'An 'A'. Dunno how!'

Jay seemed rapt: 'Nice one! Have you kept it up?'

'What Shakespeare? Yeah, I'm reading *As You Like It* at the moment.'

'Bit of a change from *Lear* as well, eh?'

'True, but they've got one thing in common.'

'Go on…'

'Heroines!'

The conversation petered out to baffled expressions either side of them, but Jill had been agreeably surprised by his admiration for Cordelia. It was in stark contrast to the sexist dinosaurs in her class who'd branded her a feminist merely for sticking up for the tragic princess…

Wary about walking far in unaccustomedly high heels Jill appreciated the chivalrous manner in which he'd shepherded her along the heaving high street, linking arms as they crossed the slippery tarmac, still treacherous from the earlier rain. And by the time they turned off onto The Grove he'd somehow requisitioned her hand. She hadn't withdrawn it after they'd navigated Moor Lane and finished up on Rectory Road where the do was.

They pressed the intercom on the porch of a large Victorian semi.

The party was in full swing and seemed to be occupying all three floors. It was difficult to establish who their hosts were, given the easy access to food, drink and drugs. The murky atmosphere was permeated by the sweet smell of cannabis. Jill had tried it before at her friend Sally's. She hadn't expected to enjoy it and didn't. Still, later maybe. For now, there were drinks and dancing. Stephen and Deborah were clearly on for the evening and other than worrying briefly about where she'd sleep if it wasn't going to be with Stephen Jill was relaxed. They weren't serious, after all: they were good friends and free agents. She'd probably come across someone from the hospital and if all else failed there was Jay who seemed more than a little smitten, judging by his keenness to attend to her every need.

'If yer as good at getting drinks as in the pub yer can line me up a vodka. You choose how.' It was a test: see if he'd the gumption to mix something she liked. He came back with a tall glass full of ice and what tasted like almost neat Smirnoff with a smidgen of tonic and a large slice of lime. God knows where he'd procured that lot so quickly. He'd got a large bottle of Amber. First test passed! Now let's see what sort of dancer he was. The music was pretty standard stuff – Manfred Mann, the Bee Gees, Georgie Fame. But before she could drag him onto the bare boards that passed for a dance floor an arm entwined her and she was whisked off by Stephen. She didn't mind as long as Deborah didn't object. But there was nowt to worry about on that score: she could see the blonde's head bopping up and down with one of the housemen from gynaecology. And Jay had had his chance, after all.

Stephen returned her to her drink – there was no sign of Jay – and headed back to his consort. Next time she spotted them they were smooching to Bobby Goldsboro. Deborah smiled over Stephen's shoulder and blew Jill a sassy kiss. She banked it. A vacant armchair materialised and she subsided gratefully. She was vaguely concerned about Jay, which surprised her, considering she wouldn't have given you tuppence for him at the start of the evening, and faintly relieved when he drifted over to her grasping his Amber in one hand and two spliffs in the other.

'Thought I'd take the liberty. Hope you don't mind,' and he held out one to her. She smiled and patted the arm of the chair.

'Yer a mind reader! Smelled 'em as soon as we came in. Use 'em much?'

'Nah, just at parties. Like the effect but not the afters. Get a bit morose sometimes.'

'Oh…right.'

'Only when I'm on me own,' he added hastily.

'Well, we'd best make sure that doesn't happen, eh?' Jill gave him a dazzling smile and was rewarded by his wilting visibly. 'Keep the chair,' she instructed, 'I'm gonna find some more drinks. Amber, or fancy something a bit stronger?'

'Brandy, if you can find some. Please!'

When she came back he was recumbent and gazing cheerfully into the distance. Without thinking Jill slid onto his knee and presented him with a flask of Remy Martin.

'Christ! You're a star' he announced admiringly his eyes dilated with the cannabis and fixated on the broad expanse of thigh her short skirt was exposing. Jill couldn't remember why the possibility of such a brazen display had once seemed significant! She thought for a second he was going to rest his free hand on her knee; she doubted she'd remove it. But it was merely to steady himself as he rose slightly in the chair so he could use both hands to open the recalcitrant Remy.

'Cheers, hinny!' Jill gave him another inviting smile as she clinked her glass against the neck of his bottle and they each took a generous slug. It was the first time she'd addressed him with any affection.

God knows how much later they all poured out of the taxi at Morpeth Court and staggered up the stairs to Flat Three. Helped along by Jay, Jill felt delightfully light-headed. Maybe he wasn't such a pillock after all. In fact, if he played his cards right...

They slumped into chairs. Stephen announced he was making coffee, then promptly disappeared waving vaguely in the direction of the spare room. Deborah mouthed something that could've been 'Later?' Jill pulled Jay up and they careened into the spare bedroom.

'*You* can sleep on the floor' prescribed Jill loftily. But then conscious of how ridiculous, and mean, that sounded she relented, giggling, 'Oh all right you can share the bed. But no funny business!'

'Course not,' muttered Jay. 'Er...bathroom.' And he padded off, giving Jill time to strip down to her underclothes and slip into bed. She didn't hear him return. She'd woken needing the loo and feeling randy. Back from the bathroom she could see the outline of his body by the faintest of lights from the landing. She pushed him gently aside, pulled the bedclothes from under him and got back into bed. She unbuttoned his shirt and pants and removed them. All he had on was a pair of dark boxer briefs through which she could just make out the bulge of his dickery dock (as her Cockney cousin, Robert, called it). Jazzed in a cannabis-cum-vodka haze Jill leant across and stroked it very gently, so as not to wake him. She watched in fascination as it began to grow and debated drunkenly whether she might free it from the briefs so she could see it. And touch it properly. Maybe even give it a little kiss! She was getting that worked up she slipped her free hand inside her panties.

However, just as she was becoming thoroughly inflamed a shadow loomed in the doorway and then over the bed. It seemed to be checking out proceedings and a hiss of breath told Jill it liked what it saw. A hand ran down between her shoulder blades and under her arm, cupping each breast in turn. Another hand joined Jill's inside her knickers, stroking her briefly.

'You hot for it? C'mon! Come an' join us, pet' whispered Deborah.

Bewildered but almost delirious, Jill allowed herself to be led along the corridor by her predatory chaperone. They stopped once and she was pushed up against a sideboard. Deborah kissed her avidly, simultaneously caressing her breasts. Jill nearly sank to her knees and was bundled, unceremoniously and uncomplaining, into Stephen's bed. Deborah climbed in on the other side...

Six

Professor Bleasedale was icily unequivocal. Any further misdemeanour by either of them and that was it. Finals in four weeks or not. Jay suspected his father had intervened but he hadn't let on to Pard that he'd told him. So he had to accept his friend's version: that what had saved them was the rumour Pard had circulated that the two JCR stalwarts had been celebrating and were themselves so arseholed that they were equally responsible for the subsequent ruckus. Whatever their salvation it certainly had a salutary effect. Jay knuckled down like never before. He even attended the odd lecture, though since he'd lost his gown he was censured roundly for that.

Just before exams, there was a message in his pigeonhole: did he fancy a trip to Holy Island that weekend? Ed and Jill were driving up and he was very welcome to join them. There being nothing to be gained from any further revision ('Two weeks is too soon and two days too late,' his big brother used to advise!) Jay decided the break would do him good.

He was a tad ambivalent. The last time he'd seen them, Jill was wrapped in an over-sized dressing gown emerging from Ed's bedroom. It was the morning after the party and there was no sign of Deborah. Jay's throbbing head and parched mouth impeded clarity of recall but he was pretty sure *he'd* gone to bed with Jill. He remembered being told to behave himself and subsequently falling asleep on the bed with Jill already snug under the covers. At some point he'd half-woken to find himself nearly naked and not on, but under the bedclothes. After that…zilch! He'd been a bit embarrassed but the pair of them had behaved as if nothing untoward had happened so, although miffed, Jay had left on good terms. And now this! It was all a bit baffling.

Having recently been promoted, Ed was the proud owner of a brand new silver Cortina 1500 (VAR 108G, noted Autolycus the Archivist). It was quick and he was an excellent driver so Jay was looking forward to the trip. He might even get a go himself, though maybe Ed wouldn't risk that with Jill in the car. Moreover, Jay remembered Ed was teaching her to drive so he'd probably have to wait his turn.

They bombed up the A1 cheek by jowl on the Cortina's bench seat.

'Like The Three Musketeers,' remarked Jill brightly, an arm along the top of the seat each side of her. She looked stunning, as usual, with a tight tee shirt that accentuated the curve of her boobs and a broad belt, which nipped the top in at the waist. The only disappointment was the maxi; at the party she'd worn a mini-skirt and Jay had ogled her pins all evening. At one stage he recalled engineering an excuse to touch them, but he'd chickened out at the last second. Still, at least this skirt had a slit in it so periodically he got a flash of knee!

The Cortina's most prestigious accessory was an eight-track stereo player which Stephen had fitted himself between the centre console and the dashboard. He recorded his own tapes and Jay searched, as directed, in the glove compartment until he found one labelled *Pet Sounds*. He'd liked the Beach Boys since he'd discovered he and Carl Wilson had been born on the same day. Great! He inserted it in the eight-track. It was good driving music. They purred through Alnwick to the strains of *Wouldn't It Be Nice* and ten minutes later Ed gunned it past Budle Bay at ninety with a *Sloop John 'B'* sing-along. They gave a spirited rendition of *God Only Knows* and it was only as they swung off onto the C-road that ran through Beal that Jay realised the last track was *Caroline, No*. The melancholy lyrics always reminded him of Caroline Tillotson. Caro had been his first love – in Norfolk. They remained friends. She'd been the surprise guest of honour at his twenty-first; his mother, bless her, being under the impression they were still together. Without his move to Durham, they probably still would have been.

He sloughed off his reverie as they ran out of road. The Causeway was still covered, although only to a depth of maybe eight or nine swiftly flowing inches. Jay was despatched to check the tide schedule, which was nailed to a post by the last outlook station.

'It's okay, it's going out. Five or ten minutes and it'll be clear.'

'Sod that!'

And Jay just had time to scramble back in, slamming the door as Ed nosed the Cortina into the receding waters. They made it safely to Primrose Bank although there were a few dodgy moments later skirting the bay to the main island. Jay assumed they'd head for the pub – The Ship, apparently – but before they reached Chare Ends Ed pulled confidently onto an unmade track, which cut through the sand-hills. He drove circumspectly down the path and just as the soft sand threatened to engulf them they broke through the dunes. He parked on a hard stand surrounded by marram grass and low hillocks above the sea. They had their very own bay, maybe a hundred yards across and just feet away down a shallow cliff. It was completely private.

'You'll find a cool box in the boot, mate, if you'd do the honours.'

Jay ferreted amongst the detritus. Along with the fencing kit and medical samples there was a hamper that, on inspection, was stuffed with goodies and so neatly packed that Jay suspected Jill had assembled it. (Later he discovered she'd been given £20 by Ed and told to hit the high street delicatessens. He was nothing if not generous!) The cool box was wrapped in tartan blankets and contained six bottles of Muscadet, still cold enough to be gleaming with condensation. Jay uncorked one and unearthed three wine glasses – not plastic, proper ones. He filled them, and gestured to Jill to help him. Draping the blankets over her arm, she carried them across to Ed who swiftly organized the soirée.

The day was perfect: the sky cloudless and the early June sun already hot. Another Beach Boys tape serenaded them softly through the open windows of the Cortina and the first bottle of Muscadet seemed to dematerialize. They wrangled cheerfully over whether to go for a swim straightaway or open another bottle. Jill thought swim but was outvoted and, as a penalty, despatched to procure the second bottle. Surprisingly, Jay didn't feel like a spare part. Perhaps the other two would've preferred their own company. But if so, why invite him along? Maybe they didn't worry about the jealousy thing. Everyone knew Ed had loads of girlfriends and Jill didn't seem like the possessive type. Indeed, from what Jay could remember of the night in the flat she wasn't entirely averse to his company. Perchance she just liked them both. *She* was the one who'd called them 'three musketeers'! One for all and all for one! Hmm…maybe the wine was beginning to go to his head!

Ed was droning on about Lindisfarne fauna; Jill seemed entranced. Still, he was a biologist. He'd graduated three years back, in '65, just about the time Jay was going up and, presumably Jill was embarking as a Cadet at the RVI. The age difference was significant. Not only was Ed more mature than him, he was more accomplished and considerably better off. And better looking: Ed was the original tall, dark and handsome, Jay was shorter, slightly overweight and wore specs! No wonder Jill preferred Ed. The only advantage Jay had was he was more intelligent. Better read, more articulate and certainly nimbler intellectually. He could always best Ed in a discussion. His only problem was he couldn't resist doing so even though it didn't major as his most attractive trait. In fact, whatever that was eluded Jay although he'd felt once or twice that Jill was warming to him. Not the bed thing. They'd both been stoned as well as pissed and nowt had happened. No…it was just the way she'd looked at him once or twice. As if she was kind of weighing him up; though whether that was weighing up as in 'against Ed' or just generally analysing him, Jay hadn't a clue. Though obviously he hoped it was the latter… He yawned: all this psyche stuff was making him sleepy or maybe it was the wine. He dropped off.

Only for a few minutes. Ed was proposing a swim and Jill seemed game. Since he hadn't spotted any bathing suits this could be interesting. He tried not to gawk too blatantly as Jill yanked the tee shirt over her head to reveal a red-and-yellow bra which, anticlimactically, was a bikini top. She unclasped the belt and the midi-skirt dropped to the blanket. Jay was faintly disappointed: he'd hoped she'd be wearing knickers but the matching pattern indicated a bikini bottom. She looked ravishing though, and watching her undress had given him a hard-on. Fortunately, Ed grabbed her hand and they scampered over the fine sand to the bay. By the time Jay had his jeans off he was able to follow without embarrassment.

The water was bracing but exhilarating and after frolicking about in the shallows they set off to swim to the other side of the bay. Jay was a proficient swimmer and hoped not to be left behind. He was – but not by Ed. Jill struck out strongly for the reef with Jay in frenzied pursuit. He arrived soon after and was rewarded by a flashing smile and an eyeful of Jill's bikini failing excitingly to conceal her stiff nipples.

'Colder than you think, eh!' he chortled, making no attempt to avert his gaze.

'You're a naughty boy, Jay Fincher. But I like you,' she mimicked, appearing to glance down through the crystal clear water before playfully planting a kiss on his lips.

He hadn't realized you could manage an erection under such conditions; but it promptly revived as Jill's knee accidentally brushed against him in the current. Before he could take matters any further, however, a breathless Ed spluttered up to join them. Jay noted appreciatively that Jill dipped modestly below the foam. Strewth! Was that for his benefit? Did it mean there was hope for him yet?

Seven

Jill was enjoying herself.

The drive up had been fun. The music enhanced the holiday atmosphere and even though she was no great fan of the Beach Boys their songs were quite catchy. The boys, particularly Jay, became notably more relaxed and it felt perfectly natural to rest her hands on their respective shoulders. Stephen was driving fast, which was a bit of a turn on, especially when combined with loud music, and being sandwiched between two boys she might fancy.

She'd been wary for a sec when she saw the stack of bottles Stephen had brought. That was two each, and in the afternoon! Jill wasn't used to drinking through the day and the few times she had it seemed to take her no time to get tiddly. She hoped Stephen wasn't planning to get her sozzled and take advantage. And Jay? He wouldn't, surely? Then she remembered he was there at her suggestion so he could hardly be part of some Machiavellian plot. Even so she shuddered to think what Sue would say: sunbathing in a bikini and sozzled in the afternoon with two fellas. *Asking for trouble, hinny!*

Dismissing the conspiracy theory, Jill nevertheless sensed a certain tension in the air. Stephen was describing the birdlife. His explanations of the differences between various types of tern and gull, as well as kittiwakes, fulmars, razorbills and gannets, were fascinating. Although Jay didn't seem to think so.

In spite of herself she drank more than her fair share of the second bottle and was enthusiastically matching Stephen glass for glass on the third when he returned to the swimming suggestion. Jill had come prepared. Can't see that they have, she thought, but she wasted no time in removing her tee shirt and skirt. She was conscious of being slightly aroused and was unsurprised when Jay, whose eyes had nearly popped out watching her striptease, started to develop an erection as he stripped down to his boxers. To save him embarrassment she grabbed Stephen's hand and dragged him down the low cliff into the bay.

After the predictable larking about the challenge of swimming across to the far – sea – side of their private cove was taken up without discussion. Jill simply set off. She had no fears about being shown up; her brother Rob swam for United Services and had schooled her well on their hauls around St Mary's lighthouse. She glanced back once or twice and was pleasantly surprised to see that Jay was much the stronger swimmer of the pair. That was good. She suspected he felt physically inferior to his taller, sportsman-friend: this would even them up a bit. By the time she reached the reef, which turned out to be nearly twice as far as they'd first estimated, Jill was elated and excited in equal measure: a combination of the sensuousness of the swimming and the alcohol. Jay was just a few yards away now but Stephen was lagging a long way behind…

It must've been the fourth bottle! Everyone was in a state of dishabille. Well, to be strictly accurate, the boys had just their boxers on whilst Jill had her bikini bottoms on and her top all skew-whiff from where they'd been playfully trying to remove it.

It was just a game: a bit of nonsense as she pretended to egg them on.

'Why, boys, I do believe you're trying to see my boobs!' Jill moued, crossing her arms and covering her bosom; and then as they shook their heads in denial uncrossing them again as if to display the goods! Except that she still had her bikini top on. Well almost. She'd calculatedly hooked a thumb in the side of the material and as she threw her arms wide once more it scooped one breast half-clear of its gaoler. She chuckled in mock embarrassment and popped it back undercover, accidentally brushing it with her fingers.

'Ooh that's not very comfy,' she moaned. 'Better try again!'

Jill anticipated some assistance. Sure enough Stephen pulled the top down and, when in a fit of giggles, she pretended to remonstrate, Jay chivalrously attempted to restore it. As a result of their combined efforts it came off completely and two separate hands roamed lasciviously if briefly over her breasts. Her protests were somewhat undermined by her nipples betraying her excitement and she was in danger of getting carried away when she slipped and subsided gently to the rug. They all collapsed laughingly into a drunken coma…

Jill was first to come round. She felt deliciously light-headed and mischievous. In the no-man's land of half-sleep, images of the Jesmond party were swimming in and out of her consciousness. She'd been going to give Jay his deserts. He'd been really nice to her all night, looking out for her every need and accommodating her whims even when she'd condemned him to sleep on the top of the bed. Poor Jay! He was the only one who missed out and the only one who didn't know!

Fully awake but ratted, Jill felt as horny as hell. It was now or never. She removed her bikini top completely and poked Jay's shoulder gently. As he came round, all agog, she put her finger to her lips and nodded towards their bay. Earlier, Jill had spotted a shallow inlet only thirty yards or so from the water's edge. She led Jay swiftly into it. Satisfied they were hidden from view she put her arms around his neck and kissed him lingeringly. Out of the main inlet the water was crystal clear and calm. The breeze had subsided and the sun beat down on their heads and exposed shoulders. The cries of the gulls and kittiwakes seemed not so much mournful as romantic. Jay returned her embrace keenly but not intrusively and they remained cemented together for some time gradually exploring each other with their tongues. Jill's breasts were pressed against him and she felt her nipples harden as she rubbed them backwards and forwards. She groped behind her until she located a smooth ledge in the rock. Then she hauled herself onto it so that her boobs were level with Jay's face. Let's hope he's not slow on the uptake...

Jay was circling her salt-wet nipples with his tongue.

'Mmm...thas nice, pet...doan stop!' She moaned appreciatively and felt them licked, then sucked more vigorously. She slid her hand down between their bodies and discovered him sticking rigidly through the slit in his briefs. She squeezed affectionately and began to ripple him. Jay groaned with stifled gratitude and kissed her again, passionately. He was panting, his breath roaring like the waves beyond the reef in her ear.

'Oh God,' he moaned, 'Oh, Jill...thas wonderful...you're so... Oh bugger! No...no... Sorry!'

Jill smiled indulgently. Typical! If ever she'd fancied it herself, it was now and instead she'd pleasured him so expertly it'd all been over before...

'No, no...don't worry! As long as you enjoyed it!'

'Enjoyed! It was incredible...' He was trying to find the right words to explain how he felt. Not just physically but emotionally as well. He'd almost worked it out...

'We should be getting back. If Stephen wakes up he'll be wondering what's happened. Least said, eh...'

The caution proved unnecessary. Both Jill and Jay slept most of the return journey, their heads resting together on top of the plastic bench seat. Stephen smiled avuncularly and drove more slowly, more considerately than usual.

Much later, relatively sober, they were driving back to the flat having dropped Jay at Newcastle Central. Jill, hung over, felt slightly nervous. She didn't think Stephen would be unduly worried even if he knew about the illicit swim: he was pretty broad-minded. Even so she saw no reason to raise the topic.

'Well you two seem to be getting on a bit better. Changed your mind about him?'

'Wouldn't go that far. But you were right: he's just shy.'

'Yeah, and prone to introspection. Well certainly since his brother died.'

'You never told me that! What happened?'

'He was in the Navy. Submariner. Killed out in Singapore. Jay doesn't talk about it much. Well not to me.'

Hmm, that explains a lot, thought Jill. Wonder if he'd talk to me? She sensed something almost protective in Stephen's tone; perhaps he saw himself as a surrogate elder brother. 'You really like the bloke, don't you?'

'Yeah, he's okay! Always getting into scrapes, though: needs looking out for. Talking of which, I'm on a course and then working in London for the next month. Why don't you go down to Durham and see him?'

'Oh, dunno about that. Wouldn't you mind?'

'No course not. We're all mates, aren't we? Anyway I reckon he'd be pleased.'

'Well…if you say so. Maybe I will.'

Eight

The results were posted on adjacent notice boards outside the library. Jay, with Jules as moral support, was searching for his name. Firsts, Two-ones, Two-twos...surely the arseholes hadn't given him a Third? They couldn't do that; not after the standard of his essays. He scanned the next notice board for Thirds, but there weren't any. Nothing! What the hell was going on? Then Julia spotted it: *Jay Fincher: RP.*

'The swine!' she exclaimed passionately. 'The pathetic, unprincipled, pusillanimous bastards!'

'Steady on, Jules. It can't be that bad. What does it mean, anyway?'

'It means, you poor sap, that they've had the last word. It stands for *Received Pass*. They didn't dare fail you, but they wouldn't award you Honours.'

'Oh, is that all.' Jay was genuinely relieved.

'All?' screeched Jules, furiously. 'It's a cop-out, a disciplinary degree. They dish 'em out once in a blue moon!'

'So...bit of a rarity then?' grinned Jay. 'Like my namesake, J-for-Jonathan Swift with his *ex speciali gratia* degree from Trinity, eh!'

That seemed to further provoke Julia who, dismayed by her friend's lack of concern, elected to compensate by taking some action.

'Come 'ere you chump!' she instructed, holding out her arms. Jay allowed himself to be enfolded and they hugged each other. At length she released him but only so she could put her arms round his neck. Then when Jay summoned up what he hoped was the correct expression of gratitude-cum-hopelessness she kissed him fulsomely on the lips. When she finally released him she still held his head in her hands and his gaze in hers.

'And don't ever forget how fond I am of you. I'll always be there for you. Always, okay?'

Jay was gratified by her indignation and touched by her show of affection. He'd always liked her; could easily have pursued her if she hadn't made it plain that she did actually love her straitlaced solicitor and would not be led astray by the likes of Jay! Just for a second during the kiss he'd felt her lips open ever so slightly. He wondered whether it was a sort of goodbye-invitation and that if he'd escorted her firmly down the Bailey she might've been persuaded to express her sympathy in more sensual terms. Getting it right for once he dismissed the fantasy and replaced it with gratitude. Then it crossed his mind, uncharitably, that the kiss might encompass a tinge of guilt. Julia had got a First, the only one awarded that year. He was just pleased they hadn't failed him, and if it really was so rare then it was distinctive. He was Autolycus after all: different, unique, a snapper-up of unconsidered trifles! And when his certificate came through the post – he wouldn't bother attending the ceremony – it'd presumably be plain *Bachelor of Arts*. No fancy classifications. Yeah, that'd do for him. As his brother used to say, 'In the words of the Bessarabian prophetess: Stuff 'em!'

He congratulated himself afterwards. He wasn't pretending. He really wasn't that upset. If he had been, like when Caroline had split up with him, never mind when his brother was killed, he'd have gone on the piss. He weighed the possibility fleetingly but rejected it. It being only eleven wouldn't normally have stopped him; he just didn't feel like it. But he needed to do something. Something symbolic, something to demonstrate, to himself at least, that they hadn't won, that he still remained in control. True to himself, as that old fool Polonius had advised, uncharacteristically prescient. Yeah: his tables... *Meet it is I set it down, that one may smile, and smile, and be a villain. At least I'm sure it may be so in Denmark.* Durham, Hamlet's English Elsinore!

It wasn't a question of revenge. Their sort – Swift's Lilliputians – didn't merit that. More a case of expurgation... He could've burned his gown in Palace Green...except he'd long since lost it. But his books... yeah, that was it. *All saws of books, all forms, all pressures past...* His books were the symbol of their intellectual hold over him. Get rid of *them* and there'd be no symbol, no hold. But not get rid of as in throw off Prebend's Bridge into the Wear. That would be a waste. He'd sell 'em. And, even sweeter, he'd sell 'em back to the second-hand bookshop where he'd acquired most of them originally. That was doubly sweet; cause since he'd half-inched most of 'em in the first place he'd be making pure profit. Money-back on cost-nothing. Infinite riches! Autolycus the Avaricious would be proud of him! What's more, he could do with the money – especially what he'd get for Bloody Beowulf! Pukka edition:

should've cost him three guineas and the going rate was thirty bob. Twitchin', man!

Course he could always try a few after that…

Nine

Stephen had been gone a fortnight and she'd heard nothing from Jay. Jill was depressed. Not clinically, as Stephen would've pointed out, just down. She was on a split shift so had nearly four hours to kill and she fancied a break. Get out of the hospital and down to Reg Dobson's café on Percy Street. It was only a five-minute walk. But she'd have to change out of her uniform: they weren't allowed to wear them outside. It was a shame, as Jill was really proud of being a nurse and would've revelled in advertising it. But rules were rules and it was pointless getting into trouble over something so trivial, especially this close to Finals.

She opened her locker to see what civvies she had and there it was underneath her jeans and jumper: the lit twins' handsome edition of *As You Like It*. Oh great! I'd forgotten about you! Changing her mind, but not her uniform she took the book through to the big lounge. It was virtually empty so she bagged a small table on its own in a recess overlooking the grounds. They were pretty just now with the lawns neatly mowed and the shrubs (Stephen would know all their names) in full bloom. She scuttled through to the kitchenette, brewed a mug of Nescafé and reclaimed her spec. Good! Now she was completely on her own. She was keen to get started but as she carefully opened the front cover out fell a letter. Jill smiled tenderly: it was the grovelling apology Jay had sent her after that first calamitous meeting. She'd been touched. And amazed: one, that he'd written at all; two, that he'd managed to track her down to the RVI, even if it had only reached her courtesy of Sister Watson.

Already cheered, Jill laid the letter aside and opened the book. Now that she'd got something to get her teeth into she was no longer depressed. Only thing was the Introduction was almost as long as the play. If she had to trawl through that she'd never reach the text itself. She was about to skip the lot when she noticed from the contents a section on Rosalind. Joyce's description of the heroine suggested this might be critical so she plunged straight in expectantly.

Jill knew that the female parts in Shakespeare were played by young boys. What she hadn't appreciated was just how much fun the playwright, and his audiences, had with the gender bending! So this Rosalind was going to dress up as a boy, then as a boy pretending to be a woman and then as a jaunty boy reflecting on events! Bloody hell! This was just up her street. No wonder Joyce had praised Rosalind; pronounced differently it seemed, with the last syllable to rhyme with hind or kind.

Now Jill *was* ready to start the play!

Two days later she still hadn't heard from Stephen and was debating whether to follow his advice and visit Jay. She mentioned it to Sally when they bumped into each other in the canteen.

'Why man, course yer should. If yer like him.'

'I think I'm starting to, but it's a big step.'

'How come? That Stephen's gannin oot with other girls apart from you, pet. Yer do kna that, divn't yer?'

'Course! I'm not stupid. But this'd be different.'

'Why?'

''Cause if Jay likes me as much as I'm starting to like him he wouldn't want to share me.'

So?'

'So...I'd have to decide between the two of them.'

'Canna see it mesel, hinny. I mean it's not as if yer never look at other fellas...'

'Whaddya mean?' Jill's indignation was mock, and they both knew it.

'Oh aye? What boot that Gay?'

Gay Adeyemi was a houseman on orthopaedics. He was from Nigeria. Very handsome. Jill didn't have the hots for him or oot. It was just if he came onto their ward when she was taking round the meds trolley it seemed inclined to shake so much half the pills finished on the floor instead of inside the patients. She'd confessed to Sally who teased her mercilessly. At a recent Nurses' Ball, he'd asked her to dance and they'd proved such a hit – Jill being a sexy mover and Gay blessed with a similar sense of rhythm – that there was speculation about their going out together. Trainee nurse and doctor would have been highly irregular and Sally had mocked her accordingly. However, it was just after the rumours had surfaced about Sally and the theatre sister so she'd soon piped down. She needed Jill's unswerving friendship.

It worked both ways. Sally had always looked out for Jill even though her motives were not entirely unselfish. She was openly bi whereas Jill was more ambivalent, and discreet. Sally was forever trying to lure Jill into bed. As she had her own flat and held the best nurses' raves that was not too difficult. Jill had succumbed a couple of times, but not recently. She'd enough on her plate what with still worshipping Sue and being unable to choose between Stephen and Jay!

But Sal was right. She'd settle nothing if she didn't try, so down to Durham it was. She didn't have a 'phone number for Jay, or his address and Stephen had been a bit vague about his whereabouts mentioning both St Cuthbert's on the Bailey and digs in Allergate at different times. She didn't know the city well: just a few of the pubs and those mostly in the dark with Stephen, so she hadn't clocked their whereabouts. She was grateful Sal had accompanied her; although a bit anxious about what might happen with Jay. The last thing she wanted was Sally chatting him up!

It was still early so they started checking out the coffee shops around the Market Place and up Saddler Street which she knew led to several of the colleges. An hour later they'd drawn a complete blank, even after a daring recce of men-only Cuthbert's. They were headed back to the centre when it occurred to Jill that, since it was now past opening time, Jay might very well be in his local. She remembered it was the Buffalo Head and moments later she and Sally were squeezing down the constricted corridor. There was no sign of Jay in the dingy bar and the only person she recognized was his mate from the ill-fated darts-cum-climbing evening back in February. She was trying to recall his name – Tawd? Tard? – when he came over.

'Hi, you're Stephen's girlfriend aren't you? Sorry don't know your name. I'm Pard, remember?'

'Yeah, course. I'm Jill: this is Sally. You haven't seen Jay Fincher, have you?'

'Yeah, as it happens.'

'Oh good. Where?'

'He was up at the Green with Julia.'

'Julia? Who's she? Not his girlfriend, is she?'

Pard smirked, 'Not exactly… But they're pretty friendly. Or at least they were when I saw 'em,' he added maliciously with a smile that was more of a leer.

'We might go and meet him, that's all. Where's this Green?'

Again Pard eyed her up blatantly. She was glad Sally was there.

'It's a bit hard to describe but I'm on me way there to meet me wi…er…someone. You can tag along if you want.'

Jill didn't want, but could see no alternative.

The Green was picturesque. It had a castle on one side and a fine cathedral on the other. Jill vaguely remembered traipsing round the cloisters with her friend Morag who'd been at St Aidan's. On the other two sides ranged university buildings, including the library. As they reached it the main door opened and a small, brunette woman emerged.

'About time! It's bloody freezing in there… Who's this?'

'Oh just some friends of Jay's.'

'I'm Sally. This is Jill, Jay's girlfriend', intervened Sal pointedly.

The woman ignored Jill and gave Sally a dazzling, c'mon smile: 'I'm Jorja. Pard was just gonna take me to lunch. You can join us if you like.'

Sally nodded keenly before Jill, who thought she'd just glimpsed Jay at the far side of the Green, could demur.

'You go ahead if you want. Think I just spotted Jay.'

'Okay, catch you later, flower,' and Sally linked arms with Jorja as they headed back towards the pub. Pard trailed behind, glaring.

By the time Jill reached the Bailey Jay had disappeared.

Ten

Back in Chester, Jay found his parents weren't over-chuffed with his degree, but they didn't make a huge fuss either. The summer dragged by, mountaineering proving more fruitful than job-hunting. He didn't have a clue what he wanted to do next, so it wasn't as if he'd lost out on some coveted career. Opportunities? The only advert that had caught his notice was for an international firm of copywriters. They wanted only *Firsts. Or people who thought they should've got one!* Just the job: but he lost the clipping and they were deprived of his genius.

He joined the staff of Woodbridge High. English and Maths were shortage subjects and you could teach either as an 'untrained graduate'. If Jay took to it, he could always get a professional qualification later. Probably wouldn't pertain: he was only on a six-week contract. Even that, he knew, had been secured through his father's influence. As Her Majesty's Divisional Inspector, with oversight of every school in the North West, Ray Fincher numbered scores of local authority chiefs within his purview. The local headmaster, reckoned Jay, would be small beer. Besides, his mother already taught geography there and Mr Jenkins, the head in question, seemed a decent enough bloke. Jay didn't have a formal interview but understood that he was on probation and that it was Mr Jenkins, not Raymond Fincher HMI, who would decide whether the contract was to be extended beyond half term. That suited Jay. If he were successful it would mean a permanent post and his parents would be pleased. If not, he'd head back to the north east. Stephen had said he could share the flat and apparently they were desperate for teachers around Newcastle. Either way he was welcome to come up for half term.

Woodbridge was an early '60s, two-storey, flat-roofed monstrosity. But it was situated in a village and had a middle-class catchment area. It housed seven hundred kids and around fifty teachers. Two of them started on the same day as Jay and, like him, were rising twenty-two. There the similarities ended. Sid Baxter, the maths man, was okay, if a bit studious.

Sarah Lines was a history teacher: very pretty, very Welsh and a pain in the arse. Both had been to teacher training college and were therefore qualified. But on a staff with scarcely any graduates Jay was nevertheless given the benefit of the doubt. Except by Miss Lines.

'Got your teaching plans all sorted for this first term, Mr Fincher?' she enquired snidely? What will you start with today?'

Jay, was needled. 'Oh I thought perhaps a soupçon of romantic poetry with a scintilla of Jacobean drama.' It shut her up for the time being.

Sid was more sympathetic. 'If you want any tips, Finch, just say the word. It's not the easiest job to start with.'

'Cheers, Sid, much appreciated' he responded, making sure Miss Smarty Pants heard.

He actually had all the advice he needed; but it didn't do to mention your parents. Especially *his* parents! Strangely, he was more concerned about the staffroom than the classroom. Justifiably, as it turned out, because the kids were mostly great! The school was divided into four houses – Buckley, Oxton, Spann and Yoxall – all nineteenth-century Cheshire worthies apparently. As a subject specialist he got to teach top streams: B1, O1 and S1; then in order, perhaps, to balance any suggestion of favouritism, Y4. In the fourth year they specialised so he acquired 4T2 and 4C2 as well. He was also Oxton 1's form teacher.

The Head of English, Tess Bailey, was supportive. She contacted him in August and they met in her deserted demountable. She dismissed the surroundings with a laugh.

'Yeah, most of the senior staff opt for the main building. More prestigious. But these rooms are quieter; plus, being more isolated you get fewer unwanted visits! Soon as you can, move out to one.'

Miss Bailey ('No, no, call me Tess!') was attractive an all: red hair, high cheekbones, sexy voice. Why wasn't she married? She couldn't be more than thirty... Anyway, she laid out the whole syllabus for him: grammar, comprehension, set books – the lot. He borrowed the four set books for the first half of term and read them the following week, not least to impress Tess. She just smiled.

Jay's dad was from Birmingham and his only piece of advice was based on teaching in the rough backstreets of pre-war Sparkhill. 'If you run into any trouble pick the biggest bully in the class and belt him!'

Jay wasn't sure if it was a joke. By the end of the first month he'd got the measure of all his classes except 4T2. Discipline, he decided, was based on silence; not the class's – his. He'd tolerate a low, purposeful buzz, but if anyone got too loud or interrupted him he'd simply stop in mid-sentence. The first few times the malefactor might continue but when the rest of the class fell silent and the culprit became aware that everyone was looking at them, they shut up. Except in 4T2. There were three of 'em and they were apparently renowned for taunting new teachers. Baxter had already had a run-in with them, and Miss Lines had had to resort to reporting them to the head. Jay wasn't having that.

The most disruptive was a lad called Crofton. He was tall and burly, bigger than Jay, and blatantly contemptuous. The first time Jay had given him the silent treatment it'd worked: Crofton didn't know what to make of it and piped down. It happened again the following week. Same result. But the third time Crofton not only took no notice but turned his back on his teacher and carried on talking, only more loudly. The rest of the class was deathly. Jay couldn't let it go. He moved swiftly from the front to Crofton's bench. Still nattering, the lad didn't see him coming and was caught off guard by a swift and forceful blow to the side of his head. The effect was dramatic. Crofton was lifted out of his seat, across the next, empty desk (he wasn't popular) and ended up in a heap in the aisle. Hushed anticipation as 4T2 awaited Crofton's reaction. The lad struggled to his feet, gave Jay a look of venom laced with fear and resumed his seat. He didn't speak again that lesson; and Jay had no further trouble with him. Or 4T2. Or anyone else...

Come October a couple of the older blokes took him under their wing. Peter Jackson was Head of Art, James Warburton of Drama.

'Wanna come along on Thursday, young Finch? We generally slip out to the Haymakers for a couple. Breaks the week up, like.'

The pub was in a neighbouring village and as Jay's mum drew the line at him borrowing her Hillman Imp to go out drinking he had to rely on a lift. Vic Burrows, the head of history and Bill Molyneux, the head of PE, made up the regular crew so he was usually okay. Apart from the first week when mention was made of the Crofton incident and Jay complimented on the outcome but advised not to employ that tactic again, there was no shop. They played doms and cards and drank Greenhall Whitley: usually four or five pints, nothing excessive. The talk was of birds, though Bill was the only other bachelor, and sport, especially football. The latter was problematic: they all supported Liverpool whilst Jay, following Pard's lead, had been supporting Leeds United for a couple of seasons. The two clubs were archrivals and when Vic suggested going to Anfield the next time they met Jay was ambivalent. Then it transpired the fixture wasn't until

December. He probably wouldn't even be there by then.

Half term was late October and the week before Jay was summoned to Jenkins' office. He feared the worst, which was a shame as, completely against expectations, he was enjoying the job. Typical, he thought. Find summat you're okay at and some bastard'll bring you down! Though he hadn't helped himself by missing a Monday.

It was his mate's twenty-first that'd done it. Malcolm Armstrong – Malc – was Jay's oldest friend. They'd lived opposite each other as children; Malc had been the star guest at his fifth birthday party and they'd kept in touch ever since. Even when Her Majesty re-located her Inspector to Norfolk for ten years, and when Jay had been up at Durham he and Malc had contrived to meet up. Usually to walk, and later to climb together in the Lake District. So when a party was announced, Jay was included.

Malc still lived in *The Croft* with his parents, Neville and Marjorie. So Jay borrowed the Imp and drove up to Wilpshire first thing on the Saturday. The party was at a posh hotel by the River Ribble and Malc's father, an exceedingly successful dental surgeon, spared no expense. The food and wine were lavish and no one should really have been driving back to Neville's. However, once there, elder brother Hugh took over as sommelier and good intentions – Jay was supposed to be back by Sunday lunch, latest – began to evaporate. The champagne was Veuve Clicquot Ponsardin '55 which would've been fairly innocuous on its own. But Hugh was mixing cocktails: soaking cube-bergs of Demerara sugar in Angostura Bitters and then adding Hennessy VSOP before topping them up with the Clicquot. The result was lethal. Jay didn't remember much after eight o'clock, not even crashing out on a camp bed in Malc's room.

No one stirred until late Sunday morning, when Hugh decreed that the hair of the dog was required. Two hours in the Wilpshire Hotel and spirits were restored sufficiently to revisit the Clicquot. It wasn't until seven when they were about to repair to the pub once more that Jay was handed the 'phone by Neville. His dad was livid. If he wasn't in school the following morning Jay was jeopardising all the good work so far. What the hell did he think he was playing at? Was he deliberately trying to make his father look a fool? Jay was in the middle of assurances that he'd be down early doors when Hugh intervened, clicking down the receiver and hauling him off to the boozer.

The next thing he registered was Marjorie shouting up the stairs to come and get their Monday brunch. It was three in the afternoon before he felt ready to drive; and dark when he got home. His father cut him dead and he went straight to his room in a haze of alcohol and guilt.

'Come in, young Fincher. Sit down.' Mr Jenkins' tone was friendly enough and his expression affable. He was a small man but solidly built and looked older than he was, probably cause he was bald. Jay glanced quickly round the office. It was sparsely furnished: a round coffee table with three arm chairs in the corner and a row of grey stainless steel filing cabinets along one wall. The walk across to the chair in front of the head's desk could've been designed to intimidate but Jay felt more welcome than nervous.

'Thank you, sir.'

'Well your six weeks are up. How d'you think you're getting on?'

'Umm…okay…I think, sir. I like the job – especially the kids.'

'Well that's half the battle. What would you say to an extension 'til next summer?'

'Whoa! Brilliant! Thanks very much, sir. I won't let you down.'

So half term proved to be just that. His mum and dad were relieved and elated in equal measure. But they ruled out the trip north to see Stephen, insisting he attend a drama school run by the local authority whose chief education officer, Charles Fox, was a particular friend of his dad's. Jay was disappointed. In spite of his ignominious departure from Durham he was missing the illuminati – especially Julia. And he'd hoped to bump into Jill as well. He must ring her.

Eleven

It had been a hectic start to September and Jill and Sally were away on holiday the following weekend. She'd seen nothing of Jay, but she'd heard from him twice: once to give her his home address – in Chester, apparently; the second time to let her know he'd got a teaching job. It wasn't much by way of contact, yet the more she thought about him, the more Jill realised she was falling for him. God knows why him not Stephen. Jay was nothing like as good-looking; he could be immature and selfish and inclined to sulk when he didn't get his own way. But he could also be charming with a warm, winning smile when he chose to employ it and, mostly, he was considerate and sensitive. Plus, he had nice hands and kept his fingernails clean! He was certainly intelligent. Far brighter than Stephen, even if he'd apparently finished up with a disastrous degree, whilst Stephen was the proud owner of a 2.1. Jill smiled at the double irony, partly of their respective degrees inversely reflecting their intellects, but mainly of her even giving a toss. She wouldn't have a few months back: degrees weren't something she ever thought about. But Joyce's talk of a University of the Air and her plans for them to enrol had made Jill more aware of others' potential as well as her own. Not that anything would come of it if it were left to her. She wasn't pushy enough. Joyce was though.

Meanwhile both study and Jay would have to wait, cause Tenerife here we come!

Jill had been abroad before. Two trips to Southern Germany. The first had been a school visit, the second, two years back, a solo follow-up. She'd spent several tiresome days escaping the clutches of the lovelorn but terribly proper Wolfgang, and a much pleasanter few nights falling into the embraces of the bounteous Adrianna. Sally had never been beyond Tyneside. So it was Jill's responsibility to get them there!

Just as it was getting light, the train from Newcastle rolled into King's Cross. From there they had to negotiate their way across London. A taxi was out of the question, and they hadn't a clue which bus route to take.

The Underground wasn't yet open so they found a coffee bar that was and whiled away the time.

'Okay,' Jill tried to sound authoritative, 'from this map I'd say we get the Piccadilly Line to Leicester Square and then the Northern Line to Charing Cross.' She traced her finger over the royal blue and black lines for Sally's benefit. 'Then if we change again there, it's three stops on this yellow-and-green job to Victoria.'

After a minor panic when they realised you didn't just wait for the next train – you had to find a different platform, miles away from the one you'd come in on – they arrived safely at Victoria. The station was autumn-chilled and draughty and they were relieved when they located the bus terminus and could scramble onto the coach for Gatwick. The wait there seemed interminable.

Jill had really enjoyed her flights from Newcastle to Dusseldorf and back. It hadn't crossed her mind that Sally wouldn't like flying. But when they finally started taxiing out to the runway she saw her friend's hands were clasped tightly together and her eyes screwed shut in terror. She scrabbled around in her handbag until she found her trusty mints and putting an arm around Sally's shoulder persuaded her to suck one.

'Take your mind off things, petal. And it'll stop your ears getting bunged up.' Unaccountably, Sally seemed to find this prospect a hoot and rapidly relaxed. By the time they touched down in Tenerife she was quite the seasoned flier, pointing out the coastline of the island from her window-seat. Jill leaned across. The contrast between the shimmering, azure sea and the dry as dust beige vegetation and grey hills was amazing. No green, Northumberland fields to be seen! There was a round of applause as the captain landed the jet smoothly on the gleaming tarmac and then, after a short delay, the stewardess opened the main door and they stepped out onto the rickety steel steps. The blast of hot, dry air took their breath away and they were grateful for the relative cool of the terminal before collecting their bags and queuing for the dilapidated tour coach that would deposit them in Puerto de la Cruz.

The Hotel Las Vegas was just off the main road overlooking a public lido, the beach and the open sea. It had just three storeys surrounded by compact grounds but there was a lot of bright, purple bougainvillea and all the window ledges were bedecked with red and orange trailing plants that Jill didn't recognise. The reception was small but welcoming and there was a tiny shop selling beach stuff, drinks, sweets and postcards. You had to buy the stamps separately. Jill bought three of each, intending to write them straightaway, otherwise she'd be back before they were! They were soon installed in their twin room. It was quite spacious and best of all had an en suite shower, so you knew you were really on holiday!

The next morning, whilst Sally lingered over breakfast she dashed off a card home, and then a couple of days later one to Jay.

Holiday going quite well. Weather marvellous and hotel good. S'pose the food could be better. Nightlife is non-existent, but there's a BBQ by the lido tomorrow. After breakfast at nine we spend the day by the pool. Be a lot more fun if you were here. Take care, flower. All my love Jill.

She reviewed the postcard – *Vista General de Garachico* – and wondered whether she'd been a bit over-amorous. But it was how she felt just then and, besides, she'd already stuck the 3.5 PTAS stamp on.

A few days later, things were looking up. There *was* some nightlife at the hotel club: the Palomino. You went down a steep, winding, iron staircase which deposited you straight onto a small, square dance floor surrounded by plush, brown couches with low tables in front and between. The bar was a bit of a crush but served bottled beer, wine and spirits: both Spanish, and English. The latter were really pricey. On their second visit, the girls were chatted up by four wide-boys from West Ham. Jill's knowledge of football, instilled by her Magpie-mad dad and their visits to St James' came in handy. She even knew some of the Hammers' players as they'd featured in the World Cup Final which, ironically, Jill had watched on her trip to Germany. The lads were impressed and when it transpired they, too, were stopping at the Las Vegas Sally and Jill suddenly found they had company at the bar. Then at breakfast. And later at the pool. Especially at the pool. The first few days, with nothing much else to do, they'd spent hours sunbathing. They couldn't afford suntan cream but had heard Johnson's Baby Lotion produced the same effect for a fraction of the cost. Neither gave going topless a thought and both had acquired deep tans. They were very popular with the boys who competed to get the beds closest to them.

The banter was mostly good-natured, although both girls' breasts figured prominently, especially of an afternoon when a lunchtime session had emboldened the Stratford swains. Jill took it in good part whilst making plain she wasn't interested and then, when that failed to deter her would-be suitors, claiming she was engaged. Sally raised her eyebrows but didn't betray her; she was preoccupied with her own fan club. After a particularly heavy session on the local red, recommended by their waiter,

Marcos, Sal was persuaded to accompany two of the boys to the twin they shared. Jill staggered to bed alone. She didn't seek the lurid details when Sally surfaced later the following morning. But she did make the mistake of referring to the six, or 'El seis', as Marcos had dubbed them, in her next postcard to Jay.

Jill never discovered what had caused the fall out but things cooled down markedly after the night-of-passion and although the quartet would swing by their sunbeds for a chat there was no further risqué banter and no more propositions. Jill enjoyed the last few days but was ready for home.

Jay's letter was waiting for her. The chump must've told his parents about 'El seis' and his dear mother had insinuated that Jill must be somewhat 'flighty'. That were typical. Apparently, she'd been reet snotty when she sussed Jill was seeing Stephen as well as Jay. Sounded a proper Tartar! Why on earth did Jay reveal the secrets of his love life to her? Jill wouldn't have dreamt of telling *her* mam! She thought about dashing off a curt reply but decided it would just make things worse. She'd give it a few days 'til things calmed down and then write him a proper love letter, hinting he was the one for her!

Besides, with only six weeks to go to her Finals she needed all her energy for work. *Study Block* was the last push before the exams. It was like being back at school and if the test questions were any guide Jill was going to fail miserably. What would Jay think of her if that happened? It'd certainly postpone any hopes she was beginning to harbour of moving down to Chester; apart from making it more difficult to find a placement in one of the local hospitals a further three months of separation was a miserable prospect. She wondered whether what passed for their relationship could survive it. Things had been a bit rocky since Tenerife…

Still half term was imminent and once she and Jay met up she was confident they'd be okay. Problem was there was no room at St Peter's Road. Uncle Bill and Aunt Elsie were down from Glasgow. Normally Jill would've been delighted at drinks down the Labour Club with her favourite uncle, but not at the expense of missing Jay.

'So why don't you both stop here?' Stephen had called by as she finished work and whisked her off to the Collingwood. Typical! She didn't see him for weeks but when she did they just took up where they'd left off. Still, that was what friends were for.

Jill pondered the offer, 'If you're sure that'd be okay? Don't wanna put you out.'

'You wouldn't be. Jay knows he's welcome any time and now Alistair's on sabbatical there's loadsa room. If it doesn't work out for him at Woodbridge, he might come up permanently. Believe there's a pile of vacancies round Newcastle.'

This was the first she'd heard of the possibility. 'Wow, that'd be terrific! I mean not that Woodbridge didn't work out…but that he might be based up here! Don't think his mam and dad would be very happy, mind. Especially his mam, she doesn't like me. Or you, for that matter.'

'But I've never met her!'

'Nor me, but that doesn't stop her. I reckon she doesn't think I'm good enough for her precious son. Too *flighty*, whatever that's supposed to mean.' Jill gave an expurgated version of the Tenerife correspondence. 'Plus, she doesn't think I should be seeing you if I'm going out with Jay.'

'That's daft. We're all friends.'

Jay would be on the Friday evening train from Manchester and since Stephen was working in Hexham he'd pick him up at Newcastle Central on the way through. Jill was nervous. She'd heard nothing from Jay. Would he know she was even there? What if he wasn't pleased to see her? She inspected Stephen's fridge and located a corked half-bottle of Muscadet. She poured herself a glass and was about to take it through to the lounge but first gulped most of the glass down, then refilled it and put it on the little hexagonal oak table by the easy chair. In the absence of a telly she reviewed the flat's reading matter. Gone were the piles of archaeology journals and the other tomes that Alistair had accumulated. Gone, too, was his poetry collection. That left just Stephen's bird books and fencing manuals. Not exactly her glass of plonk!

Remembering he had a bookcase in his bedroom she wandered through and began to scan the possibilities. It wasn't promising: a bunch of climbing guides and half-a-dozen trashy looking paperbacks, which wasn't the sort of stuff she wanted Jay to *discover* her reading. Then she noticed it on the bedside cabinet: *Delta of Venus: Erotica* by Anaïs Nin. The name was vaguely familiar. Hadn't Sue mentioned her? Something about an affair with Arthur Miller. And the racy subjects she espoused – sadomasochism and lesbianism – had stuck with Jill. Hmm…any port…

Talking of which she needed a refill. The Muscadet was almost empty. It wasn't fair to polish it off. Unless…she recollected from the picnic it was Stephen's favourite so there was a fair chance… The crate in the corner still had seven bottles in it. In which case… Jill decanted the dregs and stuck a replacement in the fridge door. The 'phone was ringing. She reached it but just as she said, 'Hell...' it went dead.

She settled down with *Erotica*. It comprised short stories so she opened it at Stephen's bookmark. Half an hour later Jill felt distinctly flushed. The wine? Or the reading matter? It was a lot raunchier than she'd expected and all the more arousing for being understated not explicit; quite sophisticated, more Jay's style than Stephen's. Where were they anyway? Much more of this wine-erotica combination and she'd jump on Jay before he got past the hallway!

Another half hour and they still hadn't arrived. Jill was on a third salacious chapter and halfway through the second bottle.

Finally! She heard the front door open and hurtled out of the lounge and down the stairs. 'Where's Jay?'

Stephen looked perplexed. 'God knows! He wasn't on the six-fifteen. Or the six-forty- five. I waited for two more, but...'

Jill burst into tears, punctuated by stifled gulps of, 'Swine...bastard!'

'Look, I'm sure there's a perfectly reasonable explanation,' Stephen suggested.

'Huh! Well I'd sure like to know what it is!'

'He'll probably ring any minute.'

'Well he'll get no answer then! C'mon, we're going down the Brandling.'

In retrospect Jill couldn't imagine why she'd suggested that. The last thing she needed was to bump into some of the RVI crowd. Fortunately, they didn't and after a couple of Dubonnet and lemonades Jill had simmered down. After all, how could Jay know *she'd* be there? They discussed the possibilities – the favourite being that, for some reason he'd decided not to come. Missing one train was easy, but missing a whole string? Then, irrationally, she began to blame herself. She'd obviously done something to upset him. But what? Their recent 'phone calls had been all lovey-dovey and his letters their usual mixture of affection and erudition. Hers had been...well, just loving...

She was going round in circles.

'Sod 'im!' she announced finally. 'Let's talk about summat else? How's yer love life?'

When they got back to the flat her almost-empty glass stood, warm, by the open *Erotica*. Jill gave Stephen a fierce look, defying him to comment. He looked about to put his foot in it but rescued himself.

'Nightcap?'

Two glasses later, Jill slid elegantly down the sofa and ended up with her head in his lap. The next thing she knew it was two in the morning. She'd woken up in the spare bed. Randy-ratted, she careened into Stephen's room.

Twelve

Jay had called Jill's home on the Thursday night. She was out and there seemed to be a party going on. Battling the noise, he left a message with her dad, though it could've been her brother. He couldn't come up but he'd 'phone tomorrow and explain. He tried to get hold of Stephen but there was no reply.

The following evening, he tried again. This time there was no reply at St Peter's Road. Same at Stephen's though someone might have said hello just as he replaced the receiver. It was only during the third game of bagatelle at the Dog that it struck him. The voice had been Jill's! What the hell was she doing there? Don't say she and Stephen were back together again? Maybe he should give it another go. But there was no payphone in the pub and by the time he got home it was past eleven.

Over the weekend he read the prospectus for the drama school and started on some of the background material. It was heavy going. The section on role-play was particularly dense. He could see that language played a central part in identifying people's roles and how they exercised them. Obviously what you said to someone and how they responded would reflect what kind of relationship was involved. The same person might be referred to as Mr Jenkins, sir, Leslie Jenkins, Les or Hey you! It'd depend largely on the context and language was nothing if not contextual. That was okay. It fitted Jay's philosophy of relativism summed up for him by his big brother, 'Things are rarely black and white, kid: more an intermediate shade of grey.' Like when Hamlet claimed there was nothing neither good nor bad but thinking made it so. Or summat like that. But turning all that into a group exercise for a bunch of fifteen-year olds sounded like hard work. Certainly if Saturday and Sunday were anything to go by.

To begin with he'd been bewildered. But by the Thursday it was starting to make more sense. The exercise he devised on situations where individuals misunderstood their roles in relation to the rest of the group and betrayed the fact by the language they used actually received some approbation.

Then the letter arrived.

Dear Jay,

I don't know how to begin this and perhaps it'd be better if it was left unwritten, but I have to tell you how desperately sorry I am about Friday night. I seem to have a knack for spoiling things but this is the biggest mess I've ever made, and the only person to blame is me. I'd gone up to Stephen's flat specially and had been waiting for you forever and had drunk far too much so when you didn't arrive I was really upset.

Couldn't you at least have 'phoned? I didn't know what to think. I was so narked I stupidly suggested going to the Brandling. As if we'd find you there! When we got back... I can't believe how stupid I was ending up in bed with him. It's not as if I even fancy Stephen any more.

But it was my fault, all of it. Not his. Jay, please don't let what happened break up Stephen and you. The last thing I want is for your friendship to be wrecked by a stupid girl.

I can't ask you to forgive me but I hope that one day you won't think so badly of me. I find difficulty expressing myself at the best of times and writing this letter has been especially hard. I haven't been able to say what I wanted but I hope you get the gist.

Look after yourself, Jay, and good luck with the job.

Take care and God bless, Jill.

Jay let out a heartfelt sigh. He needed to clear his head. It was cold and the first splintered ice of the autumn had formed at the edges of the canal, where he and his dad had marched in Indian file and silence the morning after his brother's death. At first he stomped along angrily. Then the beauty of the morning gradually calmed him down and he became pensive. After an hour of walking along the towpath he came to a bench by a lock. It was hard and uncomfortable: conducive to mature reflexion.

A cold, perspective-grappling while passed...

No one person was to blame for everything as Jill had tried to claim. All of them were responsible. He certainly wasn't going to reproach Jill for getting pissed. Then again he didn't get the impression that Stephen had taken advantage. He would usually of course, but not with Jill. They were all too close for that. In any case, she wouldn't have ended up pie-eyed if Jay hadn't upset her in the first place. He should've made sure she *knew* he couldn't make it.

Jay shivered and resumed his walk. By the time he got back to the house he was clear: it was just one of those things. Nothing to be gained by recriminations. He sat down at his dad's desk and wrote back to that effect.

Four days later came the reply. Most of it reiterated her feelings of guilt and regret but gradually the negativity was replaced by relief.

> *Anyhow, that's enough excuses. I just hope we can both put it behind us and, if possible, start again. Thanks a bunch for writing like you did, Jay. It meant so much. Made me so happy I gave the cat a huge kiss, but I don't think she appreciated it!*

> *Take care and God bless.*

> *Much love, Jill.*

Jay was elated. For once he seemed to have done the right thing! He wrote back immediately saying that of course they could put it behind them. They'd meet as soon as they could; then she'd see how much he cared for her...

The term flashed by. He was relishing the work and getting on really well with the kids. Even 4T2! His favourite class was his own though: Oxton 1. There were forty of them, which made his classroom a bit of a squeeze, but they were so bright and lively, so keen to learn. At the beginning of December, the form captain, Maxine, a cutie with long black hair and a disarming smile, put a request to him. Could they decorate the classroom for Christmas? All the other first-years were going to and they'd come in on Saturday if that was okay? Momentarily, Jay wondered whether he should consult someone.

''course, Max, I'll come in myself and help.'

Jay loved December. Ever since they'd lived at The Lodge and he'd helped his mum decorate the entrance hall. Their gardener, Buck, used to lop off a massive bough from one of the *Cupressus* trees and his dad would attach it to the banisters which marched down the winding staircase. Then, whilst his mother draped the lower branches with all their old favourites – the green leather rabbit, the yellow deer and, best of all, the miniature axe – Jay would climb up the outside of the banisters and attach the Christmas angel to the most inaccessible point. It always had to be in place, at the very latest, by the twenty-first: his birthday. That was a Saturday this year, advised his *Collins Gentleman's Diary*.

Meanwhile, there was the traditional school play masterminded by the heads of drama and art: Jim Warburton and Pete Jackson. They were joined by Kate Almond, the music mistress. Their production was to be *My Fair Lady* and Jay was welcome to pitch in. He was hesitant. The only live drama he'd encountered was on the course and he didn't feel qualified to fulfil any role as a result of that, although it was a good chance to contribute beyond the classroom. Which was one way to get on. Plus, insofar as he'd got any mates on the staff, Pete and Jim qualified. Okay, he was in.

Initially it seemed a mistake. Listening to lines didn't amount to much and the dress rehearsals became an increasingly titillating torture. The leading ladies were dazzling and with elegant dresses and make-up looked at least as old as him. He was in danger of falling seriously in lust with Katrine, who played Eliza Doolittle. He hoped it was not too obvious when she was teasing him with her interrogative smiles and flagrant décolletage.

Musicals were a closed book, although he knew this one was based on *Pygmalion*. He procured a *Piano Selection*. Its cover was a garish black and white and pink, portraying an angelic Shaw (a likely story!) pulling the strings attached to Professor Higgins and Eliza. Rex Harrison played the professor, Julie Andrews the flower girl. It cost Jay 3/6, which was two pints, but he judged it a good investment and it wasn't long before he could play every number. He'd long ago passed his Pianoforte Grade VIII. He'd have gone on to professional qualifications if some idiot at grammar school hadn't persuaded his parents that he must concentrate on his academic studies to gain a Cambridge Scholarship. Since he hadn't, Jay felt a double failure. Still, Durham had been okay and he could still play to an acceptable standard even if he didn't practise much these days.

A fortnight before the first night, Miss Almond failed to turn up for rehearsals. Panic stations all round! Some of the girls were quite tearful and even Katrine seemed at a loss.

'Er... I s'pose I could step in,' offered Jay tentatively.

'Didn't know you could play, Finch. Sure you're up to it?'

He nodded and slid onto the piano stool. The introductory medley was fine, but he found it hard to concentrate on the music when Katrine was chirping about how 'luverly' it would be. Receiving a ravishing smile at the end of the song, Jay wondered if there'd be any chance of shielding her against the winter chill when they'd finished. He swallowed hard: that way madness lay, not to mention instant dismissal. Still, his substituting for Miss Almond had certainly got them out of a hole and even though she recovered from her 'flu in good time for the actual production Jay gained a lot of kudos. And he just about managed to keep his hands off the leading lady.

Thirteen

The festive season loomed and Jill was back with Sister Watson – *Trish*, off duty – who had always been her favourite. She was pretty and vivacious and gave her nurses huge encouragement. She'd already promised Jill her first staff role once she was qualified. Jill was on the ward when beckoned into the cubicle they called an office.

'Yer not really supposed to take calls on duty but it's yer mam. She sounds quite agitated.'

'Thanks, Sister. Sorry… Hi Mam, what's up?'

'It's yer letter, our Jill. From the RCN. Yer said to open it.'

Oh God, she'd failed for sure! She took a deep breath.

'Okay, Mam, give it to me straight.'

'Why man, yer've only passed with flyin colours. Yer a proper nurse now, pet!'

Jill was so convinced she'd bombed that she gave an unintelligible yelp and burst into tears.

Sister Watson waited for her to calm down and then smiled: 'So you've passed then, hinny? Congratulations, Staff Walker!'

More tears.

'Well I canna have me staff nurse cavorting around in blue and white stripes. Get yersel doon to the laundry: they'll be expectin you.'

Jill returned twenty minutes later in the light-grey uniform of a staff nurse of the Royal Victoria Infirmary. It was the proudest moment of her life!

The next morning when she started her shift there was a huge bouquet of flowers waiting for her on the office desk. The patients had clubbed together. They were mostly young men in with accidents from the shipyard or from their motorbikes, so medically they were fit, and cheerful. Jill lost count of the number of pats and squeezes her new uniform received! That weekend she started writing round to hospitals in Cheshire, starting with the Chester Royal Infirmary…

She'd been reading *As You Like It* intermittently and was greatly impressed with Rosalind (rhymes with hind and mind, she prompted herself). Now she had an added incentive to finish it. After 'phoning Jay, who seemed genuinely impressed with her news, Jill called the lit twins. Delighted, they announced a party in her honour the first Saturday everyone was free.

A fortnight later the three of them were enjoying high tea in the elegant Edwardian living room at Moor Crescent. It reminded Jill of Delaval Lodge where her Aunt Louisa used to entertain her to tea when she was about seven or eight. She hadn't really been her aunt; she'd been a friend of Granny Johnson's under whose roof Jill, Al, her little brother, and her mam were living at the time. Her real name was Mrs Smellie, which used to make all the kids, except Jill, laugh. She was a widow and dead rich: the only person in the neighbourhood to own a TV. Jill's mam said that was the reason Mrs Smellie invited her back; cause when they'd all gone round to watch the coronation, Jill was the only one who'd remembered to say thank you. Crust-less sandwiches and chocolate cake they used to have, on fancy plates. That's what'd reminded her: they were Royal Doulton just like Joyce's.

'So…Rosalind would've been played by an apprentice in the Chamberlain's Men…'

'That's right,' interrupted Joyce, 'probably in 1599, quite possibly on Shrove Tuesday.'

'Right. So a young man was dressed as a woman, Rosalind, who then dresses as a man, Ganymede, when he, I mean she and her cousin Celia retreat to the Forest of Arden.'

'Exactly!' Sue's turn to intervene, 'But don't forget the significance of the name.' Jill looked blank. 'Ganymede was Jove's cupbearer in Ancient Greek myth. He was besotted with the boy's beauty so he disguised himself as an eagle and carried him off to Olympus. Juno was furious.'

'But what's that got to do with Rosalind?' Jill was getting thoroughly confused.

'Ah that's the clever bit. Shakespeare's having his usual joke. The debased version of Ganymede is *Catamite*, a boy hired for his services. You know – sex.'

'So it's to make Rosalind seem even sexier?'

'Yeah…and funnier. The audience found the whole boy-dressed-as-girl routine hilarious even without the girl then passing herself off as a youth whose name evoked dubious connotations.'

'Got it! So when the boy who's dressed as a girl who's disguised as a man pretends to be a girl for Orlando to practise his lovemaking on…the whole place would fall about laughing!'

'Precisely,' cut in Joyce, 'and then Rosalind tops off the performance by playing the *Epilogue* which as she admits is *not the fashion* but…'

'No, no! Don't go on: I haven't started Act V yet!'

'Oops!' laughed Sue. 'Sorry, we can get a bit carried away…'

'Just a tad,' conceded Jill, as the 'phone shrilled from the hallway.

Joyce slipped out to answer it and Sue smiled, 'So now do you see why I suggested *As You Like It*, pet?'

So it was Sue's choice, not Joyce's. She'd just been the intermediary. Jill chose to look puzzled.

'Rosalind, of course. She's a feminist's dream! Plus, she's you *exactement*: high-spirited, imaginative, full of fun and…beautiful.'

Jill was conscious of the blood suffusing her face as Joyce returned looking grave. 'That was the Police. Mother's been involved in an accident. Struck by a vehicle in Acomb. They think she's been taken to Hexham General.'

'Oh no! What d'you wanna do?'

'I'll try the hospital first. See what they can tell me.'

Sue and Jill were left alone again but the atmosphere had changed. 'Shall I help you clear away?' offered Jill.

They took the plates through to the kitchen and washed up.

Joyce returned from telephoning the hospital. 'It doesn't sound too bad, but they're keeping her in. Sorry, girls, I'm going to have to break up the party.'

'Of course, love. Shall I come with you?'

'No, it's okay, thanks. You stop and look after our guest. I may not be that long.'

Sue came across and seated herself in the opposite corner of the settee. 'So how have you been, my sweet?'

Short question: long explanation! By the time Jill had run through the twists and turns of her complicated relationships she was bemused herself!

Sue looked at Jill, 'So…my turn to be confused, chicken. Are you going out with Stephen, with Jay, or with both of them?'

'Oh dear, it sounds awful when you put it like that. But no, the three musketeers are over. I've decided. It's Jay I want.'

'Hmm…that's if you want a man at all. Have you actually told this Jay about us?'

'Well, no…but then, does Joyce know about you and me?' she countered.

'Okay, point taken. What say we keep it that way, hin?'

'Probably best,' agreed Jill, risking a yearning look towards her mentor and would-be lover.

'As I said, just like Rosalind: impetuous as well as cheeky!'

'Well…?'

Sue leaned across and kissed her gently on the cheek.

'It'll happen when it's meant to, sweet: just not now. It's not the right time. Besides Joyce could be back any minute.'

Jill sighed acquiescently. Sue was right, of course… Meanwhile, she'd keep her side of the bargain. What possible good could it do for Jay to know?

Fourteen

Well, he'd got through the first term. *My Fair Lady* had been a resounding success and he'd navigated the perils of the Last Night party. There'd been sentimental kisses all round, but if his clinch with Katrine had been that intimate someone would've commented. The whole cast was there, after all.

Anyway, that was history; tonight Jay was due at the Black Dog.

Since he'd moved home permanently he was playing for the Dog's first team in Division One of the Chester & North Wales League. He was currently third in the Dog averages, with seventy-three. The team'd gathered for a pint or two and a practice stick before going into town. They were away to the Axe. Jay knew the table just like he knew all the others cause Charlie had told him the key to becoming a top player was away-form. Any fool could knock up seventy or eighty on his own table but they were all different and you had to get to know, and remember, their quirks. The Axe was a prime example.

'No good going in at lunchtime, though,' cautioned Charlie. 'The bar'll be empty.'

Jay was puzzled: surely that'd be a good time. No one to see your mistakes, plus you could practise key shots like the break repeatedly until you had 'em off pat.

'Not in the Axe. You'll see. On the left side of the table there's a bench seat. Come the match there'll always be three or four blokes sat on it. Makes the table play to the left!'

'So getting the break right when the bench is empty would be no use! Crafty sods! Is it legal?'

'Legal...yeah; but it's frowned on. When you go to sus it out take some mates. But if anyone shows too much interest just pretend you're playing doubles.'

Unable to conjure up mates impromptu, Jay had gone alone the previous weekend. The saloon was empty but he still shot a couple of sticks before five or six blokes arrived all together. Three sat on the bench, the others played a game of singles. Jay saw his chance and chalked the slate. The first stick he missed the break and struggled to a thirty-five/forty-one deficit. Second time he overhauled his opponent and stayed on the table. He beat the next chap convincingly, but starting to feel less-than-welcome, declined further wagers.

'Nah! Gotta go, thanks. Only came in for a quick pint.'

When the Dog team arrived that Friday the same blokes were there. They were all in the Axe team! It turned out to be a needle match. The Dog won five-four; but only after Charlie pulled out a ninety-six in the final match. The result left them top of the League going into the mid-season break.

The following morning, a slightly hung over Jay drove to Manchester. Jill was due in at 12.30. The train was late, Jay anxious. Not that she'd stand him up; it was the prospect of the arrival itself. The debacle at half term meant they hadn't seen each other for over three months. Letters and 'phone calls were all very well, but... In the summer she'd still been going out with Stephen. Then, after Tenerife she'd written to say Jay was the one. They'd all stay friendly, of course, but she'd made up her mind. Then she'd gone to bed with Stephen again! Still, he was proud of the way he'd handled that setback. Surely, they'd be okay now? And Christmas was on his side; he'd always loved it, it put him in a good, more confident mood, made him less self-centred and more considerate.

The platform was crowded; he didn't see her initially. Then they almost bumped into each other and suddenly they were hugging and kissing, oblivious to the people flowing either side of them. They ran out to the car park and reached his mum's Hillman Imp.

'Stop! I wanna look at you!'

She giggled and curtsied. God she was beautiful! Her jet-black hair was cropped in curls to frame her face and she'd a beige coat on he'd not seen before. Its belt was tight and showed off her figure. He held her at arm's length. She was stunning: just as gorgeous as that first time in the Buff. Christ! What a twat he'd been!

By the time they reached home it was after three, which was maybe as well. Jay couldn't imagine Jill was ecstatic at the prospect of meeting his folks. Well, his mother, anyway. But it went surprisingly well. His mum had laid on a splendid high tea and received Jill's offers of help warmly; both carrying stuff through to the drawing room and washing up afterwards. Jill's case, a smart leather grip, was still in the hall. When

Jay offered to take it up for her his mother's direction was pointed.

'You're at the far end of the corridor, dear, on the left by the guest bathroom.' Jay's own room was next to his parents', as far away as it could be...

They were due at the Woodbridge staff dinner dance at eight. It was formal and Jay was sporting his birthday present: a brand new DJ from Gieves & Hawkes. He was particularly proud of it, partly because he knew that Gieves were based in Savile Row, but mainly because they'd also made his brother's naval uniforms. He had a moment's misgiving as he was tying his bow tie when he couldn't remember if he'd mentioned to Jill that it was evening dress. He needn't have worried. He and his father were sipping Tio Pepe when she walked in. Jay's dad nearly dropped his glass. She looked sensational: in a figure-hugging black satin dress that was low-cut but with a crochet halter neck. She looked like the world's most elegant spider! Jesus! Was she really going with *him*? She'd be the belle of the ball, all right!

The Woodbridge staff do was held at the Grosvenor Park. Its ballroom was arranged with tables for a hundred or so around an elliptical dance floor. Each table was for eight and Jay made sure he and Jill joined Pete, Jim and their wives, together with two strangers who didn't seem that friendly. The hotel was noted for its cuisine and the Christmas menu, whilst traditional, was extremely tasty. More to the point, the wine list was superb, although on formal occasions, restricted. Even so the Pouilly Fuissé they enjoyed with the prawns was light and refreshing; whilst the Nuits-St-Georges complemented the turkey perfectly. Jay didn't like puddings and made a bit of a fuss about a cheeseboard. He was rewarded by their waiter bringing a large oval platter with Cheshire, Lancashire and Shropshire Blue together with an assortment of biscuits and sticks of celery. Turned out Jill preferred that, too.

Jay planned to drink just enough wine to stifle his anxiety about the dancing. He'd had classes once but could never get the hang of it: a quickstep was tolerable, waltz ditto especially when smooch-time loomed, but the foxtrot was beyond him and the samba and tango complete mysteries. He had an uneasy feeling that Jill would be a proficient dancer and he'd let her down. Fortunately, she was understanding and patient, though after a couple of especially inept performances she graciously accepted invitations first from Pete and then from Jim. He knew he should ask the wives up but pretended to need the gents and, by the time he returned, was relieved to see them with other partners. Jill meanwhile, as Jay had anticipated, was whisked around by a stream of partners. From being relieved he gradually grew narked, as she was obviously enjoying the attention as much as the dancing. Fortunately, before he could develop a monumental sulk, the band progressed to a series of waltzes, which Jill elected to sit out. When it dawned on him she was declining offers for his benefit Jay cheered up enough to take to the floor once more. The Last Waltz was wonderful: they were intimately entwined and Jill just smiled when the inevitable happened, kissing him lingeringly.

They shared a taxi with Pete and Jean. Jay instructed the driver to drop them off at the corner of their cul-de-sac. Only the landing light shone at *Jedka* and they let themselves in circumspectly. As he closed the front door gently Jay felt Jill's lips nuzzling his ear.

'I'll go up first, but don't be long.'

Almost unable to contain himself Jay made a show of closing, and then silently opening, his bedroom door. He undressed in the dark and put on his pyjama bottoms, in case he was intercepted by his mum or dad. Their upstairs bog was half way along the corridor and he'd already rehearsed disappearing into it or emerging from it if he were rumbled on either journey. He'd also memorised exactly where the creaking floorboards were.

'You won't need those,' murmured Jill, playfully tugging at his pyjama tie. She shuffled over to the far side of the double bed as he wrestled off the bottoms and slipped in beside her. She was naked.

'Oh boy!' he sighed. 'I've waited so long for this, sweetheart...'

Fifteen

My Darling,

Just a short note to let you know I arrived back in Newcastle safely after an uneventful but bloody cold journey. The train didn't leave Manchester until 5.20 but made up for it after, so I wasn't that late.

Thank you so much for seven wonderful days, darling, I really did have a marvellous time. It was hell leaving you mind; sorry I made a fool of myself in front of your parents. All I want to do is to make you happy. Sometimes I feel so darn inadequate when I'm with you that I find it difficult to know why you're still going out with me. If only we were more alike, my love. We're so different in so many ways. Silly little things that you don't even need to think about worry me sick. I'm so afraid of disappointing you...

Jill re-read the rest of the letter and, as so often, wondered whether she should send it. She always seemed to be apologising when there was no need, according to Jay. But she really meant the bit about being different. They were like chalk and cheese! Still, maybe that wasn't such a bad thing. Stephen had once told her some law of physics about like poles repelling and unlike ones attracting. Perhaps that was her and Jay? It'd better be, because she'd made her mind up. He was hers! She was going to move down to Chester, get digs and take up the offer of a post at the Chester Royal Infirmary.

Her friend Sheila was already there, flat spotting for her. Jay was, too, but Sheila being based at the nearby West Cheshire Hospital was better placed to identify somewhere close at hand. Jay'd probably find her a palatial pad in deepest Wales! He wasn't terribly practical in such matters. Well, come to think of it he wasn't terribly practical full stop! There! Chalk and cheese again!

A fortnight later, Jill took a call from an elated Sheila. She'd found just the place: a one-bedroom, furnished flat on Liverpool Road close to the hospital. It was one of four in a Victorian semi and at least one of the others was occupied by a nurse so she'd have some company. It was on the second floor and shared a bathroom and kitchenette. And it had a nice big garden separating it from the main road. Should Sheila go in that weekend and put down a deposit?

Jill didn't hesitate. It would mean moving away from home. But after three years of intermittent flats and the nurses' home she was used to being independent. She'd miss her dad and to a lesser extent her mam. They were getting along better these days, partly she suspected, cause her mam was pleased Jill had found a nice young man to settle down with. She wouldn't particularly miss her little brother, Al, who was a pain in the neck. Her older brother, Rob, was married now. She would miss the lit twins. But she felt their paths were destined to cross. If her mam thought she'd lost touch with them, especially Sue, so much the better. She still had no plans to mention them to Jay.

As for the rest of the gang from the Infirmary, she'd miss Sally, although she was always nervous lest she and Jay met up. Sally was so indiscreet she'd think nothing of teasing Jay about his girlfriend's bi-sexuality. Jill wasn't sure how he'd react. He might be appalled; he might be excited. He was so unpredictable! And she'd miss Trish Watson. Trish had been a sister for five years and was destined for higher things. She was hard working, efficient and demanding. But she was also lively and fun to work for. Jill had learned so much from her. Both were sorry to see her go, but they'd keep in touch. Jill was to let her know if things didn't work out in Chester and she needed help re-establishing herself in the RVI. Or the General. Or in a private nursing home or hospital. Trish had loads of contacts.

By March she was installed in 66, Liverpool Road and on the first Monday she started at the Royal. Female orthopaedic, eight o'clock sharp. For the rest of the month she worked with Sister Roberts who was old-school and liked everything just so. But once she established that her new staff nurse was dedicated and reliable she began to cut her some slack. By the end of her probation they were on first-name terms off the ward and come April, Sister was confident Jill would manage on her own after the Easter break.

Meanwhile, she was establishing her own routine at No.66. Her co-lodger turned out to be male: a thirty-year-old charge nurse at the West Cheshire. Jill was a bit apprehensive. He seemed pleasant enough but she didn't know how Jay would react to his girlfriend sharing a bathroom and kitchen with another, undeniably good-looking, man. It would be difficult to conceal the arrangement: they'd be bound to meet sooner or later. Still, she'd cross that bridge when she came to it. Besides male nurses were rare, charge nurses even rarer, and the only two she'd encountered at the RVI had been gay. And really nice. So she could be worrying unnecessarily. The kitchen wasn't an issue as Alan hardly ever seemed to cook anything; although he took turns with tea and coffee. Initially Jill had been startled when he wandered into her flat without knocking just as she was getting dressed for her shift; but if he clocked owt he didn't embarrass either of them by saying so. She should've put him right straightaway, but when he presented her with a steaming mug of coffee she couldn't find the words to complain. The next time it happened she made an even bigger mess of things.

'It's not that *I* mind, Alan, but I don't think Jay would be too impressed if you sauntered in without knocking.'

His cheeky grin suggested he'd deliberately misunderstood her so, anxious not to make matters worse Jill left it at that. It wasn't as if it happened every day. Alan worked different shifts at the West Cheshire so they could go a week without encountering each other.

Jill had finished unexpectedly early one Saturday and although not a devotee of afternoon drinking had been inveigled into 'just a quick one'. It turned out to be someone's leaving-do in a private room above the Feathers. The drinks were free and it was after eight when the carefree staff nurse wobbled up the stairs at No.66. She was pleasantly knackered. She'd had no time to change and was dying for a long soak. Alan was on duty so the bathroom was hers for ages. She poured herself a glass of the Rioja she'd liberated from the party and collapsed briefly into an armchair, stripping off her uniform in between slurps. Down to her bra and knickers, she lay back feeling randy. Hmm, maybe later: bath first... She wrapped her fluffy, cream robe around her and swayed squiffily across the corridor.

As she neared the bathroom door Jill realised she'd been beaten to it. Bummer! She was about to slink back to her flat when she noticed the door was ajar. Curious, she peeked through the gap. Alan! She wondered why he hadn't closed the door, but remembered she wasn't supposed to be here. Nor was he, come to that. What was he doing usurping her bathtime? She was about to turn away when her eye was caught by a sudden movement. Behind the bath, at the opposite end from the taps, was a broad ledge onto which Alan was languidly hauling himself. Jill was intrigued and knowing she really shouldn't be spying on him made it irresistible.

She took in his glistening-wet body as he slid backwards onto the ledge and her eyes widened: she definitely shouldn't be watching this!

But she couldn't detach herself. He had a much better body than she'd imagined: sunburn-brown, lean and muscular. Mesmerised, Jill gulped as his hand emerged from the water grasping a bar of Pears. He proceeded to soap all around his stomach. No…this was too much; she must stop peeping. But she was transfixed. He was sliding his curled soapy hand around… He casually arched his left knee and rested his foot on the side of the bath. Why? Dammit! Now she couldn't see properly unless she nudged the door open a bit more. Too risky! Jill craned her neck. She found she was rubbing herself abstractedly up and down against the door jamb. Oh God! she moaned silently, if this goes on for long… Making a determined effort to tear herself away, she found she was still enjoying the show sometime later.

Almost too much later. Jill drank in the expression of abandonment on Alan's face. She'd never seen that look before, but she was pretty sure what it meant. Inexplicably, the door jamb was massaging her more vigorously now. Simultaneously, Alan groaned urgently; his whole body went taut, then started jerking just as the offending knee finally relinquished its purchase. Jill groaned, audibly this time, her imminent rapture threatening to expose her. Then, as Alan's shining-wet torso slithered back beneath the bubbles, she finally tore herself away and scurried back to her room. She slumped in the nearest chair and massaged herself frantically, relief flooding her in a matter of seconds. When she came round, she sighed deeply and smiled; at least she hadn't given herself away.

The following morning, she was awoken by Alan drifting into her bedroom in a dressing gown bearing a cup of tea and a digestive biscuit on a small metal tray that proclaimed *Guinness is good for you!* She was about to remonstrate with him for overstepping the mark.

'Mornin, Staff, thought you might like a restorative after the evening's exertions!'

Jill had to admire his insouciance. She tried to look innocent.

'Dunno what you mean, Staff!' Alas! she couldn't stifle a snigger and when she broke into a smile it was clear that they both knew what had happened.

Jill's hospital routine was a little more conventional. (Quotidian, even, she mused, a word she'd picked up from Jay. Reminded her: she must resume her Shakespeare study now that she was settled in.) Her first task was to read the ward report from the night staff: condition of their thirty-two patients, any admissions and so on. Then it was the bedpan round, followed by bed-baths for those unable to walk. After that the sheets were changed. Then there were dressings to be inspected and re-applied before the ward round with the consultant (or 'God' as Mr Keiter, an orthopaedic surgeon, was popularly known). Mr K was a legend. Ascetic and unapproachable at work, he was reputed to throw the most Bacchanalian end-of-year parties. An invitation to one of those and you were made: or possibly unmade, rumour had it. Jill had already listed it as a secret ambition! He was also a heavy smoker and had no truck with regulation. Rebuked by a senior sister for smoking in theatre he had allegedly responded, 'Sister, my cigarette ash is the most sterile element in this room!' He was also unbelievably handsome in a remote, horror-movie fashion. Christopher Lee's Dracula, say. Jill was in awe of him; but whilst the young housemen who hung on Mr K's every word would frequently flirt with her, the great man himself seemed impervious. Except…was she imagining it or was there a certain esteem in the way he invited her to conduct him on her ward?

Then lunch. Thirty minutes. Just long enough for her favoured curried eggs, with cheese and biscuits, washed down with a glass of water. After that a mad dash to the nurses' home for a quick fag (she'd finally succumbed) before the afternoon bedpans. That was followed by a pressure pads round. The more elderly women were prone to sores-where-they-touched so Jill and her nurses took particular care to check bums and heels.

After that came the best bit of the day: tutorial sessions. Although Jill had only qualified herself six months previously it seemed an age since she'd been a first-year, all wide-eyed and receptive. The youngsters' enthusiasm was just the tonic towards the end of a nine-hour shift. Jill never thought of herself as a teacher but maybe her willingness to share her expertise and sympathy for her charges made her one. She'd had no training, unless you counted what she'd picked up from the lit twins; perhaps that's what they meant by *transferable learning*.

Then it was a final round of meds, bedpans and pressure points; and suddenly it was six o'clock.

Sixteen

It was the 'Sonny' that did it.

Jill was throwing a belated flat-warming party for her friend, Sheila, and husband, Barry, plus of course Jay. He'd walked into town and met them at The George, partly because it was nearest for him but mainly for the bagatelle. The Dog played there in the League so Jay knew the table. He anticipated at minimum showing off his expertise and, if he didn't like Barry, taking some money off him. Maybe both! Turned out Barry didn't play; but some of the locals were in so Jay, courting Jill's irritation for being antisocial, played them instead. In less than half an hour he'd won two quid, but Jill's expression suggested it was time to depart. That didn't go down so well with the vanquished, who were still muttering about re-matches when the party left.

They'd work their way back to Jill's flat via the best pubs, so next stop was The Ship Victory. Barry might not be a bagatelle player but he could sup. Jay was impressed; he was only half way down his barrel-glass of Hydes' when Barry got 'em in again. They'd had four pints in less than an hour; Jay decided it would slow things down a tad if they kept crawling. He still liked a pint or eight but preferred to take his time.

'Bull & Stirrup, all right?' he offered, forgetting he was in company for a moment. The Bull had recently displaced the Haymakers as the preferred destination on a Thursday night. Its drawback was its location in the centre of town: bad for driving home; its advantage was Brenda who served a mean pint of bitter and had magnificent breasts. She wasn't shy about displaying them either and invariably wore tight, low-cut blouses. His fellow teachers demonstrated their appreciation variously, in a light-hearted, bantering fashion, which Brenda took in her stride. None of them, as far as Jay could tell, suffered from the same affliction as him; it made returning from the bar with a tray of beers quite awkward! He'd recently taken to going in on his own, just for a swift one, on his way to Jill's. He reckoned Bren was starting to take a bit of a shine to him and fantasised about asking her out. She must be about thirty though.

By the time this had flashed across Jay's consciousness it was too late to turn back. Let's just hope Bren didn't drop him in it. She didn't; merely advised them that the snug was empty. There was a nice fire, so they'd find it cosier. There was also a darts board and a fair chance Jill would propose a game of doubles. She was a useful player, taught by her brother, Rob, apparently. Jay really liked Rob in spite of their having little in common apart from drinking and his sister! He was a handy bloke to have in your corner as well – boxed for the RAF – although usually he was really placid. Just as well because Jay was aggressive enough for two. Jill proposed *Micky Mouse*. They complemented each other. Jill was adept at scoring singles and trebles from twenty down to twelve, Jay was ace on the doubles. They were rapidly three-nil up. It was all very friendly, no money involved, though it did encourage faster drinking. By the time they moved onto the Liverpool Arms Jay calculated he was on his sixth; Barry had slipped in a couple of fliers.

Fortunately, Jill's last instruction was not to be later than eight thirty. She and Sheila would go on ahead and put the finishing touches to the meal. It was 'just salad' (Jay had noticed 'just' was Jill's favourite word: she was a mistress of unconscious self-deprecation). It wouldn't take much preparation.

The conversation dried up. He tried football but Barry was a rugby fan. League, too. Jay knew little enough about Union let alone League. They were reduced to domestics.

'How's Jill finding the hospital? Pretty different from Newcastle, eh?'

'Yeah, guess so.' Jay realised guiltily that he'd hardly ever asked her. 'Seems to be enjoying it though. Likes the extra responsibility.'

'Yeah, Sheila said she would.' His wife was a Sister. 'What about the flat? She's sharing, isn't she?'

'Yeah, another nurse.'

'What's she like?'

'Dunno, never met her.'

'Oh, right.'

'Reckon she's a right stunner and Jill's worried I'd fancy her,' chortled Jay and silence fell once more. It was a relief to have to leave.

They clambered noisily up the stairs and tumbled into the flat. Jill was being modest as usual: on the table was a banquet of cold meats, various salads and a load of rabbit food; and next to the sofa and the easy chair she'd set two side-tables with crisps, nuts and twiglets. She must've been saving up. There were three litres of Nicholas Wines: Chasspré, Canteval and Vieux Ceps. That was thoughtful, she knew the Vieux Ceps was his favourite. Additionally, Barry and Sheila had brought a bottle of Blue Nun whilst Jay had purloined one of his father's stash of Châteauneuf du Pape. It looked like being a good evening.

'Bet you're glad you didn't live in Edward VI's reign,' advised Jay portentously as they tucked into the cheese and biscuits.

'Go on then. Why?' Barry was a sport.

''Cause he introduced a limit on the number of pubs. London was restricted to forty and Chester to TWO!'

'Strewth! See what you mean.'

'Yeah. Swings and roundabouts, though. A century ago there were forty in Northgate Street alone!' Jay was into his stride now, 'And back in the Middle Ages there was a huge brewing industry round here. It's mentioned in the Mystery Plays. I've been reading 'em with Oxton 1.'

'What's that when it's at home?' enquired Barry good-naturedly.

'Not it – they! They're my form at Woodbridge. They're only twelve but bright as buttons.' Jay puffed with pride.

'They must be if they can cope with that stuff. They tried it on us at school: couldn't make head nor tail of it. Anyway what's it all got to do with beer?'

'Full of references. Like when Christ redeems a load of sinners but condemns a brewer to the flames of hell. Let's see, how's it go?

> Sometime I was a taverner
> A gossip and a tapster
> Of wine and ale a brewer
> Which woe hath me bewrought...

Summat like that anyway.'

'How does he know all this stuff?' Sheila's tone was of incredulity tinged with impatience.

'Oh it's all to do with Autolycus. Tell them, darling,' prompted Jill.

Dimly aware of his tendency to hog the conversation, Jay elected for the digest, 'Oh he's just a character from Shakespeare. A cutpurse who acquires pennies, or in my case trivia.'

Jill looked faintly disappointed, but she'd have been pissed off if he'd started quoting reams of *The Winter's Tale*.

'Oh, cherub,' she quipped *'the retort courteous* – how very considerate!'

'Strewth! Or should that be touché, Touchstone?' Jay had noticed she seemed to be getting pretty interested in Shakespeare these days. But quoting *As You Like It*? What the hell? It was puzzling, her being a nurse, an all. He must quiz her sometime.

By now both their friends were looking perplexed, much to Jay's satisfaction. Dinner seemed to morph into music, and conversation into dancing. For once Jay was relaxed enough not to be embarrassed by his ineptness and they were all enjoying themselves when a loud rap on the door broke the spell and Jill's landlord burst in.

'Can't you buggers turn it down a bit? I'm getting complaints from other tenants.'

Jill started to apologise but Jay, remembering she'd chosen this Saturday because her neighbours beneath would be away, was less accommodating.

'Bollocks!' he shouted.

'Yer what?'

'You heard. It's bollocks. The place is empty. It's only you complaining. Obviously can't stand anyone enjoying themselves!'

'You can't talk to me like that!' Mr Blundell's voice had risen an octave and Jill was worried. Not least for his blood pressure: she knew he had a heart condition.

'Oh push off, Blunders!'

Her landlord was shouting now: 'Now you listen to me, sonny...'

'Don't call me sonny, you superannuated prat!' Jay was in full flow. 'Piss off or I'll lay one on you!' Blundell was a good six inches taller, but Jay strode towards him and waved a clenched fist under his nose.

'All right, all right,' blustered the proprietor, 'there's no need to be like that. Just tone it down, that's all.' And he beat a retreat, trying to muster his dignity.

'And you, young lady, you come and see me tomorrow.'

Jay just laughed but Jill appeared mortified and Sheila and Barry embarrassed for her. It occurred hazily to Jay that he could possibly be responsible for spoiling the evening, but instead of apologizing he remarked forcefully, 'Well, good riddance to him!'

Jill looked pained: 'You can't just ride roughshod over people like that, Jay: you really can't. You should go and apologize.'

'Bollocks!!' muttered Jay even more vehemently. 'That's it. I'm off!'

Seventeen

She was on her way out when Mr Blundell summoned her. Sure of his ground now, he was sharp to the point of rudeness. As Jill tried to close proceedings with another apology he spelt it out: if her boyfriend, or any of her friends, caused any disturbance in the future she was out.

She'd been looking forward to exploring Chester. It was the first Sunday she'd had off and a cool, bright spring morning. Ideal for a walk along the city walls round to Grosvenor Park and down to the River Dee to buy a sandwich and a newspaper and relax in the sun. If it was warm enough. Now it had been spoiled by her stupid boyfriend! What the hell was he thinking of? It wasn't even his flat. It was all very well playing Sir Galahad but why couldn't he just be chivalrous instead of downright offensive. And he was so aggressive. She didn't doubt he meant it. He'd have punched Blundell if the man hadn't backed down. She remembered a tale he'd told her from his Cuthbert's days. Him and his friend Pard, whom she neither liked nor trusted, getting into a similar situation and nearly getting sent down. Terrific! He'd have left before they'd had a chance to get to know each other. And whatever his faults, Jill did love him. Most of the time. But, Jesus! he could be infuriating.

It was so beautiful she began to calm down and by the time she was pattering through the park's cherry blossom she was cheerful again. But she was still angry with Jay. She needed to pay him back somehow. Teach him a lesson. As she chewed her ham and cheese roll, a roguish thought... she'd treat Alan to a return fixture! Monday he'd still be on nights but Wednesday and Friday were his bath slots, too. She'd get there before him and pull the same stunt with the door just ajar. Then when she heard him approaching she'd be lying back in the bubble bath...

She was still daydreaming wicked when an elderly lady parked herself on the bench and pulled out a bag of seeds from her carrier. She offered Jill a handful and within seconds they were joined by assorted spuggies, starlings, tits and blackbirds. Jill had always liked birds: even as a kid she'd learned the names of all the common ones from old Bowly who used to frequent the burn where she played. An unpleasant memory was associated with it, though, so Jill thought instead of Stephen, who was virtually a professional ornithologist and had taught her loads of the Latin names. She wondered whether to share some of her knowledge but, as suddenly as she'd arrived the old duck arose abruptly and disappeared without a word.

Jill tried to revive her reverie but its attraction already seemed passé. When she'd spied on Alan it had been a drunken impulse. The idea of *planning* such an escapade was…well, a bit creepy. She could have a few drinks first of course: that had a tendency to get her in the mood, but it seemed too calculating. Besides even if she succeeded in carrying it off suppose it didn't stop there? Suppose Alan was bolder than her and far from worrying about giving himself away did so deliberately, striding into the bathroom and offering to 'give her a hand?' It was just the sort of thing a man would do. No! The whole idea was lunatic.

There had to be a better way of teaching the teacher a lesson.

Back at the Infirmary Jill was still ruminating over her lunch break. It wasn't just about helping Jay grow up a bit. He was that sort of man: he'd probably always be immature. Maybe it was the downside to his imag-ination, his impulsiveness, his creativity. It still didn't excuse his being a pain in the arse, though. If he wanted to upset people that was his lookout; there'd be times when he'd have to suffer the consequences. That didn't mean Jill had to. This was about her as an individual. Her independence. But how to demonstrate it?

She was still deep in thought when Bronwyn set down her lunch-tray.

'Hello, Staff. How's tricks?' Sister Roberts liked to tease Jill by being formal, even though they'd been on first-name terms since she'd shown Jill the ropes on Ward Six.

'Oh, hi Bronwyn. Okay, thanks. Everything all right with you?'

'I'm fine but mother's not so good. She was admitted to Bangor General last weekend. Some sort of heart problem, apparently.'

'Oh, bummer! Sorry, Bron. Is it serious?'

'They're not sure yet. Done a load of tests but nothing definite. Whatever transpires she's not going to be able to manage on her own. Not for a while, anyway.'

'Right…what're you going to do?'

'I've already spoken to matron. She's says to take as long as I need.'

Sister Roberts had been at the Royal for yonks and was highly thought of, so Jill wasn't surprised by matron's latitude.

'Well that's a relief. Is there anything I can do?'

'As a matter of fact, cariad, there is.'

'Great! What?'

'You could look after my flat. It's just as handy as where you are now and it'd be much nicer for you. No landlord, for starters – I own it!'

Jill's mind was racing. Positives? Loads. Negatives? None that she could see instantly. 'That's really nice of you, Bron, but what about family? Isn't there anyone else you'd sooner have looking after it for you?'

'No, my sisters are in Cardiff and married. I'm nearest, and we old spinsters have no ties!'

Jill snorted her derision. 'Well, in that case…I'd love to. I'll pay the going rate, of course. I guess I'll have to give notice at No.66, but that'll be a pleasure.'

'So I believe. You're well out it. That Blundell's a reputation for putting on nurses. So you'll take me up on it?'

'Absolutely! It'll be brilliant! Where is it?'

'Handbridge. Just across the river. Why don't you pop round after work on Thursday? We can sort out the details.'

'Love to. Whereabouts exactly?'

'Just off Mill Street: really handy for the Bridge Inn. Tell you what: meet me there. Say, half-six in the Lounge?'

'Great! Thanks a bunch! See you then, Sister!'

'Look forward to it, Staff!' And Bronwyn left, her step a tad jauntier than when she'd arrived, fancied Jill. There was no time for her curried eggs. She could squeeze in a coffee and a plate of cheese and biscuits whilst she considered this unexpected opportunity. Of course, she needed to see the flat, but knowing how meticulous Bronwyn was at work Jill imagined it would be spick and span.

But what about Jay?

It was suddenly so obvious: don't tell him, at least not yet. The flat would be furnished and she didn't have much stuff to move. A car-full at most. She knew just the person. The Nurses' Ball was looming and one of the housemen, Monty Wilson, had been pestering her for weeks. Quid pro quo: she'd go with him if he transported her belongings to Handbridge. That would deal her delinquent boyfriend a double blow. Perhaps he'd get the message; but, if he didn't, he could cool his heels.

The flat was over a butcher's shop.

'It gets a bit noisy through the day, but by six it's like a morgue. Plus, Roy's a good butcher. I've been going to him for years. I'll make sure he

knows you then you'll get preferential treatment. Does fabulous steaks…
if you like that sort of thing?'

'Should do,' grinned Jill, 'me mam's a butcher!'

They paused as they climbed the narrow stairs and Bronwen pointed
out a lumber-room-cum-loo on the half-landing. Jill feared the flat
might prove similarly cramped but when Bron opened the door into the
living room she was astonished. It was huge and had a terrific view of
the river and the Old Dee Bridge. To the rear was a small, but fully fitted
kitchen and a box-room with a bunk bed. Above was a spacious double
bedroom with a bathroom leading off it.

'Bron, it's perfect! Thanks ever so much for thinking of me. I'll really
look after it for you. Promise!'

'I know you will, cariad. And if you're worrying about the rent, don't.
I only want a peppercorn. You'll be doing me a favour keeping it safe and
sound.'

'That's really generous, thanks. Just one thing. Would it be…?'

'Okay if your young man stays? Of course, love.'

'I don't mean every night, just now and again. He doesn't even know
I'm moving yet!'

The best bit of all had been telling Blundell.

'Come to ask a favour, have we?' he leered. 'Want to throw another
party for that precious boyfriend of yours?'

'Oh no, Mr Blundell,' Jill gave him her sweetest smile and handed
him a buff, hospital envelope. 'There's a week's rent. I'm moving out.
Tomorrow!'

Eighteen

Jay hadn't intended to eavesdrop. But when the conversation was about money! He'd never heard his parents discuss the subject before. So he couldn't help loitering on the bottom stair as his father's muffled tones rustled under the drawing room door like errant pound notes.

'It's an increase of £500, Mu. Not to be sniffed at.'

'But it's not as if we need the money, darling, what with your DI's salary and my teaching. And now Jay's earning too.'

Jay knew roughly what his father earned cause he'd seen the report on his desk: *Select Committee on Education and Science. Part 1: Her Majesty's Inspectorate.* The blue-jacketed HMSO publication looked as dry as dust but it happened to have a bookmark fairly near the front. *'satiable curtiosity* opened it at Page 2: *Pay and Conditions of Service.* There was some boring stuff about links to the administrative class of the civil service and then the nitty gritty: HMI pay scales. He knew his dad wasn't a standard inspector any more, though there were only about 500 of *them* nationally. He traced down the list: there it was 'DI' – divisional inspector, the ones with oversight of a whole region. Salary £4,325 per annum. Shit! Not bad! About five times what Jay was on. Still, fair enough: he had a helluva lot more responsibility. Jay recalled there were only two ranks higher: chief inspector and senior chief inspector, or SCI, as he'd heard his father refer to the current incumbent, Sir Wilfred Pound.

'It's not the money, sweetheart. I agree we can get by without the extra dosh. It's the prestige. There are only six CIs in the whole country.'

'But that's my point, Ray. They're not in the *country*, are they? You'd be based in London.'

'Only during the week. And Pound said there was provision for that. Staff flats near Green Park at a very reasonable rent, source-deductible. You're pretty much guaranteed to be on the four o'clock out of Euston come Friday with no requirement to be in the office before ten on Monday. Some weeks I wouldn't be needed at all and could work out of Manchester, just like now.'

'I don't know, Ray. I'd get awfully lonely during the week.'

'But it's no different from a Full Inspection. Except then I usually have to leave on Sundays.'

'Hmm… I don't know…' Jay could tell his mother was weakening and heard his dad go for the jugular.

'Besides you've got Jay now. You can keep an eye on him and he'll be company for you in the evenings.'

Jay smiled thinly. So that was his nights mortgaged for the foreseeable future.

'Anyway, let's think it over. I don't have to let them know 'til next weekend.'

Jay padded softly up to his room.

By the end of term, however, it was his mum who'd prevailed. Raymond Fincher did not become one of Her Majesty's chief inspectors. Instead, he had a tailor-made staff inspector's job and could remain in Chester.

'You remember Sir John, don't you, son?'

'Course! D'you still see much of him?' His dad had been friends with John Hunt for some time. They'd met through the Duke of Edinburgh's Award, which the pair of them had championed. From being an elitist qualification for public school types it was now available, largely due to Ray Fincher, in most secondary schools in the country. And he'd mainstreamed it for less-able kids via the Record of Personal Achievement he'd created. It was this, apparently, that had persuaded Curzon Street that, rather than lose the specialist skills of one of their most accomplished inspectors, they should create a new post for him: Staff Inspector for Geography and Outdoor Education. Ray was jubilant. He hadn't really wanted to move to London, much as he liked his regular trips there. And his wife's intransigence had won the day; not to mention a rise of over £300 p.a. Not a bad outcome!

Jay was chuffed. He didn't fancy his dad living down in the Smoke. It wasn't that he'd have to look after his mum. After his big brother was killed he'd got comfortable as man-of-the-house during his father's frequent absences. But he missed him, too. He was a pretty sound bloke and they enjoyed climbing and drinking together, as well as the occasional round of golf. Although on the links Jay felt a disappointment. Unlike Chris who'd been proficient, though nowhere near the three-handicap their dad played off, Jay struggled round the local courses, rarely breaking ninety and, more often ending up with a frustrating three-figure tally.

Didn't detract from their enjoyment of the nineteenth hole, though!

Moreover, his father's responsibilities would continue to include the annual DES camping course, which this summer was to be based around Plas y Brenin. The warden there was a good mate of his dad's and had been on the preliminary Everest expedition with Sir John so the climbing and the craic would be high quality. Jay was looking forward to both.

Meanwhile, he was puzzled. He didn't worry when Jill failed to call for a week after the ill-fated party. On reflexion he shouldn't have threatened to deck Blundell or, when he had, he should at least have been apologetic instead of storming out. So he was probably in the shit. (*Semper*...he grinned!) Better to let Jill calm down. Besides, she was likely on nights and they could often go a whole week without meeting, or even talking, given the antisocial hours. When the second silent weekend arrived though, he was worried.

The front door to No.66 was ajar, but he didn't have his flat key. His knocking brought the porter-from-hell lumbering up the stairs. Jay detected a malicious glint and was half expecting a sarcastic put-down.

'You'll get no answer, sonn...er...mate. Yer girlfriend's gone.'

'Whaddya mean gone?'

'What I say. Gave me a week's notice and buggered off.'

Jay was panicking now: 'Where to? Where did she go?'

'Dunno, mate. But she's not here anymore so yer wasting yer time.'

Jay was flummoxed. But the last thing he wanted was Blundell crowing over his discombobulation, so he muttered a face-saving: 'Yeah, right of course,' and launched himself down the stairs half-a-flight at a time. Then he strode purposefully out to his mum's green Hillman Imp, jumped in and gunned the little beast up Liverpool Road so that, if Blundell was spying out of the flat-window, his departure would appear decisive.

In reality he didn't have a clue where to go or what to do.

His first reaction was to repair to the Bull & Stirrup and work things out over a pint or six. But it was only eleven: bit early for him these days. Besides if he had a skinful he'd have to ditch the wheels. Then there'd be the required explanation, followed inevitably by recrimination. He could try the hospital, find one of Jill's friends. But where to start? He didn't know his way around the nurses' home and he could hardly stroll onto Ward Six asking for Staff Walker. Plus, he'd look a bit of a twat mooching about trying to find his girlfriend. Without a convincing alibi he'd have to concede he seemed to have misplaced her. Shades of Lady Bracknell. Misfortune at least, probably carelessness!

The Imp had spirited its way to the car park by The Ship Victory. Well, maybe just a couple of jars wouldn't do any harm. Not in the Ship, though; he'd be bound to bump into a bagatelle crowd and the next thing it'd be closing time. He'd likely be a few quid richer but undoubtedly the worse for wear. No, what he needed was beer-and-sympathy: had to be the Bull after all. There was no sign of Bren, but it was mercifully quiet. Jay ordered a pint, scrutinising the badge on the pump handle as the barman pulled it. He knew Higson's was brewed in Liverpool but had never noticed it dated back to 1780. Not bad; though hardly threatening Shepherd Neame. He was pretty sure that was 1690-something but it came from Kent. Southern beers didn't really count. Still 1690-odd, made you think. Dryden'd be Poet Laureate still and *Absalom and Achitophel* would be all the rage. He liked Dryden. He was a conundrum: politically capricious, full of praise and blame and notorious for his indecent writing. For the first time that disconsolate day, Jay chuckled:

In pious times, ere priestcraft did begin,
Before polygamy was made a sin,
When man on many multiplied his kind,
Ere one to one was cursedly confined…

And right on cue, in walked Bren! He certainly wouldn't mind multiplying his kind on her!

'Hello! Not your usual time, Jaycy.'

'No. Drowning me sorrows, Bren.'

'Why, what's up, love? You can tell your Auntie Bren.' She parked herself on the stool opposite, giving him a right eyeful as she did.

'Oh, it's me own fault. I've been a ruddy berk. I upset Jill that much she's left.'

'Whaddya mean, left? Left Chester?'

'Dunno, Bren. She's gone from her flat.'

'Sure we can think of something. I'll be back when I've served this lot.' She gestured at the crowd of Liverpool supporters who'd spilled raucously into the public bar; and rose from the stool, giving Jay another basinful of beautiful Bristols.

Yeah, King David had it right!

Two pints of Higson's later Jay had devoured most of the unfamiliar Times. It wasn't his cup of tea, too Establishment, but it never hurt to see how the other half lived. Even if they were a bunch of un-reconstructed

Fascists! It had only been a divertissement though: he was no nearer working out what to do.

Bren returned, sparkly-eyed. 'You must have her 'phone number back north.'

'Yeah, but what use is that? Surely she wouldn't have returned to Wallsend?'

'Maybe not, but her mum'll know where she is. Honest! Just try.'

Inspirational! Jay downed his pint, kissed Bren much more hurriedly than he'd have liked and sprinted down to the Imp. The house seemed deserted but he still installed himself in his dad's study and used the extension.

'Hello hinny. Luvley to hear from yer, pet. Aal reet?'

'Not really. I've lost Jill.'

'Why wor Jay, that were a bit careless,' teased Mary. 'Spose yer'll be needin my help to find her, eh?'

'Please, Mary! Any ideas?'

'Wey-aye, man. Yer divn't need to look far. She's still in Chester.'

'Oh, thank God for that! Whereabouts?'

'Handbridge? Know it?'

'Yeah, yeah.'

'She said to be in the Bridge seven o'clock Satdy. An divn't be late!'

Nineteen

Jill didn't get much post, just the occasional card from Sally or Trish Watson. Nothing from the family, except at Christmas time, but that was weeks yet. Her heart skipped when she saw the letter was franked with a Newcastle City Council stamp. The writing was Sue Lambton's.

Inside was a pretty card of Warkworth Castle and a brief but exciting message. Sue had applied for the post of assistant county librarian with Salop County Council and had an interview in Shrewsbury on Friday 5th December. She was thinking of staying over the weekend in Chester. Would they be able to meet up?

Jill's initial reaction was to ring her there and then. Saturday morning: Jay was away climbing for the weekend and Sue'd be at Moor Crescent for sure. But so would Joyce. Sue would certainly have told her partner about the interview (wonder how she feels about *that*) but would she have mentioned a stopover in Chester? Not wanting to risk any awkwardness Jill decided to postpone calling until the next day. If she left it until eleven Joyce would be at All Saints, Gosforth; besides it would give her a chance to figure out how to play it. She wanted to see Sue of course, although the infatuation of Lindisfarne had dimmed somewhat. She'd been young and impressionable and got carried away with the romanticism of the island fling. But if Sue stayed in the flat, there was the possibility of consummating their relationship. It would doubtless be a wonderful experience but at what cost? It felt like Sue should look out for Joyce, although Jill loved her too in a grateful, asexual way. She had so much to thank her for and couldn't bear the thought of their falling out because of her. Then there was Jay. In theory, he'd only find out if Jill told him. Surely? But Handbridge was a close community. If she and Sue went to the Bridge they'd be sure to bump into someone both Jay and she knew and complications would inevitably follow.

Nuts! It was all so difficult.

She decided to go for a walk, clear her head, reach the right decision…

As she emerged onto the pavement she walked straight into Roy, the butcher.

'How's my favourite nurse?' he enquired cheerily.

'I'm fine thanks, Roy. Seeing you has just given me an idea though. Can you look me out a nice fillet steak, please? I'll pick it up on my way back in, if that's okay?'

That was it. She was going to treat herself. Living virtually rent-free in Bron's flat left her with spare cash for the first time. (She didn't count her savings, courtesy of Aunt Louisa. They were a secret. A big one!) If Jay chose to desert her for the weekend, he'd be the loser. She walked over the bridge, pausing in the centre to watch the swirling eddies beneath and that year's still-dappled-brown cygnets swimming wilfully against the current. The day was bright enough but cool and the fluffy white clouds were intermittently mirrored on the water's surface. Starting to get cold Jill crossed the remainder of the bridge and strode up between the Georgian frontages towards the city centre. She would pick up some titbits to make a salad and drop in at Quellyn Roberts to treat herself to a bottle of decent wine. She'd been there with Jay's dad, so knew the ropes; otherwise she'd probably have been a bit overawed. She sauntered through the vaults until she came to the Bordeaux section. Remembering what Jay's dad had told her about château-bottled clarets she engaged a dishy and frightfully well-spoken young man, until she saw the cost. Panicking, she made an excuse and beat a hasty retreat. Maybe Raymond Fincher could afford those prices but Jill would have to be content with some plonk from the corner shop! Eleven-and-nine-pence rather than six-pounds-ten! True the Canteval only came in litres so there was a fair chance she'd end up tiddly, but so what? Whilst the cat's away...

Besides Jill hadn't completely forgiven Jay, and the prospect of getting up to something faintly wayward appealed to her. So she prepared coleslaw, potato salad and tomatoes to go with the steak and deposited the lot in Bron's fridge for later.

It was too early to go out. She cast around for something to read. Not in the mood for Shakespeare. But under last weekend's papers lay her clandestine copy of *The Autobiography of a Flea*. Jay had given it her; it was quite the most salacious book she'd ever encountered, provided you were in the mood. Jill thought she was, but after ten minutes she was singularly unstimulated so she stashed it under the scatter cushions and wondered what to do next.

She didn't want to spend the whole evening in. Maybe the obscene text had worked subconsciously as, on a whim, she decided to go out, pretending she was on the pull. She changed into her shortest mini-skirt and her lowest-cut jumper and slapped on some make-up. She strolled back up town to the Bull & Stirrup. She was quite comfortable going into most pubs on her own, but preferred somewhere she knew people. She'd been in with Jay and knew that Brenda, the barmaid, was friendly enough. She had what Jay would call 'a fine pair': no doubt the reason for him and his teaching mates frequenting the place! You couldn't get Newcastle Amber in the Chester pubs; if she'd been with Jay she'd have ordered a pint but on her own she didn't quite have the nerve, so settled for a bottle of Worthington White Shield. Quite a few of the nurses drank it; reputedly the best value for getting merry quickly, on account of its innocuous taste and high alcoholic content. Just the job, she thought impishly. There was a free table in the corner. It wasn't long after opening time and she began idly flipping through the pub copy of the Chester Chronicle. Not much of interest, though a piece about an extension to West Cheshire Hospital caught her eye and, armed with a second Shield, Jill soon became absorbed in it.

'Looking for pastures new already?' Her former flatmate looked quite dishy: tight beige flares – Farahs, by the look of them – and an orange, silky-looking shirt. The outfit showed off his black hair and dark olive eyes. He'd already shouldered his brown suede jacket and stood over her, grinning admiringly.

Cheeky bugger's ogling me boobs, thought Jill indignantly. Then she remembered it was her choice to show 'em off in the first place so she just smiled. She hadn't actually wanted to pull some complete stranger; company she knew and liked was far preferable.

'Hi Alan, what brings you here?'

'Just slipped in for a quick one: glad I did, too!' He smiled broadly fixing his gaze even more deliberately on Jill's breasts. 'If I'd known you were here I'd have come in earlier! No boyfriend tonight?'

'No he's had a better offer!' she joked. 'Gone climbing in the Lakes.'

'More fool him: mind if I join you?'

'Feel free; but whilst you're still on your feet, mine's a White Shield.'

The bar was more crowded now and in the time it took the charge nurse to get back with the drinks Jill adjusted her clothing, yanking the jumper down and letting her skirt ride up. There, she grinned mischievously: that should give him something to gawk at! The prospect of teasing a man she knew to be susceptible in the secure environment of a public bar was both risqué and enticing.

'Phwoar, Staff: you're looking a bit tasty tonight! That boyfriend of yours must be crazy letting you out dressed like that.'

'He doesn't know. Besides I don't dress to order.'

'Well it certainly works for me! Anyway, if I can tear myself away from the view for a moment...what were you reading about the Westie?'

'Oh it's just about the new extension. D'you reckon it'll mean more jobs?'

'Sure will. Want me to put in a good word?'

'Depends what you're after in return!' laughed Jill suggestively.

'Why, Staff, the very idea!'

The banter continued and, although Jill bought only one round, the drinks kept flowing. There being only so much beer a girl could consume Jill switched to vodka and orange. She was on her third...or was it fourth? But she was still caught out by Alan's change of tack.

'So what're we doing for supper?'

Jill should tell him to get lost but heard herself inviting him back to the flat. There'd be enough to go round.

'I'll get a bottle on the way,' he promised.

She was about to observe they didn't need another one but failed to: couldn't have too much booze, after all.

The cool December air did nothing to sober her up, or to stifle the excitement that had been fuelled by her unaccustomed exhibitionism. As she unlocked the front door and switched the lights on Jill was momentarily aware that Alan would have a fair shufti as she ascended the steep stairs. She'd ask him to go first but it would seem a bit feeble, so she set off a tad unsteadily. She half expected to feel a guiding hand on her derrière and was almost disappointed when they reached the living room without mishap.

She poured two generous glasses of Alan's Beaujolais and waved airily towards the sofa.

'Make yourself at home. I'll just prepare the salad. Won't be two ticks.'

Jill checked the fridge: she retrieved the bowl of salad, got the steak out, cut it into two unequal parts and put it ready under the grill. Downing her wine and filling up the glass, she sidled through the hallway to the sitting room door. It remained as she'd left it: ajar. Through the chink she realised Alan had found the ill-secreted copy of the *Flea* and was avidly devouring it. His face was flushed. Should she burst in now, or give him a bit longer?

Back in the kitchen Jill deliberated. It was bizarre, but ever since she'd witnessed Alan's antics in the bath at No.66 she'd had an irrational desire to see, even handle, his dickory-dock. Actually it went back a lot further. There was the orderly in the laundry room back at the RVI. What was his name? Yeah, Stirl. She'd been dozing on the blankets after a heavy night out and he'd been perving over her when the staff nurse had blundered in. Jill had been both scared and relieved but had harboured an inchoate craving to reach out and touch the offensive weapon. Her colleagues on the psychiatric wing would have had a ball!

The recollection confused Jill. She really didn't know what she wanted to happen but she felt delightfully tipsy. Anyway it was a shame to have got this far... She padded back to the half-open door and glanced through. Alan looked excited but was still reading. As she watched impatiently he undid his zip and fumbled around inside. That was it, she decided boldly: she was going to give him a hand. But just as she'd prepared her entrance, including a suitably astonished reaction, the doorbell sounded.

It could only be Jay. No one else would call at this time on a Saturday night. Sod it! She'd never bothered to tell him about Alan. If they met under these circumstances, there'd be trouble for sure. She strode hurriedly into the sitting room just as Alan was re-arranging himself. She pretended not to notice.

'Quick! Downstairs! There's a loo on the landing. Hide in there whilst I see who it is.'

Commendably composed he did so without demur; Jill continued past the half-landing to answer the door.

Twenty

Most of the teachers claimed to hate report writing but Jay liked it. He knew he was privileged. Oxton 1 were such a bright bunch; it wasn't difficult to find encouraging things to say, and with the minority who hadn't exactly covered themselves in glory he made a point of accentuating something positive. You couldn't have favourites, of course. Maxine was his. On her report Jay wrote: *Maxine has settled in extremely well and made an excellent start to her career at Woodbridge.* Then he took the pile round to the office and deposited them with Miss Brierley, the school secretary, for Mr Jenkins to countersign. When they were returned to him for issue to the kids on the last day of term he found a slip of paper in Maxine's report. On it, in the head's own handwriting it said, *And the same could be said of her form teacher. Well done, Fincher.* Jay didn't mention it at school of course; nor at home, though he knew it would've been well received. He folded it in half and taped it to the inside back-page of his *Collins Gentleman's Diary.*

At the beginning of the Michaelmas Term (Jay still clung to his favoured nomenclature) the three new recruits were summoned to see the head. His deputy, Graham Bewcastle, was there too. It felt like a job interview. Jay feared the worst even though it could well be an opportunity: they wouldn't all have been called in if some indiscretion were to be investigated.

'You've all made a good start, so congratulations are in order!' smiled the head. Bewcastle nodded ever so faintly, as if he knew he had to agree with his superior but that it pained him to do so.

'Here's the situation. We've conducted our annual staff review over the holidays...'

Jay's heart sank: someone was superfluous to requirements and as the only untrained teacher, it'd be him.

'As I say, it's an annual event, nothing to worry about...'

That sounded better.

'We have one Scale Two post available for last year's new intake. We'd like each of you to think about your strengths and weaknesses and this time next week tell us why it should go to you.'

Jay breathed a sigh of relief; at least he wasn't being sacked and in theory, since he'd now passed his probation, he was as eligible for promotion as the other two. Wouldn't happen though. He knew Bewcastle would favour Sid, they were both mathematicians; whilst staffroom gossip claimed Miss Lines had 'caught the head's eye', whatever that meant. Still, he'd give it some thought and maybe discuss it with his dad.

The first chance was on Saturday over a pint in the Dog.

'Something's come up,' he began gnomically, employing subconsciously an expression his father used. The latter just smiled and waited for elaboration.

'Yeah, there's a promotion to Scale Two available. The three who started last year have to justify why it should be us to Jenkins and Bewcastle on Monday.'

A long silence whilst his dad pondered the matter.

'Well the first thing to say is well done! Even to be considered is a feather in your cap.'

'Thanks...but any advice on how best to present my case?'

'That's easy, son: with modesty and concision. Another pint?'

Later, as Jay ran out bagatelle winner and they collected their coats to head back, his dad added thoughtfully, 'And think about what you can bring to your post over and above your undoubted subject expertise.'

Two days later he was back before the board.

'So, young Finch,' began the head, indicating this was to be an informal chat not a stuffy interview. 'Why should we promote *you*?'

'You shouldn't, sir.'

'I beg your pardon?'

'You shouldn't. Sid Baxter should get it: he's best qualified.'

'Well thanks for the recommendation, but you're not making that decision. We are! What, for example, could you add over and above your English skills?' Bewcastle's tone was not unfriendly and the question was exactly what his dad had predicted. Clever ole bugger!

Jay took a deep breath, 'Well two things, sir. Mr Warburton's departure leaves us with no drama teacher and the school play coming up in ten weeks. After that programme last October, I volunteered to help out at the county drama course during the summer. I really enjoyed it and I learned a lot. They've invited me back to teach on it next year. I reckon I could step in and help Peter... I mean Mr Jackson put on the school play this Christmas.'

'Hmm, point taken, Fincher. Anything else?'

'It's longer-term, sir, but more significant.'

'Go on.'

'Well it's not so long before they raise the school leaving age. That means our current second-years, say, instead of becoming our bored fourth years will be even-more-bored fifth years. What are we going to do with 'em?'

'Well, you tell us!'

'Outdoor pursuits, sir. Reckon it'll really appeal to 'em. Build up enough equipment – tents, climbing gear, canoes, dinghies – over the next couple of years and instead of vegetating, disgruntled sixteen-year olds we could have kids enthused by the great outdoors. Competing to get on activities that took them away from school. I know there's no post to cover it but I'd do it for free! And if we started before ROSLA becomes official, we'd have a head start on everyone else.'

'What about the head of PE? Wouldn't he have something to say?'

'I've mentioned it to Bill...to Mr Molyneux, sir. He's all for it. Besides it'd go way beyond PE: it'd link with geography, Biology, Literature...'

Head and deputy raised a collective eyebrow: 'Literature?'

'Yes sir, it's what De Bono calls *lateral thinking* – seeing connexions between apparently unrelated things. New uses for old ideas...that sort of stuff!'

'Well one can't fault your enthusiasm, young Finch...but *Literature?*'

'Absolutely, sir – *Shakespeare on the Rocks* – just give me a chance!'

And they did. Later that day he was called back in and a beaming Mr Jenkins promoted him to Scale 2.

'You'll be in charge of drama and the development of outdoor pursuits! Well done, young man. Keep it to yourself for now; I've not had a chance to tell the others.'

Sid took it very well: came and congratulated him. But the noxious Miss Lines didn't. Moreover, she was foolish enough to broadcast her reaction before storming into the head's office demanding to know why *she* hadn't been promoted.

Dissatisfied with the explanation she'd huffed.

'Well, if that's all you think of me I may be forced to look elsewhere.'

'In that case I can give you an excellent reference, Miss Lines.'

Much to Jay's amusement she'd left at half term in high dudgeon.

Twenty-One

'Sorry to call unannounced. And so late. I wasn't sure if you had company.'

'Bronwen! How lovely to see you! Come on up.' Jill was relieved, and puzzled. She went ahead, checking the landing light was on and the loo light off. She ushered Bron into her own living room, fussing around her self-consciously.

'What a lovely surprise! What are you doing in Chester?'

'Long story, cariad. Probably best told over a drink, if you've got anything. If not, we could go back to the Bridge.'

'Not unless you want to, I've got some wine.'

'Perfect,' murmured Bronwen. She'd already had several rum and cokes at the pub and didn't particularly want to show her face again. Besides, the flat was more private.

If she noticed the half-empty glass on the side, Bron didn't say anything so Jill fielded it on her way through, taking a slurp from it on the way. There, now Bron would assume it was hers, she thought fuzzily. Surely there was no other sign she'd had a visitor. She selected the biggest glass she could find and poured a generous measure of Canteval into it. She topped up her own and took them through. Bron had closed the curtains and switched on the standard lamps at either end of the sofa. She looked peppered, her eyes momentarily closed.

Jill had never seen her out of uniform. She was wearing a modishly short, brown skirt and a tight beige jumper. Crikey! Jill was slightly dazed: she hadn't realized before what shapely legs Bron had. She was just thinking how attractive her boss looked when a sound from downstairs startled them both.

'What was that?'

'Maybe I didn't pull the door to; I'll just go and check.' Anxious to make sure Alan had gone Jill went down the stairs at a fair lick. She opened the door silently and then shut it firmly.

'Must've left it on the sneck by mistake. No problem, all secure now.'

'Oh good.' Bron sounded knackered, 'Cheers!'

'Cheers, boss. So what's up? You're not gonna throw me out are you?'

'No, just the opposite. But that'll wait. No…it's mum. She was doing so well I was planning to come back soon. But she was out shopping in Bangor and she must've had a stroke. Fell quite badly.'

'Oh, no! Poor her…poor you!'

'Yeah, they took her back into the General and she seemed to make quite a good recovery so they discharged her within the month. She's lost a lot of movement on her right side though and she's finding the house difficult. She says she can manage but I don't want to risk it. A friend's looking after her whilst I'm away, but it's only a stopgap.'

'Course.' Jill couldn't think of anything else to say and figured the best sympathy was another glass of wine. It would be easier to bring the bottle through. Bron didn't add much more and Jill didn't like to pry so they reminisced for most of the rest of the Canteval, gossiping about the ward and their mutual acquaintances. Jill pottered off to the kitchen in search of more wine but came back empty-handed to find Bron snoozing at the other end of the sofa. Did she wake her up or drape a blanket over her? Jill didn't even know whether Bron had intended to stay. She was pondering the options when her guest yawned, stretched and came around.

'Ooh sorry, cariad, just dozed off for a mo. I must get off and leave you in peace.'

'Hang on, where you going?'

'Back to Bangor.'

But you can't. You've had far too much to drink.'

'Hmm, hadn't thought of that; guess you're right. I'll maybe curl up here for the night if that's okay with you?'

'What in your own flat?' Jill was indignant, 'I'll make up the bunk bed and sleep there.'

'No way! I'm not turfing you out of your own bed. *I'll* sleep in the bunk bed.'

'No, that's not right either.'

'Well, we're not going to fall out over it. We'll share the double. It's big enough, after all. You're not shy, are you?'

'Course not! If you don't mind, I don't.'

'Well that's settled then. Nightcap?'

Jill was at a loss; they'd finished the wine and she'd nothing else in.

Bron chuckled. 'You obviously haven't stumbled on my stash then! Wait here.' And she disappeared through to the kitchen emerging swiftly with a bottle of Captain Morgan and two shot glasses.

Jill smiled nostalgically. The bottle reminded her of the first Walker family holiday at Seahouses. They'd stopped in a caravan and each night after their fish and chip supper her dad would suggest: 'Summat to keep the cold out, Mary?' and produce a bottle of Captain Morgan. It had been a holiday treat from her Uncle Bill, who ran a hotel, and the sham was that it was just the one bottle, whereas they'd actually been given two or three. Jill liked the label. It was connected in her mind with *Treasure Island*, which the lit twins had prescribed for holiday reading. And she'd always liked the smell.

'Iechyd da!' toasted Bron raising the glass to her lips and throwing it back in one.

'Salud!' responded Jill sipping it cautiously and then, seeing the expression of mock disapproval on Bron's face, downing the rest of it. She allowed herself to be poured another shot and this time, when Bron threw hers back in one Jill followed suit.

Bron refilled the glasses but this time put them on the low table in front of the sofa. She lounged back and smiled warmly at Jill.

'There is something else, love. I called in at the Royal earlier. Saw matron. And Mr K Separately.'

Jill knotted her eyebrows.

'Yeah, wanted to clear it with them before I said anything to you.'

Now Jill was properly hooked, 'What, for heaven's sake?'

'Well you know matron told me originally they'd keep my post open as long as I needed?'

Jill nodded supportively, 'Quite right, too!'

'Thanks, pet, appreciate the vote of confidence! Seems there's a time limit after all, though. They want to appoint a temp with the promise I'll be considered if and when I can return.'

'Oh no! That's not fair. They should...'

'No, think about it. They can't hold the vacancy forever, now can they?'

'Well, suppose if you put it like that... D'you know who they've got in mind?'

'You, cariad! You!'

Jill was stunned: 'Oh Jesus! What...? I mean...how d'you know?'

'Easy, pet: I recommended you. Matron agreed, and Mr K had no objection. He was almost animated! You must've made some impression there, love.'

Jill blushed. 'I don't know what to say.'

'How about *Yes*?!'

'Well, yes...yes...yes! Absolutely! But only if it'll give you a better chance when you're able to come back.'

'That's very generous! I'm sure it will.' Bron rose a tad unsteadily and picking up both glasses presented one to Jill: 'Iechyd da, cariadfab!'

'Iechyd da!' echoed Jill '...carriadfab??' she puzzled.

'Darling!' explained Bron. 'Come here!' and depositing their empties on the table she put both arms round Jill, drawing her in close and treating her to a warm hug. Jill responded, wrapping her arms round Bronwen's ample waist. The cuddle intensified until Bron abruptly removed her hands from behind Jill's neck and cupping her cheeks affectionately planted a brief kiss full on her lips.

'Wow!' gasped Jill, her arms still round Bron's waist, 'If that's the seal of approval, I wouldn't mind getting promoted every day!'

'Go on with you! Shameless little hussy!'

Bron was making light of it, but Jill thought her eyes sparkled with more than just affection. Perhaps that debate about who-was-sleeping-in-which-bed had not been merely an exchange of pleasantries. Then again, it might have been the Captain Morgan!

'One last nightcap and then bed, cariad; some of us have to be up in the morning!'

Twenty-Two

Jay sat beneath the broken walls of the keep. Beeston Castle was closed to the public, certainly over the winter anyway, but you could get in illicitly with a modicum of scaling tactics. (Only very mild Severe, smiled Autolycus the Ascendeur!) The leaden sky looked full of snow and it was freezing, but his climbing trousers and down jacket kept him snug and he rewarded his enterprise with sips from a flask of his mum's broth. Looking westwards across the dreary Cheshire plain he could just make out Chester's cathedral tower and, more alluringly, the Welsh hills beyond. He was in reflective mode.

Strewth! The Seventies already! What'd they bring? And what'd they be dubbed? They'd just lived through the 'Swinging Sixties' according to the tabloids. Jay couldn't see it. The permissive society had passed him by. Well maybe not completely: he'd had his share. But not without downsides. His first love, Caroline had initiated him but then when he'd departed for Durham she'd transferred her affections. They'd kept in touch, mind. She'd even been the guest of honour at his twenty-first but any aspirations he'd had of rekindling the flame had been rapidly extinguished. They were, and hopefully would remain, good friends.

He'd spent the next term at Durham moping after Caroline; then, after his big brother had been killed he didn't have much time for anyone. In the final year, he'd got pretty pally with Julia. But she was engaged and twenty-three so he was never really on there. Sweet though, and dead bright!

There'd been the occasional, drunken one-night stand; and then he'd met Jill. It probably wasn't the most auspicious encounter and the fact that she was going out with one of his best mates didn't augur well. But although she'd seesawed between them for several months her move down to Chester seemed to have settled matters. Until recently when their sex-life had run into the sand, propelled by his crass behaviour, admittedly. And now her flat in Handbridge was more like a foreign country to which he no longer had a visa.

They'd missed out on the Christmas party but had met up for a New Year drink in the Bridge. Not a watering hole he frequented, Jay had felt very much on the defensive and when she didn't invite him back afterwards he'd been seriously deflated. The new regime was reinforced when he asked her for a key.

'No, sorry love, not this time.'

'Why not, you were okay about it before?'

'This is different.'

'Why?'

''Cause it's not just any old flat I'm renting. It's Bronwen's and I said I'd look after it. And that means *me*, not *we*!'

Jay was gobsmacked. He was sure there was a flaw in her logic but doubted it would matter. She'd made her mind up and he wasn't going to change it. Stuff a stoat! He'd never seen her like this before: it was like a declaration of independence!

Initially he wasn't over concerned. He was the dominant one and sooner or later she'd come round. But when the festive season had come and gone and he'd still not stayed overnight in Handbridge, Jay was thoroughly addled. The key seemed to be to resume their physical relationship; but how to persuade her? It wasn't the sort of thing you could ask your parents: his mother would have a field day, whilst his dad would just be embarrassed. Once upon a time he'd have asked his big brother, but although he still spoke with him often in his head, it wasn't something he'd broached. His only corporeal friends were miles away: Malcolm in Lancashire, Pard in the north east, Tom Hood in Norfolk. He'd largely lost touch with Tom, and wasn't sure he could trust Pard, who seemed for some reason to be envious of Jill. That left Malc. He was his best mate by a street, but Jay didn't think his expertise ran to agony aunt stuff.

For once even Autolycus was no help. A reliable Touchstone in matters intellectual, when it came to affairs of the heart he had nowt to vouchsafe. And as for Hamlet, he was clearly a non-starter: if he couldn't cope with Ophelia he was hardly going to explain a much-feistier Rosalind, whose muse Jill seemed increasingly to espouse. He was just going to have to work it out for himself.

Not exactly in Don Giovanni's league! The closest he'd come symbolically to the permissive society was a shopping spree to Carnaby Street. The floral shirts he'd purchased with such panache – well it was late afternoon and he'd been in the Admiral Duncan since opening time – still graced their plastic hangers. They'd be all right for beachwear; if he ever found himself on a beach. Still, if youth was wasted on the young (I wish I'd said that, Oscar!) sex was undoubtedly overrated. Particularly if you weren't getting any!

There were more important things, after all, and as the new decade dawned the main one was work. The promotion had gone well, especially financially. Coupled with his annual increment it'd put Jay on nearly £1,000 a year and had enabled him to negotiate a part-share in his mum's new car. It was a little cracker: a brand new, bright red Mini with an easily logged registration plate of RUJ 505H! He'd persuaded his mum in the interests of safety that they should fit a couple of fog-lamps, which looked dead sporty, and a huge reversing light fitted to the boot. It was great when you'd burned someone off: compounding your superiority with a flash or two!

The Christmas play had gone well. They'd moved up-market with *The Yeoman of the Guard* and Jay's penchant for Gilbert & Sullivan had given the production his own imprimatur. Feedback had suggested that some of their audiences had preferred the previous year's *My Fair Lady*, but what did they know? It was a matter of education: their business, surely? Anyway, the head was happy, and that was Jay's main concern; he'd delivered on the first of his promotion promises already.

The second was trickier, and more strategic. Picking up the info from his dad he was prone to toss the acronym ROSLA (the raising of the school leaving age) around the staffroom. He was pretty sure some of his colleagues didn't know what it stood for, let alone have plans for implementing it. Well, they bloody well should. It had been announced way back in '64, and was looming large. With his dad's expertise in outdoor education – a concept he'd invented nationally, fusing rugger-bugger outdoor pursuits with academic field studies – came equipment. Jay was frequently asked to, 'Just test this for me, son,' and handed the latest Vango tent or spanking new Viking No.4 climbing rope. It wasn't yet enough to kit out a whole year facility but it helped persuade Jenkins. Just handling the equipment gave the head a feel for Jay's enthusiasm. When the budget allocation became available that summer, Jay would be at the front of the queue.

Then there was the new sports hall, which Autolycus the Opportunist was quick to exploit. Bill Molyneux, as Woodbridge's long-serving and highly respected head of PE, was consulted extensively about the design. Taking advantage of their Thursday night camaraderie, Jay mentioned the possibility of a climbing wall, persuading his senior colleague that if you incorporated it into the initial plans it was a really cost-effective investment. By the time they had the climbing equipment, they'd have somewhere to use it; although unbeknown to anyone apart from his dad, Jay's climbing ambitions were far wider than the sports hall. And with the arrival of a new female games teacher he recognised the possibility of involving girls as well as boys.

He wasn't sure if girls could actually climb: were they strong enough? But Jill had given it a go during their three musketeers phase, when they'd cram happily onto the bench seat of Ed's Cortina and tear around Northumberland with him on his client-round. The outings were fun but a source of jealousy, too; not an emotion Jay was used to experiencing. The roads were narrow and winding. Ed drove fast. A rash right-hander would find Jill's thigh pressed firmly against his own with Jay fantasising briefly about how she was going to make out with him later. Then a lurching-left would throw her against Ed, where she'd remain longer than seemed necessary. It was frustrating.

Ed was due to make several calls in Hexham. Jill was off duty and fancied a look at the Abbey. However, before she and Jay could start exploring, Ed was back.

'Two calls cancelled. I'm done here. Fancy slipping out to Crag Lough?'

'How about a pint at the Twice Brewed first?' suggested Jay.

'And maybe a sandwich or something?' prompted Jill.

Three rounds later they turned off the Military Road and headed up to High Shield Crag.

'To give it its Sunday name!' joked Ed. 'It's part of Hadrian's Wall' he added, for Jill's benefit.

They parked up and retrieved the gear from the boot. Ed jettisoned his rep's uniform and they both changed into jeans, draping their rocks-shoes round their necks. Jill was already in jeans, though they were a trifle snug for climbing. They strolled along to the wide gully, which split the first section of the dolerite sill.

'That's the Appian Way. There's a few easy routes to choose from. Just to get you started.'

After an easy romp up a Diff called Fifth Avenue, which Jill accomplished with poise, they scrambled along towards Raven's Tower. Ed paused beneath Hadrian's Buttress.

'The Chimney's Severe, mate. D'you wanna lead?'

Their Northumbrian Mountaineering Club guide described the route as 'Strenuous' but scanning it Jay reckoned he could overcome the steep groove and show off his skills simultaneously.

'Sure!' he said confidently, without thinking a thrutchy chimney might not be the best route for Jill. He revelled in the steep rock with its small but positive holds, pausing briefly to place a stonking runner underneath the chockstone. Then, feeling securely protected, he swung cockily into the chimney proper. It went easily.

'Piece of cake!' he crowed.

Jill was roped between them for maximum security; Jay would ensure her safety from above, with a tight rope if she got into difficulties, whilst Ed would point out the holds from below dispensing encouragement as required. The theory worked well until Jill moved into the chimney where she got stuck. There wasn't much Jay could do to help – hauling her up like a sack of potatoes risked jamming her in more tightly – and advice from below was superfluous. Ed soloed up to help her. It seemed to take some time to free her and, although Jay hadn't an uninterrupted view from his eerie, he suspected Ed was making a meal of it. Bloody hell: his hands were all over Jill's bum and, far from complaining she appeared to be enjoying it. By the time he'd freed her and she'd conquered the chimney she'd emerged panting and pink. And not just from exertion, thought Jay uncharitably.

Still, she'd proved she could climb…

So, including girls must be a possibility. Give Miss Grayling a fortnight to settle in and he'd engineer some excuse to sound her out. Not that he viewed the project with anything other than opportunist professionalism: she was as plain as a pikestaff. Although, dawdling past the gym Jay did note that she had a cracking figure, accentuated by the sports-top and short gymslip she espoused. Hmm, maybe not such an unattractive prospect, after all.

His chance came one weekend. Unlike weekdays when the swimming pool was fully booked with classes, Saturday mornings were reserved for staff use. Normally it was popular and fairly disciplined, training in lanes, that sort of thing. Bill and the other blokes had just left and Jay was ploughing up and down his forty lengths' breast-stroke when he realised Miss Grayling – Linda – was about to join him. Abandoning his schedule, he broke into a swift crawl, emerging at the foot of the steps just as she was entering. She was wearing a pale blue, cotton bikini and he couldn't help noticing the effect of the cool water on her nipples. She submerged herself beside him before heading off down the adjacent lane.

The next Saturday, Jay ensured he was still in the pool at eleven-thirty. Once again, the others had left for their marital chores and he and

Linda had the place to themselves. She didn't seem averse to his proximity, however, and he was beginning to harbour visions of helping her out of her bikini when she challenged him.

'Come on, Finch: I'll race you!' and dipping under the lane rope set off without warning for the far end. Caught unawares Jay was several yards in arrears when Linda tumble-turned for the back length. He set off in pursuit, employing his no-breaths crawl technique, which he couldn't keep up for long. Fortunately it turned out to be only a fifty-yard contest though he still failed to overhaul her before they regained their starting point. Dipping under the rope he emerged laughing and spluttering. He pretended to stumble into her arms and tried to embrace her.

She was still gulping for air: 'Why Mr Fincher, I hope you're not trying to take advantage!'

'Why, Miss Grayling: whaddya *you* think?'

'I think…time's up,' she smiled gesturing over Jay's shoulder to where the pool attendant was signalling midday. 'For now…'

Still, it was progress and, in the absence of any present encouragement from Jill, must be counted a nod towards the 'Sexy Seventies'! Maybe, at the end of a rope… Jay would dangle his outdoor education plans before the plain but curvaceous Miss Grayling. Meanwhile, his putative girlfriend's behaviour continued to perplex him. They'd never got round to exchanging eternal love-vows, although she'd been more than affectionate in her letters. Now they appeared farther away than ever: friendly enough but in a polite, almost reserved way. Was she going out with someone else?

Twenty-Three

New Year shindigs were notorious at the Royal: even Bronwen endorsed Jay's caution. Well Jill had been wary. And all had gone smoothly: a little drink and dancing but nothing untoward, until the orthopaedic consultant had called by. Jill's attitude towards Mr K had burgeoned from fear to respect to a deep desire for his good opinion. Latterly, her attitude had morphed into an adolescent crush; the slightest expression of praise from him was enough to make her blush. Bron's confidence that he'd endorsed matron's good opinion of her was thrilling. Not that she'd ever let her feelings show; whilst Mr K remained courteous but distant.

This evening, however, he seemed full of bonhomie, though still officially on his white-coated rounds. Anyone not actually on duty had changed, albeit in a hurry. Odd combinations of casual wear and nurses' uniforms abounded. Their boss was so relaxed that the informality didn't seem to matter, and if he'd still got work to do it certainly wasn't interfering with the social whirl. He chatted to all and sundry, sipping from a large glass of Chablis. Maybe this wasn't the first party he'd dropped in on.

Then, after twenty minutes or so he was on his way, scattering good-will and New Year kisses. Fearing he was going without a farewell to her, Jill gave him a friendly wave. He turned, strode over to her and, slipping a discreet hand under her elbow, ushered her into the side ward.

'A quick word, Staff.'

She was mildly surprised when he didn't remove his hand but assumed that she too was in line for a polite festive kiss. Well, she'd better be, she thought indignantly. If others' undeserving cheeks had received a brush, the least she should merit would be a peck! Once in the side ward, however, the boss encircled her slim waist and drew her towards him.

'Sorry, Staff…and an especially Happy New Year to you!' He planted his lips firmly on hers. Jill, needing to put her arms somewhere, reached up and entwined them around his neck. When they uncoupled, she swallowed hard to regain her composure.

'Compliments of the season to you, too, Mr K!'

'Oh, and Staff, if you have time perhaps you'd leave your report in my office on your way out. Only if it's convenient that is…'

Then he was gone, leaving Jill in disarray.

Back on the ward the party was in full swing and no one appeared to have missed her. Thank God! It was one thing having a swift goodnight clinch with a houseman or two, quite another to be caught snogging the senior consultant! She poured herself a large glass of plonk. The report could wait: she wouldn't be calling into Mr K's office. Several more glasses and the inevitable goodnight cuddles and Staff Walker was relaxed but ready for home. She was just passing the staff lounge on her way out when Dr Wilson, the houseman whose antics at the Nurses' Ball had almost landed them both in trouble, spotted her.

'Hello, Staff, was hoping I'd bump into you.'

'Why Dr Wilson! How nice to see you!'

'Time to pop in for a celebratory drink?' he inveigled, clutching her arm and manoeuvring her into the lounge. It was heaving and extremely noisy. He mouthed something, which could've been an invitation to dance, and when Jill didn't demur she found herself clutched tightly round the waist. One waltz followed another and the young houseman grew increasingly amorous. He didn't try to kiss her, just pressed himself hard against her. *Hard* being the operative word! What was it about men and dancing? Ever since her first encounter as a kid at the Catholic Club when she was lined up by her friend Gina to dance with 'Hardun' Dodd, Jill seemed to encounter erections whenever a dance entailed contact. It wasn't so much flattering as tiresome. Except when she was stottin, and then it had a tendency to get her turned on. Her ardent medic was grasping her ever closer; quite brazenly impaling her as they rotated tipsily amongst the crowd. Fortunately, before Jill could get carried away the music petered out. She made her apologies and high-tailed it.

Time for home. Straight home, too. No reporting to Mr K.

But inexplicably, there she was, report in hand. She paused briefly, took a deep breath, and tapped gently on the office door. It opened swiftly and there stood Mr K still in his long white coat but with a balloon glass half full of dark ruby wine.

'Ah, your report, Staff,' he smiled. 'Do bring it in; and, now you're here, you'll take a nightcap before dashing off, eh?'

Jill hesitated. Caution and the Jay-on-her-shoulder said, No way! But drink and the devil spoke louder.

'Thank you Mr K, that'd be nice,' she smiled, looking for somewhere to sit. A plush red captain's chair or a too-cosy-looking sofa? She opted for perching on the edge of the large, leather-bound desk and glanced round. It was more like an apartment than an office, with a luxuriously thick cream carpet and an even thicker-pile Persian rug by the desk. The lighting was subdued and the walls adorned with paintings, two of which she recognised from a visit to a Grasmere studio with Jay, as Heaton Coopers. Mr K seemed a tad more reserved than he had been earlier. He poured Jill a generous measure of the claret and settled himself before holding her gaze momentarily.

'Cheers! Thank you so much for coming, Staff, I was really hoping you would. I've been monitoring your progress carefully. Your attitude and application are admirable. Plus, you may be surprised to learn, it was a proud moment for me when you became the highest-achieving staff nurse this hospital group has ever recorded!'

'Thank you, Mr K, I had no idea...'

'You have a great career ahead of you in nursing; I think you'll find the New Year brings your own ward.'

Reckoning she wasn't supposed to know, Jill stammered: 'Wha... what? You mean I'll be a Sister?'

'Yes, Staff. You're exceptionally talented. You could go to the very top, and I don't just mean in this group of hospitals, or even this region, I mean nationally. With the right support and guidance, of course. You're also, if you don't mind my saying so, a beautiful young woman. You remind me of my daughter...'

Everyone knew the story. The boss's wife and only daughter had been killed in a car crash some years earlier and, ever since, he'd apparently had no time for relationships other than professional ones. She felt highly flattered by his solicitude; should she afford him some indication that the feeling was mutual? But she didn't know what to say or do, other than give him a warm smile and mutter some banality about being extremely touched. Her boss's thoughts were on loftier matters, however.

'Here, let me top you up and then I'll tell you what's on my mind.' He refilled their glasses. The claret was delicious, much better than anything Jill had tasted before. This time he settled back in his captain's chair, a discreet distance away from her, before proceeding quietly and at considerable length to adumbrate his proposal.

After a while Jill found she was feeling distinctly light-headed and her attention was drifting. Nevertheless, she got the gist, which was basically his patronage, no strings attached. He'd clearly taken to her and was anxious to promote her career; he was an influential figure in the medical world and was doubtless perfectly capable of delivering what he was advocating. All he asked for in return was absolute discretion – she should tell *no one* of their arrangement – and the satisfaction of seeing talent rise to the top. A long pause ensued as they quaffed their wine, and Jill realised her would-be mentor was waiting for some sort of response.

'Goodness, Mr K, I don't know what to say,' she started lamely. 'I'm very flattered by what you're suggesting. You've no idea how much I've learned from you and how much I admire you and your work.' (Oh, God, this was coming out all wrong; it sounded so wooden and polite, when what Jill was feeling was soaring exhilaration.) She took a deep draft of her wine and started again.

'What I mean is, Boss, I'd absolutely love to take up your offer; no one else would know and I'd do whatever you wanted in return. Anything.' she concluded breathlessly, a deep blush suffusing her face and neck.

Her host smiled warmly and for the first time she detected real affection in his expression.

'That's wonderful, my dear, I think we understand each other. Now I really must let you go. I shall be in touch in the New Year – indeed, in the new decade! I'm sure it will prove momentous…'

Twenty-Four

'So what do you think, Miss Grayling?'

They were huddled in a quiet corner of the staffroom where Jay had been outlining his plans for introducing outdoor pursuits for future ROSLA cohorts. It was quite disconcerting when everyone else wore formal teaching garb to be addressing someone in a tight, low-cut tee shirt and body-hugging tracksuit bottoms. Jay was poor at disguising his fixation and more than once Linda caught him out.

'I think you need to pay more attention to what I'm saying and less to gawping!' she murmured, not unkindly. 'Seriously though? I think it's a great idea especially for the less academic. They're already bored with conventional PE and games long before the fourth year. God knows what they'd make of having to endure 'em for another year! What does Bill think?'

'Same as you; he's all in favour.'

'And Jenkins? We're gonna need extra equipment. Where's the funding coming from?'

'Ah, that's the best bit. I happen to know that the DES are making huge one-off grants to LEAs. And the Authority'll channel the funds to schools with the best-prepared plans. Ours'll be one of them, for sure.'

'You seem to have it all worked out.'

'Only the boys' activities. I'll need your help with the girls.'

'Fair enough. Obviously makes the case stronger.'

'So you'll help me? We can work together?'

'Deffers!' She caught his gaze wandering again: 'Why don't we discuss it further on Saturday? Not here, though. Bill's got an away fixture: the PE office'll be free.'

'Brilliant! What time?'

'Eleven? I'll have the coffee on.'

(And not too much else, he fantasised fleetingly.) 'Great! See you then.'

It was only afterwards that he remembered he was supposed to be taking Jill out for the day. It was the first weekend she'd had free for ages. Bugger! No woman for weeks and suddenly he'd got two! Well...in a manner of speaking. Still, it was three days away: something'd turn up. But by Friday, nothing had. He was just about to put Linda off but decided to call Jill first.

'Oh, I'm glad you 'phoned. About tomorrow.' She sounded a bit tentative, as if she half expected him to change his mind. Fat chance!

'Yeah, great. My parents are away so I've got the Mini for the weekend. Where'd you like to go?'

'Well that's it. I can't I'm afraid.'

'But we've had it planned for ages. I thought you wanted to?'

'I do. Course I do!'

'So what's up?'

'I've gotta go on a course. Um...administration.'

'Oh. Well what time's it finish? I could pick you up afterwards. We could go out for dinner. Or if you're tired we could just come back here,' he suggested hopefully.

'Love to, pet, but it lasts the whole weekend. In Manchester,' she added faintly.

'Manchester! Why on earth d'you have to go there?'

'It's a regional programme, for new sisters from all over the North West. There'll be some top people on it,' she added hurriedly.

Jay sounded genuinely deflated: 'Oh well, if it's that important I guess you've gotta go. No, I mean course you have. When will I see you then?'

'Not sure. I'm working next weekend. I'll give you a bell.'

And the conversation fizzled out. Jay puckered self-critically: he'd hoped summat would turn up! Well it had, so it was no use moaning. Oh well! Maybe he'd take up Miss Grayling's offer after all... Mind's eye racing, Jay pictured the scene. He'd enter the PE office to find her perched on the treatment bench, with her skimpiest tee shirt struggling to hide her beguiling boobs and a ridiculously miniscule gymslip on. She'd smile invitingly and, crossing her legs, give him a tantalising glimpse of bright red knickers. The project would assume its appropriate priority...

Jay shook his head. Was it such a good idea, after all? He was well aware of his propensity for getting into scrapes. So far it'd been just good-natured banter with the homely but voluptuous Miss Grayling, but he knew if she gave him the least encouragement he'd be sorely tempted. He'd no idea what the PE office was like but it'd surely be private enough for more than a tactical discussion on outdoor pursuits! He wasn't worried about Linda; she'd never mentioned a boyfriend and lived with her mum and dad in Tarporley. If she was as amenable as he hoped, that was her business, no one else's. But he'd never gone behind Jill's back before. Well, nothing serious anyway: just flirting with Bren at the Bull & Stirrup. All the lads did that; when Jill sussed she just laughed it off. She certainly wasn't one to be straight-laced. Besides what about her and Dr Thingy? The one she'd gone to the Nurses' Ball with? Bet that didn't end with a peck-on-the-cheek goodnight! And what about Ed? She might not be seeing him anymore but when the three of them'd knocked around together she'd been screwing 'em both for months! Sod it! He'd keep his appointment and see what transpired.

Right or wrong, once he'd decided Jay rarely wavered. Saturday found him stalking down the long, main corridor towards the gym. He didn't actually know where the office was and, loath to blunder into somewhere verboten, he padded cautiously through the changing rooms. A distant radio piped out light music so he followed the sound and there it was: 'Head of PE. W Molyneux.' He knocked and receiving no response hesitated, half expecting to encounter Bill. Linda had said he was away in Malpas with the first team, but supposing she was wrong or the fixture had been changed? He'd better have some plausible excuse.

He knocked again and a female voice answered: 'Come in.'

Miss Grayling sat demurely in the office chair, wearing a dark blue, two-piece tracksuit zipped up to her neck. Jay stifled his disappointment with difficulty.

'You look like you lost a pound and found a penny, Finch! What's up?'

'Er...um...nothing... Nothing, I'm fine.'

'Okay. How d'you like your coffee?'

'Er...strong and black, thanks. Two sugars.'

Linda clicked the kettle back on and in the time it took to boil she'd unearthed two, non-matching mugs and doled out the sugar from the Tate & Lyle packet. She took hers black and straight and proffered Jay his.

'So...what've you got in mind?'

(Christ! thought Jay if I tell you that you'll throw me out for sure!)

'Er...well...we're gonna need allies: we can't run a full programme of outdoor pursuits for all the fifth years on our own. I mean think of the PTRs for one thing. They're gonna have to be generous, especially for rock climbing.'

'Yeah, and sailing. It can be fairly hazardous too, y'know.'

'S'pose so,' conceded Jay, who hadn't really thought much beyond his own forte.

'Well, I can help there, if you want me to… And with canoeing. I took courses in both at college.'

'Oh, brill! Didn't know. And Peter Jackson's a keen orienteer. I'm sure he'd help. Bill an all of course: nice of him to loan out his office by the way! I think he's persuaded to incorporate a climbing wall in the new sports hall.'

'Yeah, he told me. Said it'd help reassure the sceptics! Y'know, safety first and all that.'

'Course, but the wall'd be just for starters. Later we'd get out to the limestone crags at World's End and the sandstone walls at Helsby and Frodsham.

'Brilliant! It'll give me an entrée!'

'How d'you mean?'

'Well we PE types can read and write you know! My second subject is geography, specialising in geology. It'll strengthen my case for broadening the classroom curriculum.' She paused glancing at him anxiously, not expecting from previous reactions, that he'd understand.

'Got you! Terms like carboniferous limestone and old red sandstone would come to life if the kids had experienced them for real. Handled the rocks, felt the difference.'

'Precisely! Though if you want to be pernickety that old red sandstone is micaceous, cross and flat-bedded sandstone of fluvial and Aeolian facies! Anyway, how's an English teacher knows anything about geology?'

Jay grinned sheepishly: 'It's my parents: they're geographers. Fact that's how they met: both in the first geography school at Birmingham apparently, way back in the thirties. 'spect there's a plaque on the university clock tower!'

'So how come you didn't follow in their cartographic boots?'

'Could've done. Got accepted at Leeds, and Birmingham but I was only sixteen so it seemed like a good idea to try for Cambridge.'

'And…?'

'Failed to get a scholarship and ended up as a farm labourer for the rest of the year! Reckon I learned more then than the whole time at Durham!'

Linda looked as if she might be impressed. Jay couldn't tell.

'Anyway you get my point about the curriculum?'

'Absolutely! I made the same case to Jenkins and Bewcastle about English. Said it'd be *Shakespeare on the Rocks*!'

Linda laughed appreciatively, 'There's just one problem, though…'

'What's that?'

'I can't climb! You'll have to teach me first!'

'No problemo! Soon as you're ready and we've both got a free weekend I'll take you to Frodsham.'

Linda had become quite flushed during this exchange and Jay's overactive imagination had him helping her cool down. It was pretty hot in the small office; perhaps if she removed... It was only then that he clocked the way her tracksuit suggested the curves of her limbs; she might have nothing on underneath! But he hadn't the nerve to ask her and she certainly didn't let on. The moment passed.

Back home, alone, Jay was relaxing in his dad's study. He mused on recent events. Story of my life, he grinned, pouring himself another glass of his father's eminently quaffable Château Lynch Bages. The old man certainly knew how to organise himself. In addition to the small wine rack a bookcase at right angles to the desk housed his latest toy, a Garrard open-reel tape recorder that currently featured the mellifluous strings of the *Introduction & Allegro*. Gradually superseding Beethoven, many of whose sonatas Jay could still play, Elgar was a favourite composer. He'd never forgotten attending the *Last Night of the Proms*. Chris had been in full-dress uniform, which had secured them a spec right next to the platform. Relatively subdued in the first half of the concert, they'd later belted out all the popular tunes majoring, *naturellement*, on *Rule Britannia* and *Land of Hope and Glory*! And afterwards they'd ended up at Ronnie Scott's, gloriously drunk and still singing at three in the morning! What a night!

The *Introduction* had soared to the summit of the Malverns and his eyes pricked with tears as nostalgia overtook him. He leaned forward to reposition his brother's photograph and studied the handsome naval officer, his eyes fixed steadfastly on the viewer, right hand clutching his hat, epaulettes shining proudly. He raised his glass deferentially.

'Cheers, big brother! You'd have known how to play this one...but I'm fucked if I do!'

Twenty-Five

It was dead on two o'clock when Jill opened the door of her flat (Mr K had stressed punctuality) and there it stood in her modest Handbridge street. An Aston Martin. It was deep blue, with two doors and four seats, though you'd best be titchy if you sat in the back. It looked brand new. Jill knew that nowadays you could tell by the number plate but this one wasn't much help: *AWK 1*, it read. Mr K materialised beside her and the boot seemed to open automatically, revealing a burgundy valise. She silently thanked Aunt Louisa: her own grip didn't look out of place at all.

Jill had loads she wanted to ask but Mr K seemed preoccupied so she settled down to enjoy the drive. They were quickly out of Chester, heading through a string of small villages – Tarvin, Kelsall, Sandiway – before they crossed over the M6 and reached the prosperous suburb of Altrincham. A while later they were pulling up outside Manchester's Midland Hotel and a uniformed porter was offering to park the Aston. Jill assumed they'd be stopping at the hotel (separate rooms, of course) and wondered why their bags weren't being extracted from the magic boot. Before she could ask, however, Mr K was guiding her into the lobby where a large billboard listed amongst other events: *North West Regional Hospital Board Opening Session & Reception.* They checked in at a lace-covered table to collect their name-badges. Jill was tickled pink. Although the badge itself was a tacky plastic affair it had inscribed, in copperplate, blue writing: *Sister Jill Walker.* Much more impressive however, was Mr K's which read *Professor Sir Anton Keiter.* Jesus! She didn't even know he was a professor, let alone a sir! Kept that pretty quiet! Still 'Anton' was nice. Suited him.

Jill feared a lecture theatre, but the ballroom wasn't organised like that. There were twenty or so round tables, each encircled by chairs in such a way that everyone could see the low dais at the front, with its table, four armchairs and a lectern. The audience-tables were covered in maroon velvet and had bottles of water and glasses clustered in the middle. Before each seat lay a foolscap pad and pencil. It looked very smart, very professional.

Jill was impressed, but apprehensive, more so when they were ushered to a table marked *Reserved*. Oh God, right next to the stage; what if she was expected to ask a question?

The platform party comprised a fusty-looking man in his sixties and a younger, altogether more vibrant woman whose smart uniform resembled that of a matron with fancy shoulder-decorations. Jill's hopes rose when it became apparent that the man, who announced himself pompously as the president of the regional hospital board, was only to chair the meeting. Hopefully, the striking matron-type whom President Pomp introduced as the chief nursing officer for the North West would be less stuffy.

Dame Dorothy Bowles regaled them with stories of her training in post-war London and her rise through the nursing ranks in the fifties and sixties. She wasn't in the least bit self-important, considering her job; maybe that was a reflexion of her relative youth: she couldn't be much over forty. Moreover, she was using her own experiences to illustrate the opportunities available to an ambitious young nurse. Her speech was entitled *Sisterhood & Supervision*, which might sound boring, but proved a real eye-opener.

As the applause died down a re-arrangement of the platform party ensued: President Pomp and Dame Dorothy moving to the outside of the row of chairs, leaving the middle two empty. An expectant buzz coincided with Mr K whispering that he was sorry to desert her, as he rose to meet the entourage that swept down the side of the room. Two of them sat down at Jill's table whilst their boss, presumably, greeted Sir Anton warmly and accompanied him to the dais. Whoever the speaker was, Mr K was clearly in charge of proceedings now.

'Ladies and Gentlemen, it gives me great pleasure to introduce the Secretary of State for Health and Social Services, the Right Honourable Richard Crossman.' Cue tumultuous applause from the star-struck audience. His speech was a bit of a let down. It was mostly about recent developments in the health service only some of which, such as the idea of primary health care, Jill had heard of. There were some in-jokes that soared over her head, although Anton (could she possibly call him that?) seemed to appreciate them. The best bit was about Harold Wilson.

Now Jill *had* heard of him. She remembered her dad's delight when he first became Prime Minister.

'Howay man, Mary,' he'd chided Jill's less-than-enthused mam, 'at least he's a Northerner! Not like them London intellectual pansies!' Although he was less impressed by the PM's support for Huddersfield Town! Her smile of reminiscence happened to coincide with one of the minister's jokes, which the aide sitting next to her promptly misinterpreted.

'I noticed you enjoying the Secretary of State's little joke,' observed the suave young man handing Jill a glass of champagne subsequently. 'I'm Aubrey Semblance, the minister's PPS.'

Jill hadn't a clue what a PPS was and felt distinctly ill at ease. 'Nice to meet you. I'm afraid I'm just a humble sister.'

'But one with a future, I imagine, if you're a friend of Sir Anton's. He and my boss go back a long way. He's extremely influential, you know.'

That was better: Jill was happy to talk about or listen to anything on that subject. Unfortunately, before he could impart words of wisdom or gossip Aubrey was called away.

'His Master's Voice,' he quipped, with the ghost of a wink, 'hope to catch you later.'

Before she could decide whether to be disappointed or relieved Jill spotted Mr K heading towards her with Dame Dorothy on his arm.

'Well, I still say it was very clever of you, Anton. Getting Dick to speak at an event like this was a real coup. Oh...aren't you going to introduce me?' Dame Dorothy concluded, smiling warmly at Jill.

'Dot, this is Jill Walker, one of the brightest young stars in our region's firmament! She's just the sort of person your talk had in mind. Jill, meet Dame Dorothy Bowles.'

'Delighted, my dear: I hope you enjoyed the minister's speech?'

'Enjoyed yours a lot more! It was great! But you're a Dame: and I'm just a sister. And a temporary one at that! D'you really think someone like me could aspire to those heights?'

'Of course! Any case, I wasn't always a Dame. I was brought up in Becontree, in the East End of London. My family were penniless: my dad was a docker, my mum a cleaner. So of course you could! Especially with Anton's support.' And to Jill's relief she released Anton's arm and allowed herself to be whisked away by some other worthy.

Before she could start quizzing her boss, however, the cocktail party syndrome struck again; he was returning a distant wave and murmuring: 'Bound to be a bit hectic, my dear, at least until the ministerial train departs. Let me point you in the direction of Molly Shawcross, and then I'll have to leave you for a while.'

Unlike Dame Dorothy, Molly turned out to be a real matron; and in charge of nursing at a cluster of hospitals in Liverpool. She, too, was a revelation and Jill spent an informative and entertaining ten minutes with her.

She was about to embark on a visit to the States sponsored by a private sector healthcare company. She mentioned the name, but in the hubbub Jill only half-heard it and didn't like to ask again lest she seem ignorant. It sounded dead interesting though, something to do with Virginia. Maybe she could ask Anton?

Finally! He returned, having escorted his ministerial charge to the official car, and announced they were leaving. Jill downed her flute of champagne in one and was swept through the lobby to the cool of the early spring evening. The Aston drew up and they were on their way again. Jill noticed a sign to Piccadilly station. It reminded her of Jay but she shut her eyes, denying him entry. They turned down Oxford Road past a sign to the university. But before they reached it the boss swung the Aston left onto Grosvenor Street. That sounded familiar, but then she recalled there was one in Chester. Still, she knew it had links with the Duke of Westminster so odds were it'd be posh! Mr K pressed a keypad on a column to the driver's side of the entrance and the wrought-iron gates swung slowly open. There were just four numbered parking spaces, all empty; the car came to a halt in the last one. The magic boot sprang open for their suitcases.

They took the lift to the fourth floor and Mr K let them into the apartment. Several rooms led off the central hall. The first, a large lounge, had an enchanting view over the city where the evening lights were just starting to twinkle. Then, an intimate dining room, with a kitchen beyond. Three further doors led to a study, and two bedrooms. Mr K opened the door to one and ushered Jill through, depositing her grip on the queen-size bed as she wandered across to another picture window.

'I hope it's to your taste, my dear, I've done little entertaining these past few years. You're the first person to stop here. But Mrs Brayson is very thorough so I'm sure you'll find everything you need. I've taken the liberty of booking dinner. Eight o'clock. Should give us time for a drink first.'

Slightly overwhelmed, Jill just nodded and her host withdrew.

She unpacked rapidly, first priority being to hang out any creases in her dress. Then she took her toilet bag through to the bathroom. *Her* bathroom! Apart from a toothbrush she needn't have bothered: everything you could possibly need was already there, courtesy, presumably, of Mrs Brayson. There was a separate shower and Jill dispensed abruptly with her business-like trouser suit, luxuriating in the hissing cascade. She'd drunk more champagne than she'd intended and the shock of the sparkling water revived her. She stepped carefully out and retrieved a blue bath sheet of Egyptian cotton, savouring the soft feel of it against her skin. Then she was back in her bedroom locating the bra and knickers she'd chosen earlier to complement the dress.

An eighteenth birthday present from the lit twins: dark blue, sheer silk with a plunging neckline, nipped in at the waist and flared at the skirt. The latter hung a trifle longer than was fashionable but although she'd had no occasion to wear it for a couple of years, Jill was relieved to note it wasn't tight, except at the bust. She knew she looked special in it as both Joyce and Sue had said so.

'You look stunning, my dear. *Jsi krásná!*'

Jill raised an interrogative eyebrow, but he just smiled: 'Tell you over dinner. Champagne?'

'Hmm, please.' Jill noted the bottle, already opened in a traditional ice bucket.

'I think you'll like this: Pol Roger '55. A little better than the Midland's modest, though well-intentioned offer! And, don't worry, I'm not driving!'

No need. Charterhouse was only ten minutes' walk away, although at the rate they'd consumed the champagne Jill fancied it might seem further on the way back. It was old-fashioned and discreet although her boss seemed to be well known judging by the fuss the *patron* made. Both the starters and the main course arrived so promptly and were so delicious that they ate in silence until the coffee was poured. A bottle of apparently unordered Hine XO materialised and her host, having enquired considerately whether Jill minded, proceeded to clip, then light up a Romeo y Julieta.

'So tell me about these lit twins. Judging by the dress they must think a great deal of you. How long have you known them?'

'Oh, forever…well it seems like it. Joyce was my infant teacher and I met Sue a bit later at the library. They've taught me so much: far more than I learned at school. They encouraged me to become a nurse and, well…they've just always been there for me.'

'And are you still in touch with them?'

'Oh yes, just before Christmas. Sue was down for a job with Salop County Council, assistant county librarian, I think. She got it, too; and now Joyce has applied for a headship in Shrewsbury. So hopefully they'll both move down and we can all see a lot more of each other again.'

'And which one are you in love with?' gimleted her host.

Anyone else, Jill would've told to mind their own business but coming from…what the hell was she supposed to call him now?

'Before I tell you – and I'm not trying to prevaricate – please boss/ Mr K/Professor/Sir Anton. What on earth do I call you these days?'

'Anton will be fine, *láska*. That's Czech for 'love', by the way.'

'Okay. Well since you ask…er…Anton, both of them really. In different ways. Joyce is going to get the two of us on a degree course, with the University of the Air. I expect you've heard of it.'

'Indeed I have: what're you going to read?'

'English. It's always been an interest. Especially Shakespeare. Have you read *As You Like It*? It's my favourite.'

'Really! Rosalind's one of Shakespeare's finest heroines. Which twin put you onto her?'

'Well Joyce, but it was Sue's copy. And, yes you're right: she's the one I'm in love with!' Anton said nothing, just smiled understandingly so Jill felt compelled to add, almost defensively: 'Doesn't mean I don't fancy men. Well some of them, anyway… I'm choosy!'

'*I can love both fair and brown*…eh? Nothing wrong with that. And if you haven't read any Donne, try him. Before he came over all devout he was engagingly licentious!'

On which lighter-hearted note the conversation and the dinner concluded. Anton wrapped his arm around her waist as they strolled back, but as much to keep the evening chill at bay as to presume on their earlier discourse. Back at the flat he made no attempt to kiss her. But he did gaze at her intently at her bedroom door.

'*Jsi krásná*…you're beautiful, Jill. *Dobrou noc!*'

Twenty-Six

'So our standard comprehensions aren't your cup of tea?'

Tess Bailey was giving little away. Even though he'd known her for eighteen months she remained an enigma. She seemed impervious to his charms; or at least his brand of intellectual flattery. He soon realised he was better read than her but she was Head of English, and therefore his immediate boss, so he had to refrain from indulging his more coruscating proclivities! He couldn't tell yet whether he'd been summoned for a discussion or a bollocking. He played for time.

'Sorry, not with you. I'm not in the proverbial, am I?'

'No, not at all. Just want to hear first-hand what you've been up to with our less-able pupils.'

Jay was partially reassured by the clue, 'Oh who's been talking?'

'Brothers and sisters, Jay: they do you know! Some of my top-stream have been complaining that they're stuck with the text book whilst their less-gifted siblings seem to pick and choose!'

'Oh…is that all?' Jay relaxed, confident he could justify his departure from convention. Better be able to, cause I'm not about to revert to the norm, he thought. 'I brought in some back copies of *Reader's Digest* and left 'em on the side when I had comprehension with 4T2 and 4C2. One of the brighter sparks picked one up and came to me afterwards. Showed me a story about an airman falling 18,000 feet without a parachute and surviving. Reckoned it was pretty interesting. Got me thinking, so I brought in a load more mags and asked both classes to spend a whole period browsing through them in groups of four and marking any that looked okay. Finished up with about forty articles.'

'And then?'

'I cut 'em all out, cadged a load of thin card off Peter Jackson and stapled each article to make a folder. Then I drafted questions designed to test their comprehension of what they'd read. But open questions, so they could use their imaginations a bit; not the usual barristers' closed-jobs whose predictable answers bore the pants off 'em. Come the end of the year I'm gonna calculate the average percentage score and compare it with the traditional textbook comps they all loved so much. If increased enthusiasm so far is anything to go by they'll be a lot higher.'

'Hmm...interesting. Hope you're right. Won't the open questions invite responses that entail a subjective approach to marking though?'

'Maybe, to a degree; but it's a small price to pay for creativity!'

'Well, it's certainly a novel approach. Mind if I mention it to Geoff Thornbury; he's coming in next Monday.'

Jay shrugged: 'I don't mind, 'specially if I knew who Geoff Thornbury was.'

'Oh, sorry: he's the county's senior English adviser. I'll introduce you if there's an opportunity. But just in case there's not...let me have a sample of the most popular ones for him to peruse.'

Mr Thornbury's schedule proved too tight to incorporate a meeting with Jay, but a fortnight or so later he was invited to a meeting of heads of English at Tarporley Teachers' Centre: *To discuss the county's response to new and controversial developments around CSE Mode 3.* Jay hadn't a clue what that was but he was thrilled to get the summons. And if Tess Bailey was miffed she didn't show it.

Meanwhile his bibulous colloquy with his big brother had failed to resolve his amatory dilemma, although he had at least crystallised it. He wanted to be with Jill; insofar as he was capable of loving anyone after his brother's death, it was her. But he fancied Linda as well. So then again... maybe he hadn't! Perhaps he could find a way of discussing it with the old man...

'The thing is, son, it's all the rage in London.'

It was half term and they'd met at Jay's suggestion. The Pied Bull wasn't far from his dad's office and they'd just started doing pies: cheese and onion, and steak and kidney. Claimed to be the first in Chester. Jay'd offered to buy lunch.

'What's all the rage...pies? I thought you went to Tiddy Dolls?'

'I do in the evening but it's more of an eating house. Very cosy and welcoming, not at all your average Mayfair ambience. No, I meant the pubs. There were three of four within walking distance of Curzon Street; they all did proper lunches – shepherd's pie, bangers and mash, chicken in the basket, that sort of thing. Been doing it for years: it's just that the provinces are starting to catch up at last. Anyway, Cheers!'

'Cheers, glad you approve. Er... I wondered if I could pick your brains?'

'Fire away, son.'

'Well…I've been invited to a meeting in a few weeks' time. It's sup-posed to be for heads of English so I'm not quite sure why it's me not Tess.'

'Sounds promising: what's it about?'

'Well I don't really know! That's why I wanted to quiz you. It's summat to do with *CSE Mode 3*?'

His dad laughed, 'Oh, don't worry about that. I can give you plenty of background. You know about CSE, yeah?'

'Not much, I haven't taught any exam classes yet. It's an alternative to GCE, isn't it?'

'Yes: stands for *Certificate of Secondary Education*. Thing is, the more egalitarian minds at the Ministry twigged that GCEs might be okay for academic kids but once ROSLA loomed we were going to need something different for the conscripted!'

'So are they just watered down 'O' Levels?'

'I should hope not! I helped develop the geography model via the *Secondary Schools Examinations Council*. We were trying to be a bit more creative than that!'

Jay's ears pricked up; he liked the sound of creativity! 'Sorry! So the actual exam's more imaginative, not just the syllabus?'

'Exactly! Best example is the one you're talking about: Mode 3. Once you explode the myth that everyone has to be assessed externally by anonymous examiners against abstract criteria you're in business. Teacher assessment and coursework are much more exciting alternatives! I mean… who knows your kids best? You or some examiner at the AEB?'

'Yeah, I get all that but what about Tess Bailey's query on subjectivity? Won't teacher assessment lead to charges of bias?'

'Not if you incorporate a reliable system of moderation.'

'Okay, so how d'you do that?'

'That, I imagine, is what your meeting'll tackle!'

'Brilliant! Fancy another Guinness?'

Jay spent the rest of half term trawling through HMSO bulletins. He started, with uncharacteristic logic, at No.1 on the CSE itself. By the Wednesday he'd progressed to No.3 on techniques of examining. By lunchtime he'd developed a seriously jaded headache; why on earth was he struggling to master the Spearman-Brown and Kuder-Richardson estimation formulae? He taught words, for fuck's sake, not sums! Out of the blue, however, came salvation in the guise of Autolycus the Arithmetician. These seemingly arcane calculations were of course scholarly trifles: to be snapped up and deployed subsequently for the assembled teachers' company to marvel at Jay's scintillating intellect! Enthusiasm rekindled, he soldiered on through Bulletin 5 on school-based exams to Bulletins 11 & 16, which covered oral and written trial examinations respectively. He might not be the most senior English teacher come the meeting but, by God, he'd be the best informed!

He was still no further forward on the romantic front, though...

It was Saturday – the first weekend off Jill had managed in ages. They met in the Bridge, in late-evening sunshine. Jay was already seated by the window, trying to look casual but in smarter-than-usual brown slacks and a short-sleeved cream shirt with a paisley cravat. The bar was quiet and although apparently absorbed in the *Guardian* crossword he spotted her immediately she came through the entrance. Her jet-black hair was cut in neat curls, which framed her face, and she was wearing make-up. A bright scarlet blouse was tucked into a navy-blue flared skirt.

'You look lovely!' He rose and they embraced warmly then, whilst she made herself at home, he strode across to get the beers.

Initially the atmosphere seemed a bit strained. It was that long since they'd been together it was almost like a first date: politely enquiring about how she was, and the family back in Wallsend, and what she was up to. He tried sharing his own news but she didn't seem very interested in alternative assessment methodology. Then he remembered she'd got career developments of her own.

'How's the job going? How was your conference? Manchester, wasn't it?'

'Yeah, it was really interesting! Met some fascinating people.'

'Oh...right. How did you get there? Train?'

'Er...no, I got a lift.'

'Who from?' demanded Jay, more peremptorily than he'd intended.

'Oh just one of the consultants,' offered Jill airily, 'he was speaking and wondered if I needed any help getting there. Saved me the train fare.'

'That was thoughtful. Anyone I know?'

'Don't think so. I hardly knew him myself. Old bloke, bit of an academic. Pretty tedious, but it turned out he knew everyone. Even introduced me to the chief nursing officer. Now she *was* interesting. Told us loads about the transition from ward to management. D'you know...'

But Jay, already bored, had spotted someone. 'Look,' he interrupted, 'there's Peter! Peter Jackson – you know our Head of Art. Shall I see if he'd like to join us? He seems to be on his own. Oh no...there's a few of 'em coming in.'

'Sure…' it was Jill's turn to be bored. The last thing she wanted was to sit and listen to a load of teachers rabbiting on about their respective charges.

'I've gotta go pretty soon, mind. I've some ward records to catch up on.'

Jay was just about to employ his powers of dissuasion when the pub door opened again to admit Linda. Bollocks! He didn't think she'd spotted him yet so he could offer to see Jill home, and bundle them both out of the side door. He tried to sound disappointed and casual simultaneously.

'Oh, shame! Still if I can't tempt you…how about I see you back to the flat before they descend on us?'

'Thanks, but I really do have to work. So no night-caps, I'm afraid.'

'Sure, sure…understood!' And he bustled them out into the Handbridge gloaming.

Twenty-Seven

Jill liked Raymond Fincher. He was generous and warm-hearted and treated her with respect. He also had a lively sense of humour and was much easier to be around than Jay's mum, who could be rather distant, reserved even. She never said as much, but Jill always got the impression she wasn't good enough for Muriel Fincher, or her precious son. She would probably have disapproved of her husband's habit of taking Jill out to lunch occasionally, and she wondered whether he'd actually mentioned it. From something he'd let slip she doubted Jay knew either. Not that there was anything untoward in the arrangement, even if they did get a few looks...

Their rendezvous was the Eastgate Street entrance to the Grosvenor (uh, oh...Grosvenor, again!) which also happened to house an up-market jeweller's: Boodle & Dunthorne. Jill, punctual as always, was there at five-to-one and was scrutinising the displays as Raymond arrived.

'Sussing out the rings?' he joked.

'No...no... I was admiring the watches. There's some right bobby-dazzlers? Is this where you got Jay's?'

'His Rolex? Yes, it was actually. They'd only been open a year or so then. Twenty-first present you know. Think he likes it, though he doesn't give much away, does he?'

'Oh...and I thought it was just me,' pouted Jill. 'No, seriously, he's very proud of it. And very careful with it too. It goes back in the special green box if he's climbing or anything!'

'You two getting on okay these days?' It was a friendly enquiry over the Gordon's Export gin and tonics Raymond had ordered before lunch.

'Yeah...course we are. Why, has he said something?'

'No, no...as I say he doesn't give much away.'

Jill thought he looked a wee bit uncomfortable and, as if regretting he'd raised the matter, he changed tack.

'Anyway, how's your mum and dad? And your brothers? Keeping well, I hope. And how's work? What's it like being the youngest Sister in all of Cheshire?'

'Bloody hell, Raymond, since when did you join the Inquisition?' He laughed apologetically so she continued. 'Well let's see…mam and dad are both well, thanks, and Rob and Al. Going up to see them all at Easter. The job's great and as for the *youngest Sister* bit, I guess there'll be another one along soon so I can pass the burden on!' Jill's natural modesty masqueraded as self-denigration; secretly she treasured the accolade.

'Don't be so unassuming: it's a remarkable achievement. Jay's as proud as Punch!'

Hmm…be nice if *he'd* told me that, she thought, but before she could let it cloud the atmosphere the pâté arrived.

They opted to skip mains and over cheese and coffee Raymond opened up a new front. 'You got a spare half hour when we're done here?'

'Yeah, no probs, I'm on a split shift. Don't have to be back 'til five.'

'Good. There's something I think might interest you.'

They cut through the precinct and emerged on the Rows above Bridge Street, heading towards the river and crossing at the traffic lights that divided Pepper and Grosvenor Streets. Anton's flat flitted across Jill's mind. What on earth would Raymond think: they were probably about the same age! Dragging herself firmly back to the present Jill remarked this was the way she walked home from work as Raymond put a guiding hand in the small of her back and pointed to a steep flight of steps leading to an imposing Georgian portico. Jill must've walked past a hundred times and never noticed it.

'Auction rooms: there's a sale coming up. I thought you'd be intrigued by some of the lots.'

Jill was mystified. She didn't know the first thing about antiques and had never expressed any interest; but as they went into the main hall and Raymond led her through to an elegant, pillared side-room it began to dawn on her.

'But these are like the ones you've got at *Jedka*. Japanese something-or-others!'

'Japanese Imari,' smiled her guide, 'been collecting it for twenty years or so. Back then nobody knew anything about it. I've picked up pairs of eighteenth-century vases in Norwich for thirty bob! Worth a lot more now!'

'Look at that table there!' exclaimed Jill. 'Those blue and white plates are just like yours, aren't they?'

'Well spotted: they're *Sometsuke*. They're under-the-glaze Imari from North Kyushu. It's the Japanese island closest to China and Korea. You've heard me talk about Ming?' Jill nodded. 'Well the Ming dynasty and the Ching one that followed it influenced the Korean potters who'd already been working in Kyushu for hundreds of years. It's some of the simplest and most perfect Imari porcelain.'

'And those with all the colours – three, four, five different ones – you've got some of those, too,' cried Jill excitedly.

'*Nishikide*' pronounced Ray authoritatively, 'sometimes called Brocade Imari.'

'What you mean sort of lace, as on blouses or dresses?'

'Yes, or fancy waistcoats!'

'Like Jay's you mean?'

'Precisely! Most people think that's why it's called Brocade Imari. But it's not! The Japanese also refer to the autumn tints on mountains as brocade. *That's* where it comes from!'

Jill shot him an admiring glance: that was another thing she liked about him – he was so darned intelligent. Obviously where Jay got it from: shame he didn't always measure up in the generosity and warm-heartedness stakes!

They parted and Jill dawdled back over the bridge, pausing to gaze at the river, keen to avoid spending any longer than necessary in her solitary flat before the evening shift began. Had Raymond gathered they were going through a sticky patch? He was shrewd as well as intelligent: that was why he'd enquired. And then backed off, recognising it was none of his business. Jill doubted anyone else would've realised but she and Jay were about as far apart as they'd been since Jill had followed him to Chester. And although she could pinpoint the overt cause of their *froideur* – the row with Blundell, which led to her moving flats – there was more to it than that. Otherwise why was she even considering Anton's offer?

They'd been easy together, but not intimate, in the apartment. Anton had a meeting at the university and Jill was invited to make herself at home. Disappointed to find no books she'd been reduced to trawling through a week-old copy of *The Daily Telegraph* (or *Torygraph* as Jay dubbed it, mainly to irritate his mother). Jay was right: its politics certainly weren't to Jill's taste, and her dad would've had a fit! An article on cigars caught her eye. It was about some bloke called Zino Davidoff, the son of a Jewish tobacco trader who dealt mainly in gold-tipped cigarettes. Made from Turkish tobacco: they'd be those things Jay smoked when he was trying to impress people! Black Russian, I'll bet!

The family had left Kiev following some anti-Czarist plot shortly before the First World War. Kiev? Was that in Czechoslovakia or Poland? She wasn't sure where Anton came from but it could be one of those Eastern European states behind the Iron Curtain. Absorbed, she read on. The Davidoffs had settled in Geneva and in 1926 Zino had been sent to South America with a load of introductions, and instructions to learn the tobacco business. He travelled from Buenos Aires to Brazil and then to Cuba, which was apparently *the* place to learn cigar making. Come to think of it, she'd heard of Havana cigars. Would that one Anton smoked last night count? Zino had allegedly claimed he'd *discovered Cuba's perfume and her sensual warmth, as an immature adolescent discovers an ardent, knowledgeable woman*. So a bit like Jay and her then! There was quite a bit more but Jill persevered if only to impress Anton; however, the imagined conversation about the relative merits of Davidoff and Romeo y Julieta never transpired!

Instead, as the Aston growled gently through the Cheshire countryside Anton casually mentioned how he envisaged their understanding. There was no pressure to meet him just because she had a weekend off. She would have her own key and, apart from alerting Mrs Brayson to any intended visit in his absence, Jill was free to use the place as she liked. There would, Anton assured her, be regular regional health events, which would be worth her while attending; he would keep a look out and notify her accordingly. She jibbed slightly at the business-like feel of the arrangement but was conscious of the opportunities Mr K was creating for her and decided that a tactful acquiescence was called for.

Back in her own flat, in the limbo between shifts she wasn't so sure. Manchester had been great and she'd met people who could give her career a real boost but hadn't she moved to Chester to be with Jay, not to become a chief nursing officer? Maybe she could do both? Jay was always saying, when two apparently exclusive options occurred: 'It's not an either/or – it's a both/and!' But then his philosophy of life seemed to be based on having your cake and consuming as much of it as possible before anyone pinched it off you! And if they did, thumping them before they could eat it!

Still, maybe given time he'd become more like his father…

Back on the ward, as the quiet of the evening settled in, she gingerly picked up the office 'phone.

'Chester 35106,' announced the voice Jill fervently hoped would answer.

Twenty-Eight

Jay'd never admit it to anyone else, but the agreement to share the blame attached to what they laughed off as the 'defenestration of Durham' had not just saved Pard's university career; it had scuppered his own. Dr Wallace had confided as much subsequently: before the incident he'd been defending Jay's academic record to his critics. True, his attendance at lectures and seminars might be lamentable but his written submissions were of the highest standard. The worst the Lilliputians could have belittled him with was a Lower Second. But the opprobrium attached to the brawl resulted in Dr Wallace being unable to prosecute his charge's claims further. Hence the disciplinary degree that had so incensed his friend Julia.

By contrast, Pard had escaped with an Upper Second.

Subsequently, whilst Jay had started as an untrained graduate at Woodbridge High, Pard had stayed on and completed a year's teacher training. Then, much to Jay's chagrin, he'd secured a history post at the Royal Grammar School, Newcastle upon Tyne. A boys' independent school, it ranked as the city's oldest centre of learning receiving its Royal Charter from Queen Elizabeth I. In short, just the seat of academe to which pre-Peterhouse aspiration would have beckoned Jay!

It just didn't seem fair...

So when he received the invite he was in two minds. Particularly as Pard had written it out painstakingly in his admittedly elegant italic script on RGS-headed notepaper (which he'd doubtless nicked from the school office). It was typical Pard: designed to impress and goad simultaneously. Well stuff him and his superiority complex, Jay wasn't going.

Later, in the snug of the Bull & Stirrup waiting for Jill to finish her shift, he mentioned the invite to the bounteous Bren. She'd not met Pard but had listened to Jay singing his praises in the past. Without actually bad-mouthing his varsity buddy, Jay managed to convey his ambivalence about accepting Pard's invitation.

'Don't be daft! You were best mates at college, of course you should go. You'll have a great time. And if you don't believe *me*, here comes the boss. Ask her!'

Jay was even more dubious about Jill wanting to go, even if she were included. For some reason, there was friction between the two of them, though according to Jill it was more on Pard's side than hers. Something to do with Pard's wife, Jorja, though she wouldn't disclose what. He couldn't fathom anyone not taking to Jill.

'Course you should! You've not seen each other for, what, eighteen months? It'll be great to catch up. And even if I'm not invited it doesn't matter: it's Easter and I was planning to see my folks anyway. We can go up together regardless!'

Jay still hesitated but could offer no concrete excuse.

'That's settled then. We'll aim for Easter Saturday, eh?'

The drive up was uneventful, and much quieter than normal: none of the usual nursing v teaching banter. It seemed like they were on a second date, the excitement of the first having subsided into a state of not-quite-knowing-what-to-talk-about. It was a relief when they reached St Peter's Road and Jay pulled across to No.124.

'Aren't you coming in? They'll be expecting you. Me mam said she'd do us a proper tea, like.' (Jay smiled, not at the invitation but at how Jill's Geordie accent surfaced back on Tyneside!)

'Nah! Thanks anyway, but explain I had to get straight on to Cullercoats, will you? I'll see them tomorrow, I expect.'

He gunned the Mini diagonally across the tarmac, relishing the squeal of the tyres and the snarl of the engine. To maternal disapproval he'd recently had a straight-through exhaust fitted: sounded more like a Cooper 'S' now than a commonplace 1071cc. He just hoped Pard still had his '66 Triumph and hadn't graduated to a sports car. Jay was confident of seeing off the cumbersome 1300! He dropped down to the roundabout under the A1058 and screeched all the way round in second, hugging a really tight line and only straightening out when he reached the slipway that led to the Coast Road. Then he bombed it all the way along to the front where he swung left until reaching Cullercoats. There was a free parking space outside the fisherman's cottage and Jay was relieved to see the Triumph next to it. He was still anxious about meeting Jorja again; they'd never really hit it off, even though Jay had tried his best.

'Not here just now, mate. I'll explain later. Beer?'

And Pard, who seemed genuinely pleased to see Jay, pulled a couple of Exports out of the fridge and offered him one. No glass, of course!

'Cheers, squire: all the breast!'

'Cheers, Pard, good to see you mate. You look fit.' It was true: Pard had lost weight and appeared more sculpted than Jay remembered. He was casually smart in beige cords and a tight black, short-sleeved shirt, which displayed his biceps. 'How's tricks?'

'Pretty good, mate. Yourself? Still going out with that nurse?'

'Yeah – 'cept she's a Sister now. Youngest in Cheshire,' bragged Jay proudly.

'Strewth! Good on her,' Pard actually sounded impressed. 'So, is she with you?'

'Yeah, stopping at her parents' place. Wasn't sure if the invite included her?'

'Course! But we'll have this first night to ourselves, eh. Then see how the land lies. How long you up for?'

'Depends. Didn't know what you'd got in mind. No hurry to get back though. Jill's got the whole week and I've a fortnight like you.'

'Three weeks, mate: longer vacs in the independent sector!' The first hint of one-upmanship; Jay decided to let it go for now.

'So where're we off tonight?'

'Tynemouth. The totty's summat else in the Sausage!'

'Sausage?' Jay didn't know Tynemouth particularly well.

'Cumberland Arms, squire. You'll see!'

The Sausage was heaving but Jay luckily secured a small wrought-iron table whilst Pard elbowed his way through the four-deep crowd at the bar. He got one or two looks but no one was brave enough to complain and he was back in no time with four pints of Vaux clutched in his boxer's grasp.

'Save waiting! We'll have these and if we don't score here we'll head across to the Salutation.'

A lot of the girls looked like right boilers; they were dressed to the nines with skirts like belts and boobs hanging out of their tee shirts. It didn't seem to worry them that it was bloody freezing for April. No luck though. Their track record failed to improve in the Sal where Jay bought the Exhibition; after which Pard announced they'd try the Stuffed Dog.

They threaded their way down Front Street until they reached a once-white-tiled building on the other side of the road. 'Turks Head Hotel' it read in large grey capitals above the windows. Jay looked puzzled but Pard shrugged.

'You'll see why inside.'

The bar was packed, but through the smoky murk Jay could just make out a stuffed dog mounted in a glass case on the wall.

'Various versions,' explained Pard, 'I like the one about the Shields ferry. They reckon the dog's owner fell in, pissed like, and the dog jumped in to save him. They both drowned but the bloke's friends decided to have the dog stuffed in his memory! Anyway, cheers!'

'Cheers, mate. It's good to see you again. What's the Royal like anyway? You made many friends?'

'Nah! It's a bit stuffy. Y'know, old-fashioned. How about you? What's…?'

'Woodbridge? It's okay, much the same. Kids are great though: gonna introduce outdoor pursuits for the ROSLA cohort.'

'Nice one! I've revived their defunct boxing club.'

'Thought you were looking pretty sharp.'

'Cheers, squire. Pint?'

They had another couple of Youngers No.3 after which Pard declared it was time to lose the wheels so they drove, a tad erratically, back to Cullercoats and parked up. A final session in the Last Orders was rounded off by a Chinese. Just like old times!

Jay expected the Sunday to be a lazy day and fancied dragging Pard down to the Labour Club where Jill's dad and uncle would doubtless be good for a game of doms and a few free beers.

'No way! Go west, young man! Tell Jill we'll pick her up in an hour.'

This was less like old times. Certainly not The Three Musketeers revisited! There was no way an already-reluctant Jill was about to be squashed between them and she ended up being chauffeured in the back. She spent much of the journey alternating between studious ignoring of the front-seat chat and screwing up her face trying to decipher half-heard snatches. She felt distinctly ill at ease. Their destination was Chesters: quite close now, somewhere this side of Hexham apparently. After that all she gleaned was something about *The Clayton Collection.*

'So what's this collection? And how come you're in on it?'

'Connexions, squire: whaddya think? You remember old Birley?'

'What ex-Master of Hatfield? Wasn't he one of your tutors?'

'Do me a favour: bit more than that! He was Professor of Romano-British History and Archaeology.'

'Stand corrected, but what's the link to Chesters?'

'Well it seems Birley made his reputation on Hadrian's Wall; his first site was way to the west at Birdoswald.'

'That anywhere near High Shield?' Jay was anxious to recover some ground and doubted Pard, as a non-climber, would've heard of that bit of the Wall. But Jill had and would therefore feel part of the conversation.

'Dunno. Anyway the point is that Birley's mentor was FG Simpson who was excavating Milecastles on Stanesgate way back around the turn of the century. Not long after Clayton died.'

'So?'

'So there's a direct link, yer gowk! That's how we're gonna get access to the private collection. That, plus the fact that our head of history at RGS is leading a new dig there this summer.' Pard paused before the knockout blow: 'And I'm on it!'

Jay could think of no rejoinder besides which he was grudgingly impressed.

So was Jill once Pard had presented his credentials and they gained entry. He noted her interest and quickly capitalized on it.

'Look at this. It's one of a group of milestones from Vindolanda. That's where my professor's done most of his excavations. This one's dedicated to *Caesar Flavius Valerius Constantinus*. That's Emperor Constantine to you!'

'Mint!' exclaimed Jill, fascinated. 'How old d'you reckon it is then, Gregory?'

Jay's antennae twitched: he couldn't recall anyone ever using Pard's first name. It sounded somehow intimate.

'Early fourth-century. Constantine was born around 274 AD and died in 337. And it's Greg, by the way. Well to you anyway.'

'And this one: isn't it from Vindolanda, too? It looks like a tomb.'

Pard laughed, 'It's an altar! But why d'you think it comes from Vindolanda?'

Jill squatted beside the dais and pointed to the inscription: 'There, look: it says *VINDOLANDESSES*.'

'Well spotted!' admired Pard crouching down close to her (unnecessarily close, huffed Jay).

'But what's the rest mean? Can you translate it?'

Pard was quick to oblige, gratuitously taking Jill's hand and pointing her forefinger to each word in turn.

'*PRO DOMV DIVINA ET NUMINIBUS AGUSTORVM...* It means *For the Divine House and the Deities of the Emperors...*'

He was interrupted by Jay, anxious to disrupt the tableau: 'Strewth! Look at this one: it's massive! Another altar...to Jupiter, I think.'

It failed. Pard droned on, still clasping Jill's hand, which she made no attempt to withdraw: '*VOLCANO SACRUM VICANI VINDOLANDESSES...*

the villagers of Vindolanda (constructed) this sacred offering to Vulcan.'

'Crikey! Didn't know you could speak Latin, Greg!'

'Can't be much call for it in Cullercoats, eh, mate?' interjected Jay sarcastically.

'No, but it comes in handy in archaeological circles,' dismissed Pard triumphantly. He leant across and put his hand under Jill's elbow and they rose as one.

'Who's Vulcan, by the way?'

'Son of Jupiter and Juno. He's the Roman God of fire and forging. Greek equivalent's Hephaestus: sometimes called Mulciber, the softener.

'The softener, eh...' murmured Jill thoughtfully.

'Bastard!' muttered Jay.

Twenty-Nine

Unexpectedly, Jill had enjoyed the day.

She'd been interested in ancient artefacts ever since she'd met Alistair, Stephen's flatmate! Not the theory in the stuffy academic magazines that littered every worktop, but the prospect of a dig. Once you got Alistair onto that, his habitually sombre expression would dissolve and his eyes would sparkle with fervour. Jill fancied trying it, but the opportunity had never arisen. Alistair was always too preoccupied with his postgraduate studies, Stephen had no interest in the prospect, and Pard...well she didn't particularly like him – bad influence – even though he was apparently an archaeologist. The trip to The Clayton Collection had been a revelation.

Had she planned to incite the green-eyed God? She was always impressed by scholarship, including Jay's, but combined with an obvious yet effective charm offensive it'd cast Greg in a new light. He had charisma and the instinct of a good teacher. He was also physically attractive. He wore rimless glasses which, with his long sideburns, gave him a raffishly erudite air and although little taller than Jay was much more muscular. Oh, and he had nice eyes! But most fascinating of all were his marital arrangements. Jill had met Jorja just once when she'd been down in Durham looking for Jay. They hadn't hit it off, mainly because Jill's focus was elsewhere and Jorja struck her as needing to be the centre of attention. But there was surely more to it than that: Jill would quiz Greg when the opportunity arose.

At Jill's insistence they'd called at St Peter's Road, so Jay could pay his respects. Her dad was down the Labour Club. So whilst her mam fussed around the boys histrionically Jill slipped up to her old *den* and selected the most tantalising outfit she could muster, smuggling it into her trusty grip past any prying maternal eyes.

Back at the cottage the blokes broke open the beers. Jill puckishly swiped each boy's bottle in turn, taking large swigs to their amusement. She repeated the performance on the second round – to Greg's admiration and Jay's inchoate concern. Then she took a bottle of Newcastle Amber up to the spare room. She necked a third of it and, after a strip wash, downed another third or so. She dressed with uncharacteristically roguish care, rolling on the sheerest black stockings and attaching them to the midnight-blue Guipure suspender belt Sue had given her, along with the matching knickers and half-cup bra. The brown midi-skirt looked very demure but had buttons most of the way up the front; whilst the thin taupe jumper had a plunging V-neckline. It was revealing, before she donned her tight brown-leather biker's jacket and zipped it almost to the top. It felt thrilling but looked positively prim. Then she finished the Amber and applied her make-up. No wonder she felt frisky: a combination of several weeks of abstinence – and archaeology! Mr K's intentions had proved far more honourable then she'd hoped; whilst the night with Bronwen had not realised any subliminal fantasies. They'd both crashed out and Bron had left early the following morning without waking her. Meanwhile, she'd been deliberately keeping Jay short. The unfamiliar caress of Greg's fingers had left her feeling distinctly febrile…

To compound it she eschewed her normal drinking plan. True, she'd started on beer: you couldn't not in the Tynemouth Lodge, their Bass was legendary. But after a couple there and one in the Priory she'd switched to rum and cokes. Always a dodgy sign. As her mam used to pronounce, 'Rum makes you randy!' Well she should know, thought Jill spitefully. Her hint that they should have something to eat went unnoticed and she had to make do with crisps and peanuts. By the time they came out of the Gibraltar, she was feeling merry; which probably accounted for her suggestion as they reached the Grand.

'Howay, you two, there's a do on. Let's crash it!'

The board in reception announced the wedding celebration of Mr and Mrs Roger Dixon.

'Locals then,' proclaimed Jill confidently, recalling Joyce's long ago guidance, 'Dixon's a Border Rievers name. Bound to be a good party.'

'Bonza!' Greg was addressing Jay: 'Bride or Groom?'

'Groom!' advised Jay decisively. 'The family'll be less protective. Easier to con. Yer know: the old schoolmates routine!'

Jill giggled: her consorts had obviously pulled this stunt before! Sure enough they strode haughtily up the imposing staircase and into the ballroom, commandeering the nearest half-empty table. Doubtless they could've fallen straight into a 'Yeah, known-him-for-years routine', but the party had reached the stage where nobody gave a toss. Jay summoned a waiter, announcing high-handedly that they'd only just arrived from London and had some catching-up to do. He was about to bridle when a bottle of Asti Spumante materialised but, on a glare from Jill, stifled his snobbery. The bubbles sufficed whilst they reconnoitred; a process hi-jacked when Jill provocatively unzipped her biker's jacket.

Greg turned out to be a passable mover and she enjoyed the sensation of whirling round the parquet in a state of mild intoxication. She knew it was pointless trying to get Jay up. She just hoped he was relaxed enough not to start a grump. The signs were unpromising: whenever they passed his table he seemed increasingly glum. Accordingly, Jill cut short her pleasure and they returned to base. Jay brightened up immediately and gestured under the table. He'd already purloined two bottles of spirits: one a brandy Jill didn't recognise, the other a reassuringly familiar bottle of Captain Morgan!

They decided to quit whilst they were ahead, Jill wrapping the Captain Morgan inside her rolled-up jacket, whilst much to her amusement the brandy disappeared down Greg's trousers. Jay grabbed a waiting taxi and Jill shuffled across the back seat, only to find him already in residence. Greg instructed the cabbie and parked himself on her other side. Oh sardines! They'd no sooner set off than she discovered she'd run out of cigarettes: she leant forward to get their driver's advice and noticed his badge. 'Ralph Walker', it read. Coincidence! Anyway, according to Ralph Walker, the only place open would be the Shell garage at the far end of the Coast Road. Helluva fare then, but no one seemed bothered; as if to underline their alcoholic unconcern the brandy bottle emerged from Greg's trousers. They each took a hefty pull and Jill settled back between the two boys, exhaling contentedly and feigning shuteye.

Having set up the situation she was miffed when nothing happened straightaway. However, the trip via the Shell station would take at least twenty minutes and as they slowed down to negotiate the roundabout leading to the slipway she felt Jay's fingers caressing the back of her upper arm. Although she went all goose bumpy she gave no other indication she'd noticed and he graduated to stroking her jumper between her arm and her breast. She wondered whether Greg had noticed and, if so, what his reaction might be. She squinted through her eyelashes just enough to check: he wasn't moving but was staring avidly. She gave a sigh and stretched, accidentally pulling down the jumper to expose more of her boobs. Jay's fingers, unimpeded, slipped inside the soft material. She felt her nipples stiffen. Surely Greg would suss…

His hand brushed her buttock lightly. The contact was so faint it could've been either accidental or exploratory. Jill decided it was the latter and dropping her hand to his, she pressed it gently on the outside of her skirted-thigh. Her libido was rising steadily and it didn't help when she caught sight of Ralph twisting his mirror so he could clock what was going on. Somehow a fourth-party watching proceedings made it even raunchier. This could easily get out of hand.

They were overtaken by events; the neon of the Shell garage lit up the taxi briefly. It occurred fleetingly to Jill that she should adjust her top, but they parked in an unlit corner, having manoeuvred past the row of vehicles waiting to fill up. Looked like quite a delay: hope they weren't going to get charged for it. Maybe she could sweet-talk their driver – Ralph? – into pausing his meter! Anyway, she wasn't going for her own cigarettes! Jay, however, seemed reluctant to leave her alone with Greg, who could hardly be expected to volunteer himself.

'Oh, for God's sake! Don't be so childish. You can both go!' and she handed Jay a ten-shilling note. 'Howay: get two packs of Embassy and don't forget me change!' Should be about three bob, she calculated. She exhaled loudly and lay back in a brandy-haze: they'd be a while.

'Why yer divn't get many of those to the pund' chortled Ralph.

Sober, she'd have told him to get stuffed. Drunk, and already aroused, she just pretended to be affronted.

'Well you shouldna be looking!'

'Howay, man, they're bootiful.'

He was obviously just trying it on but he had a certain saucy charm about him. Recklessly, she reached for the brandy bottle and took a double-swallowing slug. It burned her throat, hitting her stomach moments later and rekindling the fire that was already smouldering there.

'Why thank you, kind sir! A'am glad yer like 'em!'

'Don't s'pose yer'd let me have a feel?'

'Yer cheeky sod.'

'Sorry, pet. I didn't mean owt...'

'Nowt like being forward, I s'pose. We'll see...' Jill's mind raced: it wasn't exactly what she'd meant by sweet-talking but if it served her purpose...

'It's just when yer fella were playing with 'em like, yer seemed pretty turned on.'

'Oh did I?' she enquired coquettishly. Jill was minded to indulge him. But not for nothing!

'Hmm… I dunno. What's it worth?' she posited warily.

'Free taxi ride?'

Jill was agreeably surprised. That must save them at least fifteen quid. Just for a quick fumble?

'What both ways?' she confirmed cautiously.

'Yeah, from the Grand to here and back to wherever you want!'

'Well, aal reet then. But only if you promise to be good!'

'Why I'll do me best, hin…'

'Just a quick feel, mind – no groping!'

Ralph seemed to materialise beside her. It was an obvious move but its suddenness took her by surprise. He put his arms around her so they were close up against each other. He was clean and smelt good… She'd made it clear it was just a quick fiddle. But Ralph's shivery fingers were turning her on, and instead of wanting him to get it over with as swiftly as possible she found herself glancing out of the back window, hoping the boys weren't returning. She sighed audibly and turned to face him, just as Ralph's quivering digits brushed against her nipples.

'Hey! I said just a quick feel!'

'Sorry, hinnie: didn't mean it. I'll stop if you want…'

'Hmm…'

He lowered his head and tried to kiss her breasts.

'Whoaah, steady on! Thas a bit morean a feel, bonnylad,' she protested without conviction.

'Howay, gan on, pet. Aa'l stop if tha doan like it.'

Jill couldn't help but smile. Should she let him?

'Doan yer think yer've had yer money's worth?'

She was squirming with pleasure but had to call a halt. Whether her decree would've sufficed was fortunately not tested; the boys strolled across the forecourt and Ralph retreated to his cab.

'What was *he* doing?' demanded Jay.

'Wanted the full fare in advance, in case we did a runner,' was the best Jill could summon.

'Cheeky bugger!'

'Hmm…you could say that…'

'Yer what?'

'Nothing. I mean, yes…he was…'

Then they were mobile again; she tried to calm down and enjoy the shorter journey back… Fat chance! Soon after the brandy bottle had circulated yet again, the boys clearly had other ideas.

'You'll let us pleasure you again?' whispered Greg.

'Don't be naughty...' But Jay was already unbuttoning the midi-skirt and, with a delighted snort, exposing her suspender belt and stockings.

'No Jay, not now... Maybe later pet.'

'Oh, go on. You know you want to.'

'Howay, yer buggers,' complained the taxi driver, 'Yer can give o'er treating me cab like a brothel!'

That's rich, coming from you, she thought, but mercifully they were almost back. Jill was scrabbling for respectability as she stumbled out onto the pavement. The solicitous Ralph held the door and pressed a card into her hand.

Then they were congregated in the living room. Feeling she had to regain control Jill announced she needed the bathroom. She should go to bed now. That's what she should do! She glanced at the card. On the front was printed: *Ralph Walker Taxis: 091 66777*. On the back was scrawled: *Free ride anytime for you, pet!* Cocky blighter, she thought, but she couldn't help grinning. Maybe next time she needed a taxi and was skint as well as drunk... Suddenly she felt far too dissolute to retire.

'Anyway, you can forget any ideas about a repeat performance! I don't know what came over me!'

'Well, whatever it was you seemed to enjoy it!' remarked Jay crudely.

'Well...it was a one-off! All right?'

'If you say so, pet.' Jay sounded grudgingly unconvinced, as if Jill's having enjoyed the episode would somehow demonstrate a subconscious yearning for more. Jill sensed a sulk coming on.

'Of course,' offered Greg, ingratiatingly.

'Anyway, that's it! Enough talk. Are we going to open that rum or just look at it?' And when both her paramours looked agreeably surprised: 'Right, who's for a special coffee?'

Not waiting for a response Jill seized the bottle and marched into the kitchen. Whilst the kettle boiled she located three mugs of assorted sizes. She put a heaped spoonful of Nescafé into each and then measured out the Captain Morgan – a small one for her, a medium-middle-sized one for Jay and a geet big 'un for Greg. Just like the three bears! Leaving hers on the draining board to make sure she didn't get them mixed up she returned to the living room to find Greg sprawled on the sofa.

'Howay, man!' she prodded, 'where's Jay?'

He blinked lazily: 'Oh...gone t'bed. Said he was knackered.'

Well that simplified matters. She handed him his mug and placing the other one in no-man's land on the table turned for the kitchen to retrieve hers.

'Aren't you having one?'

'Yeah, I'm just gonna get it.'

'Have that one.'

'Nah, it's got sugar in it.'

When Jill returned Greg was sitting upright and alert.

'Hey, great coffee, Jill! Take a pew,' and he gestured towards the far end of the sofa.

They slurped lethal doses of the rocket fuel, periodically emitting grunts of approval. Greg finished his and was about to start on Jay's.

'So…' she began nonchalantly, 'where's Jorja then?'

'Wondered when we'd get round to that,' he grimaced, ''s'pose you want all the gory details.'

'Natch! Spill the beans!'

'She's left me…' he began bluntly, '…dunno when she's coming back. Or even if…'

'Oh! Greg, I'm so sorry, pet!' Jill snuggled compassionately closer and gave his thigh a sympathetic squeeze. There was a long silence punctuated only by occasional slurps.

'So what happened? Yer can tell me.'

Another lengthy pause made her anxious she was pressing him too hard before he seemed to decide: 'Yeah yeah…okay. Fact I'd like to, 'specially with you being partly responsible.'

'Me? How come?'

'Remember that time we met in Durham when you were looking for Jay? Jorja was with me. And you were with your friend Sally.'

'Yeah…don't see how that makes me responsible though.'

''Cause they wouldn't have met otherwise. That's who Jorja's gone off with: your mate Sally.'

'Oh shit! Greg, I'd no idea. Poor you!' Jill half-turned to face him and stretched up to plant an understanding kiss on his cheek. As she relaxed, his arm slid off the back of the sofa and onto her shoulder. She nuzzled closer.

'Jay's a lucky bastard! You're a man's woman. At least if you fancied someone else it wouldn't be a lesbian…'

'Oh, Greg…' she turned her face to his. Not that she much liked kissing men: it just seemed the easiest way out. Particularly as his fingers were already wriggling inside her jumper.

'What the fuck's going on here, then?' Jay's face was contorted with rage.

146

Thirty

Lady Caroline Lamb, Viscountess Melbourne. What was it she'd said after meeting Byron? *Mad, bad and dangerous to know!* Autolycus the Antagonist, eh! He'd bloody show 'em!

On reflexion the only thing he'd have done differently would've been to put one on 'im. He'd wanted to. Then again, he'd probably not've got out of the cottage alive! But what the fuck was Pard playing at? Just because Jorja had left him for some other bloke didn't give him the right to touch up Jill. They were supposed to be mates, and she was supposed to be his girlfriend! So they'd had a few drinks and Jay'd got a bit sportive in the taxi, which Pard had maybe clocked. Didn't give them carte blanche for carrying on without him. And if his girlfriend was so horny she had to spread it around as soon as his back was turned, well...

He'd have been totally justified in dragging Jill off home. But whose home, at that time of night? Then he'd have been the one left stranded. No he'd done the right thing: given them a piece of his mind and stormed out. Shouldn't have driven, of course. But he'd been super careful along the Coast Road and through the city centre, and once he was on the A1 he hardly saw another car. By the time he'd crossed the Pennines it was light and he'd reached Bridge Drive just in time for breakfast. His mother had been a bit surprised but at the faintest of headshakes from his dad had said nothing. He pleaded exhaustion and went to bed 'til they were both safely out of the way.

He used the rest of the Easter holiday to good effect: mugging up on CSEs and soloing a load of routes at Helsby and Frodsham. Even before the start of term he was well prepared, academically and physically. The 'phone call from Linda still came as a nice surprise, however; Jay had anticipated having to make the running. Instead she'd enquired whether he was up for that climbing lesson on such a beautiful sunny day!

The Frodsham buttresses were easily accessible from the main Chester-Runcorn road and were much quieter than Helsby, especially on a weekday.

It was always easier for beginners if they weren't being watched by a crowd of other climbers. She'd asked him what to wear so, rather than alarm her with some risqué fantasy, he'd advised whatever she was most comfortable in. When he parked the Mini outside her parents' semi she emerged in her uniform of tracksuit and trainers, with a small rucksack, which she swung behind the passenger seat. Twenty minutes later they were the sole car beneath the crag. Jay extracted a ninety-foot Viking No.4 and some slings from the boot and led the way past the first three buttresses – *Hoop La, Neb* and *Changing Room* – explaining that most of the routes there were too hard for a first outing.

'This is *Long Buttress*. It's got about a dozen lines. Some should just suit us. We'll top-rope 'em.' Linda looked blank so he explained: 'I'll take the rope up to the top and find a good belay: a rock or a tree to fix it to. Then I'll run it through a karabiner, come back down, tie you on and guide you from here. That way you'll be protected from above and I can point out any holds that might help you. If you need any help,' he added hastily, not wanting to sound patronising.

'Sounds ok, but you'll have to show me how to tie on. Don't know any climbing knots.'

'Yeah, course. D'you think you'll be okay in those?' He pointed to her trainers, which had thick, ribbed soles and broad welts. 'They don't like you wearing boots here, the sandstone's so soft; that's why I'm in PAs.'

Another bemused look.

'Oh sorry: stands for Pierre Allain. French alpinist from Fontainebleau. Expert boulderer. Developed these specially for rockwork. Look at the bottoms: completely smooth. Adhesive, too. My mate Ed calls 'em sticky boots.'

'Well, unless you've got a spare pair?' enquired Linda, smiling at the mountaineering lesson. Then she rummaged in the sac and brought out a pair of gym shoes. 'Will these do?'

'Perfect! Plimsolls: just like they used before the war instead of hobnails. You'll be fine in those.'

'Great. Whadda we gonna do first?'

'See that corner with the wall above and the tree at the top, very originally called *Tree Wall*? Let's see how you go on that.'

'Okeydokey.'

Jay tied the rope round his waist and shimmied up the corner so quickly there was no time to see how he did it. Then he arranged a belay and threw both ends of the rope down to Linda. In a flash he was back down beside her. He pulled the rope through until there was about six feet slack.

'We'll use a bowline. It's old-fashioned but with a couple of half hitches it's foolproof. Just face the rock and I'll show you.' He stood behind her and passed the rope round her waist. Then with a twist of his hand he created a loop through which he passed the rope before wrapping it round the lead and threading it back through.

'Hang on, you did it too fast.'

He shook the still-loose knot out and showed her again. 'Look. The rabbit comes out-of-the-hole (the loop) runs round the tree (the vertical rope) doesn't like what he sees and burrows back down the hole! Easy!'

Jay had made the most of the second demonstration, brushing her sides gratuitously.

'Is your fiancée okay with all this? Yer know: you off showing the ropes to another girl?'

'Well, I may not've mentioned it… Any case, she's not my fiancée. Who told you that?'

'Bill, I think. So you're not engaged, or anything?'

'No! We're not even together at the mo. Had a bit of a falling out.'

'Oh right… Shall we get started?'

Jay took in the slack so that Linda had a reassuringly tight rope if needed and she stepped off the grassy bank onto the rock.

'That's good,' encouraged Jay, 'nice and upright. And always keep three points of contact with the rock.'

She moved confidently up the corner, then paused uncertainly at the bottom of the steep headwall.

'You're doing fine. Try not to use your knees, keep your body clear of the rock and look for small steps up. Don't lunge for the holds.'

Reassured, Linda moved onto the headwall and climbed it smoothly. They tackled three more routes before calling a halt in a small clearing at the top of the buttress. Jay had reconnoitred it on a previous visit, enclosed by trees, totally secluded. Linda fished out a Tupperware container from her sac, and unwrapped two rounds of chicken sandwiches, which they washed down with beers artfully provided by Jay.

'God, it's hot here! D'you mind?' Linda removed her plimsolls and shimmied out of her tracksuit bottoms to reveal a pair of gym shorts. They were designed for comfort not style, but the sight of her bare legs more than compensated. When she peeled off her top and he saw how snugly her tee shirt hugged her breasts, Jay was rapt. Before he could betray himself by a characteristically crass comment, however, Linda produced a small rug from her Tardis-sac and spread it out. Evidently sunbathing was to take precedence over climbing, at least for now.

'You can share it, if you want, but no funny business!' she smiled, patting the rug next to her.

Caveat taken, Jay needed no second invitation and the combination of the hot May sun and the beers soon saw them both asleep. There was a promising moment when he woke up to find Linda's arm splayed across his chest; he managed to restrict himself to gazing at her breasts rising and falling gently as she dozed.

'I might've guessed you'd be admiring the scenery! What is it about my boobs, Jay?' It was the first time she'd used his Christian name.

Unable to muster a convincing alibi he stammered: 'They're…they're… oh, bugger it…they're superb! Sorry!'

'Don't be. I don't mind. But it's climb-time again. Let's try that *Heather Wall* you showed me.'

Relieved to have escaped censure, Jay collected up the gear rapidly and arranged a belay before traversing round the side of the crag to position them under the patch of heather thirty feet up that marked the route.

'I need to master this bowline before we take the kids out! You'll have to show me again…'

She turned to face the crag and Jay passed the rope around her waist. Anxious to avoid upsetting her, he tried to keep his distance, so far as the tying-on manoeuvre would allow. Just as he was completing the half hitches, however, her tee shirt rode up and the inside of his arm brushed sensuously against her bare skin. His already burgeoning erection hardened instantly and she swivelled round to face him. Bugger! Blown it again!

But she was grinning. 'You're a naughty boy, Jay Fincher! But I like you! I like you a lot!' and she stood on plimsoll-toes and kissed him gauchely on the lips.

'Christ, Linda! The feeling's entirely mutual,' he gasped as she broke away. But when he attempted to return the compliment she eluded him.

'That's enough for now, lover boy. *Heather Wall*!'

Thirty-One

The journey back reminded Jill of her childhood. She couldn't have been much more than five when they moved to South Wales. Pits and shipyards – her dad's livelihood – had been closing all over Northumberland and they had been forced to move to Aber-somewhere. They had been on their way to lodge with her aunt Florrie. Jill had unpleasant memories of interminable waits on cold, draughty platforms.

This wasn't much better.

After Jay had stormed out she and Greg had come to their senses. He'd retired to bed and she drifted off uneasily on the sofa. Waking soon after dawn she'd collected her few belongings and headed for the Coast Road. It crossed her mind to call the cheeky taxi driver, Ralph, but she was afraid he'd interpret a 'free ride' more literally than her sober self would countenance. Eventually she spotted a yellow Lynemouth chara and even though she wasn't at a designated stop she waved it down. The terminus was the Haymarket, only a short walk to Central Station.

Timetables weren't her forte but it looked like the Manchester option would take forever. It was further, but apparently quicker, to go via Carlisle. It'd be a nice run, too, all along the Tyne valley through Corbridge and Hexham. Just a shame it was such a drizzly day: she'd not see much of the fells, or the Roman Wall.

Still, the dreary weather mirrored her mood. Whilst she didn't condone Jay's outburst, or dramatic departure, she had to concede it was mainly her fault. Getting pissed had not been clever and the cavorting with Greg was asking for trouble. Thank God she'd managed to keep the crazy episode with Ralph quiet. First and last time she'd bargain with a taxi driver, drunk!

They meandered into Carlisle where she had to pick up the London train, which stopped at Crewe. From there she thought she could get a connexion to North Wales, which would go through Chester. But she got on the wrong train and ended up mooching around Manchester

Piccadilly before realising she needed Oxford Road, by which time it was already mid-afternoon.

Walking between stations she realised she would almost pass Mr K's – sorry, Anton's – flat; but the treasured-though-yet-to-be-used key was safely locked away in her bedside cabinet. She had no number for Anton and didn't even know if he was in town. So she continued miserably on, finally arriving in Chester for teatime. Even the walk from the station took half an hour. What a bloody awful journey!

Amongst the bills and free newspapers was a small grey envelope. Jill didn't recognise the writing and tossed it on the table along with the rest. Then she unpacked her grip and hung up her clothes before running a hot-as-she-could-bear bath. Soaking in the soapy bubbles, she gradually felt more relaxed.

She lay there 'til the water was tepid and it was starting to go dark. She'd nothing in the fridge, and didn't fancy a solitary evening anyway so she dressed quickly in her comfiest trousers and jumper and set out for a hair of the dog, stuffing the mystery envelope in her bag on the way out.

She eschewed the Bridge and strolled all the way up to the Cross before deciding on the Bull & Stirrup. With luck it would be busy enough to get lost in without encountering any of Jay's mates. Bren she could cope with; a friendly shoulder might be just the ticket.

'Higson's, love?' was reassuring. The first one was a bit of a struggle but when she went for a refill the bar had emptied that much Bren offered to bring it over. She plonked two halves down on the circular table and parked herself opposite Jill.

'Phil can cope on his own for a while. I could do with a sit-down. I'm knackered.' Jill smiled warmly and they sat in friendly silence a moment.

'So, how's his lordship? Not giving you a hard time, I hope?'

'Er…no…other way round, if anything.' Bren raised her eyebrows. 'Yeah, 'fraid I've blotted my copybook somewhat,' and Jill began unburdening herself.

Bren didn't interrupt and, feeling both unjudged and supported, Jill gave a fairly full account of proceedings. Only when she recounted the denouement in Greg's cottage did Bren comment.

'Well you certainly enjoyed yourself, hon! I shouldn't worry. He'll get over it.'

'You reckon? He was pretty riled.'

'Yeah, but when he's calmed down… I mean it's not as though he caught you in the act, or…'

'No…another few minutes…'

'Yeah… I was going to say: or with another woman,' and Bren gave her a searching glance.

'Huh!' snorted Jill, and covering her confusion, 'he'd probably have joined in! Reckon he'd have liked that…'

'Maybe at the time, love. But later it would've gnawed at him. Men can't handle that sort of thing…not with their girlfriends anyway…'

Discretion and curiosity conflicted Jill, but the bar got busy again and Bren had to get back to work. Shortly afterwards Phil was hovering, a bottle of White Shield in his hand.

'On the house. Bren says you've earned it!'

Confession had unwound Jill; the beer helped. She sighed and lolled back in the chair. Then she remembered the letter.

> *Miláčku,* [it began], *I trust this finds you well. There have been developments. I believe you are free next weekend. If you could meet me at the flat around six on Saturday, it could well prove to your advantage. Dress for dinner! Ahoj! A.*

Eyes-wide, heartbeat missing, Jill craved spirits. Rum & coke? Perhaps not! Brandy & Babycham. She transferred what was left of the Shield to a neighbouring table and strode to the bar. Both Bren and Phil had disappeared and the unfamiliar barman looked taken aback at the order of a large Martell and a small bottle of Babycham. Jill's tone clearly brooked no comment, however, and after a withering look to his query about ice the barman served her in silence. She returned to her table, sat down rather too quickly and took a slug of neat brandy. What the hell was Mr K up to now?

Thirty-Two

Jay swallowed hard. His tongue felt like sandpaper, and a Bactrian hump was blocking his throat. The hairs on his neck were prickly and his palms sweaty. It hadn't struck him he'd be this nervous. Presumably it was the unfamiliarity. Or the repeated postponements when he'd psyched himself up for the meeting. Now he had to make the most of it. Otherwise the term would be over and he couldn't capitalize on it before the new school year in September.

Departmental meetings were okay. He'd got over his nerves there a while back. Just five of them sitting round the desk in Tess's classroom wasn't intimidating. This was more like a staff meeting, and he hated those, never said a word. He didn't know anyone here, though, might make it easier. But being seated in armchairs in a large oval that occupied the main meeting room at Tarporley Teachers' Centre *was* pretty unnerving.

'Fincher? How's it look to you?' Geoff Thornbury was giving him just the entrée he needed.

'Er…um…thanks, sir… I mean Mr Thornbury, sorry. Seems to me the moderating arrangements are the key.' The adviser nodded encouragingly and Jay, gulping his nerves away, plunged in. 'Well, I mean even the traditionalists concede that – for less-able pupils especially – there are advantages to continuous assessment. Exams are okay for people who are good at them, right? And by and large secondary modern and lower-stream comprehensive kids aren't. For starters the system's already rejected them. Especially in two-tier areas. Nothing against the grammar schools themselves of course…' He was conscious that some of the attendees were from Altrincham and Sale where single-sex grammars prevailed. 'They've not written the rules. But the eighty per cent of kids who don't make it already feel like failures.'

'Don't think anyone here's going to dispute that, Fincher. Can you expand on your moderation point, though?'

'Sorry, just trying to set the context. My point is that those who oppose continuous assessment do so from an academic standpoint. Exams were good enough to get them to university so they ought to be good enough for everyone. In other words, they – we – are judging the system from the perspective of success.'

'Obviously,' drawled a public school voice, in an expensive tweed jacket. 'What's wrong with that?'

'Nothing, as far as we're concerned. But it's not about us: it's about the kids. We need to look at the system through the eyes of those who fail. What's best for them?'

'I'm sure you're going to tell us!'

'We already know – continuous assessment. So they've a chance to build steadily on any success throughout the course instead of committing everything to memory and regurgitating it in three sickly-hot July hours.'

'S'pose you've got a point, but what then?'

'Oh c'mon, if you admit continuous assessment provides more encouragement to the majority then why can't you accept it's the best way to assess the new courses?'

''Cause we're concerned about standards.' The woman from the girls' grammar school sounded patronising. She looked it, too: all permed hair and twinset pearls.

And her fellow dinosaur chipped in: 'And rightly so.'

Jay emitted a frustrated sigh but before he could let rip, Geoff Thornbury intervened.

'Well that's a consideration, of course. But some of us think we can overcome it. Finch?'

'Course! I mean who knows the kids best? Us, or some anonymous academic from the AEB? Once you admit it's the classroom teacher, the rest follows.' He turned to the sceptics. 'Surely you know your own kids best?'

'Well of course. That's not the issue. We might know our *children* (Jay noted the stress in the put-down) best but we know nothing about yours. How can we be sure we'd apply the same standards?' She fingered the pearls self-consciously: maybe she wasn't as confident as she let on.

What she was really saying was that standards in a girls' grammar were likely to be higher than in a secondary modern. Or, even more pointedly, that her standards were higher than his! He bottled the temptation to dismantle her.

'But that's exactly the point.'

'Well, I'm glad you agree.' Her tone dripped acid.

'No, sorry,' Jay's tone was frigidly polite, 'you misunderstand me. The crux is not whose standards are higher. The crux is making sure we all apply the same methodology.'

Miss Snooty Drawers looked perplexed and Jay pressed home his advantage. 'Suppose we as a group identified the standards required in the various aspects of the curriculum and then devised a method of applying them across all our schools?'

'But there are more than thirty of us! It'd take for ever.'

'But if we could do it, then would we have a common standard?'

'Well…possibly. But…'

'So you agree in principle?' He swivelled round, conscious that he was soaring beyond his authority, that this was Thornbury's role. 'I mean, c'mon…do we all agree if you could establish a system that applied to us all, and more importantly to all our kids, then we'd've cracked the standards issue?'

Enthusiastic nods from opposite – a gaggle of secondary modern teachers from Ellesmere Port – and, crucially, albeit grudgingly from the grammar school contingent at the far end of the room. Gradually the nods spread round the group.

'Well if we can agree the principle surely we sort out the bloody details!'

The meeting concluded with refreshments and an invitation to all those interested to form a steering group, which would meet early in the Michaelmas Term. It would continue to be chaired by Geoff Thornbury, who sought Jay out amidst the coffee cups.

'I'll have to watch out for you, young Fincher: doing my job already!'

'Sorry, Mr Thornbury, I didn't mean to exceed my…'

'You didn't! You did us all a favour. We got the outcome I wanted without it appearing to have been imposed from above. You know, County Hall…that sort of thing.'

'Yeah, point taken. I did get a bit carried away though. Sorry!'

'No need: that's why I wanted you there. A dose of enthusiasm never hurt anyone. And you've got plenty of that!'

Jay smiled appreciatively but his bubble was punctured as Miss Snootypants, who was apparently called Fiona Manning, interrupted.

'Sorry I've got to dash, Geoff. Some of us have got departments to run! Bye, Mr Fincher, no doubt we'll meet again.' Her tone indicated she sincerely hoped not and Jay was busy framing a disparaging rejoinder…

'Bye, Fiona. Give my regards to your headmistress.'

Jay turned to go as well, but Thornbury intercepted him.

'Don't let our grammar school colleagues ruffle your feathers, Finch. Have a good summer. I'll be in touch soon.'

'Thanks, Mr Thornbury.'

'Geoff!' he corrected and swept out to the car park and a 1969 Lotus Cortina, noted Jay with approval – 5.5 J steelies and all! Be a talking point next time.

Later he wanted to tell someone! Unfortunately, his dad was running a course in mid-Wales and his mum was busy with some fête she was helping organise for St James's. Not that she'd be that interested anyway. She'd be pleased for him, of course, in her faintly distracted way. But she was a geographer, for God's sake: couldn't expect her to appreciate an arcane topic like CSE Mode 3 English!

Jill would. Especially now she seemed to be keen on advancing her own studies. Something about the *University of the Air*; he should've listened properly. She was clearly excited by the prospect which he'd gleaned had something to do with one of her former teachers. Not that he was likely to find out in the near future. She wasn't answering the 'phone and the twice he'd called round at the flat, she wasn't in. Just as well, maybe: he hadn't a clue what he'd have said.

He was pretty sure it was Pard's fault. He'd obviously got her pissed, well, even more pissed, after Jay had gone to bed, and then taken advantage. Though you couldn't blame him in a way. I mean his missus had run off with some bloke, so he'd naturally be feeling a bit sex-starved. And Jill was so bloody attractive...any guy'd want to get it off with her. Maybe it was the taxi business. She had seemed pretty turned on, even allowing for the drink. Perhaps it was his own doing...getting her all worked up and then buggering off to bed like a wally. She'd be easy meat... Plus it wasn't as if they were actually screwing or owt; they were both fully dressed after all. Yeah...he'd probably over-reacted. Again!

He was still racked-off though and he didn't know what to do about it. Chris would've known, of course, his big brother always did. But it was a bit of a one-way conversation these days. Obviously! Plus, this wasn't one of those occasions when he already knew what he should do deep down. Then he'd talk to his big brother's photo and be reassured (or not!) about what the advice would be. It might seem strange to anyone else – not that he'd ever share it, of course – but he always knew...

Even if his dad had not been in Wales Jay couldn't really talk to him about this. Most things, yes: but not this. How'd you even start: *Bit of advice, Dad, please. Came downstairs to find Jill and Pard havin' it off. What d'you reckon I should do?* Hmm…hardly! And as for his mum…totally out of the question. She'd never really taken to Jill (for ages she'd professed to think he was still with Caroline) and this would just compound it. Nah! Definitely not a case of keeping it in the family…

Friends? Communications with Pard were clearly suspended ad infinitum and Malc was miles away. Not the sort of thing you could discuss on the 'phone. Or face-to-face, really. It just wasn't summat they'd ever talked about. That left…well…precisely no one!

It occurred to him a woman might understand better. But again, who? He could usually talk to Mary. Jill's mum was nothing if not broad-minded but, same thing, not the subject for a 'phone call. Linda was out of the question, of course. That just left Bren.

Maybe time for a pint or six of Higson's!

Thirty-Three

Jill's key, with its handsome blue leather fob lay in her purse. But Mr K's Aston was neatly parked in Lot No.4. Somehow it didn't seem right just to let herself in. Supposing he was busy. Or had visitors. She didn't want to seem pushy so she rang the bell. Waiting to announce her arrival through the intercom she realised how tense she was. What if Mrs Brayson answered? Did she know Jill was coming? Worse still if a stranger responded. A woman…

She needn't've worried. Her host's cultured, Mittel-European tones invited her to come right up. Her heart was pounding. It was some weeks since she'd seen her mentor and the uncertainty surrounding her visit made it worse. She was swiftly installed in her room however, luxuriating in the comfort of her surroundings and Mrs Brayson's attention to detail. She would have to wear *that* dress again, but recalling the reception it had received last time reduced any embarrassment and, sure enough, Mr K was as charmingly complimentary as before.

'Low on the old champagne stocks, my dear. Dry sherry okay with you?'

Jill was relieved to see a bottle of Tio Pepe cooling in the ice bucket. It was Ray Fincher's favourite aperitif so she knew she liked it.

'Mmm, lovely thanks, Mr…er…Anton.' And, as he poured her a schooner generous even by Ray's standards: 'Cheers!'

'Na zdraví!'

'You promised to tell me last time. Is that Polish?'

'Czech, láska – my love. Cheers!'

'How come, if you don't mind me asking?'

'What? How does a Czechoslovakian émigré become a surgeon in Chester and end up a professor and knight of the realm?'

'Er…yes, exactly!'

'My parents came from Praha, father was a doctor, mother a teacher. The Jewish Quarter was unhealthy so they moved out to Karlovy Vary when my sisters were born. When the Third Reich's territorial ambitions became clear they fled, first to Austria, then France and finally to South London. I'd already trained as a doctor and Guy's were recruiting as fast as they could, especially during the blitz. It was hard work but fascinating. I fell in with a group, which included Ludwig Wittgenstein. He'd deserted academia, disgusted with the pampered Cambridge environment. He was a hospital porter, though we all treated him as a fellow professional. After the blitz there wasn't the same supply of air-raid casualties to study and a few of us moved north, initially to your stamping ground.' Jill looked puzzled but didn't interrupt. 'Yes, Ludwig became a lab assistant at Newcastle's Royal Victoria Infirmary. I believe you know it, láska?'

'I'll say! I trained there!'

'And no doubt lived close by. Ludwig and I shared a flat in Brandling Park. I expect you know that, too.' Jill nodded vigorously, recalling how close it was to Sally's ménage. 'He introduced me to several of his philosopher friends and that's where my interest originated. I'm not a medical professor. We went to Cambridge after the war, then when Ludwig died I moved north and took up a post here in Manchester. That's where I met my wife. We were idyllically happy... But when she and our daughter were killed in the accident I wanted a change. So I moved to Chester.'

'Strewth! You have led a full life! And the knighthood?'

'Can't shed much light on that, I'm afraid. You'd have to ask Dick Crossman.'

Jill remembered the name from the seminar she'd been to. He was the health minister or something. But her mentor's apparent reluctance to discuss the subject dissuaded her from further enquiry. Instead, emboldened by two schooners of Tio Pepe she switched to the present.

'So...apart from the obvious pleasure of my company...what am I doing here, Anton?'

'It *is* a pleasure, my dear. But you're quite right. There's more to it. You recall our original chat last Christmas?'

'What about your patronage, and my discretion?'

'Precisely Sister Walker: both are about to aspire to the next level.'

Once more Jill looked perplexed.

'Don't be alarmed. It will, I trust, be an enjoyable experience. We're having dinner with Molly Shawcross.'

'What...the...er...Matron from the ministerial reception? Oh that's okay. I liked her.'

Anton was clearly, as Ray Fincher would say, a creature of habit. Same time, same restaurant. The only difference was that Charterhouse's small private dining room had been requisitioned for the three of them. The flowers on the table and in high vases at both sides must've cost a bomb so what the dinner set back Anton! Rich as well as gifted, eh! Jill remembered something about his wife being an heiress but she'd dismissed it at the time as jealous gossip. Maybe not...there wasn't *that* much money in surgery, surely; not even if you were a knight.

Molly arrived a few minutes after eight. It hadn't struck Jill at the reception when she'd been in uniform but she was strikingly attractive. Tall and slim, her brunette hair perfectly framed her pretty features in the kind of Jean Shrimpton look Joyce had espoused that time on Lindisfarne. Recalling what a Bacchanalian event that had turned into, Jill was determined to stay sober, at least until she knew what the score was. Her resolve was immediately put to the test as a bottle of Pol Roger arrived. On top of the Tio Pepe it was hardly designed to promote sobriety. It went perfectly with the lobster bisque, though; as did the Sancerre that accompanied the Dover Sole. By the time a gargantuan platter of Beef Wellington arrived, to be washed down by Château Latour, Jill's good intentions had crumbled.

'Well, Molly, are you going to share your plans with our young friend?'

'Certainly. Fairer to call them *our* plans though, Anton. The original idea was yours, after all. And most of the initial research. Not to mention the contacts.'

'Perhaps, but you're the one who's going to make it happen.'

Jill's patience reflected her fraying concentration: 'What, for heaven's sake?'

'Charlottesville, my dear!' exclaimed Molly enigmatically and when Jill continued to look confused she added: 'That's where I'm headed. And you too, if I can persuade you to join me.'

Damn! Jill recalled it was in Virginia, though she'd only the vaguest idea where that was.

'Allow me to explain,' Anton offered. 'When I came to this country, the NHS was still a twinkle in Nye Bevan's eye. Now twenty years on it's the envy of the world. But like all grandiose institutions it's beginning to suffer from bureaucratic tendencies. Not least in its monolithic exclusion of alternative forms of provision.'

This was starting to sound like a politics lesson. Jill stifled a yawn, but Anton ploughed on.

'In the States it's quite different.'

'Yeah,' interrupted Molly, chuckling, 'you have to pay!'

'Well yes,' conceded Anton, 'but suppose you could have the best of both countries' systems. A service free at the point-of-need but not encumbered by the machinery of state.'

'Exactly! And that's what our trip's all about. Some of Anton's big pharmaceutical contacts are falling over themselves to finance us. They reckon that if we're successful they'll get the lion's share of the action.'

'Sounds expensive. Who are these firms exactly?' Jill's detachment had survived the politics but not the £-signs. Or maybe that should be $-signs!

'Glaxo here and, on the other side of the pond, Pfizer.'

Thank God for Stephen: Jill had heard of those!

'Well I can see they'd have the funds all right. But where do we come in?'

'Thought you'd never ask,' smiled Molly. 'Glaxo have already promised to underwrite all expenses for the trip and Pfizer will provide the premises and facilities.'

Jill dredged her memory for details Stephen had shared on their peregrinations around Northumberland.

'But aren't Pfizer based in New York?'

Molly looked impressed, Anton proud.

'Very good! Though their main facilities are in Connecticut now. But they're currently developing a research centre in Charlottesville. It'll link into the local hospital, the Martha Jefferson. Dates from 1908, 'bout the same time as the RVI, eh Jill?'

'Only the Leazes site,' remarked Jill, 'the original hospital dates back to 1751.'

'Right! Anyway the project is designed with the European market in mind, specifically the UK. That's where we come in.'

'But how?'

'Well, they've already got a small team of UK medics, but they haven't got any nurses. They want people used to running both hospitals and individual wards – especially orthopaedic wards. That's your speciality, isn't it?'

'Sure is!' Jill was more enthusiastic now that she could see herself making a personal contribution. She didn't want to be viewed just as Anton's protégé, or worse, *fancy bit*. She recalled from her chat with Dame Dorothy that two-week experience placements were already available in some UK regions and wondered whether this would be similar.

'So how long would we be there for?'

'Six months, initially.'

Thirty-Four

Brenda had been curiously unhelpful.

It wasn't as if Jay had been his usual Bull-at-a-Stirrup, either. He'd planned what to say then gone in when he knew they'd be quiet. She'd been serving so he'd not attempted to quiz her; just ordered his usual pint touch (the lemonade took the edge off the cheapest bitter) and found a corner table. Out came his furled Guardian and three pints later when he'd given up on the crossword and the evening staff were arriving, he asked her if she'd like to join him. Deeming preliminaries unnecessary he plunged straight in to his account, omitting any reference to the taxi ride other than implying vaguely that Jill had seemed pretty randy. When he came to the bit where he'd gone to bed and left them to it Bren snorted derisively. Not exactly the support he was hoping for.

More confused than ever he finally rang Mary.

'Yer'd better get yer skates on hinny, otherwise she'll be away to America!'

That sounded as baffling as it did unlikely; surely Mary had got it wrong. He resolved to drop off a note on his way home promising to call by at eight on Saturday evening if she didn't respond. Meanwhile, he'd be at his parents. When he rolled home his mother informed him, a trifle curtly, that Jill had been on the 'phone and would meet him in the Bridge at seven o'clock Saturday.

Christ, she was beautiful! She'd clearly gone to some trouble: she had more make-up on than usual and a dead sexy combination of black, flared mini-skirt and saffron silk blouse. Not having smartened himself for the occasion Jay felt at a disadvantage straightaway. They had a couple of drinks and caught up in a desultory fashion before he could stand it no longer.

'Your mum mentioned America. You off on holiday?'

'Not exactly. I'm gonna work there.'

'What some sort of exchange?' Jay recalled mutual visits he and a French friend had made five years earlier. He'd spent three weeks on the Riviera.

'Not really, more like research.'

'Research? What into?'

'Alternative healthcare provision.' Then when he still didn't ask she added matter-of-factly: 'It's for six months, initially.'

'Six months!!' Heads turned in the bar as Jay blared it out. 'Bloody hell, Jill, nice of you to let me know! When's all this supposed to happen?'

'Not *supposed* to, Jay: it's all arranged. I leave at the beginning of September.'

'Huh!'

'I'd have told you earlier, if we'd been talking. But it's been a little difficult these last few weeks.'

'Not surprising when you haven't been answering my 'phone calls!'

'I can't see any point in raking it all over, Jay. I'm going and that's that. But I don't want you getting upset about it.'

'And you didn't think I might? I thought we were going steady?'

'More like unsteady lately, don't you think?'

'Well *the course of true love never did run smooth*!'

'Huh! Hardly the most tactful quote, Lysander! From one of two blokes in love with the same woman!'

Bugger! Was Shakespeare her bedtime reading these days! 'Well you should know!'

'Oh come on, love. This isn't getting us anywhere.'

'Agreed. Pax?'

'Pax!' And she blew him a kiss as he rose to return to the bar. 'No more beer, love, I'm all blown out. Something short: you decide.'

The lounge was crowded now and it took Jay some minutes to get served. Figuring he was likely to be driving home at some stage he opted to stay on the Hydes' but switched to halves (Christ! Don't say I'm getting sensible in my old age!) with a large vodka and orange for Jill. You never knew: if cards were correctly played she *might* invite him back to the flat.

Such hopes were promptly shattered, however, by the arrival of Jill's erstwhile boss.

'Isn't that Bronwen, just come in?'

'Oh yes. Good, she's seen us,' as Jill waved her friend across.

'Thought she lived in deepest Wales somewhere? Bit of a coincidence, eh?'

'Not really, once I knew I was going I obviously had to talk to her about the flat. Best behaviour now!'

With any chance of sealing their rapprochement diminishing rapidly, Jay's immediate reaction was to brood. But Jill must have a reason other than politeness for her instruction so he swallowed his frustration manfully. The talk inevitably turned to Jill's trip and, whilst interested initially, Jay soon found the detailed nursing issues boring. Once it became apparent Bron was stopping over he invented an excuse and departed as gracefully as he knew how.

A few days later Jill rang with the news: Bronwen, who had no use for the flat in the foreseeable future, was amenable to Jill's suggestion that her boyfriend should occupy it whilst she was in America. On certain conditions! It was to be strictly a bachelor pad: no female visitors (Jill was compellingly certain she'd know if that particular rule was broken). And no stag parties either. He was to pay a market rent and undertake to keep it clean and tidy. And yes, as a special privilege he could move his books in, provided he acquired or built a bookcase. Heart crossed and hoping to die, he could move in as the new term started.

Deal!

Meanwhile, they'd both be busy: Jill with preparations for her trip and Jay with cementing the progress he'd made with his CSE-moderation plans. But if they wouldn't see much of each other, they did seem to have crossed a significant bridge. It was almost as if the prospect of being apart was bringing them closer together. Surely she knew how much he loved her? But he wasn't very good at expressing his feelings: he'd really have to try harder.

'Something's come up.' The time-honoured formula signalled to his dad that he needed to talk. But before they could get down to the nitty gritty there were certain formalities to be observed. Like a session on the bagatelle table, which Jay edged narrowly. No matter how much his own game improved through the League, when it came to their family tournaments it was always close. Must be that degree in snooker, he reflected aloud, much to his father's amusement.

'So how was Wales, Dad?'

'Excellent! We made a lot of progress.'

'What were you doing exactly?'

'Well you remember meeting Sir John that time on Kinder Scout?' Jay nodded appreciatively. 'And that he and I have been developing the Duke of Edinburgh's Award scheme? You'll recall in the early days, despite John's best efforts, it was seen as elitist. But once the DES had adopted my Record of Personal Achievement we could expand it, especially in the comprehensives that have been springing up at Labour's behest. It's going to be a key component in ROSLA, too. All those newly-imprisoned sixteen-year-olds will need something positive to keep them occupied beyond the traditional academic curriculum.'

'That's why you've been encouraging my efforts at Woodbridge.'

'Of course, but we can't rely on the isolated initiatives of young enthusiasts like you, son. We need every LEA to support its secondary schools in embracing outdoor education.'

Jay was well aware that the concept was still at the developmental stage.

'Well you can count on Cheshire surely? Didn't you say that new CEO was keen on climbing?'

'Charles Fox? Absolutely! We must get him to North Wales. His eldest son's not much younger than you and keen to learn rock climbing. But Cheshire's only one of scores of LEAs and we need them all on board ideally. Which brings us back to your original question.'

'What? You mean that's what your course has been about? How come?'

'As Staff Inspector for Outdoor Education I do have a certain pull, you know! The department were persuaded to support the course and every county in England was invited to send a representative. Some were already advisers like your man Thornbury.'

'What Geoff?'

'Yes. The key is they work for the local authority, not the department like me. That model wouldn't work.'

'Why not?'

'Two reasons; first, there aren't enough of us. Second, it would be seen as dirigiste. This way the DES effectively gets an agent, an advocate in every county in England.'

This was exciting stuff, but it wasn't actually what he wanted to discuss! Still…

'So in a way I'm trialling locally what you're aiming to achieve nationally.'

'Exactly, son. Which reminds me: you going to be teaching on that drama course next month?'

'Hope so. Why?'

'Cause I'd like you to look in on Nelson.'

'Who's he when he's at home?'

'Not he…it! Next door to your drama centre is HMS Nelson. It's a former Navy training school but Cheshire County Council have acquired it and it's got the makings of an outdoor centre. I want you to go down and introduce yourself. Give it the once-over and maybe get in a bit of mountaineering at the same time. The warden's called Gwynn, Caradoc Gwynn. Good bloke; used to be an instructor at Plas y Brenin. We've done a few routes together; just mention my name. Though I'll try and 'phone him in advance. There's a potential chief instructor, too; a lad called Colin…something…Yates, I think. Serious climber by all accounts.'

'Sure, Dad. I'd be glad to. Need to borrow a car, though…which reminds me there was something I wanted to mention.'

'Of course. What?'

'Well it's about Jill.'

His dad's already relaxed features brightened appreciably. He adored his future daughter-in-law and didn't mind who knew it.

'What's my favourite Sister been up to? Not promoted again, surely?'

'Sort of…she's off to America.' And Jay explained the plan and how it was only for six months and they'd keep in close touch, of course. Maybe he could even go over at Christmas? Not that he'd broached the possibility with Jill yet. He tried to sound positive, giving the impression that it was something they'd decided together.

'And she wants me to look after the flat whilst she's away.'

'Well that's splendid! You could do with your own place. Spread your wings a bit. Not that your mother will necessarily see it that way.'

'Yeah, I was wondering whether you'd talk to her first.'

'Course. Leave it with me.'

'Cheers, Dad. Thanks a lot. Oh…just one other thing. I'm gonna need some wheels…'

Thirty-Five

Ideally, Jill wanted to see everyone before she went: her mam and dad and her two brothers, Sally – though if she and Jorja were still together that could be tricky – and, of course, the lit twins. There'd be some housekeeping arrangements to run through with Bron, but they could do that at the flat. Jay she sort of took for granted: he'd already promised to run her to the airport. They'd talked about how they'd keep in touch and what they'd do when she returned; as if her absence would automatically ensure the course of true love *did* run smooth once again. Although the stream of their affection had always been a bit turbulent, it was part of their mutual attraction. Maybe it would calm down a bit with an ocean apart to sort out how they truly felt. Not that Jill was in any doubt; she'd made it clear that she loved Jay. And she was certain that, in his own singular fashion, he loved her too: he just wasn't very good at demonstrating it!

The arrangements were complicated. She would visit the family around her birthday on 24th August. It fell on a Monday so the celebrations would have to be scheduled for the weekend. Jay was a problem. She obviously wanted him there, but where would he stay? There was definitely no room at her mam's, and stopping with his mate Pard wasn't an option. Maybe one of her aunts could put him up? Something'd turn up – it always did…

Meanwhile, how to break the news to the lit twins? Jill wondered whether Sue's move to Shrewsbury was partly to do with its proximity to Chester. She didn't have a 'phone number so she wrote explaining what had happened and that the opportunity was too good to miss and how she'd love to see them before she left. She ended by inviting them to her birthday-cum-leaving party at Wallsend Labour Club.

Sue's response was enthusiastic. Of course she'd come, they both would. Joyce didn't take up her new post until September so she still had the flat in Gosforth and they'd stop there. Jill was welcome to stay too, or they could put up any friends she couldn't find floor-space for! She'd be there by Saturday teatime if Jill would like to call by?

With a strong sense of déjà vu Jill pressed the intercom at No.2 Moor Crescent, moments later falling through the doorway into the welcoming arms of Joyce.

'Why, it's lovely to see you pet! How've you been keeping? You're looking well! Sue's not here yet; train delayed at Manchester apparently. But she shouldn't be too much longer. I'll put the kettle on.'

It was as if Jill had never left. They traded family gossip and, although they agreed that details of Jill's forthcoming trip should await Sue's arrival, Joyce couldn't resist quizzing her briefly about Virginia. Surprise, surprise she had relatives there! Joyce seemed to know people everywhere!

'Yes, but in the north, in the City of Alexandria. Well just outside actually. In Fairfax County. It's only about ten miles south of DC.'

Jill looked thrown and Joyce explained: 'District of Columbia: it's what they call Washington locally. Where is it you're going to?'

'Charlottesville. It's in Virginia, too, but I'm not sure where.'

'I think it's further south, but the Americans are so vague about distance. Dan and Vera, my cousins, think nothing of driving a couple of hundred miles and back on a day-visit.'

'Molly – she's the matron, I'm going to be working with – said it had a connexion with someone called Jefferson. But I'd never heard of him and I didn't like to ask in case it seemed ignorant.'

'Jefferson, eh? One of the founding fathers. He was largely responsible for their wonderful constitution. Lived somewhere near Charlottesville, I think. We'll ask Sue.'

'Trust you pair! Is there anything you don't know between you?'

'Loads! That's why I'm pursuing my own prospects. You remember that University of the Air we talked about a while back?'

Jill nodded.

'Well I've done lots more research. It's due to launch next year so by the time you get back from the USA they'll be inviting applications. If it's any sooner, I'll get us both signed up. That is…if you still want to?' she added tentatively.

'Definitely! Virginia should be great professionally but I want to keep up my studies too.'

'I was hoping you'd still feel that way. Meanwhile, are you up for some more Shakespeare during your American adventure?'

'Course! What have you got in mind?'

'*The Merchant of Venice*. You'll love it. It's got everything: a convoluted plot, a splendid villain, a terrific clown and a strong heroine, just like Rosalind. It's a bit more serious than *As You Like It*, with noble themes like justice and mercy. In fact, its most famous speech is all about the quality of mercy. But it's funny too and has some beautiful love poetry in it.'

'Sounds great.'

'Oh…talking of strong heroines…that sounds like Sue!'

The front door opened, followed by noisy footsteps up the hall. Sue burst into the room. Hugs all round. And Shakespeare forgotten as they grilled each other about family, and friends, party plans, and America.

'Charlottesville? Fantastic! You must go to Monticello: the *little mountain*. We've a guidebook somewhere. I'll dig it out for you. Jefferson was an incredible bloke. Third president of the United States but he couldn't wait to leave politics and get back to his retreat…'

George Walker was the current chairman of the Leek Club. That meant a seat on the General Committee and privileged use of various Labour Club facilities. The plan was to lay out the buffet in the lounge and clear the bar for dancing and drinking. Anyone wanting to play snooker or darts could use the games room as normal. Problem! Women weren't allowed in the bar and even the combined advocacy of the Walker brothers (Jill's Uncle Bill, a former Club President, was down from Glasgow) failed to sway the committee. They could use the upstairs ballroom, and serve food in the main committee room. The smaller committee rooms were off limits.

The Walkers were a large family: George was the youngest of seven and, with Mary's side similarly represented, there was an impressive number of uncles, aunts and cousins to contend with. Plus, no one in St Peter's Road, or Churchill Street, or Ridley Avenue, or Coniston Gardens had ever been to America, so the send-off rapidly gathered pace. The Walkers in general, and Jill in particular, were popular so there was no shortage of friends and hangers-on. Additionally, Sally had pinned an invitation on the notice board in the RVI nurses' home and a healthy contingent of Jill's former colleagues swelled the numbers even further. There must have been well over a hundred guests.

Jay had promised to be good. He got on pretty well with most of her closest relatives, especially her brothers, so Jill was only slightly worried when Stephen appeared. But he, too, seemed determined not to make waves, and quite soon he was whirling a delighted Mary Walker around the dance floor. (Her mam had always fancied him, scoffed Jill dismissively!) Sally and Jorja put in an early appearance, and soon after the lit twins arrived. Finally, just when Jill thought there could be no more surprises, two minibuses from the RVI decanted assorted nurses, medics and auxiliaries, including to Jill's momentary agitation, Stirl.

Music was courtesy of The Baxter Five. They were friends of Al's and for amateurs they were pretty good. They'd been banging out mainstream stuff – Beatles, Elvis, The Carpenters, Kenny Rogers, Simon & Garfunkel – which had cross-generational appeal, so the dance floor was mostly packed. Jill was in demand and it was only after an hour or so that she remembered Jay. She spotted him sitting with her big brother, Rob, with two pints of Fed Special in front of them. Nowt new there!

'You okay?'

'Yeah sure. You know I'm not a great danseur.'

'Well as long as you're enjoying yourself.'

'Oh aye, just watching the antics on the dance floor. Your mate Sally and Pard's wife seem pretty friendly!'

'Jorja?'

'Yeah. I mean look at 'em now. They're like a pair of clams!'

'So?'

'Well… I mean, they're not…?'

'Lesbians? Of course…didn't you realise?'

'No way! You mean they're together? Pard's wife's gone off with another woman?' She detected an element of gloating in his astonishment.

'Sure. What's wrong with that?'

'Well…er…nothing, I s'pose. It just hadn't occurred to me…'

Jill sought to look both exasperated and understanding; she hoped Jay wouldn't leap to similarly uncouth conclusions about the lit twins. Fortunately, they were rather more discreet. And they weren't dancing anyway. She promised to catch up with him in a bit and went off to check they were okay. She needn't have worried. They'd procured several plates of sandwiches, vol-au-vents, crisps and pies and two bottles of chilled white wine. Jill slumped down gratefully in the proffered chair and held out a spare glass. Half an hour and a bottle of Sancerre (how on earth had they got hold of that?) later Jill acceded to repeated pleas to dance. The room seemed to be whirling as fast as her, and after a particularly gymnastic rendition of Mungo Jerry's In the Summertime she found herself, ready to collapse, subsiding onto a sofa. Next to Stirl.

Must be fate. This was their third encounter. Years back as a green student nurse Jill'd been on laundry duty one Saturday morning when she'd almost fallen foul of the orderly. She'd only been saved by the intervention of the staff nurse but had inexplicably not dobbed Stirl in, allowing him, rather, to take refuge in an adjoining room. Her complicity had subsequently been repaid after the Nurses' Ball when he'd rescued her from the considerably more threatening embraces of a drunken houseman in the deserted foyer of Block. He'd seen her to her room afterwards and been a model of propriety. Neither had mentioned their first encounter, although Jill had been tempted. Only her tiredness and the instinct that then was not the time prevented her...

'Do you remember that time in the laundry?' Jill had to lean into him to make herself heard, so the question emerged as a sort of shouted-whisper.

'Course! I never got a chance to apologise. Or to thank you, Nurse Walker.'

'That's *Sister* Walker these days, Stirl,' corrected Jill joshingly.

'Oh, well done, hinny! Yer a bit young fer a sister, like!'

'Well thank you, kind sir... Anyway there was no need to apologise. You didn't actually do anything and, besides, I've my own confession to make. Just never had the chance...'

'No time like the present, pet!'

'Hmm...maybe...but not here, it's too public.' She closed her eyes momentarily. 'See what's through there.'

Stirl opened the door to a sparsely furnished cubbyhole. The secretary's office? It had a large, old-fashioned wooden desk with an office chair behind it and a padded brown armchair. Jill sank gratefully into the garish orange cushions.

'So what did you wanna confess?'

Jill hesitated, taut and apprehensive. 'Well, it wasn't about what happened but what might have...if, yer know, Staff hadn't interrupted. Thing is...I'd woken up... I knew what was going on...yer know, what you were doing and I didn't try and stop it, did I?'

'Why not?'

'Cause...cause although I were scared...I were excited an all.'

'What, seeing me like that?'

'Yeah, course...and just before Staff came in I were...'

'What? Yer can tell me now, hinny...it's okay.'

'Well I were that fired up... I wanted to touch it...' Now it was out (so to speak) Jill was embarrassed and relieved simultaneously.

'Wey, hinny, yer nivver said…ah'd've liked that, mind!' Stirl looked thoughtful and then added casually: 'Would yer still like to, pet?'

Jill'd been working round to it for so long, that now she was shocked into silence.

'I mean…only if yer wanna, like.'

She fidgeted nervously and pulling one of the cushions out from behind her stuck it in her lap. 'Er…maybe. Dunno. Can't tell 'til I see it, I s'pose.'

'Wey, yer bugger, thas easily fixed,' and the orderly promptly unzipped his trousers.

Electrified into speechlessness Jill slid her hand surreptitiously under her lap-cushion and shut her eyes, almost unable to believe this was happening. Some birthday present, huh! When she opened them Stirl was rampant. Underneath the cushion Jill's fingers snaked inside her skirt-band…

'Looks like you could do with some fresh air!' Jay was prodding her gently and laughing. Jill shook herself, uncertain whether she'd been extremely wicked – or dreaming.

'Come on, let's go for a breather.'

It was dark but warm outside. They crossed the car park arm in arm to a playing field beyond. The benches were empty.

'Well you seem to be having an exciting time!' Jill gave a noncommittal cough. 'You were fast asleep! Who was the bloke providing the shoulder?'

'Er…that'd be Stirl. Known him for ages. Where'd he go?'

'Dunno. He just smiled and got up as I took over lean-to duty. Disappeared.'

'And I was definitely asleep? On the sofa?'

'Yeah, there's no harm in that is there?'

'None at all!' Jill tried not to sound too relieved and Jay shook his head and changed the subject.

'What're you taking for the plane? I've got *Bruno's Dream*, the latest Iris Murdoch. You used to like her, didn't you?'

'Yeah, thanks. Taking *The Merchant of Venice*, too.'

'Oh, you'll enjoy it.'

'Hope it's not too heavy going! The plot sounds quite serious.'

'Well its themes are. But there's plenty of humour and some of the poetry is sublime.'

'Mmm…' Jill was thoroughly relaxed again, stretched out on the bench with her head in Jay's lap.

He leaned down and kissed her gently on the lips.

'One of my favourites, too…when you're building castles under the Virginian stars think of me!' He gestured towards the blackness above:

> …*look how the floor of heaven*
> *Is thick inlaid with patens of bright gold*
> *There's not the smallest orb which thou behold'st*

my darling Jill

> *But in his motion like an angel sings,*
> *Still quiring to the young-ey'd cherubins…*

There's more… Memorise it for me, sweetheart, it's near the beginning of Act V. The quality of mercy is fine and dandy but the harmony of the spheres is something else. Happy Birthday, acushla.'

'Acushla?'

'Irish! It means *pulse of my heart!*'

'Oh, Jay! That's so beautiful…'

Thirty-Six

'Now about those wheels, son.'

It was the weekend after Jay had waved Jill off at Newcastle Airport. She'd seemed last-minute reluctant and their final embraces were punctuated with tearful kisses. Still, Jay felt they were back on the right track again, especially after her party... Helluva long time though, six months...

He and his dad were in the Peacock. 'I think I may have the solution; but it'll need careful handling.' Jay looked suitably quizzical. 'Yes, it's...it's to do with the death of your brother.' His dad never called him Chris and it was only latterly he'd started referring to him at all.

'How d'you mean, Dad?'

'Well afterwards your mother wanted to get rid of his car: you know, the MGA.' Jay nodded cautiously. 'But I didn't want to part with it; so I had a word with Roger Hood. You remember him, don't you?'

Of course Jay remembered him, although not as well, nor as intimately, as his wife, Fliss. And their three sons. The youngest, Tom, had been his best mate in Norfolk.

'Well I asked him to keep it to himself so, knowing how cagey Norfolk farmers are, he probably hasn't told a soul.'

This was tantalizing: 'Yes...and?'

'Well that's it. The MGA's been sequestered in some barn ever since. All you have to do is get yourself down to Brooklands and collect it. If... if...you want to...' His dad sounded almost tentative, perhaps to protect Jay's feelings.

'Strewth, Dad: you must be joking! Course I do!'

'Good; I'm sure it's what your brother would've wanted. Just need to play it a bit carefully with your mother. I never mentioned it to her. Still... leave that with me.'

For once his dad had no convenient meeting, which took him via Norfolk. Jay consulted his *Gentleman's Diary*. Let's see: Chester to Crewe, then pick up the Glasgow train bound for Euston. After that a short walk along to Euston Square for the Metropolitan & Circle Line. Five stops: King's Cross/Farringdon/Aldersgate/Moorgate to Liverpool Street and then the Great Eastern up to Norwich. Autolycus the Itinerant already had it by heart. Tom would meet him at Thorpe Station, doubtless sporting the latest Mini Cooper.

All went smoothly. And sure enough, a BRG Cooper was drawn up in the no-parking zone just outside the main exit.

'Hey, man: great to see you!' shouted Tom leaping out to take Jay's holdall. 'You've lost weight. You into sport or what?'

'Yeah, rock climbing. Big time. And getting paid for it, too!'

Tom looked just the same, although it must be five years since they'd seen each other. Taller maybe, tousled straw hair all over the place; he'd always been a good-looking bastard!

The thirteen-mile journey sped past as Jay explained his teaching combination of English and rock climbing. Tom was impressed but matched it with his own exploits. Within two years of graduating from Shuttleworth agricultural college he'd landed a post with an agency. Bobby's job too: swanning round East Anglia advising farmers on seeds and fertilisers. Jay remembered to make perfunctory enquiries about Tom's elder brothers but before he need venture onto the trickier ground of Tom's mum they were drawing up outside Brooklands, and there was Fliss, looking as buxom and bonny as ever. Jay had to remind himself he was there to collect a car not to shag his mate's mother. Not that he ever had; but they'd come tantalizingly close...

They enjoyed a hearty farm dinner – stew and Norfolk dumplings – washed down by generous quantities of home brew, and afterwards Jay found himself in the parlour alone with Roger Hood who just wanted 'a word'.

'Finest man I ever met, your dad!'

Jay swelled with pride. He'd heard his dad praised once before, by a monsignor whose responsibility for a group of RC colleges overlapped Ray Fincher's.

'He's the only man I've ever met,' the cleric had confided to Jay in a mellifluous Limerick accent, 'who I've never heard anyone speak ill of!'

So to garner his old boss's praise was a rare treat, especially as Jay had always been a tad in awe of the saturnine farmer, a hard man if ever there was one. (Autolycus approved of hardness!)

'How's the brandy?'

'It's excellent, sir, thank you. Much appreciated. My dad's favourite.'

'Yes I know. He introduced me to it.'

A silence developed, companionable, but long enough to make Jay uneasy. Had he upset the older man?

'Served in Lancasters. Tail-end Charlie. Must've seen some scrapes.'

Relieved, Jay just nodded.

'Didn't have to, mind. Didn't even have to volunteer: teaching was a Reserved Occupation. And even when he'd signed up he could've been an officer. Not started as a private and worked his way up to Staff-Sergeant.'

Jay knew all this but felt it best merely to grunt appreciatively.

'Maybe that's what gave him the strength...yer know...when yer brother was killed. Not that he ever said much. Didn't need to.'

Jay was mired in ambivalence. It was cheering to hear such encomiums but he'd often wished his dad *would* say something. Especially to him. Still, at least he was consistently silent! Jay was lost for words. Feeling thoroughly out of his depth, he was relieved when a discreet knock on the oak-panelled door signalled the entry of Tom.

'You're wanted on the 'phone, bor.'

Jay assumed it was his parents but was agreeably shocked to hear the dulcet tones of his-once-upon-a-lover, Caroline.

'Caro, 'swonderful to hear your voice! How on earth...?'

'A little bird told me...well your friend Tom, actually. Just thought I might like to know!'

She was stuck in Cambridge on her own. Her parents were in India. She was at a loose end. Help!

'Can you get over to Norwich?'

'Yeah, course, when?'

'Tomorrow? Let me know when you get in: I'll meet you at the station.'

'Hadn't you better check with Tom first, see if you can borrow his car?'

'Nah! Be okay.'

Knowing smiles greeted him when Jay emerged into the living room.

'So I guess we won't be seeing much of you in the next couple of days, then,' smirked Tom. 'Dare say you'll be wanting a lend of the Cooper?'

The next morning three of them tramped out past the brick cowsheds and the blackened-oak corn barns to a row of buildings Jay couldn't remember from his farm-working days before Durham. A block of low, garage-type workshops had been built since then, faced in flint and with pan-tiled gables. They went through two rooms to get to the locked door. In the centre of the garage a pod-shaped tarpaulin was stretched tight and pinned to the earth-floor by tent pegs.

'What the fuck?' muttered Tom, just out of his dad's earshot.

Jay was excited but apprehensive. His big brother would've wanted him to have the MGA, but how would he feel when he saw it? Supposing he did summat stupid?

Roger Hood undid the ties and pulled away the covers.

'Holy shit!' exclaimed Tom, 'you kept that quiet, Dad!'

The tears welled up behind Jay's glasses; but he was bursting with pride, too. The bright red, convertible MGA 1600 Twin Cam – *MTB 620*! He couldn't wait to go for a spin but… Tom's dad quietly grasped his son's shoulder and Jay was alone. The tears cascaded down his cheeks. Eventually he wiped them clear, and smiled proudly at his big brother's car. His, now…

As he entered the kitchen Tom was just replacing the black Bakelite 'phone in its cradle. 'That was Hal. Said to drop by whilst you're here.'

Hal was the grandson of their former landlord, Lady Veronica Kirkstead, who owned The Lodge and whose sailor son they had supplanted for six years. Well, not really supplanted: he'd been posted overseas for most of the time.

'What today?'

'Yeah…well now, really. If you've time…'

Jay calculated swiftly. He'd already got plans for the afternoon with Caroline but… 'Sure! We could give the MG a run, if you like.'

'Thought you'd never ask, bor!'

Ten minutes later they swung off the main Ditchingham road and onto the concrete-paved way, which, after a couple of hundred tree-lined yards, morphed into a gravel drive across open meadows. To their left wound the River Waveney, the county border. Jay smiled at the memory of the cow. The farmer who had grazing rights kept Friesians. Sometimes one would find its way through the crisscross dykes to the riverbank. Once, an overbold heifer had ventured into the main river and, being unable to regain the bank, had swum across. Jay, who'd been spinning for pike duly reported the incident to Farmer Bradenham.

'Huh! She did, did she! Well, let the silly ole fool spend the weekend in Suffolk then!' he'd snorted dismissively, as if a fate worse than death awaited the errant heifer. It'd become a family joke.

On the other side of the drive lay a range of low, sandy hills that stretched all the way to Bath House, Lady Veronica's home. Jay silently recalled his shameful contempt at their pathetic altitude, comparing them unfavourably with the giants of the Lakes like Scafell and Skiddaw. Most reprehensible of all, however, had been his eight-year-old's initial appraisal of The Lodge as it came into view where the drive dipped under a tall, elegant elm: 'Oh, what a horrible house!' he'd protested crabbily.

'So how is the sea captain?'

'Not a captain anymore. He's been promoted. Vice-Admiral Lord Kirkstead. But he's still a decent bloke and Hal – well, strictly, *Sir* Hal now – we get on pretty well these days.

Jay resisted an anciently remembered urge to scatter the pea-gravel all over the front windows of his one-time home and they growled to a halt as a large, handsome figure piled out of the bright blue front door. (Glad some things haven't changed, reflected Autolycus the Traditionalist.)

'Now then, young Fincher, how's tricks?'

'Top notch, thank you, m'Lord. I believe congratulations are in order?'

'Oh…just recognition for having outlasted the rest of the buggers,' laughed the admiral gruffly, though Jay thought he was secretly pleased.

'So, come to revisit old pastures?' And then, as he glimpsed the bright red monster behind them: 'Smart looking rig, young man.'

Tom saved Jay's embarrassment: 'It was his brother's, sir: Jay's down to collect it. And catch up with old friends as well of course…' he added diplomatically.

'Ah of course. Fine young man, your brother. Knew his CO. Said Chris had all the makings of a top-rate officer… Anyway, need to leave you to your own devices; I've been roped into presenting the prizes at the Primrose League fête. You fellows enjoy yourselves. Good to see you again, Jay.'

Just then Hal hove into sight round the side of The Lodge: 'Hello chaps! Jay, how's things? How're your mater and pater?'

'We're all fine, thanks, Hal. How're…' Jay's enquiry was cut short as the admiral set off towards the stable yard. Jay declined Hal's invitation to take a look around. It'd been ten years since they lived at The Lodge where, contrary to Jay's expectations, they'd been blissfully happy. He didn't fancy the prospect of what his or worse his big brother's room might look like now.

'Haven't got long I'm afraid. I've to be in Norwich for one. Any case, it's too nice to be indoors. If it's all the same to you I'd sooner stroll along to the kitchen garden.'

It was only a quarter-of-a-mile away, but as a child Jay had been puzzled by its name given it was so far from the kitchen. He remembered his mum's declaration that restoring it would be a labour of love and hoped it hadn't fallen into desuetude. 'And the boathouse, of course,' he explained, 'it's where Chris and I had our kayak, *Tarka*.'

They set off along the grassy track, the undergrowth on both sides thicker and more extensive than Jay recollected.

'So how come you've got an MGA?' enquired Hal, crassly, not registering Tom's baleful hiss.

'Inherited it from my brother.' Jay was keen to curtail the conversation but Hal's aristocratic traits didn't run to sensitivity.

'Oh right...Chris? He was killed in action wasn't he?'

Jay was pretty sure it was a motoring accident, but since his big brother's sub had seen serious combat out in the China seas that version of his death had got about. Even as early as his funeral which Tom, but not Hal, had attended. Jay had been disinclined to set the record straight. Then or now. He merely grunted affirmatively, which this time even the impervious baronet took as a sign to shut up.

Thirty-Seven

Jill almost didn't go. If Jay hadn't been at the departure gate to wave her goodbye, she'd have turned back. And just because of that damn birth certificate.

Well, a copy of it anyway: *Pursuant to the Births and Deaths Registration Acts, 1836 to 1929.* But she hadn't been born 'til 1947! Did that make her illegitimate? Still, they'd got the names of her parents right: *George Frederick Walker* and *Mary Hemsley Walker, formerly Simpson.* And there was the address they shared *40 Bewicke Street* although in her dad's entry it was described as being in Wallsend, whilst in her mum's it said Willington Quay. That was a bit confusing but it all seemed in order as it was signed *Alexander Thornton, Deputy Registrar,* with his seal printed over an orangey-red one-penny stamp with a portrait of King George VI. So that was all okay. But what threw Jill completely was that it stated quite clearly at the bottom that the said Mr Thornton had registered the birth in the *Sub-District of Tynemouth, in the County Borough of Tynemouth.* And Jill always thought she came from Wallsend!

But, no…Tynemouth! Perhaps that was why she'd always been drawn to the picturesque seaside village. The memory of her first trip, with her best friend, Liz Robson, came flooding back. She'd been about ten, and Liz twelve. They'd got the train from Howden down to Tynemouth (threepence return) and spent the morning in the amusement arcade. Liz had won ten shillings – one hundred and twenty chinking pennies – on the one-armed bandit. They'd traded them in at the kiosk and Liz had promptly given her half. Jill could recall the two shiny half-crowns vividly; but not as vividly as the kiss Liz had subsequently planted on Jill's surprised lips; or of the feel of her wet body as they skinny-dipped in a hidden cove off Cullercoats. She often wondered whether that had set her on the bi-path: she'd always enjoyed the sensitive, tender kiss of a girl far more than the clumsy, invasive efforts of most boys.

There was another trip disjoining her psyche. She'd been on her own for some reason. But why? Why would she have gone all that way solo? It must've been cause she had no one to go with... Then it dawned. It was after Rob had gone off to Blackpool for the Olympic trials. She no longer saw Liz; and her later love, Marge, had disappeared to Liverpool, inexplicably. She'd taken herself off to Tynemouth on a long walk. It'd been one of those days when the sea fret drenched everything, including your spirits. And something unpleasant had befallen her...something to do with the beach. Not a person, though...

When she remembered Jill laughed. It hadn't been owt at all: she'd just got dive-bombed by a load of pikies. She'd thick curls then and when a set of scrawny claws became entangled in them she'd screeched as loudly as the terns. But she'd come to no harm and her tormenters, doubtless more scared than she was, had disappeared as swiftly as they'd arrived.

Nostalgia, eh! Well that was it then: one last visit to her birthplace before she set out on her transatlantic adventure.

It was almost the end of August but still red-hot. Jill rooted round in her old den and located a pair of rope-soled pumps. They were comfortable to walk in, she remembered. What else? Shorts and a tee shirt; she was ready. The train seemed to get her to Tynemouth station far faster than in the old days and she was soon making her way through the terraces to Prior's Park. There were some dilapidated benches set along a cinder track overlooking the river. The tide was coming in and she watched long enough for it to engulf the Black Middens and disperse the cormorants to other fishing grounds. It was roasting, but she was hungry so she doubled back to Front Street, surfacing at the Salutation. She didn't feel like an alcoholic drink but the general store provided lemonade, a couple of sausage rolls and a packet of crisps.

She knew a secret garden in the Priory. Just the place for a picnic. Shivering through the green gloom of the gatehouse she emerged into bright sunlight. The ruins of the church entrance lay ahead but she swung right, past the red brick officers' lodgings. It wasn't really a garden, more a disused corner of the old fortress walls. But nobody ever went there so once she'd settled herself she stripped off her tee shirt. May as well work on the tan before the Virginian autumn!

Jill lay back amongst the grasses and sedges and late-blooming bush vetch. Then she opened the crisps and located the little blue greaseproof twist of salt. She unfurled it and distributed the contents between the crisps and the slightly anaemic sausage rolls. Some turquoise flowers caught her eye. At first she thought they were all forget-me-nots then she realized that some were a different variety: bugloss, perhaps? She should've listened to Stephen's botany lessons as carefully as she had to his ornithological instruction; but she vaguely recalled that the bristly plant lived near the sea so that was maybe it. Gulls winged majestically on the thermals, their mournful calls belying their aggressive nature. Then, much closer, a brown-and-white flash caught her attention. Above the wall that formed the outer bastion some spoilsport had strung a line of barbed wire, presumably to prevent the kids clambering on the ruins. And the diminutive bird – no bigger than her sausage roll – was perching on the wire. Periodically it darted off, looped up and down, and snaffled a beak-full of flies, before returning to perch on its trapeze. Momentarily it was joined by its mate, but she seemed to prefer the serried ranks of the ancient gravestones. Jill screwed her eyes tight; Stephen had definitely told her and suddenly she recalled them. Not by their rather drab, almost nondescript appearance, but by their behaviour. They were spotted flycatchers, feeding either themselves or their late brood of youngsters. Flickas, announced Jill triumphantly. Her sometime bird-lover would be proud of her!

She sighed ruminatively, her mouth full, not of flies, but of sausage. It was so peaceful here…why on earth was she going to America?

The last few days at St Peter's Road – and especially the birthday-cum-leaving party at the Labour Club – had reminded her how many friends she'd be leaving behind. She'd miss some of them dreadfully. Most of all, the lit twins; she'd known them since she was five. She was still in awe of Joyce. In a way she'd never stopped being her teacher. And even now it was Joyce who'd be looking out for their joint interests when the University of the Air began to recruit. Without her she'd probably never have a chance to get a degree.

Once it hadn't seemed important, but after she met Mr K (sorry… Anton!) she seemed suddenly to be surrounded by intelligent, super-educated people. And now she was embarking on her high-flying mission to Virginia, where she'd no doubt be in the midst of academics as well as medics. She felt an inferiority complex looming. Then there was Stephen, her first serious boyfriend; and Jay, of course, who had finally supplanted him. Both of them were graduates…and yet…she couldn't help remembering her junior school teacher, Miss Menzies' parting words to her: 'You're a bright girl, Jill Walker, and don't you forget it.' Trouble was, even though she often felt she was as bright as they were – and certainly had a lot more common sense and a much sharper instinct where people were concerned – she'd no bit of paper to prove it.

Then there was Sue: not only her principal mentor after Joyce, but her lover, too. Well, near as made no difference... She'd miss her most of all. Still, at least she'd got Shakespeare to fall back on, and another beautiful Arden edition, courtesy of her paramour-librarian. Was Sue trying to tell her something by her choice of texts – *As You Like It* at the RVI and now *The Merchant of Venice* to escort her to Charlottesville? Did she want Jill to combine the wit of Rosalind with the gravitas of Portia? Hardly! It'd be a forlorn hope, though both heroines were worthy role models.

And what about the perennial issue, she wondered lazily, on the cusp of a sun-induced doze...would she return from the land of the free finally clear about her sexual preferences? Or would she be more likely to crack that one in England? After all, that's where the principal contenders awaited her pleasure!

Guiltily, she got round to her family! She'd miss dad: she'd always been his little girl. Mam less so. They got on well enough these days, provided their conversation avoided the lit twins, and she'd sort of forgiven her for the affair that'd so upset her dad. Jill had grown up a lot since that transgression; she acknowledged that monogamy was okay in theory but not so easy in practice. Though even such a catchall didn't result in unequivocal guidelines. Somehow, betraying Jay, once they were together, with Stephen seemed a more serious act of infidelity than her continuing relationship with Sue. She couldn't see how sexuality had anything to do with it, though; maybe it was just that Jay didn't know about Sue. And never would! But surely that would make it worse in most moralists' eyes – deceit compounding unfaithfulness. Oh, bummer! It was all so confusing! Maybe she needed to go to America just to sort herself out; three thousand miles of ocean to provide a sense of perspective!

Then there was Jay. And their party-time under the stars. Fancy him dredging up that love poetry. And *acushla*...so she was the pulse of his heart after all! Why the hell hadn't he revealed that sooner? And why was she still going to America then?

Thirty-Eight

'*The Duchess of Malfi*. That okay?' Caroline was reading English but Jacobean drama wasn't everybody's cup of tea.

'Brilliant! Spot on! My tutor reckons it was first performed at the Blackfriars, and they say the Maddermarket was probably based on it: indoor theatre and all that.'

'Well as long as you're up for murder, waxworks and lycanthropy!'

'All in a day's work for us Newnham girls!'

Their seats were in one of the galleries and they had a fine view of proceedings. The acoustics were amazing: perfect for a revenge tragedy featuring dark stratagems and minatory whisperings. They both knew the play well enough to anticipate some of the more melodramatic dialogue and were *Shushed!!* more than once; it only egged them on!

'What do you fancy now? We could have a few jars. When's your train?'

'Who says I'm going back tonight?'

'Well I just assumed, I s'pose. I could ring Fliss and see if it's okay for you to stop at Brooklands. They've loadsa room with Peter and James away.'

'That's kind, but it still sounds a bit crowded. I was thinking maybe if you wouldn't mind dropping me at The Manse…'

'Course not. But I thought your parents were away?'

'Exactly… Now how about that drink?'

They trundled out along St John Maddermarket and down Dove Street, installing themselves in a cosy nook of The Vine.

'S'posed to be the oldest pub in Norwich. *Dos cervesas, patron, por favour!*'

Caro giggled: 'Since when did they speak Spanish in this neck of the woods?'

'*Only connect*' advised Jay, loftily.

Caro sighed good-naturedly: 'And what's Forster got to do with it?'

But Jay was in full flight now: '*Cerevisairii*, ale brewers, servants of the

Abbot. It's where the Spanish word for beer comes from.'

'Okay, I'll buy that, but what the hell's it got to do with the landlord of The Vine?'

'Just testing!' laughed Jay. 'Point is it's a Greene King pub, right? And he serves Abbot Ale, which was allegedly brewed for the Abbot of the Great Abbey of Bury St Edmonds. It's in the Domesday Book, honest!'

'Christ, Jay! Where on earth do you get this stuff from?' Caro's question fused admiration with exasperation.

'From the Gods, love! Being *littered under Mercury, I am by nature...*'

'*A snapper-up of unconsidered trifles!*' interrupted Caro. 'Didn't realise you were still in thrall to Autolycus!'

'Hardly in thrall: he's a mate really. Anyway, you're the only other person who knows about him.' (Not strictly true, but Jill could hardly protest!)

'Gramercy, kind sir!' She blew him a kiss and raised her pint: 'Cheers!'

It seemed to seal their rekindling intimacy, which two more pints of Abbot did nothing to dispel.

'That's enough for now, you're driving later. But first, provisions. *Au marché*!'

Hand-in-hand, they skipped down past the Guildhall and across Gaol Hill to where the red-and-white striped awnings of the market stalls promised a gastronomic treat. Several stalls later they had amassed a pile of brown paper bags containing liver sausage, pâté, Danish and German salami and a wax-covered smoked Austrian cheese, along with slices of Gruyère, Stilton and Camembert, cucumber, tomato and apple. Two French sticks completed the feast, all to be washed down with litres of old-faithful Nicholas Wines: Chasspré and Canteval.

'Well it saves cooking and if we'd eaten in town you'd have been limited to the odd glass of Chablis. This way you don't have to worry; you can always stop over at The Manse. We've plenty of room...' she added hastily, echoing Jay's earlier offer.

The drive back was great. The B1332 was quite busy as far as Poringland but after that Brooke and Woodton blurred past in a whiff of hot gearbox oil with the roof down to accentuate the Dunlop Sports on the smooth tarmacadam. Jay relished putting the MG through its paces, although distracted as they reached the A143, swinging through Bungay and onto the final stretch towards Harleston. The last time Caro had been in the car was when Chris had picked them both up after the summer exams. Her hair had been longer then, streaming wildly in the wind, whilst Jay perched on the boot lid between his big brother and girlfriend. It seemed a lifetime ago.

'You were thinking about Chris back there, weren't you?' Jay nodded and she added tenderly, 'Don't be sad…'

'This outfit is killing me,' she protested later. (It hadn't occurred to Jay that the skin-tight pants and top might be uncomfortable; he'd been too busy ogling them!) 'I'll just get changed then I'll do some drinks and you can relax whilst I fix dinner.'

He subsided into an olive leather wing chair and surveyed Colonel Tillotson's LP collection. Mostly Beethoven, Brahms and Mozart: not exactly his choice. These days he preferred Parry, Elgar and the English school. He selected a Klemperer recording of the Beethoven Violin and was just manoeuvring the needle delicately over the outermost groove when Caro returned. She was dressed in a loose silk blouse, with the shortest mini-skirt and highest heels he'd ever seen. Talk about showing off the famous Tillotson pins! She was carrying a circular silver tray with what looked like a bottle of sherry and a large schooner.

'It's only Dry Sack, I'm afraid. The Colonel's tastes aren't as sophisticated as yours! But it was in the fridge and it's almost full so we won't go short. Help yourself!'

'What about you?'

'I've already got one, thanks. Be back in a tick.' She swirled out of the room with a hint of suspenders.

He scrutinised the curious Williams & Humbert bottle in its coarse sacking. Its pretension ran to a tedious quote from Pepys's Diary; but the critical information was in the right-hand bottom corner of the yellow label: 19.5°. He poured himself a generous slug and made a mental note to keep Caro's glass charged. By the time the slow movement was haunting the twilit drawing room their glasses had been refilled twice.

'Dinner is served, if Sir would care to accompany Madam to the dining room!' Caro held out her hand.

The room was half-panelled in dark pine. The wall lights had not been switched on. Candles on the table spluttered and cut glass wine flutes reflected their flickering light. Through the open door Toscanini's rendition of the Pastoral provided a no-need-to-make-small-talk milieu. Jay guided Caro's chair chivalrously under the mahogany table and they settled into their banquet.

A large bowl of olives soaked up the rest of the Dry Sack and they were half way through the cold meats, and the Chasspré, when Jay felt the inside of his ankle being gently caressed. He smiled affectionately as Caro's bare foot insinuated itself inside his trouser leg and nuzzled his calf.

'This is lovely,' he offered.

'What the meal or the company?'

'Both! Especially the latter.'

'Well, you'll have to do without it for a spell whilst I fetch the cheese-board. Why don't you put on a new LP? And take your shoes and socks off,' she added enigmatically.

The Colonel's most hedonistic selection ran to a compilation album: *Romantic Adagios* and by the time he'd jarred the needle tipsily into the first track Caro was urging him to hurry up.

She looked flushed. Not just the wine, speculated Jay hopefully.

'Would you like a bit…?'

Jay smirked inanely.

'Of Gruyère, sal copain!'

Caro's tone was teasing, and her foot was back. As it slid under his arch, Jay tried not to let his ticklishness spoil his chances. She snaked swiftly up and down his calves before hooking her toes behind his ankle and pulling it briskly between her knees. The feel of her nylons was already turning him on. Now he understood her instruction earlier! As if to reaffirm it she tossed him a small bundle of knickers. They were damp and Caromatic!

'How about a bit…?'

'Ooh, yes please,' he begged.

'Of Stilton you rude man!'

She reached under the table and grasped his heel, angling the foot upwards between her thighs. There was a brief encounter with her suspenders before his toes nestled against her naked mound. She pressed herself onto him.

'Can't beat a bit of moist Camembert…!'

The next morning Jay offered to drive Caro back to Cambridge. But first there were farewells to be made at Brooklands. It could have been embarrassing, Jay fretting over how Fliss would be. He needn't have worried: she wasn't there. Her charity work had taken her to North Norfolk and she wouldn't be back until the evening. Jay was relieved. He knew he'd be in for a bit of banter from Tom but, since he wasn't in Jay and Caro's class, when it came to persiflage he'd no worries there. They'd whiled away a pleasant coffee-time before Caro announced they should go.

'Just like old times, eh?'

'Er…yeah…how d'you mean exactly?' As so frequently with Caro, and Jill come to that, Jay was lost. Was she talking about last night or being together generally?

'The two of us, the MG, the conversation…everything.'

'Right!' breathed Jay, relieved not to have put his foot in it straightaway.

'How're you finding the drive, incidentally?'

'Great! She handles really well don't you think?'

Caro laid her slender fingers gently on his bare forearm, 'I meant driving Chris's old car, honey.'

'Oh! Yeah, sorry – see what you mean…' he prevaricated, trying to disguise the shock at hearing his brother's name used by anyone other than his silent self.

'Hmm…it's okay. I'd thought about it a lot after dad first mentioned the possibility. Yer know…would it feel right? I was pretty certain it would, but I was still nervous.'

'Nervous, hon? When?'

'Well before I actually saw it. When old man Hood was about to remove the tarpaulin. I thought… I was afraid…'

'Of what?' prompted Caro softly.

'It'll sound daft… I was afraid I might burst into tears.' Caro squeezed his arm sympathetically. Encouraged, Jay continued, 'But it's been fine since. Now, I mean. S'pose that sounds daft.'

'Of course not, sweet. If you'd sooner not talk about it…'

'No, no…it's a relief to talk to someone… I mean to you, Caro. I can't talk to anyone else.'

'Not at home?' Caro was fishing but Jay didn't notice.

'Especially not at home! When you used his name just now…that was the first time. Mum still refers to 'your brother' and dad scarcely mentions him at all.'

'Oh, Jay…'

'Worse still if I try to bring him up…yer know, in a positive way – some happy memory like fishing or climbing – he just pretends he hasn't heard and changes the subject.'

'I'm so sorry, love…but at least you've got me. You'll always have me…whenever you need to talk.'

'Remember the first time you came in the MG? When Chris picked us up from school?'

'Sure do, pet, what an exit eh! Half the school watching and the three of us cruising off into the sunset. Well, the afternoon, anyway!'

'Yeah, he was pretty dashing, huh?'

'Your Chris? Oh yes! Style in bucket-loads!'

'Glad you think so; though I wasn't at the time.'

'How d'you mean, love?'

'Well what with him being the dashing naval officer and devilishly handsome to boot I was scared stiff you'd fall for him!'

'You weren't! You silly boy! You were the only one I ever wanted!'

'What until Freddie came along?'

'Oh c'mon, hon, that's not fair. We never went out until after you'd buggered off to Durham!'

'And that time at California?' The all-night barbecue at the improbably named beach just north of Great Yarmouth hadn't turned out as Jay had hoped. He still blamed Tom, quite irrationally, just cause it'd been his idea and they'd gone in his Mini Pickup.

'Well you shouldn't've been such a tool. What did you expect if you left me on my own all night? Anyway, we were only smooching.'

Jay realised he needed to quit whilst he was...not too far behind! But the repartee continued until, as they reached the statuesque beeches lining the racecourse at Newmarket, Jay calculated they could only be twenty miles or so from Cambridge. He needed to know whether he was stopping or driving on.

'So what's job now, Caro? Whaddya doin later?' Was she up for a return fixture or had Jay still got two hundred miles to drive?

'How d'you mean?' Caro was the picture of innocence.

Dammit! How could girls always do that! 'Well, yer know...tonight? I mean this evening.'

'Oh Jay, I can't. I'm having dinner with my tutor.'

It was the first Jay'd heard of Caro's tutor, though naturally any scholar at Newnham would have one. 'Academic or moral?'

Caro blushed. Perhaps it was none of his business. He was trying to think of something witty rather than mean-spirited...

'Well, neither, really. He's more a friend.'

'Oh, sorry if I'm prying.'

'You're not. I know I can tell you...we're actually *involved*.'

Caro made it sound like an infectious disease but Jay, conscious that he'd not even mentioned Jill hardly felt eligible to judge.

'Yeah, it's been going on for a while. Obviously it's classified: he'd probably lose his job if anyone found out. Particularly as he's married...' she ended lamely.

'Your secret, Caro my love, is safe. I can, as you know, be as silent as the grave.' That didn't really come out right, thought Jay but, for once he knew when to stop digging. Besides which they'd reached the Maids Causeway and he was having to dredge his memory to find the way. Caro wasn't much help, she normally arrived by train. He threaded his way through the colleges and she waved a hand airily in the direction of Peterhouse.

'Shame you didn't go there. It might've made all the difference...' And then: 'Oh, Sidgwick Avenue. If you go past my college, you can drop me at the T-junction. My digs are just round the corner.'

The farewell was briefer and less romantic than Jay had hoped: perhaps Caro didn't want to risk being spotted getting out of the conspicuous MGA by any college friends. Then again, maybe she didn't have digs; maybe she lived with this tutor guy. His wife could be anywhere.

As he sped along the A14 between Kettering and Rugby, hood down with the early autumn leaves dappling the hedgerows and verges, Jay was disinclined to worry overmuch about affairs that no longer concerned him. They'd had a great twenty-four hours and he was due in Anglesey the day after tomorrow.

Thirty-Nine

Her wobble over, Jill boarded the London plane with no further qualms, warmed and reassured by Jay's affectionate goodbye. She'd flown several times before: to Dusseldorf and back from this very airport, and to Tenerife from Gatwick. Why should Heathrow be any different?

The flight was less than an hour and she had ages before Molly Shawcross was due. But she was nervous and wanted to make a good impression, so it was important not to be late. Only when she reached the main concourse did she panic. They were due to meet by the Hertz rent-a-car desk but Jill hadn't realised there was more than one terminal! And the forest of yellow direction signs confused rather than helped. An hour later, she was hot and sweaty from lugging round her borrowed suitcase. (No best Aunt Louisa grip this journey, although she did have a dinky little carry-on bag, which her aunt had used on a luxury transatlantic cruise with Mr Smellie in the fifties.) She established the correct terminal and finally located the yellow-badged hire-car desk. No sign of her boss, but a row of empty seats nearby. Thank God for that!

When they boarded Jill had to suppress her mouth-slack reaction to the size of the aircraft. It was enormous, with two aisles and ten seats to each row. The ranks stretched back miles. Fortunately, she and Molly were on Row Ten so they were quickly settling in for the eight-hour flight.

Apart from being roused for regular meals, Jill dozed most of the way and was relatively fresh when they touched down at Dulles International. Accustomed to cheerful Newcastle she was unprepared for both the queues and the security. The staff seemed preoccupied and when she flashed a winning smile to the immigration officer who was scrutinising her passport it was received with impassivity. No, worse – hostility! She hoped it was an airport thing not an indication of American hospitality. Best to say nothing to their hosts who, after an interminable wait at the luggage carousel, greeted them at the final barrier.

Zach Smithson, who could've been the programme chief, was in his fifties. He was tall and slim with short-cropped grey hair. His features were worn and weather-beaten: he looked more like a ranch-hand than a medic. He wasn't standoffish but he didn't smile much. Jill wondered whether he was thrown by an all-women team, as he left the formalities to his colleague, Arlene.

'Arlene Franklin: ya'll will be seeing quite a lot of me. Anything you want, and I do mean anything, you just ask me!' This delivered with a dazzling smile and a warm, lighthouse gaze that embraced them both. She was quite a bit younger: late thirties, gauged Jill, and if she was Zach's subordinate she certainly didn't let it get in her way!

'Ya'll must be tired. We've a short drive to Alexandria. That's just south of DC. We'll stop there a couple of nights. Once you're rested we figured on doing some sightseeing. Plenty of time for work after.'

They stepped out of the main terminal. Jill was excited: her first steps on American soil...well, tarmac anyway. The air hit her first: not dry and searing like Tenerife, but warm and moist. Almost like a close summer's day at home but maybe fifteen, twenty degrees warmer. And the concourse was so busy. People seemed more casually dressed than at Heathrow but in more of a hurry too. No one greeted anyone. It took a while to locate the car: a huge, silver-blue Buick with white-wall tyres and *Wildcat* in capitals on the rear wings. There was chrome everywhere, especially at the back, into whose boot (*trunk* – may as well start learning the lingo!) their cases disappeared without trace.

'Before you get in take a look back,' invited Arlene, pointing towards the main terminal, which arced from a low point near the control tower via pillars and acres of green-tinted glass to its graceful zenith at the far end.

'It's been open less than a decade. Named after John Foster Dulles, Eisenhower's Secretary of State,' she informed them proudly. 'It was designed by a Finnish-American: Eero Saarinen. He figured its shape suggested flight. Kinda pretty, huh!'

Then they were out onto the main road. It was massive: four lanes in each direction and cluttered with green signs pointing to myriad destinations.

'Lee Jackson Memorial Highway' explained Zach. 'We'll not faze you with the perils of the Interstate, yet,' he almost smiled, 'though we do cross one. I'll point it out shortly. I 66, not to be confused with Route 66. Maybe you've heard of that?' His tone didn't betray confidence.

Jill looked blank so was relieved when Molly pitched in: 'Wasn't it the main road for people moving west before the war?'

'Right on!'

'Plus there's a TV programme, isn't there. Don't know if it's still running?'

'Sure is!' Zach sounded impressed 'Mostly repeats these days. There's the Interstate. Few minutes and we'll be in Fairfax. Then we'll swing by Annandale and have you in Alexandria in no time.'

It sounded familiar to Jill. Joyce had mentioned it though she couldn't recall why. Still, as long as they could get installed in their hotel soon it really didn't matter. From feeling relatively fresh when they'd landed, suddenly she was deadbeat. Check-in at the downtown Cambridge Inn – *Alexandria's oldest and finest,* announced the brown plaque outside the porch – was mercifully efficient and she was relieved to find they'd single rooms. Well one each: the beds weren't single. As a child she'd shared a smaller one than that with both her brothers! It was comfortable too: just time for a lie down before meeting their hosts for dinner.

'If you're not too tired,' Arlene had added considerately.

The next thing Jill knew it was morning. She unpacked hastily and padded down the circular staircase in search of the restaurant. Instead she found a large lobby more like a lounge in an English hotel with a load of small tables and neat little armchairs. Breakfast was a help-yourself affair served from two extensive sideboards, which looked as old as the hotel.

'Guess you slept well, honey!' Arlene rose from the table where the others were tucking into fruit and muffins, and before Jill could apologise waved her away... 'Just what you needed. Now come and get some break-fast. The waffles are amazing.'

The day's plan, apparently, was to give them a whistle-stop of the most important landmarks, starting just down the road with Mount Vernon.

'It's sorta where it all began,' explained Arlene, assuming best tour guide mode. 'Beloved home of our first president.'

'George Washington!' interrupted Jill, keen to recover what felt like lost ground.

'Exactly, honey. It was his favourite estate. Both he and Martha are buried there and it's been preserved pretty much as it was over two hundred years ago. That was when George first leased it from his father's widow, though it'd been in the family for over a century then. An ancient monument, by our standards!'

Zach was guiding the Buick through the suburbs heading for Jefferson

Davis Highway that led south to Mount Vernon when Jill shrilled: 'Gosh! What's that?' pointing to a large cream-stone monument.

They slowed right down. 'That there's the George Washington Masonic Memorial. Erected by our fraternity as a mark of respect. Wanna take a look?'

Jill noticed he'd said 'our' fraternity and risked, 'Me uncle's a mason. Grand Master or summat?'

Zach stopped the car and they gazed at the impressive building. Its frontage was square with six pillars, bit like a town hall in England, thought Jill. And above the portico rose a three-tiered wedding-cake tower. Zach pointed out a big plaque with a bust of the president's head. It read:

> Let prejudices and local interests yield to reason. Let us look to our national character and to things beyond the present period.

'So something of a visionary, your first president!' Molly seemed to know just what to say. It wasn't ingratiating but had the desired effect.

'Absolutely, ma'am!' The pride was audible and Zach's demeanour relaxed a tad subsequently.

Even so Arlene resumed guide duties once they'd drawn up in the East parking lot and strolled through the entrance gate at Mount Vernon. They were walking down a broad avenue beyond whose trees stood various outbuildings.

'These were the slave quarters alongside the greenhouses and shoe-maker's lodging. They're reconstructions. The originals were burned down in the 1830s. On the other side here's the ice house and salt house, along with the overseer's quarters and the spinning room.' They'd almost arrived at the mansion itself but Arlene still managed to squeeze in the gardener's house and the white-servants' hall.

'Also the manager's residence,' she explained before they were disappointed by a sign informing them that the house itself was closed for renovations. 'Damn! I was specially looking forward to showing y'all around!'

Instead they had to make do with the kitchen, located apart from the main house to avoid cooking smells, and various storehouses. The smokehouse re-ignited Arlene's enthusiasm (doesn't take much, admired Jill) as she explained how Martha Washington was famous for her hams! Then they were passing through the laundry yard and down amongst the lower gardens where the vegetables, herbs and fruit were grown. It was a bit of an anti-climax, though pleasant enough exercise on a fine, warm autumn day; especially with the glittering expanse of river in the background.

'Thas the Potomac. Your Walter Raleigh was the first Englishman to sing its praises. Way back in 1580-something. He didn't get to settle down here but he did name the land in honour of Elizabeth, the Virgin Queen: *Virginia*. Once we cross the Potomac into DC I'll let Zach do the guiding. He's a Washingtonian and proud of it. Me, I'm just a Tar Heel!'

Both women looked bemused and Arlene added, 'North Carolinian!'

Sure enough after they'd left the George Washington Parkway and bridged the Potomac Zach became positively animated.

'Let's get one thing clear straightaway,' he smiled. 'Those who say Washington has all the industriousness of a southern city and all the grace of a Northern one are talking though their backsides!'

'Told you,' laughed Arlene. 'Stand by for a history lesson!'

'No, no!' protested Zach, 'just a bit a background to help you 'preciate what you're gonna see.'

'Of course,' enthused Molly. Jill nodded politely.

'Federal city!' announced Zach portentously. 'The Founding Fathers and their cohorts had been squabbling awhile about where the capital for the thirteen states should be. Then finally they agreed on Washington. Must've been exciting. Rather than squeeze all the government buildings they'd need into an existing framework they could start with a clean sheet. That's where L'Enfant came in. Pierre Charles L'Enfant. He'd been brought up in Paris. His father worked in a factory: but a tapestry factory, so he had kind of an artistic feel for things. Like he painted a portrait of Washington. And he was trained both as an architect and an engineer. Plus, he had great foresight. Broad avenues and streets, superb vistas, gardens, parks, fountains, monuments – he could see them all. Especially monuments!'

Arlene caught Jill stifling a yawn. 'C'mon Zach: let's go see 'em. You can always tell our guests more about 'em then.'

The Buick was safely stowed down a side street off Ohio Drive and they strode purposefully up to the Lincoln Memorial. Jill marvelled at the pillars (Jay would've calculated their total) and then stood in silence absorbing Lincoln's stern gaze.

'Kinda follows you round, don't it!'

'Yeah, but there's a better reason for starting here,' and they followed Zach's outstretched finger. 'You can get an idea of L'Enfant's grand scheme from this spot. Right in front of us is the Reflecting Pool…'

'It's beautiful…' murmured Jill, not intending to interrupt.

'And the parks either side are bounded by avenues: Constitution to the north, Independence to the south.'

'And beyond…?' began Molly.

'That's the Washington Monument. Tallest masonry monolith in the world! On the way you'll be able to see the White House.'

'Where the president lives.' prompted Jill innocently.

'Bit more than that, ma'am. L'Enfant designed it as a *presidential palace* and set it on its own. Said it would give it the…*sumptuousness of a palace, the convenience of a house and the agreeableness of a countryseat.* Reckon he was right.'

'And beyond the Washington Monument?'

'That's the finest edifice of all: Capitol Hill; or *the Hill*, as we Washingtonians call it. L'Enfant believed the most important building of all should occupy the highest spot around – Jenkins Hill.'

They detoured north, across Constitution Avenue and round the Ellipse until the south portico of the White House was revealed in all its splendour.

'The balcony's a recent addition. Designed by President Truman in 1948. Caused a bit of a stir back then. When we've got more time you can visit properly: most of the rooms are open to the public.'

Jill was relieved. She was beginning to feel a bit monumented already. Besides it was nowhere near as fine as the pictures she'd seen of Buckingham Palace, although she didn't think the public were allowed in there.

As they neared the Washington Monument, necks craned, Zach pointed out the *watermark* roughly half way up.

'Yeah, there was a period in the mid-1800s when all building work ceased,' he explained. Then scarcely pausing in his stride he suggested, 'We could take in the Smithsonian. It's only a short walk.'

Jill didn't know what the *Smithsonian* was but *taking it in* sounded tiring. She was relieved when Arlene cautioned.

'You'll wear our guests out, Zach. Let's make our way down to the Tidal Basin and have something to eat… First…' she added diplomatically.

They sat on the grass overlooking the Basin as Arlene unpacked the picnic she'd persuaded The Cambridge to provide: ham, and egg and cress buns, pork pies, German sausage, Danish pastries and fruit. Loadsa fruit! Across the water was…

'The Jefferson Memorial!' announced Zach proudly.

'Or *Jefferson's Muffin*' interjected Arlene, 'on account of its squashed round shape! But before Zach throws me in the Basin…seriously it's beautiful; especially in the spring when the cherry trees are in bloom. There was a near riot over them back in the forties.'

'How come?' enquired Jill, perking up at the sound of action.

'Well they'd been a present from the city of Tokyo way back before the first war. People were – are – very fond of them. So when the authorities needed to move some to build the memorial the tree lovers started chaining themselves to the under-threat trees. Then when they'd been uprooted protesters dug 'emselves in to the holes! All forgotten now, of course. The Jefferson is many folks' favourite monument.'

Later, they couldn't fail to be impressed by the statue: 'Sculpted by Rudolph Evans. He imagined the great man addressing the committee of the Declaration of Independence. One of his finest achievements. He also…'

Arlene interrupted, smiling: 'Now, Zach don't get started on your hero. We'll be here all day! Besides when they're settled down in Charlottesville we can take them to Monticello…'

Jill's turn to interrupt, triumphantly: 'I've heard of Monticello. The *Little Mountain*. It was his country residence, wasn't it!'

Zach's expression suggested Jill had finally won his acceptance. Not that she'd been trying, but still…

Forty

Jay was racing the Irish Mail on its way from London to Holyhead. It must've been doing a steady sixty, and he was pushed to keep up on the narrow, twisting A55. Then without warning he lost sight of his rival and was plunged into semi-darkness, swerving out-of-control momentarily under Penmaen Mawr Mountain. Well that's what his dad had called it. Not much more than a glorified slagheap really, thought Jay dismissively as he flung the MG through the snaking tunnels that slithered under the mountain's skirts.

It was a stunning day though and his momentary disparagement the only tiny cloud on an otherwise felicitous horizon. Well, almost the only cloud. Chugging through Colwyn Bay and Conway earlier had slide-showed the past few days through his memory. The trip down to Norfolk evoked mixed feelings. It'd obviously been the right thing to collect his big brother's MGA; he was positive that Chris both approved and would watch over him whilst he learned to drive it properly. He'd told him so. It'd been great seeing the Hoods, especially Tom, again, whilst the nostalgia that Ditchingham Lodge represented felt like mopping up unfinished business. But Caroline? Holy shit! What a girl. He still couldn't comprehend how when she was miles younger than him (well, eighteen months anyway) she always seemed to be in control.

It was the same with Jill but more so, given she'd not had the domestic or academic advantages either he or Caro enjoyed. How could he have luxuriated intellectually in three years at Durham and yet feel inferior to Jill, who'd had to scrimp like buggery to qualify at the RVI? Though she'd come on a bit since then, of course. Witness their respective activities: him cap-in-hand to Anglesey, her jetting off to Washington.

And Caro swanning around Cambridge: Newnham protégé with a tutor in tow to boot! At least he didn't need to feel guilty on her account. She'd seduced him, for God's sake. Not that he'd needed much encouragement and the sex had been coruscating! Autolycus the Athletic was out of his league when it came to Caro. Always had been! He should have a twinge of conscience about Jill; but he couldn't see it. He hadn't transgressed her rule about the flat and what she'd never find out couldn't hurt her. 'sides, it was a one-off and was it such a transgression with your first love? Surely there was some sort of exclusion clause to the fidelity contract there? Bet it was the same for Jill with her first love. Whoever he was... Anycase, it felt like something he had to get out of his system. He doubted he'd ever see Caro again. It was Jill he wanted. Possibly for good...if she'd have him...

His reverie shattered by the near miss through the tunnel, Jay promptly had to revise his judgement about Penmaen Mawr, as he exited Lanfairfechan and his nearside wing-mirror reflected the boulder-strewn mass. He slammed on the anchors at the first tiny lay-by and jumped out. He could see his dad's point now about climbing there. The slag heap must rise at least 1,500 feet in no more than half-a-mile from the sea. Some feat of engineering then, to have built both the railway and main road within fifty yards of the precipitous coastline. He screwed up his eyes and could just make out the crags on top: they looked both steep and accessible. Maybe a possible nursery for youngsters visiting HMS Nelson? Jay logged a point to score with the chief instructor. What was his name? Somebody Yates: need to check the Nelson file he'd been compiling. Show he'd come prepared!

He leathered the MG down the long straights towards Bangor, only screeching to a halt as he encountered the main road. A5, eh? All the way from London, just like the train! Then he was out skirting the North Wales capital-of-learning (his dad lectured occasionally at the Normal) and heading for the Menai Bridge. Deserted! He parked up illegally and clambered over the barriers to glimpse the Strait below. It was fast flowing, but from that height it was hard to tell in which direction. He thought northwards, and surveyed the view towards a town maybe five-miles away. Beaumaris?

South, and almost immediately under him on the bank he'd just left was a large park housing a palatial property: Vaynol Hall. And pretty much opposite, on Yns Mon proper, stood an equally imposing pile, which was surely his goal. He idled through Menai Bridge, a depressing, grey-looking village, and almost missed his turn: A4080 was signposted Newborough, which he hadn't heard of, with no mention of Plas Newydd. But that must be it: over the railway and first left by a small stream on the edge of a wood. 'You'll pass a Druid Lodge then just follow the drive round.'

Jay would've gone straight to Nelson, but the drama course was his destination and he had to cement the reputation he'd established the previous year before swanning off on any climbing expeditions. Easy enough to justify, mind: they represented, after all, the two benefits Jay claimed he'd bring to the Scale Two post when his promotion was mooted – drama and outdoor pursuits.

The county drama adviser was a flamboyant character called Anthony Gradidge-Smith. Unexpectedly – given the guy was what Pard-the-prejudiced would've termed 'a raging poof' – Jay had taken to him. He really knew his stuff and the quality of his guidance was such that, after three weeks' intensive coursework his charges habitually took their production to a professional theatre: The Gateway in Chester. This was apparently the first time they'd tried running the course on Anglesey, which seemed a bit odd given the remoteness from Chester. He'd have to find out why...

Still, Tony was okay. As were the kids. It was just one or two of the tutors who got on Jay's wick. One guy in particular, Maurice Goddard, was patronising in the extreme. A veteran of half-a-dozen courses, he seemed to know all about the other tutors and was swift to share his intelligence. It reminded Jay of when he'd started at Woodbridge and Sarah Lines had ridiculed his lack of teacher training status. Goddard, a model of solicitude, had apparently informed the rest of the tutor-group over coffee that Fincher would doubtless appreciate a bit of help, what with his having no real drama expertise. Indeed, he was allegedly an *untrained graduate* so might even struggle with basic pedagogy, never mind the intricacies of Shakespearean interpretation.

But Jay had encountered this brand of intellectual snobbery before and knew how to deal with it. He decided, as his father would say, to *cultivate* Goddard. A chance remark by the drama adviser gave him his opening. Goddard was sitting on a capstan overlooking the Strait when Jay manufactured the encounter.

'Morning Goddard. Fabulous day!' wheedled Jay, trying to strike a balance between casualness and Heepian sycophancy.

Goddard fell for it. 'Morning, young Finch. What brings you down to the water?'

'Looking for you, actually!'

'Well, you've found me. What can I do for you?'

'I was hoping you could tell me a bit about HMS Conway. I asked Gradidge-Smith but he said you were the authority. Something about a family connexion?'

'Oh, absolutely!' Goddard gushed. 'My uncle was responsible for locating her here in the first place.'

'Sorry, how do you mean *locating her*?'

'Used to be a real sailing ship, old boy! Moored on the Mersey until the air raids on Liverpool. Needed to find a new site for her, and my uncle, the ship's superintendent, recommended the Menai Strait. Out of harm's way but a perfect spot to train cadets. They said it couldn't be done – Strait too hazardous and all that – but he was a hydrographic surveyor and was confident it could be.'

'Wow! Impressive! So how come it's a stone frigate now?'

Goddard's turn to sound impressed. 'How the hell d'you know that term?'

'Er…brother was a naval officer.'

'*Was?* What's he doing now?'

'No longer with us, I'm afraid. Killed in action out in Singapore in '66.'

'Bugger! That's rough! Sorry to hear that young Finch. Er…it's Jay, isn't it?'

'Yeah.'

'Maurice.' Goddard held out his hand and Jay, seizing the moment, shook it firmly.

'So…why's it on land now…um…Maurice?'

'Downright incompetence! That's why.' Jay adopted a quizzically sympathetic expression and Goddard continued. 'Not on my uncle's part, I hasten to add. His successor wasn't as skilful.'

'So what happened?'

'See that turbulent water?' Goddard pointed out into the Strait. 'The Swellies. Underwater shoals. They're dangerous enough as the tides rip through, 'specially in the spring. But if it's stormy out in the Irish Sea they're lethal. Locals told him, but Captain Bloody Hewitt thought he knew better. Ran Conway aground, the silly bugger.'

'Christ! What a prat!'

'Yeah, but it's turned out okay now. There's talk of the school shutting down and if Tony has his way, it'll become the county council's drama centre.'

'Brilliant!' enthused Jay. 'What about HMS Nelson though? Don't suppose you know about that as well? I mean why *Nelson*, for example?'

'That's easy. When Conway was refitted she had a new figurehead – Nelson! Legend has it she was unveiled by John Masefield.'

'What the former Poet Laureate?'

'Yeah, an alumnus apparently.'

'Strewth, Godd…I mean…er…Maurice…you're certainly well informed. I'll know who to ask in future,' concluded Jay deferentially.

At dinner the following evening he was sitting next to his course buddy.

'Old Maurice has changed his tune!' confided Mike.

'How d'you mean?'

'Well I overheard him telling Tony he'd underestimated you. Said there was more to you than met the eye. That you seemed a good learner and he'd look out for you in future.'

'Oh, well. That's…nice, I guess…'

HMS Nelson was a stone frigate, too: part of the same mansion that was owned by the Marquess of Anglesey. *Some semi-detached*, smiled Jay wryly as he strode down on the Saturday morning. He'd been tempted to show off the wheels but decided against it. The bush telegraph would doubtless have alerted Nelson that their visitor was staying at Conway so it would seem unnecessary, and flash. He was relieved he hadn't: as he reached the main entrance an oldish bloke, fifty maybe, was tinkering with a battered Land Rover.

'Mr Gwynn?'

The man nodded. Not hostile but clearly expecting Jay to make the first move.

'I'm Jay Fincher, sir. My dad might've mentioned I was coming?'

Caradoc Gwynn's hispid features relaxed immediately. He wiped his hands on an oily rag and extended his right one. Jay grasped it warmly.

'Good to meet you young Fincher. Yeah, Ray said you'd try and drop by. Like a brew?'

Over white, tin, finger-print-smudged mugs that must've held a pint each Jay quizzed his host about his plans for the centre.

'Hardly a *centre*, young fella, all we've got so far is squatting rights and some ambitious ideas!'

'And a fair bit of gear!' came a lilting Welsh accent from the doorway. 'Colin Yates,' he announced. 'Come to give us the once-over?' He was a bit taller than Jay, maybe five-ten, with black hair cascading over his tartan climbing-shirt collar in abundant curls. He looked muscular and extremely fit.

Jay was impressed, and wary: 'No course not! Just wondered if there was anything we could do to help?'

'We?' Colin was not unfriendly, just naturally guarded maybe.

Gwynn came to his rescue. 'Fincher's old man's a big noise in outdoor pursuits. But he's okay: he and I used to climb a bit together.'

'Fair enough, if he can help, fine. We just doan want patronising, see?'

Jay shook his head hurriedly and Colin continued: 'You climb, an all?'

'Yeah, mostly in the Lakes but I've done a bit in the Pass and at Tremadoc.'

'Oh aye, what's the hardest route you've led?'

'In the Pass? Prob'ly Brant Direct technically, though Kaiser's more committing.'

Colin looked thoughtful: 'You've led Kaisergebirge Wall, eh? What about the Cromlech? Done much there?'

'Only the easier stuff; none of the big lines.'

'Okay, young Fincher. Next time you're down look me up and we'll do the Corner and the Gates.'

'Fantastic! You're on! Meanwhile, how about a shopping list? You work out what additional gear you'd need to get a climbing course off the ground next summer, and I'll run it past the old man.'

'Okay...though it'd be better to get the LEA on board. The county holds the purse strings, surely.'

'True; but that won't be a problem, honest.'

Forty-One

'We'll take the Interstate as far as Manassas then pick up US 29. That'll take us down through Culpeper all the way to Charlottesville. 'sonly about 120 miles but we'll take our time. Stop off so's you can stretch your legs.'

'That's if we're still speaking after Manassas, eh Zach!' laughed Arlene.

Jill wondered why but figured she'd find out soon enough. When they reached Manassas they turned off the highway and headed out west before pulling up at an imposing-looking range.

'This here's the National Battlefield Park.' Zach seemed inclined to leave it at that.

'Site of the First Battle of Manassas, July 1861.' Arlene pitched in.

Zach seemed needled: 'You'd probably have heard of it as the First Battle of Bull Run.'

'Bull Run?' queried Jill.

'It's the name of the stream, tributary of the Potomac that y'all saw yesterday by Mount Vernon.'

'It's really the Occoquan River,' corrected Zach.

'So what happened?'

Arlene jumped in: 'The Yankees marched out of Washington expecting to crush the so-called Rebellion.'

'Nothing so-called about it, Arlene,' retorted Zach tersely.

'That's as may be, but McDowell's bunch were as green as they come!'

'No more so than Beauregard's. If reinforcements hadn't been railroaded in from Shenandoah...' Zach's voice was rising. Jill shot Molly an interrogatory glance but the latter signalled caution.

'Now, Zach, you know damn fine it wasn't that. It was the Virginia Brigade standing its ground.' Arlene was becoming equally strident.

'Yeah: Thomas J Bloody Jackson!'

'That's *Stonewall* Jackson to you, sir! Finest general the South ever had!'

Zach just snorted his dismissal and Jill couldn't resist asking: 'So who won?'

'We did!' crowed Arlene, 'sent those Yankees back to Washington with their tails between their legs!'

Jill thought Zach was going to burst a blood vessel; and tried a peacemaking gesture: 'But surely it doesn't matter now? It's all so long ago.'

'Your Civil War might be, ma'am…my Great Granddaddy was killed in that battle. Just seventeen, he was.'

Molly shook her head faintly, compounding Jill's sense of ineptness. The party made its way back to the Buick and the journey resumed in silence. But only as far as Culpeper.

'We could've passed it by but maybe y'all are ready for a break.'

Jill seized on the hint of apology. 'That'd be great, thanks. Anything special to look out for?'

'Only its ordinariness!' Zach almost smiled. 'This is as good an example hereabouts of *Small Town America*!'

'Sounds like a genre!' laughed Molly.

'Sure is! Highly desirable, too. Nine out of ten Americans would like to live in a small town.'

Sensing that Zach, too, was proffering an olive branch Jill obliged: 'Why's that, Zach?'

'Well, it's an idyll really: part reality, part wish list. But created for us by all the books and movies and TV shows. You know the sort of thing: neatly painted houses, the corner store, the pool hall, soda fountain by the town green…all that kinda stuff.'

'And the best symbol of all is where we are now' trilled Arlene, 'Main Street! Every small town has one; you can sit in the store drinking coffee and watching people walk by pretty much every day.'

Christ! Thought Jill, boredom personified. 'Sounds wonderful! No wonder so many people want to live here. Mostly city dwellers I guess?'

'Yeah, but not everyone thinks the same way. To its critics, *small town* is the worst insult and small town inhabitants are seen as smug, full of gossip and, well, *small* minded.'

'Well some people are never happy,' agreed Arlene 'but if you wanna place where no one locks their doors, or their cars at night, with no hustle and bustle, it's just perfect.'

'So not much of note ever happen here?'

'Well like most towns in Virginia it figured strongly in the Civil War…but maybe enough said already!' advised Zach wryly.

'Agreed!' smiled Arlene. 'There was one other event made it famous.'

'What was that?' supplied Molly obligingly.

'Ann Maria Reeves Jarvis was born here!' Her visitors looked vacant. 'Her daughter, Anna, way back, maybes 1900, invented Mother's Day for her.'

'Oh! We have that, too. Though we call it Mothering Sunday. Usually towards the end of March.' Jill scraped the memory-barrel of her Catholic upbringing: 'When it coincides with Lady Day it marks the Feast of the Annunciation. You know when the Angel Gabriel told the Virgin Mary of the forthcoming birth...' Jill stuttered to an ambivalent halt, embarrassed at sounding like a Catechism, pleased that Joyce would've been proud of her.

'Hey! That's fascinating. But I don't think it's the same thing. Our Mother's Day falls in May; and it ain't religious. Similar though, I guess,' added Arlene, lest her guest should feel disparaged.

An hour later Zach swung the Buick off East Main Street and into the grounds of Charlotteville's Martha Jefferson Hospital. Jill, tired from a journey, which her hosts seemed to have taken in their stride, immediately perked up. If this was where she was going to live for the next six months first impressions mattered. They were favourable, too: the manicured lawns and herbaceous flowerbeds studded with sweeping oaks and conifers the perfect counterpart to the range of elegant, Georgian hospital buildings. Nothing like the RVI, but just as imposing in its own Commonwealth of Virginia way!

Forty-Two

'Head of Fifth Year. It's a new post. And it carries a Scale 3 allowance. What d'you say?' This time there'd been no interview panel, just the head and Jay. It'd come out of the blue. Jay should obviously think about it, discuss it with his parents maybe…

'I'll take it, sir! Thanks very much!'

'It's no more than you deserve.'

'Well, thanks again. What will it entail, exactly?'

Mr Jenkins smiled: 'Exactly…what we decide. You and I, Finch! You're the one with the instinct for what sixteen-year olds will take to. Without you I doubt we'd be rolling in pre-ROSLA funds. Initial thoughts by next Tuesday. There's a lot to do before the new term starts.'

'No problem, sir!'

'Oh…and…Finch, keep it to yourself for now. With so many staff away on holiday I haven't even had a chance to brief Graham yet.'

Jay smiled to himself. Couldn't see Bewcastle being too chuffed, Jay had never been one of the deputy's favourites. Clearly the proscription wouldn't apply to his dad; but when he tumbled through the front door, having parked the MG in the empty drive he was met by his mum.

'Your father's been called to London, Jay. Some special meeting. Must be high-powered: the summons came from SCI himself.'

Jay was impressed and disappointed simultaneously. He couldn't discuss his ideas with his mum: presumably the head's interdict included her, as a fellow member of staff.

'When will he be back?'

'He wasn't sure. Monday, possibly Tuesday. They're off to some country retreat, apparently.'

Well that's torn it. Have to sort this one out myself. And not in the Bull & Stirrup either. Need some space.

'I realise it's a bit selfish, Mum, but would you mind if I shot off to the Lakes for the weekend. What with the drama course being so intense and the new term starting I could do with a break!'

'Of course, darling. I wasn't expecting to see much of you anyway. Now you're installed in your own place.' Funny way of describing the Handbridge flat, mused Jay. What had his dad said?

'Oh, thanks, Mum. Knew you'd understand. I'll just get some gear, if that's okay.'

The lumber-room was even better stocked than usual. As well as three traditional Viking No.4 ropes hung two brand new Perlons, still in their wrappers, red and blue, 11mm, at a glance. He'd have to offer to *test* one next time he was going down the Pass; but he'd be alone in the Lakes so camping not climbing gear was the quarry. Sure enough in the huge wicker basket under the rope hooks were three mountain tents: two Good Companions (bit too unwieldy) and a Vango Force Ten. Brilliant! A Mark 3, too, so loads of room for one and secure in any conditions. Not that he was expecting bad weather but solo it was as well to be prepared. The Vango had only come out in the last few years and his dad had procured one straightaway. Scottish, Jay recalled, manufactured in Glasgow Govan, hence the name. Autolycus liked anagrams!

He was pondering what else he might need when his mother called from the hall.

'Just off to the bridge club, sweetheart. Shall I see you later?'

'Doubt it, Mum. I'm off soon.'

'Righty ho! Don't forget to lock up.'

'Will do. I'll be back Monday.'

Jay heard the Mini over-rev before his mother took off along the perfectly flat drive. Would she ever appreciate the relationship between clutch, accelerator and gradient? Now, what else? Yeah, course: provisions! Jay considered raiding the fridge: nothing like a fry-up on an early morning camp. But then he'd have to take a Primus and he wanted to travel light. So he grabbed some cheese and biscuits, a half-finished packet of sultanas and some large apples. He checked the climbing basket again and, sure enough, there was a stack of Kendal Mint Cakes in the corner. He took a slab of each: white, and his favourite brown, then another brown for good measure! It wasn't much for two days; he should've asked his mum to make him some sandwiches. Linda's had gone down a treat that time at Frodsham.

Christ Almighty! Linda! Why not see if she fancied the trip? It'd be company; he could bounce some ideas off her; and who knows? What the blazes was the STD code for Tarporley?

'When?'

'Bout an hour?'

'How long for?'

'Two ni…er…two days. Be back Monday. I've to be in school Tuesday.'

'But term doesn't start 'til Thursday.'

'Yeah, I know. I'll explain later.'

Jay thought he'd blown it when he suggested she bring something smart in addition to climbing kit and a sleeping bag, but she hadn't demurred and now he was edging the MGA, lid down, onto the A41 for the short drive down to Linda's.

She emerged from her parents' cottage clutching a pair of boots, a small rucksack slung round one shoulder. And dressed in an eye-catching summery outfit of dark brown hot pants and a snug beige tee shirt, both of which enhanced a spectacular tan.

Jay couldn't suppress an appreciative, 'Phwoar!'

'Just back from Alicante: gotta make the most of the Indian summer!'

'You look terrific!'

'Well, thank you, kind sir! Anyway, talking of looks when did you get this? You come into money or something?'

'No, no! It was my brother's. D'you like it?'

'It's fab! I'll bet it's fast too?'

'Top speed of 110. Nought to sixty, nine seconds. Well, when it was new.'

'Okay, I'm impressed! Now…where're we off to?'

'The Lakes. If you don't mind roughing it tonight I was thinking lose the wheels at the Patterdale Hotel, and strike out from there.'

'Sounds okay; won't it be crowded though? Last weekend of the hols, and Helvellyn?'

'Not if we do it the wrong way round!'

'How d'you mean?'

'Well it's gonna be mid-afternoon by the time we're there so most people'll be coming down. If we go up over St Sunday Crag and drop down to Grizedale Tarn we can pitch at the far end. Then, first thing in the morning we can go up over Dollywaggon and Nethermost Pike and be on Helvellyn before the plebs are out of bed!'

'What, and then come down Striding Edge?'

'That or Swirral: be even quieter and we can take in Catstycam as well.'

'Sounds great: I've done Striding anyway.'

Ullswater looked magnificent: the bright sunlight exaggerating the autumnal tints, the mountain ridges mirrored in the millpond. They skirted Glemara Park until they reached Grizedale Beck then struck up the valley heading for Elmhow Crag. Sure enough, everyone else was going in the opposite direction. Jay's plan was to get close enough to Pinnacle Ridge to judge whether Linda felt up to it. It was one of Lakeland's best scrambles but steep and extremely exposed. He paused maybe half way up Elmhow Zigzags and pointed out the rocky skyline with the starting platform at its base.

'Whaddya think?'

A long pause. 'I think we'd need a rope! It looks really hairy!'

'No problemo! If we carry straight on, we'll hit the main ridge up from Birks and that'll take us direct to the summit.' Jay tried not to sound disappointed.

Later, long after the sun had dipped behind the retaining wall of the tarn, and tracksuits had replaced their scantier outfits, they were nestled at the entrance to the tent. Jay's hardtack had been supplemented by a couple of ham rolls, and assorted packets of crisps from the bar of the hotel. In lieu of a thermos was his dad's hipflask. There'd been a choice of Remy Martin or Martell VSOP. Jay'd gone for the Remy, mainly because the bottle was much fuller. He passed it to Linda. She made no comment, just took a large slug.

'Phew! Thas good! Wasn't expecting the luxury of a nightcap at 1,800 feet!'

'One does one's best, Madam,' smiled Jay, impressed she knew their altitude. Scanned Wainwright's Guide, presumably.

'Hmm... Appreciated that earlier, by the way.'

'What?'

'Not dragging me up that Pinnacle thingy! I know you wanted to.'

'Thasokay, it'll be there next time.'

A cordial silence ensued, broken only by the faintest lapping of the lake-waves, just feet away and the distant croak of a raven somewhere above them on Tarn Crag. The flask passed back and forth.

'*He drank...he drank again...pass the bottle...*'

'Sorry?'

'Conrad,' he murmured.

'Er...right. Will the MG be okay?'

'Should be. I mentioned it to the barman when I got the crisps. He might have got the impression we were staying!'

'And are we?'

'Only if you'd like to? If not, we can head back.'

'Hmm...depends...'

'On what?'

'On you, lover boy!' And she leant across and kissed him affectionately on the lips. Before he could respond she yawned: 'I'm knackered. Ready for my pit.'

'Course.'

She snuggled into her sleeping bag and gave him a tiny, tired wave.

Jay undid the flap-ties and pulled down the zip on the Force Ten. In Stygian gloom he wriggled into his Blacks mountain bag. The distant raven bade him goodnight.

Forty-Three

After the fractious atmosphere in the Buick it was a relief to settle into their quarters. The plain, red brick outhouse could have been a stable once. It reminded Jill of the outbuildings at the RVI. Suddenly she felt homesick.

Keep busy, she told herself. Molly had already chosen her pad, though since they were pretty much identical, it didn't matter. Both rooms led to a communal area a bit like the nurses' rest rooms back home. The walls were a pale shade of yellow and graced by a number of prints that looked like they could've been New Mexico: all desert and sweeping peaks. They were by someone called O'Keefe. Beyond was a kitchen-cum-dinette. Very snug and ordered. It didn't take long to unpack. Jill pondered whether to keep Sue's copy of *The Merchant* to herself, but then decided she was being over-sensitive. For all she knew, far from being sniffy, Molly could be an avid Shakespeare reader. Leaving a trashy thriller on her bedside cabinet she wandered through to the lounge and deposited the *Arden* on the coffee table. Then, aware that Molly was stirring, she went through to the dinette and prepared coffee. When she came back Molly was handling the *Merchant* gingerly.

'Holiday reading from my mentor,' explained Jill self-consciously; instantly regretting the *mentor* and expecting to be quizzed accordingly.

'One of my school favourites,' smiled Molly and laid it back down without further comment. 'Oh, coffee, thanks. Then do you fancy a turn-around town?'

'You mean the *neighbourhood*? This might come in handy.'

'*Complimentary Charlottesville Guide*? Yeah, reckon so...'

They flicked through the pages until they reached a couple of maps. The first, of Central Virginia, included the countryside to the west: Blue Ridge Mountains with their Parkway and Skyline Drives. Beyond were two towns: Waynesboro and Staunton, the latter boasting *Woodrow Wilson's Birthplace*. It meant nothing to Jill, but Molly had heard of him.

'One of their Presidents. While back. First World War maybe? Not sure. Oh, look: here's the road we came in on, Route 29. We went right past that airport. And see, if we'd turned off at Ruckersville we could've taken in the Barboursville vineyard. Says it's got imposing ruins, too. A mansion once owned by the Governor and designed by Thomas Jefferson.'

'Jefferson again. He seems to pop up everywhere.'

'You're not kidding. Look, here just outside the town: Monticello! Wonder if we could go?'

'I'm sure if you asked Zach nicely! Anyway, I thought we were going to explore. Look, there's a town map, too. If we turn left out of the grounds and head down to the Mall we can pick up Main Street.'

'Oh yeah, remember what Arlene said in Culpeper: essence of small town America! Well we can see for ourselves! Let's go!'

Sightseeing! They admired the red brick buildings, the white, wedding-cake church and the ash-grey *sidewalks*; marvelling at the way people waited at the pedestrian crossings until permitted to walk. It really did seem to have a mentality all of its own.

'Kinda cute, huh!' laughed Jill.

'You're just practising to impress our hosts. Well, Zach, more like! Mind six months' time and you'll be speaking like a Virginian. They won't under-stand you back in Geordieland.'

Jill giggled appreciatively. If she were out to impress anyone it wouldn't be Zach. Arlene was much more fun, a lot prettier and possibly susceptible! Still, none of that, my girl: you promised yourself...

'Oh, take a peek – there's the station. Amtrak?'

'It's their national system.'

'What, like British Rail?'

'Yeah, but more extensive. Like ours used to be before Dr Beeching and his bloody axe!'

They seemed to have reached a sort of campus. A big sign announced The University of Virginia Hospital, before they rounded a corner.

'Jeepers! What the hell's that?'

That was a huge round building in red brick with white cornices and half-a-dozen magnificent pillars. Its commanding presence was enhanced by the forty or fifty steps, which led up to its frontage; overseeing all was an arresting bronze statue atop two plinths, one bronze, one marble...

Later, Zach gave one of his hen's-teeth smiles.

'That was the rotunda. The great centrepiece of Jefferson's university. Glad you liked it!'

'Strewth! Jefferson again. Your...' Jill paused, keen to get it right: 'Your third president.'

'And a Virginian through and through. So being neither a DC man nor a Tar Heel, someone Zach and I can agree about! I believe y'all would like to see Monticello so we'll tell you more about him then. But whilst it's fresh in your mind there's one story about him. If you'd like, that is...'

'Oh, please!' Jill's tone was eager and Arlene obliged.

'Well, t'wards the end of his life Jefferson was asked what he considered his finest achievements. And he's supposed to have replied: *The University of Virginia; the framing of an Act establishing Religious Freedom, passed in the Assembly of Virginia; and helping to draft the Declaration of Independence.* When it was pointed out that he'd also been president his attitude was: Hmm... well that, too, I guess...

Even Zach joined in the collective laughter.

For the rest of the week, though, there was little by way of light relief. A tour of the annexes at the Martha Jefferson proved less stimulating than Jill had hoped. And after a series of visits to vet potential wards came interminable meetings with the various medics, administrators and sponsors associated with the project. Somehow they made it through Friday.

'Christ! What a week! I could do with a drink.'

'Well, lucky old you! Whilst you were hunting around that Grocer's Store for postcards to send to your ever loving, your aunt Molly was gainfully employed. In the cupboard by the dinette sink you'll find four bottles of Virginia Wine: *Cabernet Franc*, it's branded. Fetch one through and we'll give it a try.'

It wasn't bad, bit drier than Jill liked but okay. *Quaffing wine*, Jay's dad would've dubbed it. By the time she dutifully uncorked the second bottle Jill was relaxed enough to voice her misgivings.

'Don't be silly, pet. If Anton and I hadn't thought you were up to it, you wouldn't be here. It's natural to feel diffident. You're probably still tired from the journey and all the traipsing about; everything's new; some of our colleagues will need to grow on us! Course you're besieged by doubts.'

'Yeah, but this afternoon's meeting, Moll. I couldn't understand half what was being said. An' I don't just mean cause of the accents.'

'Doesn't matter! Leave all the admin and the strategy to me. You just concentrate on getting those two wards up and running by Christmas.'

'Well...if you think I can?'

'Absolutely! Look at it this way: when was the last time you got to equip a ward – money no object – and select all your own staff?'

'Hmm…if you put it like that…maybe it could be fun. Especially if *our* business meetings are accompanied by this stuff! Cheers!'

They were half way through the second bottle when it dawned that neither had eaten since a very light breakfast. They didn't fancy the canteen again.

'Let's go out. Have a proper meal to celebrate. If you think that's okay?'

Molly was enthusiastic: 'Course! It's all on Glaxo anyway! Suggestions?'

'Arlene mentioned the *Court Square Tavern*. Said it'd suit us cause it was like an English pub!'

'Check out the guide, see where it is.'

Jill rifled through the pages. 'Perfect! Corner of Fifth and East Jefferson.' She'd soon worked out the grid system: the vertical street numbers descended from the west. It was the shortest of walks.

'Think we should dress up?'

'Well maybe slap a bit of make-up on. Skirt instead of jeans. Anything to be out of uniform!'

It was smarter than expected and Jill was glad they'd made the effort. Molly seemed relaxed, and looked lovely in a Tyrolese dirndl skirt and black-and-white-striped gingham blouse. She was clearly used to attracting waiters' attentions and Craig swiftly seated them in a softly lit corner.

'Whaddya fancy?' invited Molly.

'Ale!' Jill was decisive, and after perusing the list of draught beers announced, 'Well we can get lager back home so it's Anchor Steam or St George's.'

'No choice: our patriotic duty! Two large St George's please, Craig.'

'This seems okay. Quite old-fashioned. Wonder what the food's like?'

'Well how 'bout we get some pickle spears and onion rings with the beers and then decide on mains later?'

Craig put down the two large, frothy beers and took their starter order. A relaxed silence and further scrutiny of their surroundings and fellow diners whilst the porters were consumed and Craig, ever attentive, materialised.

'When in Virginia…well we've done that bit! Let's go Californian. Two large Anchor Steams, Craig, please.'

The beers proved a perfect complement to the starters but when it came to the main course they were already struggling.

'What say we share something?' suggested Molly.

They opted for a five-cheese macaroni casserole. It sounded modest enough but, unable to resist sides of mash, mixed greens, pretzels and mustard, they ended up stuffed. No question of sweets or coffee.

'We can always have a nightcap back in the apartment.'

The remains of the second bottle didn't last long and Jill was despatched to the dinette once more. She opened a new one and poured two generous measures before risking the question she'd been dying to ask.

'So how did you meet Anton?'

Molly smiled, as if she'd been anticipating it.

'Short answer: at a seminar in Manchester. But it's a long story, love. We'll keep it for another night, eh?'

Feeling rebuked, Jill excused herself soon after, leaving Molly to her solitary Cabernet.

Forty-Four

Breakfast was Spartan: cheese and sultanas washed down with ice-cold water from a spring just above the tarn; save the apples for later. They cleaned their teeth and doused their faces in the swiftly running beck. Then they struck camp and set off. It was just eight o'clock but already shorts-and-tee shirt-warm, apparently. Jay was chuffed but curbed himself.

Above them a zigzag path skirted Falcon Crag and climbed steeply for a thousand feet to the summit of Dollywaggon Pike. Jay was going well; but after ten minutes or so, he realised Linda was not responding to his comments. He slowed for her to catch up; and suggested she should take the lead so they could proceed at her pace. Anticipating a sarcastic retort, he was relieved when she just shrugged knowingly and carried straight on. Fortunately, the path was easily negotiated: those hot pants were so distracting! They reached the summit barely twenty minutes later, and Linda gave him an ironic smile.

'Goodness, Jay: it must've been *hard* work!'

Jay blushed: 'Well you can't blame a bloke! The scenery is stunning!'

She laughed indulgently and the badinage continued over Nethermost Pike and onto the summit of Helvellyn. As Jay had forecast the plateau was deserted; they sat on the rocks by the cairn and took a slug each of their precious water.

'So, Swirral then, eh?'

'Reckon so: what's that peak just beyond though?'

'Helvellyn Lower Man. It's another three-thousander if you fancy it?' Jay wondered whether his partner shared his passion for peak-bagging and mountain stats; she seemed keen enough though, so they took in the subsidiary peak before retracing their steps to gaze onto the razor-edge below.

'Whoah! Twitchin!'

'No…it's alright! Easier than Striding, honest, You'll be fine.'

Ten minutes saw them perched on the shapely summit of Catstycam where the view over distant Ullswater was spectacular. Across the cove the first silhouettes of the day trooped nervously across Striding Edge. Their route remained deserted and the suggestion of resting by Red Tarn was well received.

'The outlet end's marshy but if we double back under the crag there's a really good spec. I bivvied there last year, it's nice and private.'

It was true. The boulder-strewn shore was shielded from prying eyes and the configuration of the rocks provided a perfect suntrap. Pleasantly fatigued from their exertions they relaxed in the hot sun, until Jay judged a cool-off in the tarn might be acceptable. His probationary prospects still in the balance, he eschewed the suggestion of skinny-dipping, merely stripping down to his shorts. Linda just took her boots and socks off. Even in the sunlight the water looked deep and slightly sinister, but he recalled Linda's prowess from their encounters in the Woodbridge pool and had no fears on her account. He plunged in.

'Jesus!' he spluttered: 'That's cold. Good though – c'mon!'

Linda dived in much more elegantly and passed him in a strong crawl, which took them both to the middle of the tarn. Then they swam back more slowly; clambered up onto the rock-platform and lay down to dry off.

Stirring himself drowsily Jay felt his companion's gaze.

'What's up?' he enquired solicitously.

'Oh nothing…just been wondering what I'm doing here! Apart from enjoying the exercise and the company, of course!'

'Snap! But you're right. There was something I wanted to run past you.'

'I'm intrigued! Fire away!'

'Well it's work, I'm afraid. Sure you don't mind?'

'Course not. What's up? Not in trouble, are you?'

'Nah! Just the opposite. But it has to be strictly between us, at least for a few days.'

'No problemo! Shoot!'

'Jenkins has offered me Head of Fifth Year.'

'And you're not sure?' Linda's incredulity was cheering.

'Yeah, yeah…but he's pretty much invited me to frame the job description. I could do with some help.'

'Course… But why me? Surely someone like Graham? Yer know, more senior.'

'Huh! Bewcastle? He can't stand me; besides, he's too staid. This calls for originality! You remember when we first discussed an outdoor education programme?'

'Yeah, course – surely we're well on the way?'

'True, but even our supporters just see it as an accessory. Summat to keep the unruly ones quiet. S'pose we made it central? Like the core of the fifth year curriculum with everything else contributing to it?'

'*Shakespeare on the Rocks?*'

Jay laughed self-consciously, but pleased she'd remembered. 'Exactly. And geography too, the way you described it. History…cause we'd fired their imaginations about what had happened in places they'd been to. Art…reproducing wonders they'd actually seen. Music…look at the programmatic pieces inspired by memorable scenery: *Fingal's Cave, Ma Vlast, Beethoven's Sixth*.' He paused. 'Sorry, getting a bit carried away…'

'Not at all! It's brilliant! Go on!'

'Well, the point is the curriculum's there already. You don't have to invent new material. Just reorganise it. Change people's sense of perspective.'

'You mean like in primary schools…so stuff's organised round the kids not the reverse?'

'Precisely! I knew *you'd* get it. And to emphasise the change we reorganise the classes, too. None of this streaming crap. They've already had that for four years. All it's taught 'em is they're second-rate!'

'Agreed! But organising them differently? How would you do it?'

'*We* – I'm hoping you'll help.'

'Christ! I'd love to but don't you need someone more experienced?'

'No! I need you: someone fizzing with ideas! Besides we can have experience, too.'

'So…what have you got in mind?'

'Well there'll only be a hundred-odd fifth years: a lot of the older ones left at Easter. We'll just need five groups. *Groups* not classes, mind: we've gotta make 'em feel different…special. So special they sorta choose their own *group tutors*.'

'Wow! Now you are getting radical. S'pose they all choose the same one?'

'They won't; cause we'll guide their choices! They'll see the five most progressive, not necessarily most popular, though maybe that, too… the five trendiest teachers in the school. And they'll wanna be part of something new. Radical, if you like. And certainly experimental.'

'Is that fair, though? Using the kids as a trial? Won't Jenkins baulk at that?'

'No, and no! It's us who'll be the experiment. The kids'll get the best teachers *and* specially tailored assessment. And Jenkins won't mind it being seen as a bit risqué cause it'll put us in the vanguard of county practice!

Ahead of everyone else on ROSLA by a full year!'

'What about Bewcastle?'

'Huh! He'll just think it's only for one year, so who cares?'

'Count him out, then. Who're you thinking?'

'As group tutors? Well you and me, for starters. Then Peter Jackson and Vic Burrows. They're both heads of department so that adds credibility; plus, as well as covering art and history Peter's a musician and Vic read modern languages originally.'

'Good thinking! Who's the fifth?'

'Well I thought you should choose. We need another woman so the girls'll feel they're just as important. Which they are!' he added hastily.

'I get on pretty well with Wendy Plead. I know she's a mathematician but she's right sparky. Plus, she's acting head of department and – here's the clincher – she's a canoeist!'

'Great! That'll give us a broad curricular reach; and the gaps'll be filled by eager volunteers!'

'Hey! It's good fun, this playing God!'

'Or in your case, Goddess!' offered Jay, giving her a smouldering look.

'Touché! But how do we translate our desires into reality.'

Unsure whether the double entendre was intentional Jay paused. He wanted to risk: *Well we could start by sleeping together* but restrained himself.

'That's why I'm to see Jenkins on Tuesday. Don't suppose he'll have anticipated a shopping list but I'm pretty sure he'll go along with it. If I were him I'd get 'em all in and let me make my pitch. That way, if everything falls flat I'm to blame.'

'Cynical bugger, when you wanna be! But how about we brief 'em beforehand and swear them to secrecy. They'll be flattered to be in the know and far more likely to respond enthusiastically than if they feel bounced!'

'Genius! I'd never have thought o'that!'

'Well that, my sweet, is why we'll make a terrific team. Complementarity!'

'I like the sound of *that*!'

'We'll see…we'll see,' yawned Linda. The sun was red-hot and high in the azure sky. In the distance a pair of ravens, and a third intruder, circled and tumbled, enjoying the thermals. Prone on the rock, now warm to the touch, they dozed off contentedly…

'So why don't you go down first and have a pint? Then I can take my time and meet you in the bar later?'

Seemed reasonable; and even if it hadn't been, Jay would've acceded:

he needed to be on his best behaviour. After an epic trundle down from Red Tarn he'd been relieved to spot the MG still safely parked at the hotel. There'd been a tricky moment when he thought Linda would opt to drive straight back; and another one when returning from reception he'd confessed they'd no single rooms. Only a family room with a double and a sofa bed. Linda had made a show of reluctance, which extended his probation without having to spell it out. The separate bath-and-changing arrangements were clearly part of the deal. Not that Jay minded an hour's beer-start! Especially when he saw the bar.

Apart from the usual keg-poison – Watney's Red Barrel – they'd a couple of hand pumps. The bar clip on the first was reversed but the other looked available: Younger's No.3. One of his favourites! The room was furnished with comfy chairs and low tables littered with magazines. The bright yellow covers of the *National Geographic* caught his eye (mum'd be in her element). There was no one about so he parked himself and waited to be served. Normally, he would have been banging on the bar or looking for a bell, but his attention was caught by a stack of climbing mags. There were some up-to-date copies of *Climbing* (God knows how they'd ended up this side of the Pond!) and, peeping out from underneath them, half-a-dozen copies of *Mountain*. He rifled through them and lit upon Volume 1 from January 1969. Classic! Especially the cover, with its brilliant photo of Craig Pant Ifan. Looked familiar – Scratch Arête, maybe, or Pincushion – nah, couldn't be, he'd done 'em both and didn't recognise the overhang. Weird!

'What can I get you, sir?'

'Oh…pint of No.3, please. If you wouldn't mind just pulling some off first?'

'Certainly, sir; though we had quite a bit through at lunchtime.'

'Yeah, even so…'

'Of course, sir.'

He'd have to stop the barman calling him *sir*: felt like being at school! Still, he pulled a good pint: dark and with a thick, creamy, half-inch head. Jay tilted the glass and supped half of it. Gorgeous…lovely chocolatey malt and a not-too-bitter, refreshing after-taste.

'Excellent! I'm Jay: what's your name?'

'Rob, sir…I mean Jay! Just off the fells?'

'Yeah.'

'Great day for it. Get much done?'

Jay recognised the phrase: a fellow climber's.

'Nah, just walking. Camped up at Grizedale last night. Fancied Pinnacle Ridge but didn't have any gear. You done much round here?'

Rob immediately launched into a catalogue of routes. He'd been in Patterdale for the season and lacking transport had concentrated on the local stuff in Dovedale and Deepdale. Jay was just quizzing him about Extol and some neighbouring Extremes he remembered from DUMC days when Rob interrupted him, his eyes on stalks.

'Phwoar! Scan that!'

Jay had already spotted Linda in the mirror behind the bar so he smiled and said softly: 'My girlfriend...'

Rob had just time to mutter, 'Sorry, mate, didn't...' before Linda reached the bar and planted a friendly smacker on Jay's cheek.

'Hope I've not been too long, sweet. Looks like you've been amusing yourself!' She gestured at the magazine-strewn bar-top and pouted: 'So what's a girl have to do to get a drink round here?'

Jay, still stunned by her greeting, gathered himself: 'Sorry, pet, what'd you like?'

'A half of whatever that is.'

'Same again then, Rob, please. Where'd you like to sit?' Suddenly, standing chatting to Rob didn't seem favourite. But Linda did! High heels showed off her shapely, bare-bronzed legs which disappeared into a neat black mini-skirt; whilst her creamy-silk blouse was so low-cut it could've been designed to pander to Jay's fondest proclivities! She seemed far prettier...

The beer, however, was not to her taste.

'Strewth! How d'you drink this stuff? Can I have a rum and coke instead?'

Two surreptitiously large ones later they headed for the dining room. It was quiet, too: most of the residents having headed home. The view out over Ullswater as the sun began to set was stunning and, although the cuisine hardly matched it, a bottle of claret ensured a mellow atmosphere over coffee and liqueurs. Quite how mellow Jay only appreciated when it was time to retire. Linda tottered through the dining room and eschewing a nightcap set off for the room. After an initial stumble she subsided on the stairs. Then she clutched the banister with one hand and wrapped the other round Jay's neck.

'I,' she intoned solemnly, 'have had far too much to drink! You're a bad influence, Jay Fincher!'

They made it to the first landing where she paused unsteadily. Unable to contain himself Jay wrapped both arms around her waist and kissed her gently on the lips. He was prepared to be rebuffed, not for Linda's avid response. Her already-moist lips parted temptingly but before Jay could respond her tongue snaked its way into his mouth entwining enthusiastically with his. Far from pushing him away when he transferred his right hand to her breasts she simply moaned invitingly. Only when Jay began to undo her blouse buttons did she demur.

'Not here. Get me to the room! Quick!'

There was a frustrating delay whilst Jay extracted the room-key from Linda's handbag; but an encouraging hiss to make haste before they tumbled through into the bedroom. Then the planned for collapse onto the double bed, and...

'Bummer!' Linda lunged for the bathroom door spluttering. She just made it through and slammed it behind her. What a waste of a good dinner!

Dejected, but realistic, Jay was just about sensitive enough to leave her to it. A nightcap in the bar would avoid any further embarrassment! When he returned, two large Martell VSOPs later, Linda was flat out and snoring gently. With a wry smile of déjà vu, Jay crashed on the sofa bed.

Forty-Five

Jill had sent two postcards soon after she'd arrived in Charlottesville, and received an Air Mail letter which was loving without being gushing, in which Jay had droned on a bit about his educational plans. He also mentioned, rather too casually, someone called Linda. Apparently a key component in said plans. Let's hope that's all, Jill thought, resolving to give him the benefit of her doubts. She'd write properly after the break.

They had five days off and their hosts, of whom they'd seen little in the past few, hectic weeks, had promised to take them to Monticello. Arlene recommended they avoid the busy weekend and go on either Monday or Tuesday, whichever promised better weather, to take in the gardens as well as the house. Jill was wondering how to make best use of the downtime when Molly bowled in from the hospital office.

'My but you're a popular girl. Four letters! Two from your ever-loving,' in a slightly snippy tone, 'and one which looks very official.' Molly tossed them onto the table, carelessly enough for Jill to feel she was a tad piqued not to have any mail herself, and promptly strode out again.

Blenkinsopp & Marley announced the back of the buff envelope. Never heard of them, thought Jill dismissively, turning to the three pale blue Air Mail letters. One looked like it was from Jay's dad so she popped it inside the *Merchant's* front cover for later. Then she examined the post-marks on the other two to get them in the right order. Satisfied, she postponed the pleasure of opening either by scurrying through to the dinette and helping herself to the coffee Molly had pre-empted. It had been percolating for ages and smelt delicious and very strong. Just what she needed after the previous night's shenanigans.

Jill wasn't one for judging people, let alone hanging placards round their necks. The *label-libel syndrome* Jay called it, after McLuhan somebody. You made up your mind about someone, often prematurely, and gave them a label. Then because you'd already decided what sort of character they were you libelled them by declining to re-examine their persona no matter what the fresh evidence to the contrary. There! She did listen sometimes!

In Molly's case, however, she was beginning to think the label was *Tippler*! Jill had thought nothing of it when on the second weekend in their apartment Molly had again stocked the under-sink cupboard with *Cabernet Franc*. Six bottles this time: good deal from the mini-mart, apparently. Jill had crashed out after their third bottle but when she tottered into the dinette the next morning there'd been only one bottle left and five empties in the trashcan.

The same pattern each weekend, although Molly didn't touch a drop during the working week. When she first pondered it Jill thought maybe Molly had had company. She was extremely sociable and seemed to have made far more friends on the campus than Jill. Not difficult. Jill had made precisely none, so over-determined was she to remain chaste! But there were no extra dirty glasses, or chairs and tables in unaccustomed positions, so Molly had to have stayed up and drunk the additional bottle on her own. Again, Jill strove to be non-judgemental: she liked a drink as much as the next nurse did; but she'd read in some medical journal that drinking solo was a warning sign of potential alcoholism.

Then there were the nights out. Jill was used to heavy drinkers. Her dad and brothers, Stephen and Jay, not to mention her friends at the RVI all liked a drink or three. But they knew when to stop. And that, increasingly these days, was before they were pissed. Not Moll. Take last night. They'd had a couple of glasses early doors and then repaired to the Court Square Tavern, where they were now treated as regulars. Especially Molly, whose outfits had, coincidentally, been getting racier each week. Not that Jill disapproved; she wasn't exactly a shrinking violet in that department herself. Unsurprisingly they received plenty of attention.

Usually, Molly would join her protégé in a few beers before graduating to anything stronger. Tonight, however, whilst Jill indulged her newly acquired taste for Samuel Adams (*just don't tell Jay I'm drinking bottled-lager!*) Molly went straight onto some Blue Ridge Cabernet. They plumped for a meatloaf platter to share but by the time it arrived Molly was already on the second bottle. She was her habitually cheerful self, however (*not a sad drunk, then*, noted a relieved Jill) and when a couple of medics from the University Hospital arrived at the next-door table they were swiftly invited to join them. It soon became apparent that the doctors, Scott and Eugene, were out for a good time: plying two attractive English nurses with alcohol clearly chimed.

Jill was cautious; she didn't want to arouse unrealistic expectations.

Molly seemed to have other ideas and, after a couple of bibulous hours, was encouraging the party to repair to their apartment. Fortunately, the younger of the pair, Eugene, had an early shift and demurred. Jill was relieved. Molly was welcome to the older guy whose hands were already far too lively for Jill's liking. Back at the flat it got worse. After sticking some romantic Country & Western on the record player, Molly disappeared to organise more drinks. Scott apparently thought Jill was fair game and, pulling her to her feet began whirling her around the cramped dance space. When she didn't actually struggle to escape he ran his hands over her blouse and tried to kiss her.

Jill stepped back smartly and slapped him across the cheek.

Scott just grinned: 'Why, I like a gal with a bit of spirit. I'll remember that later!'

Jill scrabbled for her most excoriating put-down but before she could deliver it Molly returned, all bonhomie and *Cabernet Franc*. Jill made damn sure she wasn't left alone with Scott again; and although she was concerned for Molly's welfare she nevertheless left them to it and retired to bed.

Unsurprising, then, that Molly should seem a bit offhand the following morning.

Jill shrugged, topped up her coffee and settled down to catch up on Jay's news.

It wasn't exactly what she'd hoped. Most of the first letter featured Jay's pedagogic prowess with the aforementioned Linda far too prominent; the second, much shorter, an apology for the first. Particularly disturbing was a cumbersome attempt to assure her that the hospitality of her Handbridge flat had not been abused. Jill would clearly have to buck her ideas up! Her first instinct was to reply immediately, but she decided to postpone until after the Monticello visit. That way she wouldn't overreact and she'd be able to describe their outing.

Darling Jay,

The tour of Monticello was the highlight of the trip so far. It's an amazing place, Jay. You'd love it. In fact, it's the sort of place that, if you'd been an architect, you'd have designed. Why? Cos it's impossible! Someone, think it might've been Masefield, was he a poet? Anyway someone once said of Shakespeare that he was "a rare unreasonable" who only comes along once in a blue moon. Like Jefferson. Or you, darling! Don't get too big headed! The point is he built Monticello in a totally impossible place i.e. on top of a hill 500' above

the nearest river. Terrific for transporting all the building materials! And it took
him absolutely ages, about forty years from when he was in his mid-twenties.
Not surprising I suppose cos he kept having to go off to Washington (or "DC"
as they call it here – Zach's a Washingtonian and very proud of it) on account
of having to draft the Declaration of Independence or run the country! Did you
know he was the third President of the United States?

And even when he was here he was doing loads of other stuff like founding
the University of Virginia. It's not far from where we live. Molly and I saw it
a while back. And it's got this superb rotunda. That's what reminded me, cos
there's a similar one at Monticello, only much smaller. Not that the house is small:
it's huge. It's got thirty- three rooms and thirteen fireplaces and eight stoves. Bit
like the flat, eh! There is one similarity, mind: it's bloody cold in winter!

Jill paused and flexed her fingers. She hadn't done this much writing since
her last ward report! It was hard work and deserved…a drink! Bit early
p'raps, but Molly was still in meetings and there was an almost-full bottle
of Virginian Red in the dinette. Jill scurried through and located the wine
and a glass. She filled it half way, then feeling deliciously guilty, drained
it and refilled it to the top. Now she was ready to give Jay a piece of her
mind. Never mind Monticello, what about this Linda bird!

Anyway, where was I? Oh yes the rooms. I won't bore you with 'em all, just
the ones I know you'd like best. 'sobvious, really, his cabinet and his book
room. His library was amongst the largest in the country, six or seven thousand
volumes (even more than you, pet, 'spose you've got half yours in the flat
already). But he didn't have bookcases as such. He stored them in open boxes
with shelves in the middle.

The other best room for you, the cabinet, was kind of neat! He'd made this
sorta reading-and-writing contraption with a revolving chair and a writing table
with a rotating top. Then he had a sofa for resting his legs and a bookstand that
could hold open five volumes at once. And, best of all, it was in this very room
that he designed that rotunda I told you about. The one at the University. Just
like Durham, eh!

Pause for a refill. But only one more glass otherwise she'd be asleep.

What was I saying? Oh yes, the rooms you'd like most. Well, saved the best
ones 'til last, though they're not in the main house. In a sort of basement along
an all-weather passage are what they call the "Dependencies". You know,

kitchen, smoke house, ice house, that sort of stuff. Then there's a wine room and the cellars. Apparently Jefferson had become a bit of a wine buff during a spell as French Ambassador (I think) and when he came home he started importing the stuff from all over – France, Germany, Italy, Hungary (isn't that where they make that disgusting Tokay you and your dad rate?). And he had dumbwaiters installed so bottles could be lifted straight up to the dining room above. Pretty neat, huh! Plus, there were three cellars for brewing and bottling beer and cider. Reckon you'd approve of those.

Perhaps it was cos he was such a good host that he became inundated with visitors. So, whilst he was still president he started building another, smaller house called Poplar Forest as a retreat to get away from the crowds. (Would've suited you, love!) It's near a place called Lynchburg which is south of here, I think. But it's not open to the public so we'll have to take Zach's word for it.

At the end they took questions. Mostly on the rooms, architecture, that sorta stuff. But Molly asked how come if Jefferson was such a liberal he kept slaves? The woman totally ignored her and when we tackled her on her own she said it wasn't something they discussed. End of story! Went off in a huff!

Anyway, that's enough of me rabbiting on about Monticello! How're you? You told me loads about work but nowt about yourself. Bet you're proper settled in the flat now, eh? Loadsa books everywhere. Anything to keep you out of mischief, eh!

Time to take the bull by the horns. She was feeling mellow but determined; just a case of finding the right words: put him straight without upsetting him too much. After all he was three thousand miles away and there wasn't a right lot of good she could do at that distance. Only harm, she recalled ruefully…as Tenerife had demonstrated. One last glass and then she'd tackle him…

And talking of keeping out of mischief as long as you don't do anything I wouldn't, we'll be okay! Cos I'm being a good girl! As for the work, well done with the progress you're making. Can't say I understand all this Mode 3 stuff but it seems as if you've got a valuable supporter. That Linda sounds nice; you must introduce me when I get back.

Which, right now, seems a million miles away. I'm really missing home at present – the flat, Handbridge, the Royal, the bunch back at the RVI, even your mum and dad! And, most of all, you! Don't worry I'm not gonna go all soppy, too tired! But I'll leave you with a great quote from Jefferson:

"I am happy nowhere else, and in no other society, and all my wishes end, where I hope my days will, at Monticello." Just substitute for the last two words…"with Jay Fincher"!

Maybe the last bit's over the top! Can always change it tomorrow… so sleepy…

Forty-Six

'Well, I must say you seem to have thought of everything, young Finch. Including the need for teamwork. First though, we need to assemble the team. My job!'

'Of course, sir; I'm just glad you like the ideas.'

'And I'll canvass your suggested personnel, too. I've a heads of departments meeting tomorrow morning. Routine. Run through final preparations for the new term. Peter and Vic'll be present, of course. Oh, and Wendy, as Acting Head of Maths. Naturally you'll be there as Head of Fifth Year. That just leaves Miss Grayling, I'm sure I can rely on you!'

'I'll do my best, sir.'

'Good! Then all fifth years are due in the afternoon. Summoned last term with what I hope you'll agree showed some prescience.' Jenkins' tone was self-effacing, but Jay sensed he was pleased with himself. 'That'll be your show. Then finally, I've called a full staff meeting for five o'clock, followed by a buffet and drinks to ensure 100 per cent attendance!'

It was Jay's turn to be impressed. The head had obviously thought things through as well! Then it dawned on him.

'Strewth, sir! You mean you're trusting me to brief the kids before we tell the staff?'

'Yes, Finch, after all, it's your idea. Don't you think the students'll feel privileged to know first?'

'Absolutely, sir!'

A horseshoe of fifteen easy chairs took up half the staff room, at the far end of which stood an oak table with two carvers, occupied by the head and deputy. Oh Christ! Bewcastle! Jay had forgotten about him. But he gave Jay a friendly enough nod as he was ushered in between Vic Burrows and Peter Jackson. His presence didn't seem to register with most of the assembled heads of department; except for Keith Beaumont, the Head of Science who directed an interrogative glance which Jay interpreted as: *What the fuck are you doing here?* Beaumont was in the Bewcastle camp and no friend of Jay's.

Before he could say anything, however, the boss started proceedings.

There was no formal agenda: each HoD in turn outlined their plans for the academic year; since there were fourteen of them it took over an hour. Normally, Jay would have nodded off with boredom, but Jenkins had obviously included him for a purpose and besides, Vic and Peter featured early on, which helped cement Jay's interest. Then the penny dropped: Jay was the one who was promulgating an integrated approach to the curriculum; he was clearly being challenged to extend his theory across the board. He took out a notebook and, with no time to structure his thoughts, simply jotted down a line or two for each speaker and their subject:

Art & Design – "all nature is but art" (Pope?) – the artist's eye in the great outdoors. Cinch! Memo to self – teach Peter to climb in return.

Geography – platforms of marine denudation, re-created.

History – a gallery of pictures, real ones.

Maths – not sure, talk Wendy. Dunno though: the geometry of Cenotaph Corner?

PE – quintessential outdoor education. Bill already on board. Linda!

RI – hmm…angle? C'mon, Jay – Red Sea = Menai/Sinai = Snowdon!

Science – tricky! Beaumont's a bastard…give him a listener's sycophantic smile, yer bugger!

Crafts – nature again but with a bit of help from man. Farming knowledge?

Home economics – girlie skills for campers! Better rephrase that for Linda!

English – Tess supportive. Keep on board.

Heads of year – curricular progression. Promote buy-in.

He was still scribbling as Jenkins was about to wrap the meeting up. Christ! His promotion was being announced. There was a ripple of applause and Bewcastle stood up and beckoned him over. He was to swap seats, presumably for the next meeting.

Beaumont looked about to explode.

'Well, I can see we're all finished here, Headmaster...' He stormed out.

The silence was immediately broken by an affable Jenkins thanking everyone and reminding them of the social staff meeting later. 'Oh...Vic... Wendy...Peter if you wouldn't mind hanging on... And Tess, I think you'll find Miss Grayling loitering with intent outside. Ask her to join us, would you?'

Jay wasn't sure which of the myriad meetings that day was the critical one, but the get-together which the head orchestrated with Jay's potential group tutors went swimmingly. True it was a bit unnerving having Linda making puppy-eyes at him on the front row; but Wendy, Vic and Peter were all encouraging. It seemed to Jay that no one betrayed their prior briefing; so he was taken aback when Jenkins remarked:

'That went well, young Finch: everyone seemed admirably informed, not to say briefed.'

Crafty old sod! Maybe underneath that affable exterior the head was rather shrewder than Jay had given him credit for.

The assembly hall held at least eight hundred; the September sun streaming in through the full-length windows made a hundred and ten would-be fifth years look a bit lost. Not that they showed it. Many hadn't seen each other for six weeks and friendships were being renewed in a raucous, but good-natured atmosphere. Jay needed their attention, but didn't want to create any distance between them by speaking from the stage. He grabbed a chair and twirling it round his head strode to the centre of the hall, then leaping onto it bawled: 'Wotcha, you lot!'

There was a stunned silence as he continued smilingly, 'Bet you're wondering why we're all here? Allow me to enlighten you! We thought you might like a new start. Different way of working.' Blank stares. Not unfriendly, just uncomprehending. 'So we thought we'd get your advice *before* we talk to your teachers!' One or two smiles. And nods. Particularly from students Jay had worked with before. 'Does that sound okay?' More nods but no vocal support. 'Sorry, can't hear you,' shouted Jay. Smiles, laughter and, mercifully, a scattering of, 'Yeahs!'

'Okay, here's what we suggest...first off, we need to work in smaller groups. So just make for whichever corner you're nearest to...' (mass, uncoordinated shuffling) 'and sit down. Don't worry, the floor's just been cleaned!' More harmonised shuffling, followed by collective subsidence.

'Great! Thanks! Now...we want you to have much more say in future. So how about we abandon the traditional houses and have tutor groups instead? With names *you* choose!' Ripple of excitement tempered with incredulous looks. 'So instead of Oxton, Spann and so on…please spend a few minutes discussing other possibilities with your *tutor*. Just one proviso. We want to be identifiable as a whole year. So whatever names we all agree, they'll need to be of the same category. Like our current houses are. You know, like names of places, or people or sports teams…'

Tentative silence followed rapidly by an excited buzz…great, just like a good discussion lesson! No longer needing the altitude Jay now seated himself on the chair. He'd be a roving facilitator if needed; if not he'd just observe. A few minutes' animated conversation later up went a hand in Wendy's group.

'Sir, could we have names of pop groups?'

A wave of amusement swept the hall, immediately superseded by expectation.

'Course!' said Jay decisively. 'But UK groups only, yeah? No Beach Boys on this shore!'

Jay let the debate run until, judging they were ready, he clapped his hands for silence. It fell, impressively: Jay always liked that bit!

'Okay. What've we got?'

'Hollies!'

'Kinks!'

'Beatles!'

'Stones!'

'Excellent. Now, not everyone in your corner will have voted for those, so when I call out each name I want anyone who'd opt for that particular pop group to put their hand up.' They did; and much to Jay's relief the numbers were roughly equal.

'Magic! But…we need five groups in all. So…second choices, please.'

'Searchers!'

'Gerry & the Pacemakers!'

'Merseybeats!'

'Searchers!'

'So Searchers it is. Those'll be your tutor groups for the fifth year. And since someone has to decide – Hollies fans please join Mr Burrows; Kinks – Miss Plead; Beatles – Mr Jackson; Stones – Miss Grayling; and Searchers – you're stuck with me!'

Hall-wide hilarity rapidly descended into a free-for-all as the new clans located their chieftains.

The staff meeting-cum-social that followed was a walk in the park…

although the expressions of incredulity, contempt and admiration that greeted the news of the nomenclature afforded the five new tutors considerable amusement!

For Jay, however, the magic moment came when Beaumont, glass in hand and obviously the worse for wear, cornered him.

'So...Head of Fifth Year, eh Fincher!'

'Nice of you to say so, Beaumont.'

'Nice? It's fucking ridiculous! Don't know what the hell Jenkins was thinking of! Giving such responsibility to someone so inexperienced.'

'P'rhaps he was just looking for some fresh ideas, eh?'

'Fresh ideas?' snorted Beaumont.

'Yeah, you know...maybe *this* side of the '44 Act!'

Forty-Seven

Jill was puzzled. But the disappearance of her letter to Jay was soon explained. Molly, perhaps conscious of her earlier brusqueness, had helpfully dropped it off at the office where they'd forward it for free. One of the many perks of their Glaxo sponsorship. Jill felt she'd maybe come on a bit strong at the end but it was too late now...

The other letter from *Blenkinsopp & Marley* lay unopened. Not deliberately prevaricating, Jill nevertheless hesitated to unseal it. If Molly was right and they were solicitors what on earth could they be writing to her about? She hadn't done anything wrong! And, as far as she knew, nobody had died. Oh well...

Dear Madam, [she read]. *We are instructed to advise you of the sad death of Mrs Louisa Smellie.*

Oh no! Poor Aunt Louisa! Jill was distraught; she'd been away all this time and had never got round to writing to her! And she'd promised to when Aunt Louisa had given her a goodbye tea. It'd been just like the old days, when Jill and her friends had first watched the coronation with the elderly lady all those years ago.

Jill had been about seven, Mrs Smellie in her sixties: an unlikely friendship. But that was exactly what had developed: burgeoning from the refinement of high tea into a warm and loving relationship. Hence the *Aunt*. Not that Jill didn't have other, real aunts – she had loads – but none of them was as solicitous about her welfare and schooling. Nor as generous. In time, Jill had learned not to admire Aunt Louisa's belongings in case they accompanied her as presents!

Even when Jill moved away, her aunt's birthday and Christmas letters invariably contained lavish cheques. Jill always deposited them in her Leeds Permanent Building Society account, which she never mentioned to anyone else. The green passbook currently showed a balance of over

£800. Against a rainy day, as Aunt Louisa would've said.

And now she was dead!

Jill resumed reading with a heavy heart:

> We are further instructed to request your attendance at a meeting in our Newcastle upon Tyne offices to be arranged at the convenience of yourself and any other person(s) directly affected by our client's demise.
>
> We understand that you are currently in the United States of America and appreciate, therefore, that it may take a little time to arrange to return to England. Mrs Smellie's instructions were to expedite matters, however; and we would therefore be grateful if you could comply with her wishes. It would be desirable to conclude this issue before Christmas.
>
> It was also our client's express wish that this matter should be regarded as confidential and discussed with no one else.
>
> Thank you for your consideration. I have the honour to remain, Madam, your obedient servant.
>
> Yours faithfully George Blenkinsopp.

Holy Cow! What on earth...? Why the secrecy? And the urgency? It'd better be important if she was to hightail it back to England before Christmas. Although she'd considered taking a holiday, to which she was apparently entitled, Jill had made no firm plans and had no idea how to undertake the journey on her own. And the secrecy! What would she say to Molly? And to Jay? And her parents? Well, first things first: Molly!

'No probs, love. The contract clearly stated a fortnight's break at any time after the first three months. The presumption being it would be over Christmas and New Year. There was a verbal understanding that we wouldn't both be away at once, but I've no plans for the festivities, except maybe a couple of days in New York, so feel free.'

'Oh, that's great Moll. Thanks ever so much.'

'Think nothing of it. You've earned a break and I kinda expected you'd want to see your family, not to mention your ever-loving, rather than passing Yuletide in Virginia. Though I'm sure they'd give us a good time.'

'Yeah, I'll have to miss out on that. I was thinking of just a few days either side of Christmas Day but if you're sure it's okay I'll maybe include New Year.'

'Absolutely! Glaxo can afford it!'

'How d'you mean?'

'Well the two weeks is just the time allowance. It's all expenses paid!'

'What? You mean flights an all?'

'Yep. And taxis, meals, hotels. They'll cover the flights direct. Just keep a record of major expenses and they'll reimburse you on return. Always assuming you do!'

'Do what?'

'Return, silly! They won't pay if you bail out in Blighty.'

'Well I'm not about to do that!' Jill's indignation seemed to strike a chord.

'No, no...of course not. It's just I couldn't help noticing this last fortnight...you seem to have been a bit...I dunno...homesick?'

'Oh dear! Was it that obvious? Well, yeah...a bit. But nothing that a few days with the folks won't cure. Probably won't be able to wait to get back here!'

'And when you do, there'll only be a couple of months left anyway.'

'Right! Hadn't thought of that.'

'Meanwhile, there's a load of tasks still to do here. But worrying about the travel arrangements isn't one of them. I'll get the hospital office to sort it all out for you. What you need to do is some Christmas shopping, including throwing out that disgusting old case, and treating yourself to a new one! Something to match that natty little holdall you had on the plane.'

'Glad you liked it. It's not mine, though: it's on loan from Aunt Louisa.'

'Well she's got excellent taste. It looked a bit American: I bet you can match it at that department store on Jefferson Park Avenue.'

Jill never got the suitcase; the office secured her a local flight from Washington National to New York and onwards to Manchester. The London flights were already fully booked, presumably because of Christmas. And even to Manchester, she'd have to leave that Sunday.

'Will that be a problem?'

'What leaving Sunday? No, no...that's fine as long as it's okay with you.'

'And Manchester? That'll be easier for Jay to pick you up, won't it?'

'Yeah, it will. It's brill, thanks Molly.'

Later, Jill sat down with a strong Americano to work things out. Urgency and secrecy, Blenkinsopp's letter had stressed. Well she'd certainly meet the first criterion. But secrecy? She couldn't have Jay collecting her at Manchester. She couldn't see him at all. Well, not 'til she'd attended the solicitor's meeting and knew what it was all about. That meant she couldn't tell him she was coming. But she didn't fancy landing in Manchester on some freezing December morning and then having to trek up to Newcastle where she'd have to stay on her own anyway.

Of course! Anton's flat! Even if he wasn't around it'd be okay. He'd always made that clear. She'd send him a telegram – wonder if the office could arrange that? It'd need careful wording and Molly mustn't know. On second thoughts…United States Postal Service! She'd seen it on East Main Street, only a stone's throw. And private. Well, as private as a public office could be!

The reply was waiting for her to collect the next day:

Láska, of course, use flat. Long as you like. I can't be there but Mrs B will have everything ready. Compliments of the season! A x.

It all worked out wonderfully. Both flights were smooth, comfortable, punctual. She remembered to ask for a receipt from the taxi driver who took her from Ringway to Grosvenor Street, where Mrs Brayson had thought of everything. She woke after a few hours in the familiar surroundings of Anton's guest room and lay still whilst she absorbed her situation. It felt good to be back in England, albeit not at home. In spite of the sleep she still seemed drowsy. Jet lag, presumably, they said it was worse flying east. Time to consider her next move. She could travel light. Her heavy case could stay in Anton's flat.

It was only when she was deciding what to take with her that the *Merchant* re-appeared, falling out of the holdall and depositing an Air Mail envelope on Anton's leather settee. Oh no! The letter from Ray Fincher: she'd forgotten all about it.

Dearest Jill,

[It opened in Ray's elegant hand: much neater than Jay's frequently illegible scrawl]. *I do hope you're continuing to enjoy your American adventure. No doubt you're working hard but hopefully making time to do some sightseeing. I shall look forward to hearing all about it. Lunch at the Grosvenor? My treat, of course!*

Something's come up that I'd like to discuss with you. Not suitable for a letter. It would be splendid if you were able to get over for Christmas. Is there any chance?

I'm sure Jay's missing you terribly although, of course, he keeps such matters to himself, as you know. It might be good for both of you if your reunion were sooner rather than later.

Hope to see you soon. Much love as always, Ray.

Strewth! More intrigue. What on earth could be so mysterious it couldn't be entrusted to a letter? And what was the stuff about Jay? Was it Ray's discreet way of suggesting her boyfriend was going off the rails? If so, it'd be that Linda broad, for sure. Just as well she was already here! But first there was the little matter of a trip to Newcastle.

Feeling nervous about the meeting and needing some fresh air after a night of the aircraft-canned variety, Jill walked up to Dean Street and found a lady's outfitters. She'd feel a lot more confident in a new get up: kitten heels, sheer nylons and a black pencil skirt. Plus, a white silk blouse and blue blazer.

The train was dead on time into Newcastle Central and before grabbing a taxi Jill checked the return schedule to Manchester. Then, at two pm precisely, she walked through the front door of *Blenkinsopp & Marley*.

'Mr Blenkinsopp is expecting you, Madam; if you'd care to take a seat I'll let him know you're here.' Jill sensed the receptionist was trying to make her feel small, but a distinct Geordie twang rather spoiled the effect.

She summoned her best Virginian accent: 'Why thank you, ma'am. You surely are too kind!' That shut her up!

George Blenkinsopp was a striking, severe-looking man in his fifties, black hair greying at the temples. But he broke into a smile when Jill strode confidently across the room to shake his hand.

'Miss Walker, or should I say *Sister* Walker? How good of you to come. I trust your journey has not been unduly enervating. Allow me to introduce Mr Smellie: the *Reverend* Arthur Smellie. I take it you two have not previously met?'

Jill shook her head vigorously, struggling to regain her composure. *Rev. Smellie?* What on earth was going on? She steadied herself, realising she was being spoken to.

'Your Aunt Louisa's instructions to me were detailed, but her will was succinct,' explained the solicitor clearly addressing them both. 'I am not at liberty to divulge the details to both of you together. Should you choose to discuss the provisions of the will subsequently I cannot stop you. However, I can tell you that it would directly contravene your aunt's wishes.'

Jill concentrated hard, partly to take in what Mr Blenkinsopp was saying and partly to avoid looking at Rev. Smellie. From what the lawyer was implying he must be Aunt Louisa's nephew. Goodness knows what he must be thinking about this *niece* he'd presumably never heard of.

'I shall now proceed as per your aunt's instructions if each of you is content to do so?'

Jill nodded and risked a glance at her companion. It was reassuring: not only was he, too, signalling his agreement, but with a warm, agreeable smile. Mr Blenkinsopp produced two buff envelopes and laid them side-by-side on his green-leather-topped desk.

'These are a matter for you, and it occurred to me that each of you would like some privacy. Sister Walker, please remain here. Mr Smellie, I will show you to an adjoining office.'

Completely bewildered, Jill grabbed an ebony paperknife from the solicitor's desk and slit open her envelope. Its contents were brief. She was to receive an unbelievably generous sum...

She was still composing herself when the two men returned. Rev. Smellie gave her an encouraging smile as Mr Blenkinsopp resumed his position. He was clearly more comfortable behind his Victorian bastion. He also seemed more relaxed.

'I hope from what I have already intimated concerning Mrs Louisa Smellie's wishes in this matter that each party is satisfied with the outcome.' He paused to register their reactions and Jill was relieved to see her eager nod replicated by the affable clergyman.

'In that case our business is concluded and I can wish you both – Lady and Gentleman – all the best for the future, and a safe onward journey. Good day to you.'

Forty-Eight

The term had flown. And Autolycus the Aspiring had revelled in it.

Jay's experimental curriculum with the fifth years was a great success. The year tutors – Wendy and Vic, Peter and of course Linda – displayed an unbelievable level of commitment. And it proved infectious. Apart from a few diehards like Beaumont, who hadn't spoken to him in two months, several subject specialists offered to coach in their free periods, after school and at weekends. The last were especially helpful as Jay and Linda could vastly extend the range of activities which, in turn, made the programme even more attractive. By half term they'd acquired two minibuses and were offering rock climbing, canoeing, sailing, orienteering and field studies, in addition to the more traditional autumn sports of soccer and hockey. The last two were organised with mixed teams, which had the traditionalists shaking their heads disapprovingly but appealed to the participants as being fashionable as well as fun.

There were sceptics, naturally, led by Beamont and Bewcastle. Coincidentally they all seemed to belong to the minority of staff in the NAS. They were a bolshie lot and all men, of course. The women teachers, and most of the more progressive men, were in the NUT. Peter Jackson had persuaded an initially reluctant Jay to join. The Union fought hard for improvements to working conditions and if Jay enjoyed the fruits of their struggles he should be prepared to give something back. Apart from being school rep, Peter was the best bloke on the staff, so Jay had joined. Within a year he'd succeeded Peter; and become a committee member of the Chester & District Branch.

That entitled him to attend the NUT Conference at the Winter Gardens in Blackpool. Jay was enthralled, and somewhat daunted by the plenary sessions in the Empress Ballroom. But what impressed him most was the presidential address. Max Morris was a Communist; Jay apolitical, discounting his preferred reading of the Guardian. But Morris's educational politics resonated and his espousal of the comprehensive system was close to

Jay's heart. He'd been lent a portable tape recorder and strategically located just under the platform he held the microphone aloft until his arm ached.

At the next committee meeting he was asked to report back and played his prized recording. He was dismayed to be greeted by near-hostile silence. He'd naively assumed that as union stalwarts their stance would be as radical as his own. Perhaps they just didn't like Max Morris or maybe they felt upstaged. Most of them were class teachers in their forties.

The other memento he'd brought back from Blackpool was even more explosive, potentially. He'd attended a fringe meeting on Teaching & Subversion, which apparently was the subject of a polemic by two New York education professors. It would soon be available in the UK; the session was an extended advert for it. Jay identified with the anti-authority theme generally and the iconoclastic approach to conventional curricula. In faithful Autolyclean fashion he snapped up a flier, together with one of half-a-dozen copies of a tiny volume entitled: *the little red school book*. He particularly liked the insubordinate lower-case title: touch of the e.e. cummings, whose selected poems he'd half-inched from the university bookshop. Presumably it was a skit on Mao Tse-tung. Jay knew little about Mao, save that his quotations had been published in the west as *The Little Red Book*.

Jay didn't like the medium. The session-leader ('Bob Handyside' said the hand out: 'no relation!') looked more like a beatnik than a teacher. But he fully endorsed the message. It started from the premise that all grown-ups (i.e. old farts who were Jay's seniors) were paper tigers. The broad themes included Education – learning, teachers and pupils – and The System. It sounded bland, but the detail was admirably seditious. Fortunately, given the reception his tape-recording received Jay'd not risked any reference to the little red book. And, much to his bemusement he subsequently mislaid it.

Just before half term he was invited to County Hall to meet Geoff Thornbury. He fretted about parking but when he arrived at the barrier underneath the Romanesque portico the attendant, who'd seemed about to send him on his way, checked the MG's number plate against his clipboard and waved him through. A section was cordoned off for visitors. Jay parked self-consciously, but neatly, and walked through the serried ranks of Cortinas, Capris and Heralds. All sported yellow badges below their tax discs until he came to the rows nearest the building where they changed to red. Some sort of hierarchy?

There was more security inside the back door. He knew it was the back because the palatial front entrance was for councillors and VIPs. His dad, who always parked there, had told him; so it assumed a sort of challenge.

Whatever Jay achieved in Cheshire education he'd become senior enough to merit a red badge or be a VIP visitor! He was directed to a flight of stairs and arrived on the fourth floor, making his way along the corridors until he came to a notice proclaiming: 'Advisers and Inspectors.' He still didn't know the difference but was relieved to spot Geoff Thornbury's nameplate, having missed it on the grand tour of the rectangular building he'd already undertaken. He took a deep breath, knocked and entered without waiting for a response.

'Finch, good to see you! Come in, come in. This is Steve Griffin, senior PE Adviser and...' but before he could complete the introductions the other bloke stepped forward with his hand out.

'Martin Cross. Geography Inspector.'

Jay must have looked puzzled for the instant it took the penny to drop, as his host immediately explained, 'Word has reached these cloistered corridors, young man! We understand cross-curricular initiatives extraordinaire are happening at Woodbridge!'

'And you'd like me to tell you about them, sir?'

'It's Geoff not sir; and yes, please.'

Forewarned, Jay would've agonised over what to say, made over-elaborate notes and given a stilted, nervous presentation. As it was, he paused then cast his mind back to the interview with Jenkins and Bewcastle, when he'd first explained what additional skills he could bring to the Scale 2 post. Then he plunged in.

Soon his inquisitors were smiling and nodding conspiratorially. It seemed his ideas were about to get a wider audience. And then the icing...a head poked round the door and everyone stood up as Charles Fox, the county's education director, strode in.

'Heard you were paying us a visit, Fincher. Hope your meeting's gone well? I'd have popped in earlier but the damned Secondary Sub dragged on forever. Anyway, no doubt we'll be seeing more of you. Give my best to your father, won't you!'

Back at the ranch, the head was delighted to be burnishing the school's, and his own, reputation on the seminar circuit; whilst Jay's dad was equally chuffed that what had been just a hunch was working out in practice. And what blossomed in Cheshire could burgeon across the country, fulfilling the vision that he and Sir John Hunt had developed years before. Duke of Edinburgh Awards for the many with Records of Personal Achievement to capture the results for examinalists and activists alike.

*

'So whilst the cat's away, eh mate?'

Jay and his oldest friend Malc were installed in the snug at the Wasdale Head Hotel, waiting to go through to dinner. They were ready for some home comforts, having spent the previous night in a cramped Good Companion by the side of Sprinkling Tarn. The day had been fine and they had made the most of conditions. After pitching early doors, they'd trekked round to Skew Gill and then up under the forbidding cliffs of Great End. Even on a fine day, Cust's Gully looked intimidating and for once Wainwright had not been a great help. It said there was only one short pitch when there were actually two, the top one being considerably harder. They joked that it should go into the restricted category of 'DHADI' – 'did he actually do it?' – but in the end it had gone easily enough with Malc in top form leading from start to finish. They'd pushed onto the Pike; not that they needed to bag it or owt, just that when you were already on the highest plateau in England it seemed rude not to visit the summit.

Then they'd dropped down to Mickledore and traversed west under the bulk of Central Buttress until they reached Lord's Rake. Up the slithery stone shoot past the first chockstone and they kenched sharp left to pick up the West Wall Traverse. It was steep, especially at the exit where the rocks were loose enough to make the exposure keenly felt. A romp up to the summit of Scafell followed, and back down to Cam Spout before reversing the route over Scafell Pike and back towards their campsite.

But as they rounded Esk Hause and began to descend to the tarn, the weather closed in. A wind funnelled up Stonethwaite and then swirled round in circles as if trapped by phantom retainers on Gable, Great End and Allen Crags. They reached the tent just as the storm broke. There was no question of cooking but they had some hard tack left over. As it went dark they scurried round collecting the largest rocks they could carry and rolling them over the tent pegs and onto the skirts of the tent itself. Even after they'd retired to the relative snugness of their pits the wind was still intensifying. Sometime around midnight, as the spectres howled in a buffeting crescendo, they heard the snap of nylon. Thereafter they took turns, every hour, to check the guy ropes. First time, Malc stayed in the tent manoeuvring the storm lantern and giving Jay enough light by which to secure the guys that had slipped or broken and roll the errant rocks back over the pegs. An hour later, vice versa. If the tent blew away all together they'd shelter in the boulders until morning.

At first light they surveyed the damage: rips to the sidewalls, four broken guys and a bent A-pole.

'Christ! That was a rough night!'

Jay smiled grimly: *'My young remembrance cannot parallel a fellow to it.'*

'Yer what?'

'Macbeth!' a quote Autolycus had snapped up years before and used whenever he could!

Several pints in, Malc repeated his allegation. 'Anyway, what's she like this Linda bird?'

'She's all right. Not a stunner, but a lovely body. Cracking Bristols!'

The snug was brilliant, the walls lined with mahogany bookcases full of dark red Fell & Rock Guides. Just the place to sharpen the appetite before progressing to Abraham's Restaurant, named after the brothers whose pioneering climbing and, especially photography, had opened up the Wasdale Fells around eighty years before. Replete with mountaineering memorabilia – ropes, slings, hobnail boots and rucksacks – the room exuded tradition. The food was bloody good, too, though normally a bit beyond their pockets.

Malc tried to quiz him further but Jay was not forthcoming. It was only after he'd got back to the flat in Handbridge that it occurred to him. Talking, even to his best mate, about another girl seemed somehow disloyal to Jill. Funny old business, eh big brother!

And now Michaelmas Term was nearly over. There seemed little prospect of seeing Jill any time soon. He couldn't afford Virginia even if he were welcome and nothing in Jill's letters actually suggested that. Although her most recent one was nice. Banged on a bit about Monticello, but ended pretty affectionately.

That left him sans partner for the staff Christmas dinner dance. He was fairly sure Linda would come if he asked her; less sure he wanted to. They'd kept whatever it was they had going pretty quiet and the dance would broadcast some sort of relationship. And doubtless one of his *friends* like Beaumont would take an early opportunity of alerting Jill next time they were at a school do together. What really stopped him though was the *Handbridge Concordat*. If he took Linda to the do at the Queen's he'd probably drink too much and end up taking her back to the flat where they would almost certainly consummate the process so rudely interrupted at the Patterdale Hotel. Then he would have to lie to Jill. And likely to Linda as well. Wasn't worth it…

HMI to the rescue. There was a function at County Hall the same night. Charles Fox and a lot of his senior staff would be there. His mother had declined but Jay was very welcome to come along. Cheers, Dad!

Forty-Nine

Jill had been preoccupied before the meeting. Hardly registering the centre of town she hadn't realized the taxi had dropped her on Barrack Road, just across from Leazes Park. The day was clear and bright; but too cold to sit on a bench for long. Yet it wasn't the cold that made her pinch herself: her head was spinning with possibilities unimagined just an hour previously. She tried to organize herself, discombobulated by her good fortune. Not disciplined enough to corral her ultimate aspirations, she reviewed her immediate options.

First off, Newcastle. Across Leazes was the RVI, and beyond the hospital the Town Moor. She could wander into the nurses' home and, with a modicum of detective work, find out where Sally was. Or she could cross the Moor into Gosforth and see whether Joyce still lived in the crescent or Stephen at the flat. But…Aunt Louisa's decree?

Sally? No way! She might as well take out an ad in the Chronicle! Joyce would wax all catechistic. Stephen wouldn't. He'd accept whatever limits she placed on their conversation. Trouble was they'd inevitably end up in the pub and quite possibly in bed. Which would be bound to come out at some stage, consigning her and Jay to square one. It wasn't fair; besides which if he had been up to anything with this Linda bint Jill wanted the moral high ground!

Home? Mam and dad would be that chuffed to see her she'd probably get away with a woolly explanation. Initially. But they'd insist on her stopping for New Year and it would get more difficult by the day not to fess up. Plus, she had a distinct if uncharitable feeling that Aunt Louisa's strictures applied especially to her family. Not her mam and dad maybe, but to the endless aunts and uncles which, as a long-standing friend of Jill's grandma, Aunt Louisa would be well aware of. Secrecy? Of course! The money was meant for Jill not a bunch of scrounging relatives.

Stop in a hotel for a couple of days and indulge in a bit of festive nostalgia? Even before Jill had discovered she'd been born in Tynemouth

248

she'd loved the place. Not just the seaside itself – though a meander past the Plaza to Cullercoats would evoke happy memories – but Front Street too with its pubs like the Sausage and the Stuffed Dog. She could go in either of them solo without the risk of not being served. Plus, there was bound to be someone to keep an eye out for her. But that meant word would get back to her parents…

So, Manchester, reluctantly. Newcastle Central was only fifteen minutes away: she'd just be in time for that three-something train. She remembered you had to change at York, but then it was direct to Oxford Road. She could walk from there picking up something to eat back at the flat. Unfortunately, she missed the connexion in York and by the time she got into Manchester all the shops were shut. A weary and slightly despondent young heiress unlocked the pedestrian gate and then the front door to Anton's flat.

The note on the kitchen table cheered her up.

Dear Jill,

I've taken the liberty of putting a few things in the fridge. Sir Anton says you're to help yourself to anything you want. He's arranged a table at Charterhouse (and taxis) for you for tomorrow night. Meantime he suggests you might enjoy either the Manchester or Whitworth art galleries. They're both just off the Oxford Rd so turn right out of Grosvenor St. for Manchester, left for Whitworth. He's sorry he can't be with you until lunchtime on Boxing Day. Happy Christmas!

Ann Brayson.

So that was her name, Ann! Jill couldn't imagine using it, she was a *Mrs* if ever there was one! Although once she'd never have dreamt of calling Mr K *Anton*, so you never knew. Anyway, what mattered was that Mrs B had ensured Jill wouldn't starve. On the top shelf were cold meats – ham, smoked pork, roast chicken, tongue – and two sorts of pâté; whilst below were two steaks, fillets at a glance. In the cold box at the bottom were tomatoes, chives and cucumber; whilst best of all, in the fridge door were three frosted bottles of Chablis Grand Cru.

She located the corkscrew and withdrawing the cork with a satisfying *pop!* poured herself a modest, Waterford Crystal, glass. Savouring the cold, fruity dryness of the wine she decided to shower and get changed, then relax for a while before preparing an hors d'oeuvre. Shame Jay wasn't here: it was one of his favourites. Hmm...Jay! What would she tell him about her newly acquired wealth? She couldn't imagine Aunt Louisa's proscription included him. His family weren't short of a bob or two, there'd be no question of Jay's sponging off her. If she couldn't tell her boyfriend who could she tell? But instinct suggested someone more mature: Jay's dad perhaps? They had a close relationship, he'd be discreet. She mightn't see him for yonks though; she couldn't ring him – suppose Jay's mum answered.

Enough of such stews: this evening was for her and Jill would luxuriate in...well, what? Shower-refreshed, she couldn't decide whether to get dressed again or wander around draped solely in a bath-towel. The dressing option reminded her: she hadn't unpacked! So hauling her battered transatlantic case onto the bed (Moll was right: she must treat herself to a new one) she unfastened the clasps and proceeded to haul out the crumpled contents. Need to hang out the creases. Opening the built-in wardrobe, she was surprised to see a silk dressing gown that hadn't been there before. She hung it on the door to scrutinise it properly. Three-quarter length in heavy red silk it was adorned with multi-coloured roundels alternately depicting Chinese birds of paradise and green and golden dragons. Absolutely gorgeous! Surely she was meant to discover it? And, even if it were Anton's, she was clearly invited to don it. Dilemma solved in the most sybaritic way! (Jay's word – see, darling, I *do* listen!)

Jill wasn't antisocial like Jay, but she was quite content with her own company, at least for a day or two. The galleries were a let down. Anton must have forgotten they would be closed on Christmas Eve, but the day had passed enjoyably nevertheless. The indulgence of coffee and croissants in the lounge of the Midland was followed by an invigorating stroll in Sackville Park and the satisfaction of finding her way back to the flat via a different route! She'd long ago finished the *Merchant of Venice* but decided to tackle its fifty-page Introduction, which occupied her wonderfully until it was time to prepare for the evening.

Her table was booked for eight. She might be solo, but it was a celebration. It wasn't every day you came into money; she intended to dine in style. She showered, dressed in her *solicitor-suit* but with a scarlet blouse and higher heels, and settled down with a glass of the Chablis to await her taxi. Tickled that the fare was on Sir Anton's account, Jill nevertheless entered the lobby with some trepidation. Having been twice before only reminded her that Charterhouse was abnormally smart. Would she feel out of place?

The *patron* introduced himself as Phillippe and escorted her to her *uncle's table*. He explained that although there was a set Christmas dinner she was welcome to order whatever she liked. He did however recommend the lobster bisque with a glass of Tio Pepe, which he understood she was partial to. She smiled gratefully and a large, chilled schooner arrived a minute later served on a silver tray by an extremely dishy young waiter. Jacques would apparently look after her. Jill felt like royalty: if it hadn't been for the *Uncle Anton* connexion you'd have thought they knew she was loaded!

The menu was characteristically intimidating, which helped her plump for the set dinner. Additionally, though, she felt it appropriate: it would be the only festive meal she'd get. A bottle of Château Latour appeared unordered. Not Sir Anton's usual vintage: Jacques was full of gallant apologies. She couldn't manage Christmas pudding but enjoyed a beautifully presented cheese board, washed down by a modest glass of port. Finally, a pot of coffee: with whatever brandy Mademoiselle would like? With Ray Fincher's schooling she had no qualms and without consulting the list requested a Remy Martin VSOP. Two replenishments later she asked for her bill only to be told, in tones hushed enough to rank as reverential that Sir Anton had already dealt with it! She didn't actually remember the short taxi ride back but was compos mentis enough to tip the driver and lock the various doors after her. The flat was delightfully warm, so kicking of her high heels she subsided onto a settee with a nightcap.

Late the following morning Jill awoke in bed but still in her underwear. And horny-hungover. She slipped on the dressing gown and slunk through to the drawing room; the brandy glass was untouched. Bright sunshine flooded the room. Eschewing the hair of the dog she shuffled into the kitchen and slid the coffee pot back onto the hob. Peals of bells reminded her it was Christmas Day... She perked up instantly. She might be on her own and a hundred miles from home but she had a sudden fancy to uphold a Walker tradition.

Dead on noon her dad and her brothers would file into the men-only bar of the Labour Club. Copious pints of Federation Special would be followed by Christmas dinner back at St Peter's Road where wives and girlfriends would have prepared the spread. Jill might not manage the latter, although she was looking forward to Mrs Brayson's steak, but the former rite she could observe.

The Prince of Wales was within walking distance. The bar and lounge were indistinguishable so, hoping Geordie discrimination didn't apply in central Manchester, she plunged into the packed room. Struggling to the bar, Jill surveyed the hand pumps and ordered two halves of bitter, one of Lees and one of Robinson's. Parched from the previous evening's extravagance she downed the Lees in one and before leaving the bar, bought a couple more. Fortunate to secure a stool by a shared-table, she fished out her *Merchant* and immersed herself in Act I with renewed understanding.

When she wanted refills, she left a half-empty glass next to her overturned book – a trick Jay had taught her. Both were in place on her return. She was hoping to acquire a just-vacant chair, but a tall, good-looking lad on his own snaffled it. The packed bar was hot now. Unthinkingly, she stood up and took off her blazer to hang it on a wall-peg. A lecherous, 'Phwoar!' reminded her she'd meant to retain it. Sod it! It was too late. Putting it back on would be a gesture of weakness. Anyway, she wasn't exactly feeling prudish, or she wouldn't have worn a low-cut, see-through blouse in the first place.

'Can I get you a Christmas drink, love?' He stood over her, obviously relishing the view.

Jill should decline. 'Yeah, go on then. Rum n coke, please.' He could pay for his gawping.

He tried to chat her up after that but she made it clear, in a friendly enough way that she just wanted to read. He shrugged and left; but not without brushing deliberately against her as he did. She settled back down to her reading.

Exiting the bar had entailed a degree of seasonal bonhomie but apart from a couple of festive hugs and a fancy-dress chancer who had planted a smacker on her lips just as she'd turned into Grosvenor Street, Jill reached base unscathed. She checked the fridge for the fillet steak but opted for opening a fresh bottle of Chablis instead. She'd no one to please but herself; maybe Jay's penchant for solitude wasn't such a quirk after all. The drawing room was still bathed in sunshine. Jill sidled across and, prising off her kitten heels, parked herself on the leather banquette by the window. She gazed out, sipping her wine appreciatively, but not really registering anything from the street-scene below. What on earth was she going to do with all that brass?

Presently, she felt like reading. But not Shakespeare. On a whim she padded in her stocking-feet to Anton's bedroom, in case he had any books in there. She stole in, careful to disturb nothing and placed her glass painstakingly on the dark, bedside cabinet. Then, spotting a stack of silver coasters, she slid one underneath before the condensation could stain the mahogany.

Above the bed was a shelf with a row of leather-bound volumes. Jill shuffled onto the bed and, although fearing a collection of dry as dust medical tomes, nevertheless knelt to inspect them. Bloody hell! Medical books, my bum! She read the titles with mounting astonishment: *Lady Chatterley's Lover* – read it, *The Story of O, Boccaccio's Decameron* – never heard of 'em, *Justine* – yeah, knew the Marquis de Sade, *My Secret Life, Tropic of Cancer, Delta of Venus, Fanny Hill, The Autobiography of a Flea*…and a lot more besides. Why Anton, you old dog! Not that she disapproved; and she'd wanted something to read.

Maybe later, though.

Jill was hungry. Unsurprisingly, since she'd eaten nothing since her feast at Charterhouse. She lay on the bed briefly, eyes closed, planning her meal; then sat up, drained her glass and repaired to the kitchen. On the way she spotted a rack of Château Montrose; one of Ray's favourites. Should've uncorked it ages ago, Jay would tease her. Half an hour near the warmth of the cooker should do. Just have to stay on the white for now! She took the steak out of the fridge, pasted it with olive oil and slid it under the grill ready. Then she prepared a side salad and stuck it back in the fridge. All ready.

She poured a fresh glass of Chablis, then sidled back into Anton's bedroom to retrieve the *Flea*. Settling down at the kitchen table she scoured the pages until she came to a familiar passage. Reminded her of Jay! Back in his grammar school days he'd been sent to the headmaster for reading *Lady Chatterley* in the maths class. The head had duly caned him, a regular occurrence for Jay, apparently, but not before remarking: *I could have accepted you were savouring its literary merit, Fincher, were it not for the fact that you'd marked all the good bits!* Anton's *Flea* was pristine but Jill still smiled as she leafed ahead to just such a passage.

She tore herself away as she recognised her appetites in conflict: time to eat! But first, she must taste the Montrose. Jill toasted the mirror. *Cheers, hinny: this may not be the most sociable Christmas ever but it's certainly the most memorable! Thanks a million, Aunt Louisa! And good on you, Anton, for this!*

She really should eat. She was already squiffy and feeling as humpy as hell. Wanton blouse! Every time she moved the heavy silk caressed her breasts! It was the alcohol of course; but the *Flea* was guilty too. Knowing the best bits meant she didn't waste time trawling. She poured herself a gargantuan Montrose and plunged back in. Christ it was raunchy! With a titanic effort Jill tore herself away. Thank God the meal was already prepared. She switched the grill on and a couple of minutes later was sitting at the kitchen table. Devouring the fillet steak and salad with unseemly haste she parked her plate on the draining board. She retrieved the olive oil, skipped through the drawing room, and gathering up the Montrose and the *Flea* retreated to Anton's bedroom. She thumbed feverishly until she found the bit just after Bella had ministered to the young farm-hand...

Miss...Miss...wake up, Miss! Bella moved restlessly, as if she were dreaming. Miss, Miss...

Mmm...moaned Bella gently, still dreaming, apparently.

Oh, c'mon Miss. Please say you'd like some more...

Bella stirred and rolling her eyes coquettishly murmured, More?... Whatever do you mean? More?

Yer know, Miss, more fucking?

I don't know what you mean, muttered Bella indignantly, attempting to suppress any hint of renewed lust in her slightly tremulous voice.

That was strange. Jill didn't remember a previous encounter between the two which had actually been consummated. Maybe Anton's was an unexpurgated edition. She resumed, just as some gremlin was trailing its fingers over her silken breasts...

I can tell yer would really, Miss!

Yer cheeky sod! And then curiosity overcoming her: How?

I could see it in yer eyes: it were getting yer going.

Christ! Never mind Bella, reflected Jill breathlessly, glancing down. Some sprite had undone the buttons on her blouse. One-two-three-four.

Don't be silly...you must've been imagining it.

Don't think so, Miss...

Bella was unable to deny him... Well...perhaps...perhaps a bit...but you shouldn't be saying such things. I don't know what you think they'll achieve.

Tim just grinned.

You're not trying to make me desirous again, are you? She arched her eyebrows calculatedly.

Course I am! Is it working?

God! It sure is, whispered Jill excitedly to herself. Her blouse and bra adorned the coverlet and some mischievous incubus must've been surreptitiously playing with her nipples. They were taut and seemed to be glistening with oil. How strange...

A veritable swarm of butterflies fluttered through her tummy. A genie had removed her belt and was attempting to pull off her skirt. She raised her bum obligingly.

Don't be silly, of course not!

The boy looked crestfallen.

Well maybe…maybe a little bit. But how can you tell?

Cause you're breathing all heavy again! And you're… Tim hesitated.

The boggle had now removed Jill's skirt and was running its hands up and down her stockinged-legs. It reached their tops and started stroking her through her panties…

And I'm what? enquired Bella flirtatiously, directing a blatant glance towards the boy's truncheon. I'm what? she prompted.

And yer soakin an all.

Jill was breathing heavily. She sighed lustfully as an intrusively welcome kelpie grasped her fingers and slid them inside her knickers. It was true…

Well I may be a trifle damp, I suppose. But your member's disgracefully large! Pretty good, eh Miss?

Stop fishing for compliments! You know it is, she smiled, squeezing it affectionately and giving it a brisk little rub.

Jill was struggling to carry on; the book was shaking in her hand. Some phantom had gripped her fingers in his and was slithering them between her thighs, which also seemed unaccountably oily. She sighed resignedly, bucking towards him as yet another lascivious goblin started rubbing her…

Fifty

When his dad asked him for a lift Jay was agreeably surprised. Normally it was the other way round so Jay could drink what he wanted. Maybe it was to ensure he didn't overdo it on the freebies at the reception. It felt good swinging the freshly buffed MGA towards the knee-high, black-iron barrier that guarded the entrance to the VIP car park. Initially the commissionaire looked set to stop him, then he spotted his passenger.

'Evening, Mr Fincher, sir: got a new chauffeur have we?'

'Thought it was about time, Higgins. Merry Christmas to you!'

'And you, sir!' He waved the MG towards a space near the bottom of the broad, stone staircase, which led up to the main doors. The reception area was dominated by two large Norwegian spruces laden down with baubles and tinsel. Each was topped by a glittering white angel. Jay always liked Christmas decorations; but these were overdone: he and his mum would have made a much better job. Like when he was a kid and they trimmed the fir bough in the entrance hall at Ditchingham Lodge. Now that was classy!

They were ushered into a cavernous dining room where most of the furniture had been removed. Shunted up against the wall was just a tier of tables laden with food and drink. Maybe the old man was being circumspect after all! Didn't appear to be stopping *him* though! Resigned to being bored, Jay bumped into Geoff Thornbury and Steve Griffin. They seemed to be enjoying themselves, too; shop was out of order.

'Still got the Lotus Cortina, Geoff?'

'Sure have, goes like a bird. I'll give you a lift next time we're headed for a teachers' centre meeting.'

What d'you drive?' chipped in Steve.

'Oh, he's got a natty little Mini, very sporty!' rescued Geoff.

'Er...not any more...'

Jay wasn't angling. He just didn't want to be quizzed about his brother's velocipede. Own fault, shouldn't have brought up cars.

'Steve's got a nice line in Coopers. Is that what you've progressed to?'

'Er, no…MGA.'

'Strewth! County must be paying its teachers too much, eh Geoff? What model? 1500?'

Oh stuff him then, thought Jay and gave him both barrels.

'Nah! 1600 Twin Cam, bright red, top speed 113, 0-60 nine seconds!'

The cocktail party syndrome appeared to strike as Steve waved vaguely into the throng and disappeared with Geoff, grinning, in tow. Jay allowed himself another bottle of Bass and surveyed the scene. If it'd been packed before it was positively caliginous now! And a lot more women, all of a sudden. Most of them were studious-looking old biddies but a gaggle of much younger birds stood quite close by. They looked a bit self-conscious as if it wasn't the sort of party they normally got invited to. A keener inspection was called for. As he edged closer a redhead with an hourglass figure put an empty glass on the table.

'Can I get you a refill?'

She turned to face him. Cor! She was a bit of all right! Really pretty face framed by golden-red curls, an enchanting smile and stacked, to say the least.

'Er…thanks…same again, please.'

'Which is?'

'Oh sorry: that white wine over there.'

She pointed to the back of the table, but just as Jay was about to liberate the bottle a white-gloved arm announced: 'Allow me, sir,' and topped up the glass. Bugger! Plan 'A' out the window.

Jay had no sooner transferred it to his quarry's grasp than an older woman in the centre of the group shrilled: 'Eileen, come over here love. There's someone I want you to meet.'

Jay was still swallowing his disappointment – and a final Bass – when his dad emerged from the crush.

'Oh there you are, son. How's it going? Meet anyone interesting?'

I was just about to, thought Jay ruefully.

'Like to introduce a fellow geographer…this is…'

'Hello, Fincher,' smiled Martin Cross, 'Good to see you again.'

'Might've known it!' chuckled his dad, suddenly waylaid by an inappropriately grave wraith, who leant down to whisper into Ray Fincher's ear and then vaporised. His father's face clouded over.

'It's Charles Fox. Apparently his wife's been involved in an accident. They don't think it's anything serious. But obviously Charles needs to be with her. His deputy doesn't expect him to make it later.'

'Bummer!'

'Yeah, hope Betty's okay. Shame, though, I'd planned for the three of us to have a little chat. Still, never mind. It'll do in the New Year.'

Jay knew better than to quiz his dad so he just shrugged his shoulders expectantly.

'Oh well, I think we might make a move, son.'

'Okay by me. Straight home?'

His dad pondered briefly: 'No…no…let's have one in the Bull & Stirrup. You can introduce me to this barmaid you're always on about!'

'What, Brenda? Certes!' Jay had been re-reading *Othello* as a Christmas project and was much taken with the monosyllabic affirmation. 'Deffers!' he added for good measure.

Unfortunately, the buxom Bren was not serving, so they contented themselves with a quick couple – Jay on the Higson's and his dad the habitual Guinness – before heading for Bridge Drive.

'Why don't you stop over, son. Your mother would love to see you: especially with your not coming over Christmas Day. Can't imagine what we were doing, agreeing to stay over in Astbury. Anyway once she's safely tucked up we could have a nightcap…'

Jay would have preferred to head back to Handbridge. He liked his independence these days, but the old man seemed keen to talk.

'Sure, that'd be great. But I'll be away after breakfast. Gotta lot to do tomorrow.'

Later, after his mother had indeed elected to make tracks, they repaired to the drawing room. His father opened the walnut drinks cupboard he'd rescued from Norwich's Elm Hill antiques warehouse. After several years his mother's polishing had given it a deep, handsome sheen; it enhanced both the corner it inhabited and the drinks it contained. Particularly, when his father broke open the Hennessey XO.

'Hells bells: must be a special occasion!'

His dad smiled knowingly: 'Hmm…you could say that. Cheers!'

Knowing it would be a while before the brandy was deemed warm enough to sip, Jay just returned the greeting and waited, all agog.

'It'll be common knowledge in a week or so, son, but 'til then you need to keep this strictly in the family. I only told your mother a couple of days back.'

'Of course…but what, for heaven's sake?'

'Um…well…Some misguided diplomatic committee's decided your father should receive a 'K'!'

'A what?'

'A Knighthood, son: I'll be appointed a Knight Bachelor in the New Year's Honours List!'

'Bloody hell, Dad! That's amazing! Incredible! Well done!'

'Er...thanks, son. I must admit it is quite...er...gratifying.' His dad's creased-brown mountaineer's face crinkled with pleasure and his deep blue eyes sparkled. 'Cheers!'

Warming protocol waived, they raised their balloon glasses as one. And drained them.

'Top up?' enquired his father solicitously.

'Yes, please, Sir Raymond!' Jay'd never used his dad's Christian name before!

Breakfast was fun. Normally, they'd have grazed at the kitchen bar; his mum had other ideas. It was a special occasion, and it was Christmas Eve. They would eat in the dining room and enjoy the view over the frosty lawns and ornamental cherry trees. Befittingly, she'd made kedgeree, a family favourite; there was even a suggestion of Buck's Fizz, but that wasn't really their style. They settled for carbonated water and coffee percolated to industrial strength. There was a conspiratorial atmosphere: a tiny, close-knit family cherishing their secret. Jay teased his mum with *Lady Muriel*, at which she simpered appreciatively. He couldn't recall his parents being this relaxed, happy even, since his big brother was killed.

Christmas Day! Splendid isolation! Gazing out over the River Dee. It was a fine, crisp mid-morning: hardly anybody about on the bridge, just an assortment of moorhens, coots and mallards at the thinly-iced water's edge with the odd, mewling seagull over the weir. Perfect day for Autolycus the Acclamatory!

His plan was simple: coffee and the December edition of *Mountain*, then up to the Bull & Stirrup for opening time. Since Bren hadn't been working before there was a fair chance she'd be on today. So a good bit of craic, plenty of not-so-subtle ogling of festive Bristols, the odd pint of Higson's, and back for the main event.

It wasn't as busy as he'd expected but there was no Bren so he bought two pints and retired to a corner seat where he could monitor what was going on without being disturbed. Halfway down his second, and immersed in a fascinating article on Anglesey's Mousetrap Zawn, he became aware of someone standing, then leaning, over him.

'Merry Christmas, lover boy!'

'Bren! Great to see you. And a very Merry Christmas to you too, hon!'

He was about to rise to claim a celebratory kiss but she beat him to it stooping low over his table and planting an enticingly wet smacker bang on his lips. Left it there long enough for him to harbour some outrageously improbable fantasies, and then gave him a long lingering eyeful before straightening up.

'Phwoar! What a lovely Christmas present!'

'You're more than welcome, young man: you know I've always had a soft spot for you,' she smiled. Suppressing a coarse response, Jay surmised that one, she wasn't working and two, she'd had a couple. Maybe his carefully laid plans needed reappraisal. Any chance of indulging a long-and-dearly-held whimsy and all bets were off!

'So, what you up to this fine day, Bren?'

'Oh, just a couple of drinks, then Christmas dinner with the family.'

'What your mum and dad?'

'No silly, my own family!'

'Oh, I never realised you were...'

'Yeah...with two little boys. They're with their dad now peeling potatoes and topping sprouts! I'd invite you to join us, but I don't think Karl'd be too impressed!'

'Oh?'

'I might've been singing your praises once; he quizzed me about you for weeks afterwards...'

'Oh right. Anyway it was kind of you even to think of me.'

'So, how's the gorgeous Jill? You two not fallen out again?'

'No, no...but she's in America still. Don't know when I'll see her.'

'Well don't be mizz, I'm sure she's missing you, too. Couldn't you ring her? Say Happy Christmas? Just tell her, Jay!'

'Thanks, Bren! Don't know how, but I'll try.'

'I really think you should! Happy Christmas!'

'And a very Happy Christmas to you, too, Bren. Thanks again, love.'

They embraced warmly, if briefly. Then she was gone. Jay drained his pint thoughtfully. Hmm...revert to plan...not that bad after all...

He'd returned from the parental celebrations with an assortment of Tupperware containers. Two shallow rectangular ones held smoked salmon with capers, and slices of roast turkey and ham; whilst a deep square one was filled with pre-cooked roasties, carrots, parsnips and sprouts, all vegetables mum knew he'd eat. Two smaller tubs included pigs-in-blankets together with chestnut stuffing balls, and a selection of maybe half-a-dozen cheeses.

His dad's contributions were wrapped in his customary Daily Telegraph to prevent their smashing, and presented in a green-and-gold Harrods carrier bag. They comprised a bottle of Puligny-Montrachet, 1966, promising to be a great vintage, and two bottles of Château Mouton-Rothschild. Bloody hell, 1961, one of the best years ever! Cheers, Dad! Having toiled to learn the full 1855 Classification Jay particularly savoured the in-joke: *Premier ne suis, second ne daigne, Mouton suis!* Just like the old man to calculate it would complement both the turkey and the cheeseboard.

Not that he was a slave to routine, but he would dine – just as if it were a family occasion – at five. So an ETA of four would allow ample time for the preparations his mum had detailed, followed by an aperitif overlooking the river illuminated by Christmas lights. Meanwhile, inspired by Bren's suggestion he abandoned first his Higson's and second his intended walk round the city walls. Instead, he strolled back though the centre and over Grosvenor Bridge before cutting through the Overleigh Road Cemetery and winding his way back to Handbridge. Then, confident he was fit to drive, he jumped in the MG and took a still-circumspect route to Bridge Drive.

He made his way to his dad's study. If they'd been there he'd have asked of course: even with his old man's official allowance, a transatlantic buzz might be noticeable. He'd not bargained with having to place the call and it was some time before he was finally able to raise the Martha Jefferson. Thank God for the hospital office; not only was it staffed but they were able to connect him direct to the apartment. A sudden panic! What time was it there? No, that was okay. Mid-morning-ish…they should be…

'Hello?' the voice was English, but not Jill's.

'Oh, sorry, I was hoping to speak to Jill Walker. It's Jay Fincher.'

'Oh, hello Jay. What a lovely surprise! This is Molly Shawcross. Happy Christmas!'

'Happy Christmas to you too. Can I speak to Jill, please?'

'Well you could if she were here, love; but she returned to England last week. Thought you would've known. Sorry.'

Jay strove to disguise his deflation: 'Yes, right. Well…okay…thanks anyway. Have a nice Christmas. Bye.'

'And you, Jay. Give my love to England!'

Thoroughly dispirited, Jay leant back in his dad's desk chair and gazed at Chris's photograph. *Aye, and a merry bloody Christmas to us an all, big brother!*

Fifty-One

Momentarily Jill was at a loss. What the hell was she doing in this strange bed? She closed her eyes, trying to piece together her bizarre Christmas Day. The visit to the pub had been fun; and the afternoon on the Chablis mischievously decadent. She remembered thinking the steak wasn't as good as her mam's, which provoked recollection of the Château Montrose. That had definitely been good. But after that...? It was only when she saw the leather-bound volumes strewn over the counterpane that the full tableau unfolded. She didn't exactly blush but she pursed her lips self-mockingly. Hmm...now that bit had been scrummy!

What a way to spend... Bummer, it was Boxing Day! And Anton was due. Panic stations...she dredged up Mrs Brayson's letter. Surely it mentioned lunch. The electric clock on the bedroom wall read ten-past-nine so she'd loads of time. First job: tidy up! Then she'd have a shower and maybe go for a walk. She wrapped herself in the silk dressing gown and surveyed the damage. Hardly terminal: the bed to make, obviously, but maybe it needed airing first. She threw open the balcony doors and gazed down Grosvenor Road, sucking in restorative gulps of cold air. Yeah, a walk was definitely on the menu.

Eleven o'clock: the flat was clean and tidy, the empties disposed of and the bedroom, as far as she could tell, smelt neutral. Still, wouldn't harm to leave the doors open: they must be a good forty feet off the ground, so perfectly secure. Jill'd noticed a small park on the way back from the Prince of Wales. *All Saints* the notice said; she sidled reverently in. There didn't seem to be any benches so she parked herself on the base of a gaily-painted children's merry-go-round. In the sunshine but out of the breeze. She wasn't one for dwelling on the past, immediate or otherwise, and she hadn't done owt wrong. What she also hadn't done, however, was resolve her delightful conundrum. She would respect her benefactor's instruction, of course. But she had to talk to someone and in the absence of Jay's dad...surely Anton would understand?

The click of the wrought-iron security gates and the rumble of the Aston Martin's exhausts alerted her and she rushed to close the balcony doors. The room smelt fresh and cool, so even if Anton had noticed the doors she had a ready explanation.

'Láska, you look radiant! Happy Christmas, if it's not too late.'

'Thanks! Same to you, Mr...Anton. Lovely to see you.'

He wriggled out of his suede car coat, depositing it, and a paisley scarf on the settee, along with a black leather holdall. Their embrace was warm and comforting; Jill was both pleased to have someone to talk to and relieved it was Anton. It must've been way past lunch but, as neither of them seemed hungry, Jill poured coffee into two large china mugs and took them through to the drawing room. Anton lounged on the same banquette that Jill had street-gazed from twenty-four hours earlier.

'So my love, how was Virginia?'

'Fantastic, thanks! Molly's great and our hosts, Zach and Arlene, were really helpful. Nice folks, too.'

'And the hospital project? It progresses satisfactorily?'

'I think so. Molly attends most of the planning meetings so she'd be able to give you a better idea. But things seem to be okay.'

'And your return? To what do we owe the pleasure, láska?'

'Well, I was due a fortnight's leave,' Jill prevaricated.

'Indeed. I was just wondering why you chose to enjoy it in my flat; welcome as you are, of course.'

'You mean...?'

'Instead of with your boyfriend. Or at home in Newcastle.'

'Well, it's a long story but, if you don't mind, I've been dying to tell some...I mean you.'

'Sounds like we need to clear the decks!' smiled Anton. 'Let me just arrange dinner. Then I'm all yours.' He disappeared with the holdall.

Jill felt unaccountably nervous and it was a relief when her host returned with a reassuring smile and an ice bucket with the necks of two bottles of Pol Roger peeping out above a linen napkin.

'A trifle early perhaps, but it's Christmas after all.' He poured the chilled champagne into elegant flutes and settled back with an expectant look.

'Whenever you're ready, láska. Na zdraví!'

'Salud! Well... I think I mentioned my Aunt Louisa...' and Jill recounted the whole saga from the time she'd first watched the coronation as a child, through her aunt's perennial generosity, to the solicitor's meeting in Newcastle. Was that really only three days ago?

'That's quite a story, my dear. And I feel privileged to be the one to hear it. But why do you suppose your aunt was so insistent on secrecy?'

'Well first, I reckon she wanted me to think things through for myself. Y'know, without any undue influence. Then, when I'd done that I think...well, I hate to say it but I think she wanted *me* to have her money, not a load of cadging relatives. Not me mam and dad, but I come from a big family and I'm not sure Mrs Smellie thought that much of 'em!'

'From everything you've told me about your aunt's character, and especially her business acumen, I think you're spot on. But now you've told me, what next?'

'Well, I could do with some advice, please!'

'Certainly...but for that I'd need to know – and only tell me if you're comfortable – I'd need to know how much we're talking about.'

Jill paused. Oh well in for a penny: 'Thirty thousand pounds!'

Even Anton looked mildly surprised! 'Láska, you do indeed require some advice!' He sat back and closed his eyes, steepling his fingers as if in prayer. A minute, maybe two, dragged by, but this was no time to interrupt.

'I need to make some calls. Forgive me.' And he burrowed into his study.

The champagne, on top of everything else this weird Christmas, was making Jill sleepy. It could've been ten minutes or two hours but when next she stirred it was dark outside and Anton was studying her affectionately. More like an uncle than a lover, though.

'Been talking with a stockbroker friend who doesn't keep office-hours either.' Jill had only the haziest idea what a stockbroker did but tried to look interested. 'I won't bore you with the details but he's confident he could get you ten per cent on Treasury Gilts.'

'Sorry to show my ignorance but what on earth does that mean?'

'An income of sixty pounds a week, after tax!'

'Bloody hell! That's more than three times my Sister's pay!'

'And a rock-solid investment, too. Course, you don't have to draw the interest: you could just let the capital accumulate.'

'What live now spend later, or vice versa?'

'Er...yes! You could put it like that,' laughed Anton indulgently, 'What would Aunt Louisa have wanted, do you think?'

'I think she would've wanted me to be sensible. But to enjoy it too. Y'know not splurge, but have some things I couldn't've afforded otherwise.'

'Very shrewd. Any ideas?'

'Not sensible ones! Need to think about it a bit.'

'Of course. Now that *is* sensible.'

'Hmm…meanwhile, did you say something about dinner? I'm ravenous!'

Jill reflected later: she might have sixty-pounds-a-week's-worth of independence but she could hardly match Anton for influence. He'd persuaded Phillipe to extend his family celebration and make available Charterhouse's private dining room just for them!

Fifty-Two

Molly's news left Jay thoroughly disorientated. What the devil was going on? How come Jill was back in England and he didn't know? And where the blazes was she? Presumably not in Chester. So at her parents? He should ring them, wish them Happy Christmas and all that crap. Then demand to speak to Jill. He glanced at his Rolex: nearly five. That wouldn't work: they had their Christmas dinner at three, after the blokes were back from the Labour Club. They'd all be pissed by now. So, even if he could speak to Jill it wouldn't be easy. And suppose she wasn't there. Then what? Either way he'd look a right prat!

He replaced the 'phone in its cradle, and glanced at the photo of his big brother on top of his dad's desk. The handsome, aquiline features returned his gaze steadily, though, as always, sympathetically. *Don't do anything rash*, it said. *Get yourself a drink and ponder. Good thinking, big brother.*

Jay trooped down to the drawing room and had a recce in the corner cupboard. Hmm...bit early for spirits and he didn't fancy sherry. No, what he wanted was a beer. There'd be some in the utility room. But a root-around discovered only a half-empty case of Guinness. Oh well...what's good enough for Sir Raymond...start with a couple of bottles, save him the trek up and down stairs.

And some music...*charms to sooth the savage breast* and all that. Something to suit his mood. Serious without being sombre. Back in his dad's study he flicked through the tape index. Albinoni, Allegri, Ariosto (all Eyeties: too frivolous). Arne (English, deffers, Rule Britannia: too bombastic), Bach CPE, & JS – nah! Bártók (bit of a surprise: surely he was the Hungarian his dad referred to as 'Bloody Béla'). Bax (oh, sure! *Try everything once – except folk dancing and incest.* No temptation there – he couldn't dance, and he didn't have a sister!) Beethoven. No longer his favourite, but the Seventh would do for starters. He looped the BASF tape carefully through the head and onto the empty spool before pressing the Garrard's start button. Then he flipped the gold cap off the first Guinness.

Cheers, big brother. Happy Sodding Christmas, mate!

The slow second movement calmed him down. Think this through rationally, bor! They'd been getting on fine: her last letter had a couple of unwelcome references to someone called Zach; but it had ended very affectionately. And surely his latest message, inside a judiciously chosen Christmas card, had been the right mixture of news and endearments? True, he'd mentioned Linda: that'd seemed only fair, not to say prudent. Be open. But not too explicit. No, there was nowt in their correspondence to suggest a falling out. Just the opposite. Ergo…she hadn't rorsed back home on his account. Otherwise, they'd be enjoying a cosy, romantic Christmas in the Handbridge flat.

The tranquillity of the slow movement had morphed into the drama of the third with its crescendo of knockout bars, before the coruscating violence of the finale. Yeah, right choice, bor, he mused savouring the last dregs of the second Guinness.

He fancied some poetry; most of his favourite volumes – Donne, Pope, Wordsworth, Keats, Hardy, Eliot – were at the flat. No matter: memory would serve for now, especially as he was on his tod. Jay liked reciting poetry, but not in company. A hangover from 'A' Levels meant he could still quote some nine hundred lines of *Hamlet*, including all the soliloquies. *To be or not to be* was a tad melodramatic. Plus, Autolycus espoused chronology so he should start with *sullied flesh*. *Sullied* or *solid*? He was in the Arden camp and preferred the former. Bloody academics, eh!

> *How weary, stale, flat and unprofitable*
> *Seem to me all the uses of this world!*

He couldn't help pausing, and smiling, as he enunciated *Frailty, thy name is woman*…bit harsh in Jill's case. He didn't know owt for certain; assuredly he had no proof of unfaithfulness. Well, not on her part. And surely only technically on his… *Nymph, in thy orisons Be all my sins remembered.*

No the fault, if there were any was in himself. Or maybe in his stars! Seized with melancholy he found himself lost in Keats. September 1819: what an outpouring of emotion and poesy…

> *My heart aches, and a drowsy numbness pains*
> *My sense, as though of hemlock I had drunk*

Steady on: Guinness isn't that bad! He rattled through the next five stanzas, pausing at the beginning of the sixth:

> Darkling I listen; and for many a time
> I have been half in love with easeful Death...

And then abandoned the Nightingale and broke into celebrating Pysche. He'd called her that once. And recited the whole poem: *O Goddess! Hear these tuneless numbers...* So, why had she come back? And, more to the point, why hadn't she let him know? What the fuck could be so important, and not involve him? This was gonna be more than a two-bottle conundrum. Bloody enigma!

Yeah, some Elgar next. But not the too-cheerful Variations and not without something suitable. The *blushful Hippocrene* called... The old man's claret and burgundy stash was under the stairs. Jay located a nest of Gevrey-Chambertin, 1969. Hmm...promised to be a great vintage, according to Hugh Johnson, but too young; surely his dad was laying that down? Then he spotted them, lower down the rack: four bottles of 1961 Château Talbot. Perfect! A perennial English favourite from a classic négociant, Cordier. And just about the best year ever! Surely his dad wouldn't mind, under the circs? He took a bottle through to the kitchen and uncorked it delicately, placing it next to the Aga. An hour or so should be okay. Time for another Guinness and the Elgar Cello.

Jay wished he could play the cello. The piano was okay. Particularly Beethoven sonatas. He'd long ago mastered the *Pathétique* and the first couple of movements of the *Moonlight*; and later had risen to his father's challenge: 'When you can play the third movement, son, there's a tenner in it!' In his current mood he could've gone downstairs and rattled off the *Waldstein* or the *Appassionata*. Or even the *Hammerklavier*: that would've helped exorcise his turmoil. But even after just a few beers he couldn't promise not to play a wrong note here and there. And that'd really piss him off!

Besides, the key of the Cello Concerto, E minor, was perfectly suited to his mood: melancholic and nostalgic. Binyon was pretty much a contemporary of Elgar's (wonder if they ever met?) and the slow movement always reminded him of the burning of leaves, and wood smoke. He re-wound the tape to play it again. God! It was so sad! With some difficulty he recalled Elgar's Windflower letters. Major irony! Elgar's wife was *Caroline* but the letters were written to Alice, Millais' daughter; formerly married to that berk Ruskin. What the hell did he say? Yeah, got it... *I long for the country... I think all the time of it – and you.* But was the *you* Jill, or Caroline. Certes, it wasn't Linda. Maybe it was Chris. He still thought of him all the time and, unlike his girlfriends, Jay could never see his big brother again...Yeah, Sir Edward was right: *Everything good & nice & clean & fresh & sweet is far away – never to return.*

This wasn't helping; he needed cheering up. Something light and happy. Mozart or Haydn, his dad had plenty of them. And to escape from under the mountain of melancholia? Something slight! What could be dafter than John Skelton's laughter! But he didn't have Skelton by heart and had to step next door, where in his old bedroom serried ranks of climbing books, and just a couple of poetry vols, paraded on the shelf above his bed. It'd fallen down once but fortunately he hadn't been asleep at the time!

He reached for the Skelton and lay prone, propping it against his knees. He leafed through the first hundred pages, eschewing *Philip Sparrow* in favour of *Elinour Rumming*...just the thing to lighten a mood:

> *Tell you I chill*
> *If that ye will*
> *Awhile be still*
> *Of a comely Gill*
> *That dwelt on a hill...*

Stuff a stoat! he laughed, can't get away from that Gill no how! He closed his eyes briefly, reflecting on how enchanting she was; how very much he *didn't* want to get away from her; and how totally floored he'd been the first time he'd seen her in the Buffalo Head... And ever since...

Boxing Day broke clear and cold. He was famished. The fridge was virtually empty but the remains of the kedgeree caught his eye. And there, in the door, the perfect complement: a half full bottle of 1966 Winzenheimer Honigberg. The elegant shape of the brown bottle was enhanced by the bright yellow label: Ferd Pieroth – Burg Layer. Now there was a vintner; and a memory!

He'd bowled up at eight o'clock one morning having just hitched down from Durham overnight. An unfamiliar BMW was parked on the drive where his mum's car usually stood. For some reason she was out. He wasn't confident of his reception, having given no notice but his dad was full of bonhomie.

'Splendid timing, son! We're just about to taste some Hock. And Riesling!'

The next two hours had sped by in delightfully bibulous fashion, after which Jay had retired to bed knackered. Subsequently Ray Fincher bought all his white wines from Pieroth, and very palatable they were, too!

Not that he was hung over; but this was the perfect lift. He set himself a place in the dining room with his mum's Royal Worcester, and silver cutlery; poured out a generous glass of the Riesling and tucked into his king's breakfast. He was pretty sure the old man would approve. And his big brother certainly would…

Fifty-Three

'Tio Pepe?'

'Yes thanks.'

'Same for me please; then you can leave us to the menu and our own devices. We're in no hurry, thanks.'

Raymond Fincher was treating his hoped-for-daughter-in-law to their promised lunch at the Grosvenor. Although in the main dining room, they occupied a quiet corner table.

'So, how was America?'

'Fantastic! It's an amazing country. So big. And the scenery is awe-inspiring.'

'And our great American cousins?'

'Wonderful. Quite different from here.'

'How d'you mean?'

'Well, you know what Chester's like in the summer. Full of brash Yanks with loud voices and over-familiar habits.'

'Well some of them. Not all.' That was one of the many things Jill liked about Raymond: his tolerance.

'They're totally unlike that at home – friendly, sure, but considerate and polite, too. Especially, polite. They address strangers as 'Sir' and I was always getting called 'Ma'am': made me feel like the Queen Mother!'

Jill was animated and, not for the first time, Ray reflected on how lucky Jay was to be with her. There was something more, though. Her trip seemed to have given her a newfound confidence, a sparkle that made her even more attractive.

By the time the waiter had taken their orders – a sirloin steak, rare for Ray and a Spanish omelette with fries for Jill – she'd already conducted trips round Washington, the Civil War battlefields and Orange County. Monticello needed both more attention and a bottle of Merlot, so once the cheeseboard arrived Jill felt like an accomplished tour guide. Ray, who'd never been to America was a conscientious listener; but it became clear during Jill's judiciously censored anecdotes about the Charlottesville nightlife that the unspoken agenda could no longer be ignored. Ray, discreet as ever, broached the issue delicately.

'Darling, that was fascinating. You've clearly been making the most of your opportunities. And it's delightful to have you home but, if you don't mind my asking – why all the cloak-and-dagger stuff?'

'I was afraid you'd want to know that, sooner or later. It's a bit of a saga: are you sure you've got time?'

'Certainly. I've given myself the afternoon off. Shall we take some air?'

It was just about warm enough to sit out in a sunny Grosvenor Park. Time to spill.

'Well it's all to do with Aunt Louisa. You know, the friend of my gran's who's always looked out for me.' Ray nodded supportively and Jill ploughed on. She was guiltily conscious of not telling the whole truth; she might've given the impression she'd returned for Mrs Smellie's funeral, for example. But she'd already decided to come clean about her inheritance. Short-term financial advice from Anton was fine, but she needed ongoing counsel.

'There's only one thing, Ray... This has to be just between you and me. I don't want you to say anything to Jay yet.' She felt it both rude and superfluous, but added '...or Mrs Fincher.'

'Of course not, love.'

Either she'd grown more comfortable with the scale of her good fortune or Ray was an even cooler customer than Anton.

'Well, that sounds most satisfactory,' he smiled. 'And it goes without saying that if and when you want any guidance, I'll be here.'

'Thanks, Ray. You don't mind, do you?'

'About the secrecy? Course not. We'll simply be observing your Aunt Louisa's wishes, after all.'

'Exactly... Anyway, your letter said something had come up?'

Ray smiled; Jill wasn't sure whether he'd seen through her slightly transparent gambit or whether the new topic was a happy diversion!

'Er...yes. Imari.'

'Imari? Oh...that Japanese porcelain you collect?'

'Hmm...and Chinese. Deva Antiques have made me an offer.'

'What? As in *an offer-you-can't-refuse*?'

'Hmm...something like that. Though I'm hoping it might be one *we* can't refuse!'

'Ooh! Sounds interesting. What does it involve?'

'Initially, not too much. They've lost their Oriental porcelain man. Poached by Sotheby's. They want me to catalogue and value their collection as it develops. I'd come into their emporium on the Rows at my own convenience. In addition, I'd be able to buy in London, as I've done for years, and sell through their fairs on a regular basis. And, at zero commission. It's too good to miss; but I could do with your help.'

'That'd be great, Ray – 'cept I don't know the first thing about porcelain!'

'Probably more than you realise, and anyway you'd soon learn, what with cataloguing and pricing.'

'You mean working alongside you?'

'Exactly! It wouldn't be a big time commitment and you could grow your knowledge and experience without any risk. What d'you think?'

'When do we start?'

'That's my girl! Just one thing...'

'Don't tell me – not a word to Mrs F!'

Ray laughed: 'Touché! Nor to Jay, at this stage, please.'

'No problem – co-conspirators, eh! Sounds exciting!'

Fortunately, Ray hadn't offered to walk her over to Handbridge. Creative enough to be economical with the truth when she had to be, Jill nevertheless retained her distaste for lying. And evading the reality of her domestic arrangements would have taxed Jay's flirtations with the eternal verities, never mind hers! Besides, the arrangement (how clandestine that word sounded) was strictly temporary. She was flying back to America within days. Anton had said she was welcome to stay at the Manchester flat but she'd really wanted to get across to Chester. That, it transpired, presented no obstacle either. He was off to see his sister in Prague and she was welcome to stay at his house in Chester. It would give her a good idea of the area she could afford when she returned from Virginia. As for transport the solution was simple: she could drop him at Ringway the following morning, take the Aston to Chester and return it when it was her turn to fly out of Manchester. All sorted!

Dropping Anton off at the airport was intimidating: he'd insisted she drive so he could give any advice necessary. Jill quite liked driving but was ambivalent about mentors. Stephen had taught her on his Northumberland rounds; although the odd time she'd driven with Jay aboard had been disconcerting as he tended to maintain a running commentary. On reflexion, though, Anton's guidance was helpful: by the time she needed to go solo Jill already felt at home in the Aston. It was tempting to call at the flat in Handbridge just to see Jay's face; that, however, would undermine her plan. Instead, she drove straight to the address Anton had given her south of the River Dee. Well, almost straight – she missed the turning off the Overleigh roundabout first time and found herself heading for North Wales! Recognising her error almost immediately she backtracked to Curzon Park North and located the elegant Georgian townhouse, over-shooting the drive before realising it had a double entrance. The turn in brought her to the foot of white steps leading up between marble columns to the glossy black front door. Classy! Just as well she was in the Aston! But there were no nebby neighbours to enquire what she was doing driving Anton's car and letting herself into his light, airy mansion. Noting the stairs for later Jill opened the first door off the hall. A spacious drawing room, as Anton would term it, was sparsely but expensively furnished and led via French doors to a massive balcony. Jill flung open the doors and crossed to a white balustrade that separated it, via shallow steps, from lawns leading down to the river. Be fantastic in summer! The garden was shielded by tall evergreen hedges on both sides: great for sunbathing. And maybe swimming? The Dee was tidal though, so it might be too dangerous… Even in the failing December light, the view over the river was impressive. Open fields, and Chester's ancient racecourse, the Roodee. Then beyond that the buildings along Nuns Road that included Ray's local offices and the back of her very own Royal Infirmary. She felt oddly at home and nostalgic simultaneously. What a place to live this would be!

The following morning Jill was less sanguine. A combination of hardly anything to eat or drink and a strange bedroom had meant a fitful sleep. She decided to head out early for provisions and then spend the afternoon reviewing her options. After a restorative lunch of cold meats, coleslaw and potato salad she made herself a large pot of coffee and resolved to make the most of the view. It was calm and sunny, but cold. Rooting through Anton's lumber-room Jill discovered a voluminous fleece and several scarves. Snuggly wrapped up, she arranged a small patio-table next to her lounger and dispensed a mug of coffee from the percolator.

Bit of a dilemma, here, hinny! Go or stay? How had that clown Gobbo summarised it in her *Merchant*? Budge, said the Fiend: Budge not, said his conscience? Something like that. Jill was in the same position. The Fiend – who, she recalled gave the friendlier advice, would have her on the plane to America in a couple of days. She had, after all, a contract to fulfil and had promised Molly she'd return. Conscience would have her stay and… And what? Face the music? As in come clean to Jay about her inheritance and invite him to share her good fortune? But was that tempting him with her money? Was he definitely in love with her? She was pretty sure he was, words aside, but doubted the money would solve anything. Just further muddy the already-murky waters of their turbulent love-stream! Anyway it was fruitless speculating about Jay? What did *she* want? Embrace him now or go back to America and hope they got together later?

Hang on! What was Jay always saying about either/ors? Couldn't she have one of his famous both/ands? Not clear how, but one thing was for sure – she *did* love him. But did that mean stay or go? Bloody Gobbo! She was no further forward!

Maybe I've got me Conscience and me Fiend mixed up. Making the right decision for the wrong reason. Ironic! Reckon Rosalind would've approved though! But not Portia: too prim and proper. Full of shit, too. Quality of mercy! She didn't show Shylock much: robbed him of his fortune, his daughter, his religion. Yeah, Rosalind was still her heroine. *And* she left home to find her true love in a forest. That was it! She'd meet Jay in The Woodman and they could take it from there.

Fifty-Four

'At last! Where've you been? I 'phoned to wish you Happy Christmas but Molly said you'd gone home! How come? Is summat wrong? Jill, what the hell's going on?'

'Whoa! Steady on! One thing at a time! And yes…it's lovely to speak to you too darling!'

'Of course…of course! Sorry! But…'

'Meet me in The Woodman tonight at seven and all will be revealed.'

'Yeah, but…'

'See you then. Gotta go… No more change…'

'Hang on!' But it was too late: a metallic burr announced she'd replaced the receiver in the pay 'phone. What the blazes?

Later and calmer, Jay was befuddled but reassured. At least she was here in Chester and they were going to meet. He'd have preferred the Bull & Stirrup but he could understand Jill's choice. The Woodman was a nurses' pub. But it had a bagatelle table so he'd been in a couple of times. Not for a match: they didn't play in the League. They served a mean pint of Wrexham lager, mind. Best in Chester. And the cheapest. Yeah, it could be worse…but she'd got some questions to answer. Then again, so had he…

It wouldn't help to go in all guns blazing and…besides…he was really looking forward to seeing her! Yeah, mustn't come over all-inquisitorial; just let her explain at her own pace. And get there first so he'd be waiting for her. She didn't use to like going into pubs on her own; still that was a while ago, maybe now…be full of nurses anyway. She'd know more people than him.

He pushed through the double doors off the main street. The Woodman was noisy but convivial; the jukebox was blaring out Jimmi Hendrix: *Voodoo Child*. He'd just find a good spec and then…

Bollocks! Jill was already sitting at the bar. And not alone! She was being chatted up by some suave bastard. Quite a bit older, too. A bloody doctor, for sure. Probably that bugger who'd taken her to the Nurses'

Ball. Fucking brilliant! Not surprising, though: she looked a knock-out – hair cropped short in curls round her face, nice tan, low-cut jumper and a really short, flared mini-skirt. All for his benefit, hopefully…

He was half way across the room when she spotted him; off her stool in a flash and straight into his embrace. He'd been going to say something, something romantic – he'd worked it all out – but her arms were round his neck and she was kissing him right there in the middle of the lounge bar! Jay returned the kiss enthusiastically and their clinch continued until they became aware of applause: a group of nurses at a neighbouring table!

'Darling, darling, darling!' Jill panted when they finally disentangled themselves, 'I've missed you so, so much!'

'Me too!' he muttered inadequately. And then, more practically: 'Shall we grab a pew?'

'Course! Not at the bar though. How about in the alcove? Can you fetch my drink across, sweetheart?'

'Course. What about lover boy? He's not joining us, I trust.'

'Who Alan? Nah! He's just a charge nurse I used to work with. He'll understand!'

'Understand what?'

'That I've had a much, much better offer, silly!'

Jay remembered that he was going to listen, not interrogate, but as soon as Jill started to talk he interrupted.

'Christ! It's wonderful to see you, pet. You look stunning, by the way. And…' He didn't get any further – they were embracing and hugging and kissing again. And again! And again! Finally, Jill pulled away, laughing.

'What?'

'Reminds me of that time in the Hotspur. Remember?'

'Course! We nearly got thrown out.'

'Yeah, what did the landlord say? *Howay, yer buggers: there's plenty o'room on the Town Moor for that!*'

'Or in this case, the Roodee! We could always go for a walk if we get ejected!'

'Might be a tad cold, hinny, though I'm sure you'd find a way to keep us warm!'

The exchange seemed not so much to break the ice – the heat of their embraces had already achieved that – as to unblock the conversation. Two hours and four rounds later Jay was much happier about the American adventure and Jill considerably impressed by the Cheshire educational scene. It occurred to him they should eat.

'Fancy a Chinese?'

'Yeah, that'd be nice. My shout, though.'

'No, can't let you do that.'

'Course you can. Anyway, it's on Glaxo!'

'Oh well, in that case… One for the road, as it were?'

It proved to be two, but half-nine saw them ascending the steps of the Oriental Garden in high spirits. They tackled the banquet for two, washed down by a litre carafe of somewhat dubious Chablis. Coffee and rather better brandy seemed entirely appropriate.

Relaxed now, Jay broached what he'd wanted to all night: 'So if it's not a rude question, how come you're back?'

'Don't be daft, sweetheart: to see you, of course!'

'Well obviously! But that the only reason?'

'Not quite. Aunt Louisa died…'

'Oh, Jill! I'm so sorry, love. I know how much you thought of her. Of course you'd want to attend the funeral.'

'Yeah, she was always really kind to me. Probably wouldn't have ended up going to America without her. She used to tell me stories about Mr Smellie working on the Eastern Seaboard between the wars. Guess some of it must've stuck.'

'And your family? Everyone okay?'

'Yeah, all fine, thanks.'

'Ooh! That reminds me, talking of family. You're gonna have to curtsey next time you see the old man!'

'How come?'

'Cause he's being knighted in the New Year's Honours. From now on he'll be *Sir* Raymond!'

'Strewth! He never mentioned that…y'know…in his letters.'

'Oh he couldn't. It was all hush hush. He only told mum and me over Christmas.'

'Oh, that's brilliant. You must be so proud of him. And it's no more than he deserves!'

'Tell him that: he's too modest for his own good!'

'I will. Let's take him out to dinner when I'm back.'

'What d'you mean *back*? You're not deserting me again are you?'

'Don't be silly! It's only for two months and I'm not *deserting* you. You're such a pillock sometimes!'

Jay grinned, then painstakingly shifted the debris to the sides of the table. He leaned across and, grasping both Jill's hands in his, fixed her with his most piercing, loving gaze.

'That's as maybe…but I'm *your* pillock…if you'll have me!'

'You mean…?'

'I mean…will you marry me, sweetheart?'

'Oh Jay, I have to fly back to New York tomorrow…'

'So?'

'So can I tell you when I'm home permanently?'

'As long as the answer's YES!'

'Odds are, honey! Odds are!'

www.ingramcontent.com/pod-product-compliance
Lightning Source LLC
Chambersburg PA
CBHW031052020726
47495CB00007B/1846